# DOES THE QUEEN STILL LIVE?

A novel of Drake and Elizabeth—

To celebrate the quarter-centenary of the circumnavigation of the globe, 1577–80.

This is the story of Francis Drake, covering his humble upbringing, his daring piratical exploits on the high seas and his amazing circumnavigation of the globe. The cast includes the cruelly efficient Spaniard De Recalde, Hawkins, who hated his kinsman but grew to love him, and men such as Walsingham, Dudley, Hatton and Cecil, as devious as they were illustrious; and the women in Drake's life—his poor, ailing wife Mary, Aruba the lovely half caste who is tortured to death, and Elizabeth Sydenham, young, beautiful and innocent. Above all revealed here for the first time, is the history of the extraordinary relationship that must have existed between Drake and Queen Elizabeth I.

# *Does the Queen Still Live?*

## John Fredman

**W. H. ALLEN · LONDON**
A Howard & Wyndham Company
1979

Photoset, printed and bound
in Great Britain by
REDWOOD BURN LIMITED
Trowbridge & Esher
for the Publishers, W. H. Allen & Co. Ltd
44 Hill Street, London W1X 8LB

ISBN 0 491 02469 X

To John Eliott of Plymouth with my thanks

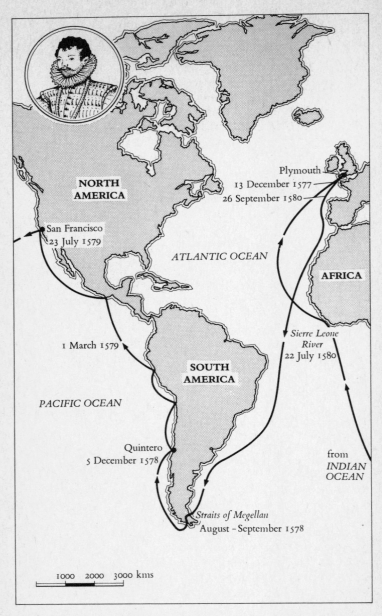

NORTH
AMERICA

Plymouth
13 December 1577
26 September 1580

AFRICA

San Francisco
23 July 1579

ATLANTIC OCEAN

1 March 1579

Sierre Leone
River
22 July 1580

SOUTH
AMERICA

PACIFIC OCEAN

Quintero
5 December 1578

from
INDIAN
OCEAN

Straits of Megellan
August – September 1578

1000  2000  3000 kms

**Francis Drake's circumnavigation of the world, 1577-1580.**

# Table of Dates

An historical novel of this kind should chiefly aim to fill the gaps left by history books. Every effort has been made to respect the integrity of famous past events, and if history on rare occasions has been bent to improve the flow of narrative, it has never been deliberately broken.

# Part One

*'Take away her merchant fleets; take away the navy that guards them: her empire will come to an end; her colonies will fall off, like leaves from a withered tree; and Britain will become once more an insignificant island in the North Sea.'*

Prof J A Froude prophesying with terrible accuracy, lecturing on 'English Seamen in the sixteenth century'. Oxford, Easter Term 1893–4

# 1

From the West they came, in the year 1549, a great, ravening, furious mob, howling blood-curdling threats in their strange, unintelligible Cornish language; and when night fell, their torches were shining in myriad needle-pointed lights as they clambered over the stark, gorse-covered, granite-strewn tors on their way to assault Exeter.

Edmund sat in the low-beamed living-room of his small farm-house at Crowndale, reading the Bible to his large brood of children. All his life it had been his habit to expound the word of God at this hour, when the cows had been milked, the hens fed, the horses watered and bedded down. He was a thin, slight man with the acid, fanatical face of a lay preacher; and as his voice droned on, his children forced themselves to sit straight-backed and attentive, for fear of the sting of their father's strap, should they doze off. As it happened the children, who were red-eyed from poring over their schoolbooks by guttering candle-light since the first crack of dawn until six each night, were soon to have unexpected relief.

''Usband, 'Usband.' Edmund's wife burst through the door. Normally she would not have dared interrupt the Bible reading, but terror had made her forget the respect and obedience she owed her husband. 'They be comin' down from the moor. If we do not flee we be as good as dead.'

'Woman, what dew yew mean?' Edmund put down his Bible, answering his spouse in the same broad Devonshire accent, so thick as to be barely understandable to one from a different county.

'The Cawnish 'ave risen and 'ave crussed the Tamar under Squire

3

Winslade of Tregarrick. 'Tis said they dew rise for the old religion.' She glanced fearfully at the Bible held in her husband's hand. 'And that the new prayer book of our good King Edward dew be the reason. They threat now, to kill all good Protestants in their beds.'

'Woman hold they tongue.' In spite of the contempt in his tone, Edmund had gone pale. His wife, who took their produce to market at Tavistock once a week, was always the first with any hard news, and Edmund did not fall into the error of failing to take her seriously.

'Marry, good husband, they dew march on Exeter and we must needs fly for our lives. And look yew over yonder tors if yew dew not believe me.'

Edmund walked over to the door and peered out into the night. He heard the tramp of marching men, saw the hundreds of torches like fireflies in the distance and came to an instant decision. 'Harness up old Lucifer, the stoned plough-horse, to the cart,' he commanded. 'All of yew run to it, now. Take only necessities, those things meet for warmth, sustenance, study and prayer.'

All was instant turmoil, and within the hour the great gelding was standing ready in harness as the family climbed into the creaking, wooden cart. They set off, resigning themselves patiently to the lurching, jolting agony caused by the spiked rims of the cartwheels biting into the hard, rutted track that led off the the moorland. Soon, from other wild tracks, more horses and carts, mules, palfreys and jennets, anything that could haul or carry refugees and their pathetic sticks of baggage, converged in a steady stream on the reliably Protestant town of Plymouth.

They were only just in time: following them down the steep, wooded banks of the river Tavy, the rebels attacked with such force that they penetrated into the town itself, looting and gutting some of the rich merchants' houses, before the militia managed to rally and drive them off in the direction of Exeter. The refugees, meanwhile, had ferried themselves out to the island of St Nicholas in Plymouth Sound and now sat there awaiting events, overcrowded, half-starved and miserable, hoping anxiously that someone would now send them relief and charity.

'And why does 'e not come?' Edmund's wife asked plaintively of her husband on the third day, when the children, growing hungry and fractious, were beginning to cry. 'Why does Sir William not come?' As 'e not been three times Lawd Mayor of Plymouth? Is 'e not a rich and powerful man and a kinsman of yorn? Will 'e not give us

Christian charity?'

Edmund spoke to her roughly and told her to be quiet. Sir William Hawkins, voyager, explorer and architect of the late King Harry's splendid navy, had more important matters on his mind than the relief of a poor and numerous family of a distant kinsman. Edmund, who also knew his relative to be a sinner, a pirate and a man removed from the word of God, looked at his starving family with distinct trepidation, guessing that Sir William would not readily welcome an ascetic, bitter, lay-preacher, together with his great brood of puling children, into his opulent household. All these things, however, Edmund kept from his wife.

When the refugees faced starvation and the rebels, who had now decided to besiege Exeter, showed every sign of needing a full scale army to put them down, the citizens of Plymouth reluctantly faced up to the appalling expense of feeding their charges and Sir William, resigned to doing his share, sent a wherry to collect his unwanted relatives and transport them to his fine house that lay close to the Cat-water.

Edmund's family were amazed at the opulence in which old William Hawkins lived. Accustomed to horn windows for the little light that glimmered into their small farmhouse, a straw palliasse for their aching bones after a day's back-breaking labour, here was beautiful glass through which to gaze at the ships in harbour, two great featherbeds for Edmund's brood to share, and with linen sheets too. Wherever Edmund looked, he saw wealth and elegance: wood panelling on the walls, plastered ceilings, and in some of the rooms real Turkey carpets. Even in the modest attic bedrooms in the high-timbered overhang of the fifth storey, where the family was quartered, the best of dry rushes covered the floor, smelling of sweet herbs, and these were often changed by the myriads of maids that Hawkins seemed to employ.

After several days of rest and good eating had restored Edmund to his usual, acid, God-fearing vigour, he began to experience violent pangs of jealousy at his kinsman's riches: a jealousy mixed with puritanical dislike of ostentation and the sheer lack of Godliness that he saw everywhere around him. What really rankled however, was the lack of respect he was receiving.

Below the salt—sat in the position of a humble servant! Yet was he not literate? Well versed in the scriptures? A yeoman who had paid four pounds a year for his land before circumstances had reduced

5

him to accepting his relative's board? Now here he was, placed in a lowly position at the great polished oak drawer table, among all the supplicants, the tradesmen, the hangers-on, the riff-raff that a rich man was accustomed to feed. That great, ornate salt, garnished in mother-of-pearl, fashioned like a warship and complete to the pieces of ordinance made from pure silver, was sheer affront, a standing reminder of his indignity every time he looked along the table at it.

William Hawkins, ageing, but still alert and jovial, made a sign to the minstrels' gallery, whereupon the musicians merrily struck up 'Pastime with Good Company,' the personal composition of William's much-mourned patron, old King Harry himself. While jigging his fingers to and fro to the lively strains, he happened to notice Edmund sitting downcast and silent at the far end of the table.

'How now, Master Edmund,' he called down. 'Why so whey-faced? Can you not do justice to this fare?'

Edmund looked up the vast distance of snowy-white, damask tablecloth covered with jewelled goblets, jugs and bowls of Venice glass that separated him from the great man. Even after the wail of the wind instruments had died away, the noise made by the liveried serving-men as they distributed plate after plate of beef, mutton, stew, veal, lamb, kid, cony, capon and assorted pastries, was enormous. It was as much as Edmund could do to see William Hawkins, let alone hear him.

'Marry,' Edmund rasped in reply, 'from this end of the table, conversation indeed becomes somewhat difficult.'

Old William seemed amused. 'And how far would you have me advance your station, pray?' he boomed. 'At my side is my dear wife, a Trelawny of noble birth, more entitled to my seat than I am myself. Opposite her, pray observe our good Lord Mayor of Plymouth, and next to him my sons William and John, heirs to all I possess.' He indicated two intelligent-looking boys in their 'teens, sitting quietly close by. 'Now sirrah.' He warmed to his task. 'Would you have me separated also from my sea captains who risk their lives on the broad seas? Anxious as I am, cousin, to do you all honour and courtesy, I cannot place you in front of these.'

'There is yet a matter more important than this,' Edmund said loudly, his voice extraordinarily arrogant. 'I see no minister of religion to bless the bounty of yor table. A bounty that dew be at variance with the simple life of our blessed Lord Jesu. What is more I also dew note that yew 'ave in this place a chapel for the saying of

6

mass: a good reason, I may observe, for why such a fine, rich house was strangely not looted by the rebels.'

Noise died away suddenly, the serving-men halted in their tracks by this impudent preacher, while the guests sat silent with amazement and some apprehension. Terrible insult had been offered to their host. Old man Hawkins was known to run quickly to anger and it would have surprised no one if he had drawn his jewelled dagger and spitted his churlish kinsman there and then.

Eyeing Edmund's large brood, who stood in imminent danger of being fatherless, William Hawkins, by a tremendous effort, kept his temper under control. 'Think not, cousin,' he said patiently, 'that the chapel is for me. Why, such worship is expressly forbidden by the King and good Archbishop Cranmer. No sir. It is there because a merchant has to deal with all sorts and I dare not make offence to a foreigner's religion.'

Annoyed at the charming way the old man had turned aside such dangerous matter, Edmund was stimulated into even greater breaches of good manners. His eyes roved bitterly over William's fine lace collar, the black velvet cap richly set with pearls and gold, his robe of purple velvet trimmed with sable, the many gold chains hanging round his neck, as befitted a man of wealth and standing. 'Also,' he continued, relishing his words, 'yew would dew well, cousin, to somewhat reform yor dress, diminish the superfluity of yor trunk hose, which is not meet either in an old man or a christian.'

It was plain from the ominous, hostile silence at the table that Edmund had gone too far. Little as old William Hawkins personally cared, he was locked into a rigid hierarchy of rank and privilege only just removed from feudalism, and from which there was no escape. 'By the cross,' he said coldly. 'What kind of man have we here, who offers deliberate insult and yet takes care to wear a Bible at his girdle instead of a sword? Take thy brood and remove thy miserable presence, keeping to thy rooms until it is safe for thee to go.'

Marching orders as explicit as that could only be obeyed. Summoning his family from the table, Edmund fairly stamped from the great hall, his children sniffing hungrily at the heaped confections of marchpane, sugarbreads, gingerbreads and sweet suckets that the serving-men were now bringing in to replace the meat course. Stiffly, proudly, he led the way up the four flights of steep stairs leading to the attic quarters allocated to him by William Hawkins.

Confined with his family in two little rooms, Edmund would now

7

spend hour after patient hour instructing his brood in the word of God and their letters. Always conscious of his duty, he had taken the education of his children very seriously, knowing that in a country where few were fully literate, literacy was the key to quick advancement. If Edmund had been moneyed, some of his elder boys would already have been at Eton or Winchester, learning French and the courtly gestures befitting a gentleman, but that had not been possible. What was more, since the dissolution of the chantries in 1547, a whole range of schools appropriate for educating older children—grammar, cathedral, monastic—had closed, thus throwing an even bigger responsibility onto Edmund's narrow, acid shoulders.

For rare moments of recreation, Edmund would for a few minutes each day relieve the children from crouching over their hornbooks and take them over to the latticed glass window, in itself a thing of wonder, and point out to them one or other of the ships lying at anchor, making sense of the tangle of masts and spars that belonged to galley, galleon, caravel, bark or merchantman. As Edmund described the perils of the journey to the Spice Islands and Africa—the cold and storms that men endured to fish the richly-stocked Grand Banks, the fearsome sea-serpents known to consume all but the most God-fearing of mariners—the faces of his children would turn round-eyed with wonder as they gazed down at Plymouth Cat-water.

Eventually, a month or so later, old man Hawkins sent a message to Edmund that he must now prepare to depart. Within half an hour the family was obediently collected at the great front gate, about to mount their cart, to which the stout gelding Lucifer had already been harnessed. Hawkins looked at them: their old clothes were scrubbed clean, mended, tidy. The old, roving seaman who had risked his life on the broad seas, where if death did not come from drowning it came from disease or some drunken knife-fight in a distant brothel, had little but contempt for their smug brand of self-contained, superior, God-fearing poverty.

'Well cousin,' he said, hiding the dislike in his voice, ''tis time to get thee gone.'

'And where should I go?' Edmund asked acidly. 'Know yew that unless I travel under some'—he managed a slight sneer—'gentleman's protection, I am no more than a vagabond looking for work. Would yew then have us whipped out of the next parish as sturdy beggars?'

At this, old William Hawkins held his ample sides and guffawed with laughter. The thought was indeed a pleasant one. 'Nay, cousin,' he said at length. 'I do more for thee than thou givest me credit. Through my intercession, the Secretary of the Navy has been pleased to appoint thee "Reader of Prayers to the Navy". A fine ship lies at Gillingham Reach, near Chatham dockyard, awaiting thy occupation. Here,' he signed to his son John, waiting at his right hand, for a piece of sealed parchment, 'this is thy passport to take thee without let or hindrance from justice of the peace or nosey beadle, safely into Kent. "Preacher to the Fleet." How does that strike thee, eh?'

'God has given me the chance to reach men's souls.' Edmund said smugly.

Now, for the first time, Hawkins really lost his temper with his ungrateful and arrogant kinsman. 'What, no thanks, sirrah?' he roared. In a gesture typical of his flamboyant past, his hand flew to his dagger. 'Then leave my door, thou mangy cur and take also all thy whining, snapping litter with thee.'

Edmund, thoroughly alarmed at the old man's behaviour, stepped back, slipped on some dirt and fell on the cobbles. Next thing William Hawkins knew was a hurricane of little fists and fingers which came punching, scrabbling, tearing at his new robe of crimson taffeta, ripping at the elegant gold buttons enamelled in black and white, and at the rich sable fur with which the gown was trimmed. His attacker was a little boy of no more than seven, incredibly sturdy, his blue eyes wide with hate. Hawkins stepped back, swore pungently—'By the bowels of Christ', tried to pluck the lad off him, but to no avail.

'Old man, do not attack my father,' the boy shrieked. 'You hear? Attack him again and I'll kill you.'

Wearying of this frantic assault on his person, William Hawkins looked at his son and said, 'John, help me.'

Now John Hawkins, thin and wiry, nearly fully-grown, joined the fight, eyes blazing. Less tolerant than his worldly father, his fury at these upstart, penurious relatives who had so abused the Hawkins' hospitality, knew no bounds. With all his strength he dealt the lad a heavy cuff across the head, causing him to stagger and release his hold on the old man. The lad, however, bounced up immediately like a rubber ball, and spitting with rage, charged at John head down, butting him neatly in the midriff so that the two of them fell heavily into the stinking, open sewer running through the middle of the cobbled street.

For a second John Hawkins' head went under, then came up dripping slime and filth, spitting brown excrement, coughing and spluttering hideously. Appalled at what was happening, Edmund finally came out of his daze and pulled his son away, fetching him a sound clout over the ears for his extraordinary behaviour, which the boy, narrow-eyed, breathing hard, endured stoically.

Old man Hawkins shook himself, eyed with disbelief the tatters of what had once been a fine robe, then roared, 'What villainy is this, sirrah? This imp is one of thine?'

'He is, sir,' Edmund replied in a quiet voice. Pale-faced, he was conscious of the enormity of the boy's actions in offering violence to one as respected as William Hawkins. It lay within the old man's power to have the boy whipped or imprisoned. For once, his acid, condemning tongue had deserted him.

'Well then, what is his name?'

'Francis.'

Suddenly, old William Hawkins roared with laughter. Turning to his dripping son, he boomed, 'John, mark this brave lad well, for we have the same red blood running in our veins. Should he return one day, you must give him employment, nay, a share in one of the Hawkins' ventures.'

'Yes father,' John said sulkily. Smelling strongly of slime and old turds, John Hawkins turned his long, fox-sharp face and pointed nose towards the lad, his eyes blazing with hatred. Not the kind to forgive injury lightly, he made a mental vow never to grant the slightest favour to his distant kinsman—

Francis Drake.

*'—she hathe bene with me a longe time, and manye years and hath taken great labor, and paine in brinkinge me up in learninge and honestie, and therfore I ougth of very dewtye speke for her, for St Gregorie sayeth that we ar more bounde to them that bringeth us up wel than to our parent, for our parents do that wiche is naturel for them.'*

Elizabeth's letter to the Council<br>
pleading for Kat Ashley's welfare,<br>
while under interrogation.

# 2

The very same year that the Drakes moved to the ship on Gillingham Reach, in the year 1549, the Princess Elizabeth sat at her writing-table in the presence-chamber of the mellow, red-bricked palace of Hatfield, awaiting the arrival of Sir Henry Tyrwhit, the envoy of the Council to whom she had graciously granted an audience. Not that there was any choice: the Council which now ruled England in the name of the young King Edward was her master also, made up mostly of scheming, ambitious men with a tried and trusted solution for all who dared to cross them: the block.

The axe. The young Princess paled as she thought of it, her heart fluttering against her ribs like an imprisoned bird beating its wings in terror against a window-pane. All love was death. She had learned that by now. The warm caress of a lover's hand soon replaced—for someone in her position—by the cold kiss of an axe blade. Not only her mother, the sensual Anne Boleyn, had paid the penalty for loving unwisely; but her step-mother, Catherine, too, had had her head cut off for loving some gay, lusty adventurer. Not that Elizabeth blamed her father. Women were wayward and lustful, and should not a man have order in his own house? She had always admired the raw, bluff masculinity of her father. She was her father's daughter and the Tudors were a red-blooded clan and the Princess, at the sweet age of sixteen, was already ruefully aware of the strength of her tumultuous emotions. Only now, however, had she realised that what to the rest of the human race was no more than a pleasant wooing followed by a breathless, healthy rutting, was to one in line to the English throne a deadly dance leading straight to the block.

She had learned the lesson too late. Only months ago she had been an innocent virgin. Now all that had changed. Seymour had seen to that. Now she was a complete woman, a maiden no longer. Terrifying thought. Now, therefore, she would have to act for her life! Using the brilliant mind that was so precociously acquiring fluency in modern languages and Greek classics, to the utter amazement of eminent academicians, she would now force herself to play the part of a pale, immature and studiously innocent girl.

As Tyrwhit was shown in, dark-robed, dark-jowled, bowing with all the hypocrisy of the great power invested in him by the Council, she sat straight-backed, imperious, her dress severely simple, her hair neither curled nor double-curled in the fashion of the court, but an auburn frame to her flawlessly pale skin, magnificent in its tawny, silky simplicity. She was careful to show her hands—Cranmer's Bible held modestly between slim, ivory fingers that entwined the pages like silken threads. She watched Tyrwhit's face change from remote severity to barely hidden admiration as he studied those wonderful fingers.

Yes, she thought. Even when I am old and withered, these fingers will never lose their power to fascinate. So long as I live, they will weave spells round men's souls and they shall do my bidding. Now, first, only let me pass this pike, for I shall never enjoy a man's body again: for all love is death.

'You have the depositions, madam?' Tyrwhit asked.

'Yes,' she said calmly. 'I have read them.' They told of the Lord High Admiral's comings and goings in his nightshirt while the Lady Elizabeth was still abed, fetching her a gay slap on the buttocks and making as though he would come at her. But that was not enough. The Council would have to prove that she had been plotting marriage with Seymour, a treasonable act for which she could lose her life: and that, she would not be scared into admitting.

'You are not concerned?' Tyrwhit asked. 'Madam, you should be.'

'Come to the point,' she said calmly. 'I have my studies to do.'

Tyrwhit looked at her with surprise. For a young girl in the shadow of the axe she bore a remarkable composure. It was true what everybody said—that she was the reincarnation of old King Harry. Expecting a submissive, frightened girl ready to admit all in exchange for her life, here was cold defiance; and Tyrwhit, never a man of great steel, found himself discomposed.

'My Lords of the Council must have the truth,' he said grimly. 'You are to relate what passed between your highness and Lord Seymour.'

If only they knew! He would come in the morning, before his wife was abroad, that rakish, red-bearded fellow. And what could a frail young girl do against his brute strength so humorously applied? Daughters of Henry VIII did not scream for mercy, for deliverance. She fought him, biting, kicking, then as excitement surged through her young body, had surrendered.

'There was nothing,' she snapped, 'and were my father alive, he would shorten you by a head for such imputation. Are you not aware that all I crave for is the peace to study religion and classical languages?'

'Your cofferer and Mistress Ashley have confessed all.'

A chill gripped her heart. The gay, silly, scatter-brained Kat Ashley and light-headed Thomas could literally be the death of her: yet they knew so little. ' 'Tis but the idle chatter of servants,' she sniffed. 'Was ever a Kingdom governed on such matter as this?'

Tyrwhit flushed. 'You deny he courted you? Wanted you?'

'I cannot be a master of men's lusts,' she shrugged. 'Go back and tell your Council that I would have none of him.'

'Even so,' Tyrwhit persisted, 'for seeking your hand, he has committed treason, and shall pay the price for it.' He looked at her closely, searching for the blush of emotion that the promised death of a lover might bring: but there was nothing.

She was heartbroken as her thoughts went back to those summer mornings: the dawn chorus of birds in the Hertfordshire forest; warm hands experienced in the art of love, squeezing her smooth, white breasts until each nipple stood out taut like the stamen of a lily; his strong body holding her, a body shortly to lie headless in its grave and eaten by worms. All love is death. With iron will she kept her face devoid of emotion. 'Then,' she said smoothly, 'and in such case, it shall be seemly for me to propose you a proper epitaph. It may be said that he was a man of much wit but very little judgment.'

Tyrwhit smiled to himself. The girl was mature for her years, every bit as clever and as hard as they said. I shall tell the Council, he thought, that she has a good wit and that nothing is gotten of her but by great policy.

'So you deny everything?' Tyrwhit asked lamely.

'Not only do I deny, but I demand redress for injury,' she said, for the first time allowing a trace of heat to enter her voice. ' 'Tis said I am with child by the Lord Admiral. I desire the Council to bring me to London where the people may see my condition as a good and seemly maiden.'

' 'Tis not the people who decide,' Tyrwhit said smugly. 'That is the prerogative of my lords of the Council.'

'You are wrong, sir,' Elizabeth said, her voice meek again as befitted a sixteen-year-old girl. 'Pray forgive me, but I think you are incorrect, for the people do love me as I do love them.'

Annoyed with himself, Tyrwhit retired, bowing, scraping, returning by such means the curtsies of the pert young maids of honour in the outer chamber. The Princess Elizabeth had prepared a little trap for him, into which he had neatly fallen, thus enabling her to remind him of the vast love the common people bore for her. No one knew why such love existed, but it was there and she knew it. Only a brave man would dare cause injury to the young princess without good and sufficient reason. She would be forgiven and he, Tyrwhit, had always been wasting his time. The people, in the end, were stronger than the Council and the Princess, by some secret, arcane magic, seemed to hold the people in the palm of her hand, a trick she must have learned from her father, bluff King Harry.

The Princess watched him go, smiling an unfathomable smile. Then she returned quietly to her books. Soon she would commence work on some pretty needlework, a demure little present she was preparing for her brother, the King. She felt the laughter rising up inside her, hysterical from relief. Tyrwhit had been ineffectual and the danger was passed: and she had been lucky, very lucky not to conceive, because a baby meant either death or submission to a husband. Now she had learned her lesson. She had the trick of it. This strange, bewitching power that she had over people, and especially over men, she would use to gain her own ends. Henceforth, all men would be her lovers: she would beguile, bewitch, flirt outrageously, but there would be no more romps in bed. That sort of love ended only in death.

*'What I am ye right well know—I am your Queen . . . like true men stand fast against these rebels—and fear them not, for I assure you I fear them nothing at all.'*

Queen Mary to her bodyguard
defending Whitehall Palace.

# 3

In due course, Edmund and the family took possession of their ship, an old hulk harboured by the Navy against such time as it might possibly be required. Damp, cold and ancient, Edmund's wife never ceased to complain about this rotting wreck and the awful conditions in which she was required to raise her large family. Her husband, however, paid no attention. He was far too fulfilled, far too busy, preaching the word of God according to Cranmer's Bible to the long-suffering sailors of King Edwards's Navy to notice.

As for young Francis, his imagination had been stirred by all those ships in Plymouth Sound, the strange beauty of that forest of masts and spars, the smell of tar and caulking, all the exotic sights of the Cat-water. Now, he would lie at nights listening to the groan of timbers as the vessel heeled over to the race of the incoming tide, the gentle lap-lap of waves against her hull and the sighing, creaking, cracking sounds as she settled back into the mud again like some old, rheumaticky animal sighing for peace and sleep. He would sniff the bitter smell of bilge-water, the odour of salt spray on old oaken planking and the sea was suddenly no longer a stranger to be feared, but a companion with whom to go through life.

Soon, as little boys quickly learn to do, he was sculling about in a small boat, oblivious to the cold, steep waves surging in from the North Sea, at one with the elements, threading his way through the dangerous channels and sudden, savage, rip-tides with all the effortless ability of a young eel.

As Francis Drake grew up he drifted apart from his father, who, eyes shining with fervour, spent more and more time at the task given him by Almighty God, of educating poor sailors in the Protestant faith. Soon young Francis, spurning the bookish scholarship of his

15

vast brood of brothers and sisters, would disappear, sometimes for days at a time, on an exciting voyage of discovery in his little cockleshell boat. Before long every hidden cove, every thickly-wooded inlet of the River Medway was known to him like the palm of his hand. If he was caught away from home at nightfall, he would doss down on the floor of some ale-house, lying quietly like a dog in front of the blazing log fire, his eyes growing rounder and rounder with wonder as the friendly seafolk drained their pewter flagons of ale and told wonderful tales of distant oceans: tales of those who had sailed with Cabot to Hudson's Bay and had found only ice and esquimaux instead of a short route to the Spice Islands; those who had voyaged with old William Hawkins to Guinea and Brazil and brought back ivory, Brazil wood, parrots and popinjays. There was even one old sailor who, in his cups, would peel off his jerkin and show the half-healed lash marks on his bare back, a reminder of the Muslim galleymaster to whom he had been sold after capture by sea pirates in the Levant.

The world seemed a wide and wonderful place and Francis was in love with the sea, longing for the music of the salt wind whining through the standing rigging. As years went by, young Francis grew amazingly: not tall, like some slender, lisping courtier—in truth he hardly grew upwards at all, his body not wasting its strength in that direction—but preferring to build bone and muscle in those parts useful to a deep sea mariner. Instead, he grew a chest which in full maturity would resemble somewhat a rounded barrel; legs short and thick enough to ride the steeply canted deck of a small vessel caught in the short chop of a wild North Sea blow. Although only a lad, he was before long doing a man's work and would go off for weeks at a time, crewing for skippers plying small sailing barks along the coast.

On one occasion, puzzled by the church bells that could be heard ringing in every village along the Medway, he inquired from his skipper as to the reason. ' 'Tis for the coronation of Queen Mary,' was the short reply. Such things meant nothing to Francis: he hauled on the sheets, spilling slack from the sail, and thought little more of it.

One bitter night, towards the close of the year 1553, he returned to the hulk, laden with presents that he had bought with money saved from his wages, only to find the old ship deserted and the family's belongings scattered all over the place in frantic disorder. Worried about the fate of his mother and his brothers and sisters, young Francis scurried into the smoky, low-beamed ale-house by the sign of the Fox and Goose in Gillingham, anxious for news from his many sailor friends who spent their time there consuming strong ale. To his surprise, however, he was hustled outside the back door by the landlord, whose face was working in terrible fear.

'Good mine host,' young Francis piped up. 'Canst pray tell me what has befallen my family?'

'Your father were taken by soldiers yesterday,' the landlord whispered, his voice cracking in panic. 'The Queen looks everywhere for Protestants and your father as Preacher to the Fleet was the first to be questioned. Asked to sample "wafer and wine", he refused, so they took him, with all his brood and all his flock.' The landlord made to shut the door, so terrified was he of being seen talking to a Protestant brat, but Francis' frantic hand scrabbling at his arm stopped him.

'Leave me,' the landlord hissed. 'We are all good Papists now.'

Francis said miserably, 'At least can yew tell me where they took my family?'

'Who knows? The "fleet" perhaps? Now go, lest I am made to join you dangling from the same gibbet.' He turned away, anxious to be rid of the boy, slamming, then bolting the inn door.

As the landlord's feet died away across the stone flags, Francis, normally so self-reliant, now knew terrible loneliness. Deprived of help, deserted so suddenly by his friends, he felt tears rush to his eyes: but, squaring his shoulders, he knew he must play the man and try to find his family. Lacking food, money or proper winter clothing, he set off down the open road that led to London.

He had gone perhaps ten miles, and could feel weariness and hunger descending upon him, when only a few yards ahead he saw a man standing motionless in the middle of the road. The man, who held a long truncheon in his hand, was well-dressed in the height of fashion with a slashed doublet, good silken hose and a velvet cap crowned by a dashing turkey feather.

'Well lad,' the man said. 'All alone, are we?' He peered closely into Francis' face. 'And I warrant you look in need of a good meal.'

'That I am sir,' Francis said ruefully. The man had the look and speech of a gentleman, and he was glad to meet somebody who appeared sympathetic.

'And to whom do you belong? You are in the employ of some nobleman, no doubt? Or possibly,' he furrowed his forehead, 'you might be of gentle stock yourself, requiring no passport to travel. 'Tis just possible. Well, which is it lad?'

Francis, not knowing what to say and resenting the stranger's over-curiosity, tried to push on past, but the man quickly grabbed him around the arm with fingers that felt like steel bands. 'I pray you not to run away when I address you, sirrah.' The man's face had turned cold and ruthless. For the first time, Francis noticed his thin, cruel mouth, the strange red glare in small, closely-set eyes, and knew that this man was outside the laws of society.

Struggling, using all his considerable youthful strength, Francis tried to break free, but the man was fully-grown and had muscles made of iron. He held the struggling boy with contemptuous ease. Eventually, bored with the boy's refusal to submit, he released him. And then, with a sudden, savage chop of his gauntleted hand, he hit Francis a terrific blow full across the face. Francis crashed into the mud, fighting back a scream of pain.

'Well, you belong to me, boy, from now on,' the man said indifferently. 'My name is Blount. Mark it well, for I am the Upright Man in these parts and you'll do well not to forget it. Try to escape and I'll put out both your eyes.' He indicated a finely-jewelled dagger caught stylishly at his waist. 'And think not that I jest,' he sneered. 'Of all my little earners, 'tis always the blind beggar child who earns the most.' He paused. 'Now what is your name, lad?'

'Francis. Francis Drake.'

'Ahead of me, Francis. Move!' He pricked the boy with the point of his dagger, so that he set off stumbling along the track, until they reached the brow of the hill. There, Francis was greeted by the sight of a cluster of tents and clapboard huts, set by the side of a running stream. The man directed Francis into one of the tents, gave him a shove that sent him sprawling into the straw, then growled in the direction of a gap-toothed old crone who sat in a corner with a young girl cowering under her arm, huge eyes saucer-like with terror.

'Hark to this, woman,' the man snarled. 'Here is a lad for you to look after. Feed him. Explain how we gain our living here. Let him escape and I'll slice off your dugs and feed them to my wolfhounds.'

'Yes master.' The woman shuddered, trembling uncontrollably as she watched the man close the tent flap behind him.

'Who are yew, mistress? Where am I?' Francis asked fearfully.

'You know nothing of this place?'

'Only that he commanded me here.'

18

'My name is Mistress Newman,' the woman said. She stopped, noticing the intent gaze with which young Drake was examining her. Even at his tender age, Francis Drake's first thoughts were that this woman had once been something better than a poor, starving beggar. 'Ah yes,' the woman went on, smiling sadly as Drake took in her straggling dirty hair, filthy shift, flaccid, unwashed and disease-scarred skin. 'I read your thoughts well enough. 'Tis true that I comes from a respectable, God-fearing station in life. Peradventure a lad like you cannot understand how I be reduced to this parlous condition. Shall I then, while you eat, tell you my story?'

The boy, worn out by the rigours of his journey and thoroughly frightened, could only nod dumbly. However, the pangs of hunger in a young stomach were still strong, and he eagerly attacked the hunk of nourishing rye bread and the flagon of ale that she placed in front of him.

'My husband,' the woman said, 'were a skilled tailor, and I a dressmaker in the household of my lord of Somerset. But on his downfall, all our lord's retinue were dispersed. Cast onto our own resources, penniless, we were travelling the highway to place ourselves with my uncle, who runs a prosperous pig-stall at Honiton market, when my husband met his untimely end falling from his horse. 'Twas then, deprived of the protection of my husband's good sword-arm, that we,' she glanced at the grubby, saucer-eyed girl in the corner of the tent, 'fell easy prey to the first "Upright Man".'

'Upright man?' Francis queried, in between mouthfuls. 'What is he?'

'I will explain,' the woman said.

Explain she did, in the good simple language of her class, so that the boy could understand her better than any bookish schoolmaster. The dissolution of the monasteries, she told him, and the ruthless eviction of tenants so that the great lords might enclose land to graze sheep, had resulted in a huge army of skilled men and small landholders being forced into mass vagabondage. These people, 'sturdy beggars' as they were called, given no choice but to live by their wits on the open road, roamed the country in great packs: and at the head of each pack was an Upright Man.

'Such a man,' she explained to the spellbound, horrified Francis, 'be king over all his people. Versed in all the ways of trickery and murderous violence, the unwritten law of the highway gives him supreme power over all those—his subjects—whom he has enslaved.'

19

'And this man who calls himself our master,' Francis said wonderingly, 'is he then so powerful that you cannot, one dark night, escape from him?'

'To what purpose?' the woman said dully. 'To meet another of the same kind? Do you know what an Upright Man does when he takes a woman? You are not too young to understand the lusts of the flesh, lad. I will explain. First, he breaks her to his ways as though she is a horse to be ridden. If she be a maiden, he takes her maidenhead, thus depriving her of virtue and any dignity. Then he will beat her daily until she is compliant, then set her to work earning him money in some ale-house brothel. Only when she is worn out and old like me will he leave her free to mess around her cooking pots, feeding the rest of his evil brood.'

For Francis, reared in the God-fearing insulation of his father's farmhouse, a whole new world of fear and terror was opening up. 'How old are yew, then?' he asked, wide-eyed.

'Thirty-five,' the woman answered quietly.

Francis went pale with shock. The life, the ceaseless ill-usage by men, had turned this woman into an aged, withered old hag before her time. 'And her?' he asked, pointing at the girl, perhaps two years younger than himself, pretty, mop-haired, with huge, brilliant black eyes, who still lay crouching silently at the back of the tent. 'What of her?'

'Mary, my daughter, she be,' the woman said tonelessly. 'No fine lessons in dressmaking or needlework for her. No chance of a respectable position as lady's-maid in the house of some lady of rank. Instead, she be trained to wriggle through a yeoman's window while her master engages him at the front door and God save her from a cruel beating, should she come away with nothing. Soon,' she lowered her voice, 'she will earn more—in other ways. When it pleases him, the master will take her maidenhead and then she will be just another doxy like myself.'

The girl, hearing what her mother had said, started to shiver uncontrollably, tears winding down her pinched, pale cheeks as she rocked backwards and forwards in silent misery.

Francis Drake found himself saying with impish courage, 'I'll rescue yew from all this.'

'You?' The woman laughed hysterically. 'A mere lad? Keep silent, I pray you, lest you put us in worse peril than we are now in. He, who loves to hurt, to break limbs, will mutilate anyone he thinks will run.'

20

'Nevertheless,' Francis said stoutly. 'I will help yew escape. You have my promise. Yew will see.'

Oh yes, he thought. One day I shall be a brave buccaneer and rove the seven seas, if God so pleases, and all shall be in terror of my sword. But I shall never hurt a woman: never in all my life. They are but sweet and timid creatures and always they shall have the protection of my strong sword arm, whether friend or foe, for I have seen the straits into which they may quickly fall through the power of bad men. It was not long before exhaustion overcame the racing thoughts of his young mind and, with his head sinking onto a straw pallet, he was asleep in minutes.

Francis' education into the crooked arts of the underworld began early next morning. In spite of himself, his boyish mind could not help but be amused at the strange tricks employed by the criminal fraternity. Within a short time he promised to prove as dexterous and light-fingered at the art of petty robbery as he was at the tiller of any boat caught suddenly in treacherous shoal water. He was taught how to recognise a rich merchant by his furs and sables; a prosperous farmer, up to town to lay a suit of litigation in the law term, by his purse bulging with crowns for the lawyer's fat fee. Not only that, before long, with a piece of sharp horn clipped to his thumb, he had learned how to slide in under a man's cloak and cut his purse faster than a flash of lightning.

One evening he returned to his filthy tent for his bread and gruel to find Mary, the silent, dark-haired girl, not there. When he asked Mistress Newman where her daughter was, the woman turned away, red-eyed and biting her lip. The only reason she did not sob out loud was because she had long ago wept away all her tears. Eventually, deep in the middle of the night, Mary came back, her body creeping painfully across the ground. By the light of a guttering candle Drake could see her curled up in a corner, knees under her chin like a baby, shivering, groaning strange noises from the back of her throat as she relived some awful, personal agony. Even in his youthful innocence Drake sensed the Upright Man had been at her. He shuffled across and awkwardly began to stroke the girl's hair. But the girl let out some strange, harsh scream like an exhausted hare dangling in a greyhound's slathering jaws and, running to another corner, crouched there, dark black eyes almost starting from their sockets. It was only then that Francis realised why Mary Newman had not

21

spoken one word to him in the time he had been there. The Upright Man had caused her to go dumb with terror.

Satisfied that their crooked arts were now practised and perfect, Blount eventually gave his subjects the order to move. Mules and wagons loaded down with their packed tents, a host of thieves, prostitutes and vagabonds moved off in a shambling, tattered line towards London. An amazing sight: the clapperdudgeon beggars, their bodies a mass of festering sores produced by the application of crowfoot, spearwort and salt, and brought to appalling lividity by a final smearing of ratsbane; stumbling whipjacks possessing forged licences to beg by reason of recent shipwreck; terribly mutilated beggars; pretended mutes; so-called epileptics, who by the well-timed insertion of soap in their mouths could induce a magnificently convincing fit; dicemen with their fullams loaded with lead and quicksilver and bristles with short hair set into one side to prevent that face from lying downwards. All this bizarre panorama of humanity, representing the accumulated and black arts of the underworld, prepared now to invade the capital.

Spending each night in some different, poxy ale-house, never less than three or four to some pustulent hay pallet, the procession of beggars wound its way into the first wretched, closely-packed hovels of Southwark. Negotiating with long practise the stinking, mire-ridden, filth-filled central ditch that received the houses' daily excrement and rubbish; impervious to the strident cry of 'gardez-loo', as some beldame emptied a pisspot full of turds onto the passing heads of those below; they passed on their right the Marshalsea Prison, already filling with the grim results of Queen Mary's religious persecutions, then on their left the Globe and Rose theatres, frequented by strolling players and rootless vagabonds; the bearpits, stews, brothels and all the other splendid sights of ancient London until, at length, a vista of the River Thames suddenly opened up before their eyes.

London Bridge—the prospect never failed to astonish, and young Francis found himself gasping at such a magnificent sight: the twenty great arches that spanned the river; the opulently handsome, timber-lined houses belonging to wealthy merchants that were built on the two middle spans; the hoarse cries of the boatmen along the river bank as they cried 'eastward ho' or 'westward ho', offering their services for a penny a journey.

Francis was not given long to admire the fascinating sights of

22

London. No sooner had he been immured, together with Mistress Newman and her daughter, in some miserable hovel, than the door burst open and Blount swaggered in. Without any warning he dealt Francis a cruel blow in the face that sent the boy crashing to the floor, his nose bleeding, his eyes full of tears. 'That,' Blount snarled, 'is just an earnest, boy, of what you'll get if you try to escape. London is a small town to such as me and there's not an innkeeper from here to Charing Cross who won't deliver you back to me in hours. Now I plan to show you what you'll get every night you don't steal me a goodly, fat purse. Come here . . .'

At this moment Drake, though little more than a child and weeping from pain, looked deep into his own soul and found there a stubborn, obstinate courage. 'Francis Drake is no dog to come at anybody's whistle,' he said.

The eyes of the Upright Man went dark red with rage. 'Well,' he said, advancing on the boy, 'now you have gone and ruined yourself. 'Tis better to break a limb or two and send you out to beg.'

He rushed at the terrified boy, but as he did so the previously dumb girl, Mary Newman, let out a sudden loud wail and without any warning threw herself protectively across the boy, her frail body stoically absorbing Blount's angry blows. 'Leave him alone,' she shrieked. 'He is but a lad. Do what you will with me, but leave the boy alone.'

Blount, out of breath, finally desisted. He walked to the door then turned and said 'I am tired enough boy, to give you one more chance. Remember, a fat purse by tomorrow eve or I'll cut off your nuts and sell you to Archbishop Bonner as a Popish choirboy.' To illustrate his intentions, he laid a meaning hand on his rapier.

As Blount's footsteps died away, Mary Newman, dazed and bruised as she was, managed to crawl over and pillow young Francis' head in her lap. Tenderly she tried to smooth away his awful fears. 'What a brave boy 'tis,' she crooned in her round, ripe Devon accent. 'What a brave lad 'e 'as bin.' She stroked his forehead through the long watches of the night, so that the stare of terror finally faded from Francis' eyes, and cradled in the girl's gentle hands he slept for a while.

Hours later, when he woke, she was still there, warm and comforting. 'Yew were struck dumb,' he said in a wondering voice, 'yet yor kindness to me, made yew speak. I will never forget that. Never, never.'

23

'Hush. Sleep,' the girl said softly.

'I mean to be a great man someday,' Drake said in a small voice. 'One day I will seek yew out and make yew my wife. Here's my oath on't.'

'Yor oath?' In spite of her misfortunes, the girl managed a small, tinkling laugh. 'And how seriously must I take the oath of a boy?'

'Yew will find the oath of Francis Drake is not easily broken.'

The girl said nothing. She lay her bruised body down beside Francis and tried to sleep. She had never before met a boy who had such a high opinion of himself, and she did not wish to hurt his feelings by laughing again. As Francis lay in Mary's arms and dreamed of the soft moorland air of Devon, the good plain food his mother baked, the lowing of the cattle as they came in off the gorse-scented tors to be milked, something else impinged on his weary senses. He woke with a start.

'Drums,' he said. 'Does nobody hear drums?'

Mistress Newman, nudged awake, sat up with a start and listened carefully. 'Bless me,' she said. 'You may be right. Or is it imagination?'

'No,' Mary said excitedly. 'I hears them right enough. They be drums.'

Distinctly carried across the cold dawn air came the rhythmic riffle of drums; then the mutter of distant cheers and the sound of marching feet; and finally, the untidy clatter of cavalry cavorting over the Southwark cobbles.

' 'Tis he, Thomas Wyatt,' Mistress Newman said with sudden excitement.

'Thomas Wyatt?' Drake said curiously.

'He plans to place the Lady Elizabeth on Mary's throne and stop the threatened burnings of Englishmen at Smithfield for the Bishop of Rome's pleasure.' Mistress Newman's face had come alive with sudden hope. 'He advances on London to save such as your father from death. Is that not good news, pray?'

'It certainly is,' Francis replied, trying to keep the emotion out of his own voice.

At sunrise he peeped out of the window and saw a small group of weary men resting in the courtyard of the inn opposite, their hauberks and arquebuses neatly stacked against the wall. Suddenly a man, booted and spurred and wearing a finely-chased cuirass, clambered down the inn steps, at which the men jumped respectfully to

24

their feet. Francis called Mistress Newman over, pointing out the man, youngish but with a high forehead caused by a receding hairline, who was now poring over a map.

'Why, 'tis he, Wyatt himself,' Mistress Newman exclaimed.

'Are you sure?'

'Of course,' she snorted. 'When we worked for Somerset, he and his father, a famous poet, would oft visit us.' Quickly, prising open the horn window, she stuck her head out and shouted, 'Sir Thomas, Sir Thomas.'

Wyatt lifted his head. 'Who calls me?'

'I am Mistress Newman, formerly in the employ of my lord of Somerset. I am here held captive by a cut-throat called Blount. I do be desperate and crave your help.'

'Well, what is this?' came a loud bellow from the parlour below. There was the scraping of boots, the sound of pewter pots clattering to the floor. 'Ask for help, will you, mistress?' Blount's voice was thick with temper and as his boots came clumping up the narrow, winding stairs, he shouted menacingly, 'I'll give you help.'

'Help me ho, sire,' shrieked Mistress Newman, 'or I am soon dead.'

Blount rushed in, a riding quirt dangling from his wrist. He aimed several lashing blows at the woman, who screamed with pain and crawled like a dog into a corner, looking up at Blount with pleading eyes. Down below there was the sound of rending timber as the inn door was suddenly beaten down, then the crash of boots climbing the stairs. Help must be coming, Francis Drake thought. He watched Blount melt into the shadows close to the door, a rapier in one hand and a dagger raised in the other, and tensed himself to act quickly. Wyatt came stumbling through the door and peered uncertainly into the gloom. As Blount's arm lunged down with the dagger, Francis knew instinctively what he must do. Not caring for his own skin, he launched himself onto Blount's back with one enormous, springing bound. The poniard clattered from Blount's hand and with Wyatt now on his guard, a furious sword fight developed between the two men.

Outside all was chaos. Drake spotted two of Blount's henchmen trying to get up the stairs to assist their leader and calmly rolled an empty firkin of ale down on top of them, sending them tumbling to the bottom of the stairs. Hearing a loud moan, followed by the sound of a body thumping down onto the floor, he ran back inside the room. There was no need to have worried. It was Blount who lay there, a thin trickle of dark arterial blood issuing from his mouth, while Wyatt, breathing hard, sheathed his rapier.

'I thank thee, Sirrah.' Mistress Newman, despite her weak and filthy condition, spoke gracefully to Wyatt, managing at the same time an elegant little curtsey. 'We have all been abused indescribably by this villain, and greet you as our deliverer.'

Wyatt nodded. 'And who is this lad?'

'Drake is his name: and he has been a brave boy.'

'Drake?' Wyatt's brows knitted together. 'I'll warrant that name's familiar.'

'Please sir, my father was Preacher to the Fleet before he was taken by the Queen's solidiers,' piped young Francis.

Wyatt smiled. 'Then I must tell thee that he educated the fleet well, for most of my men are seamen from the Medway and all my heavy ordnance comes from their ships. For that alone I wouldst do thee honour, but I trow lad, I am in thy debt for saving my life as well.'

' 'Tis nothing.' Francis dropped his gaze modestly. ' 'Tis nothing at all.'

'You are wrong, lad. 'Tis everything. So pray tell me what I can do for thee?'

'Give me your word that yew will help these ladies and give them your protection on their journey.'

Wyatt's face twitched in a smile. 'You are a knight of chivalry, already,' he exclaimed. 'What else?'

'Only let me serve yew,' Francis said, 'for like my father, I am no Papist.'

'Well, thou art too young to bear a sword, but I have need of a sturdy messenger boy. Report to me at noon, at which time I shall have what is necessary for the ladies.' Bowing gravely to Mistress Newman and her daughter, with the true nobleman's innate courtesy to those of lesser rank, Wyatt left the room.

Now, all was chattering and excitement as Mistress Newman and poor, wan little Mary scraped together their pathetic pieces of baggage and made ready to take their leave. At noon they were ready, and going down the stairs they found Wyatt had kept his word, providing two quiet palfreys for their transport, together with two attendants to escort them.

'Goodbye Francis.' Shyly young Mary kissed Francis Drake on the cheek. 'I go now to stay with my uncle who has a pig-stall at

Honiton market. One day we may meet again.' She stopped, paused as though plucking up courage, then the words came out in a rush. With a great blush reaching clear past her saucer eyes to the roots of her raven hair, she said, 'I must tell thee now, that I do love thee dearly, my sweeting.'

Francis, new to the game of love and too young to understand the emotions that could be aroused in the breasts of women, could only stand there red-faced, watching their disappearing figures.

Battle: confused, milling, bloody. Thrusting up from Southwark with four thousand men came Sir Thomas Wyatt, messenger boy Francis Drake by his side, legs wrapped round a sturdy pony that must have come from very much the same part of Dartmoor as the lad himself.

In the capital there was consternation. Winchester House, seat of the Bishop of London, had been sacked and pillaged. The Bishop's palace, so opulent from the revenue of its Southwark brothels that all London prostitutes were known as 'Winchester Geese', was expendable: but the City of London was not. Better a catholic Queen with a Spanish husband than a burning city and ruined trade! Accordingly defences, under the energetic supervision of my Lord Mayor and Lord William Howard, were soon made so stout that when Wyatt tried to cross London Bridge he found the gates closed, all the city steeples and towers topped with artillery and the massive Tower of London booming defiance from its formidable ordnance.

Wyatt's army eyed the thirty or so blackened, shrivelled heads belonging to executed traitors impaled on the southern gate tower of the bridge and began to murmur. If their revolt failed, their own heads would soon replace the delicious, stinking, bloody meat around which scavenger birds were now wheeling, screetching and fighting. Wyatt, realising that the moment had come for inspired leadership, turned smartly in his saddle and shouted 'All right, lads. So we'll take 'em in the rear. Off to the west.'

To the consternation of the Londoners, the rebel army now evaporated like the wind, only to reappear a few hours later at Kingston-on-Thames, where, equipped with planks and ladders, they quickly repaired the bridge and surged across the river during the night. At daybreak Wyatt reached Brentford and all London was in seething chaos: the Lord Mayor and his aldermen were dressed for combat, even sergeants-at-law pleading their cases in court wore full armour.

27

At noon Wyatt was at the Knight's Bridge and Francis received a wonderful chance early in his life of seeing what a dashing, resourceful leader could do.

At this point, however, Wyatt made the one mistake that was to cost him dear. Certain that the city was his, he advanced into the fields of St James without adequate scouting or reconnaissance, thus enabling the Earl of Pembroke to fall on the rear of his army and cut it off, so that while Wyatt himself advanced triumphantly across the meadows of Charing Cross, half his force lay halted behind him. This was the moment for Drake, riding low in the saddle, oblivious to the arrows and bolts that whistled past his ears, to dash back and forth across the fields with urgent despatches. With the invaluable intelligence brought by his young messenger boy, Wyatt now changed his order of battle to meet the altered circumstances: the army left in its rear, to assault Whitehall, while he, Wyatt, made a dash for the city.

Wyatt had reckoned, however, without the trained bands and their extraordinarily stubborn insistence on their rights and privileges. With a great cry of 'clubs' they rallied so stoutly under Sir Henry Jerningham, captain of the Queen's guard, that the rebels could make only slow progress along the wide, elegant Strand. Knowing the other battle to be more important, Wyatt waited anxiously for news. Once he captured the Queen the battle was won. If he failed to capture her, his own head might very soon join the others on London Bridge.

To the frantic rat-at-at of drums, Queen Mary's personal, blue-coated, gentlemen-at-arms, five hundred in all, formed into a tightly-knit group outside Whitehall Palace and gave desperate battle. Now young Francis Drake was treated to the truly amazing sight of Queen Mary courageously coming out to join her men. Small, dumpy, tight-faced, thin-lipped, she could be clearly heard encouraging them in her deep, masculine voice, the great black cross smudged across her forehead earlier at mass by the Lord Chancellor's thumb still plainly visible. The bravery of this funny little woman, standing there in the full magnificence of her coronation robes, donned specially for the occasion, oblivious to the arrows falling all around her, was something Drake would never forget, and it had the same effect on her own men. Somehow, miraculously, they held, giving the Earl of Pembroke time to fall on the rear of the rebel army with a tremendous cavalry charge and sweep them to bloody ruin, like so much chaff on a harvested field.

It was all over. Francis Drake galloped for his life across the fields that separated the village of Westminster from London, bearing terrible news. Up the Strand he went, the shoes of his flying pony striking sparks from the magnificently paved surface, lined with its many rich shops of goldsmiths and silversmiths. Finally he caught up with Wyatt, who by now had penetrated to the very vitals of the city and was besieging the Lud Gate itself, close by the stinking, foul ditch of the Fleet River. When Wyatt heard the news, that his army was destroyed, that everything was lost, he took Francis to one side. 'Boy,' he asked sombrely, 'will you still serve me as bravely in defeat as in battle?'

'Yes sir. I will.'

'Then listen. You must fly to the Princess Elizabeth at Ashridge. Somehow, I cannot tell you the way, you must gain access to her. Tell her all is lost. That Courtenay did not rise in the west, that Suffolk failed me in the north. That on my own I did my best. Can you remember all this?'

'I will try,' Francis said stoutly, although the message made little sense to him.

'There is more. Enough has been committed to paper to condemn the Princess to death already. You must tell her—' Wyatt cocked an ear, and hearing the distant clatter of Pembroke's cavalry surging triumphantly up the Strand, his voice rose frantically to a high pitch, bordering on hysteria. '—Yes, you must tell her to destroy all letters she has had from me. That within days, she will be called to answer to the Queen for her part in all this. Only if all evidence of our—' he hesitated, reluctant to use the dreaded word '—treason is destroyed, can she ever hope to survive. Do you understand?'

'I think I dew, sir.'

'Then repeat it back, lad, for on you, all England's future hopes now rest.'

Wyatt took Francis, stumbling, through the whole message. Then, satisfied the boy had it straight, passed over a great purse of jingling crowns and his own brace of finely wrought pistols, saying grimly 'Take these. They will serve you well and I warrant I shall soon have no need of such baubles.'

Francis, pale-faced, took the money and the pistols then looked one last time on the impassioned, tortured face of this man who had saved him from Blount's cruelty, who had been so good to him, this son of a poet who had lived a dream and would soon die a traitor's death. Saluting gravely, he wheeled his pony and galloped off down a side street.

Somehow, he knew, he must obtain an audience with the Princess Elizabeth. She was likely to be heavily guarded, a prisoner in her own house. So what chance would he, little more than farm boy, have of getting in to see her? The task was plainly impossible. Yet he must try, as he had promised. For Wyatt, he would do his best to keep his word.

Like the wind, Francis Drake headed west, towards the manor house of Ashridge.

*'Although I may not be a lion, I am a lion's cub and have a lion's heart.'*

Elizabeth.

# 4

It was a bitter day in early February. The Princess Elizabeth paced up and down the spacious presence-chamber before the roaring fire she had caused her attendants to build up. Normally she would dance a galliard or two in order to raise the blood, then take horse and gallop like the wind through the lush deer park of Ashridge; but for many months now she had been in agony of mind and her health had begun to fail. For almost two years she had walked a terrible tightrope with her sister, gracefully accepting her presents, dutifully attending mass and instruction, at Mary's request, in the 'old religion', but one woman does not fool another so easily, especially a half-sister.

She hated Mary: hated her with the full-blooded fury that her father would have understood. And Mary had tried to return her hate with love, because she was a good woman, virtuous, steeped to the brim in prayer and cant, and recognising the sin for what it was, had fought it down. Envy: oh yes, that was another thing. Mary had envied her all right: age to youth; withered virginity to the experienced coquetry of a slim, tall golden-haired girl—despite all her mock-modest looks. Mary was unpopular, while she, Elizabeth, with one gesture of her gorgeous hands was adulated wherever she went. And while Mary made ready to hand England over to the Pope's legate and a Spanish husband, the English looked to the beautiful Princess for deliverance. That was it: little matter who was Catholic or Protestant. What difference did it make—only small points of dogma, unless you were a frustrated, maniacal zealot like Mary. It was the insult: a people melded by the Tudors into a nation, freed from the chaos of baronial wars, energetic, patriotic, flexing their muscles, arising from sleep but still remembering the glory of Agincourt and Crécy; now to be meekly handed over to a Spanish husband—swallowed by the huge Hapsburg empire.

It was too much for her: too much for any young girl. Seven years before she had learned her lesson well. One false move by anybody in succession to the throne, the slightest indiscretion, could be quickly blown into treason by a hostile lawyer, an ambitious minister. That had been nothing—pouf—she snapped slim fingers in derision. She had made mincemeat of Tyrwhit. No danger—no real danger— although she had been frightened enough at the time, when a young girl of thirteen. No danger. not compared to this. Now, this eighth day of February, she stood in deadly peril of death; put there by events over which she had never had control.

What do you do when members of your own household are found to be plotting to place you on the throne; when you discover that members of the finest and most powerful families in the country are involved; when all England prays to you for deliverance from Mary's burnings; when all England longs for an English Queen on the throne; just exactly what *do* you do? Why you do absolutely nothing at all, except play the sweet innocent and hope they will not bungle the plot, and if the Queen grants them enough rope with which to hang themselves, it is not your hand which swings them off into eternity.

Walking. She kept walking. Exercise was absolutely necessary to her. As she walked, she tossed her head, allowing her flowing hair, silky in all its reddish-tinged magnificence, to cascade around her ears, as if reassuring herself by the infinite softness of its touch of her ability to fascinate and ensnare the opposite sex.

The men, she remembered, had first started plotting in late November and Mary had suspected almost at once, sniffing with a strange sureness of instinct the rotten canker of rebellion. So then there was the faintly ridiculous sight of good, prayerful Mary trying to give her sister the benefit of the doubt and doing nothing to scotch the plot, other than to grow colder and colder in her manner towards Elizabeth. Still, tension had grown so strong between the sisters, that Elizabeth had asked and received Mary's permission to retire to her manor of Ashridge.

What a magnificent occasion that had been! That sparkling morning of December, when she had set out for Ashridge accompanied by no less than five hundred gentlemen retainers. She could still remember the roars of laughter, when ten miles along the way, her eyes gleaming with mischief, she had stopped her journey and commanded a messenger back to Mary, in a bold, ringing voice, to supply her with copes, chasubles and all the other accompaniments of catholic ritual. But this time Mary had not been fooled, and in return she had received nothing but coldness and silence.

Christmas had come and gone in a whirl of frantic merriment: Sir James Crofts chosen as 'The Lord of Misrule'; Ashridge a riot of holly, trailing ivy, branches of yew and spruce; mistletoe branches; the yule log brought in; the traditional wassails drunk; the roast peacock borne before the company; and then the boar's head, to a frantic piping and trumpeting from the minstrels, the wail of rebecs and the thunderous riffle of drums reverberating throughout the manor house. All through the twelve days of Christmas the plotting had gone on, while she, recognising now that the plot was likely to be bungled in an excess of wine-bibbing, had frowned and refused her active encouragement. No good. She was the fairy Princess: the magic figurehead around which treason eddied and flowed. On 2 January, while Philip's emissaries arriving in England to sign the marriage treaty with Mary were pelted with snowballs, the conspirators, dressed as the twelve fools of Christmas, galloped drunkenly about Ashridge with their bells, pigs' bladders and hobby horses, conspiring openly, at the top of their voices.

By 17 January Mary, not surprisingly, knew everything, forcing Wyatt to strike prematurely from Kent on the 25th, hoping to take London before the Queen had time to muster her forces. Now, ugly rumours were filtering through from the capital of Wyatt's complete defeat and capture. Under torture, he would be certain to involve her—and the Princess knew—real fear.

Up and down the great room the Princess paced: back and forth, her thoughts racing. All this preparation, all this education, all this scheming, she thought bitterly. All come to nought. Would it be death? Preceded by the Tower? At the thought of that grim, terrible place a huge wave of bizarre, unreasoning horror swamped her senses. Right from the earliest days of her childhood, those awful words 'the Tower' had been associated with emotive frontiers of terror that only the wild imagination of a child can fully encompass. She clamped her teeth together and shuddered. Pull yourself together. To survive, you must think. A woman is born with little strength but many brains. Use them. Plan. Keep calm.

Impossible. She was ill. She swept upstairs and, burying herself deep in the rich furnishings of her huge four poster, conscious of her privacy and that she was no longer on public view, she allowed her iron self-control to desert her. Drawing her knees up to her chest, she gave way to florid, desperate, hysteria, sobbing her way through the long reaches of the night until she fell asleep from sheer exhaustion.

As for young Francis, he made the journey to Ashridge easily enough. From London it was a bare thirty miles and one night at an inn had sufficed, where, with a careful eye on the locked door and ready hand on pistol, he had managed to keep at bay footpads and all other greedy gentlemen of the road.

When he saw Ashridge for the first time his heart sank. A moated manor house, it possessed only one drawbridge, and this seemed well garrisoned by a small but resolute number of men-at-arms determined to protect their Princess, no matter what, until the Queen commanded differently. Francis Drake realised that the moment he presented himself at the drawbridge and asked for an interview with the Princess Elizabeth he was likely to be received with roars of laughter, given a smart clip across the ear and told to be off. How then, could he get in to see her? The matter was one of incredible urgency. He cast around for inspiration, brain working with lightning speed. Immediately, he began to get the germ of an idea.

Close by the manor of Ashridge a number of gypsies were camped, horse-dealers and pedlars, who had been doing good business with the many people continuously coming and going from the manor house. Francis had heard all about them from his father and the thought of entering their camp frightened him. They were desperate men, he knew, liable to be hanged or flogged at the whim of every local justice of the peace. As a result they did not welcome strangers readily. Yet Francis' idea seemed to him a good one and he knew he would have to try.

As he approached the camp, his presence was immediately signalled by the barking and growling of a great pack of mangy, half-starved dogs. They were enough to deter the stoutest-hearted intruder and Francis, with some difficulty, forced his pony to walk calmly through the mass of snapping and threatening teeth until a man came out of a tent and held up his hand in peremptory fashion. Dark and swarthy, with earrings glinting from both his ears, the man wore britches and a jerkin of roughly-tanned cony-skin; but what set him apart from others was the scarf made up of fantastic colours which he wore around his neck and the exotically-embroidered turban covering his head.

'What do you wish here?' the man growled at Francis in a strange accent.

'I seek the headman.'

'I am the jackman of this family.'

'I have to gain entry into that manor yonder. For this, I must needs have yor help to learn the tricks of a pedlar.'

The man looked at him for a long time before saying anything, then growled, 'Not from us, boy. Such tricks take time to learn and we leave tomorrow. 'Tis said the Queen's men come. My neck is not yet ready to be stretched.'

Now Francis, in the typically bold, flamboyant gesture that was to mark him so utterly apart from other and lesser men in the future, pulled out his fat purse, still heavy with the golden crowns so impulsively handed to him by Wyatt, and threw it down in front of the gypsy, the pouch bursting and laying a glittering cascade of gold on the grass under the gypsy's eyes.

The gypsy made no effort to pick it up. That would have been undignified for a man as proud as he. Instead his dark eyes seemed to close in fathomless thought. Suddenly he smiled broadly. 'That was a fine gesture for a lad as young as you,' he said. 'Very well. 'Tis done. I accept. Tonight you will lodge with me. My name is Ned Bright.' He extended a hand, which Drake, leaning forward on his pony's neck, shook. Only then did the gypsy chief allow himself to bend down and gather in the coins.

'But did you not take a risk?' Bright asked Francis, at length. 'I might have taken your money and given you nothing in return.'

'There was no risk,' Francis said softly, 'for yor reputation is well-known. Yew certainly would have robbed me of every penny before allowing me to leave yor camp and so I had nothing to lose at all. Is that not right?'

Ned Bright's black eyes sparkled as he roared with delighted laughter. 'That was indeed well said, for I like a lad with a good spirit in him and 'tis plain to see, you fear nobody. Follow me then, boy, if you will.'

The gypsy conducted young Francis into the camp, where all was frantic activity. In an hour's time, the Princess' master of horse would allow the gates to be opened, so that servants, soldiers, and gentlemen-at-arms might come to trade and to gawp. Francis, open-mouthed, gazed with amazement at the flashing, smiling, swarthy faces, painted red and bright yellow, and at the garishly calicoed scarves all the gypsy folk seemed to wear over their shreds and patches. Bright escorted him through a group of madly flying dancers, feet and leggings capped with many tinkling bells, as they prepared an exotic spectacle of 'Moorish' dancing—an art they had brought with them across Europe and now corrupted into the name of 'Morris' dancing.

It was plain that Bright had taken a great fancy to this lad, so well set-up, so full of confidence, with bright blue eyes that would look straight through a man and call nobody master. Also, he had been much taken with the fine bold way that Drake had thrown a fat purse at his feet in such devil-may-care fashion. Accordingly, he put his arm round Drake's shoulder and said 'Come share our food. You will soon find what kind of folk we are. Afterwards I will give you the sturdiest donkey we have, together with a pannier-full of trinkets to help you get into the manor.'

That night, Francis sat by a roaring fire while the gypsies taught him the pedlar's whining jargon. Soon plied and drugged with the gypsies strong ale, he collapsed flat on his back and slept the sleep of the damned. When he woke, stiff and cold, under his blanket, it was to find himself completely alone. Terrified, he looked frantically around, but he need not have worried. There was his pony, tethered to a nearby tree, and Bright had indeed kept his word, providing him with a sturdy jennet across which a double pannier-full of goods had been strapped.

Francis did not have to look too far to find the reason for the gypsies sudden departure. With sinking heart he saw the file of mounted, blue-coated soldiers, the fine gentlemen with feathered hats and embroidered riding-suits of rich taffeta; and heard the chink of bit and stirrup as their horses wheeled and cavorted impatiently for the drawbridge to come down. These must be the Queen's men, come to take the Princess Elizabeth back to London to face charges of treason: and eventually the block. If, in his own way, he was ever to help her, and so keep his pledged word to Wyatt, he dare not linger a second longer. Already he had delayed too long. Mounting his pony, and leading the laden jennet behind him, he made his way slowly down the path towards the manor house with fear chilling his heart.

He was immediately in luck: by arriving so soon after the Queen's soldiers, he caught a moment of temporary confusion when the Queen's men took over control of the house from the Princess's, so that with no proper guards posted and with Drake being little more than a harmless lad, he was able to pass in over the drawbridge without comment. As soon as he found himself in the spacious courtyard, he began to sing, heart thumping, a traditional pedlar's ditty:

'Lawn as white as driven snow,
Cyprus black as e'er was crow,
—what will you buy from me good folks?
Gloves as sweet as damask roses,
Masks for faces and for noses. . .'

The soldiers, busy stacking their arms, grinned tolerantly at the cracked sound of the lad's voice, now in process of breaking, one moment in a high treble octave, one moment low, like a man's, and indulgently strolled over to inspect his wares. They were soon overtaken by a great rush of serving maids, wenches from the kitchen, even well-born maids-of-honour, who, mostly confined by their duties to the manor house, welcomed the chance as a heaven-sent opportunity to replenish their wardrobes.

'What will yew buy, good people?' Drake sang out. 'Golden quoifs, stomachers for lads to give to their dears, pins and perfumes and pomanders for my lady's chamber? Necklaces of fine amber?' Suiting actions to words he let clothes, baubles, scent bottles and trinkets drift through his fingers in a golden flood for all to see.

Soon there was a great scrimmaging crowd as the Queen's horsemen, some of them rakish bravos with doublets slashed in the latest Spanish style, seized the moment to get acquainted with the prettier girls and ensnare their affections by buying them a little trinket or two. Noticing a stoutish woman, middle-aged, almost certainly of the Princess's court from the richness of her dress, Drake detached himself from the crowd examining his wares and walked over to her. 'Well-a-day, good lady,' he sang. 'What dew yew lack? A cambric partlet and a pair of sleeves? A cherry-coloured cloak garnished with gold buttons and loops? Perfumes? Sweet bags? Try my fine silver bodkin mounted with pearls.' Lowering his voice to a whisper, he hissed, 'Where is the Princess? I must talk with her.'

The woman tossed her head with annoyance at the boy's temerity. 'What? Who are you to see her grace?' she said scornfully.

'Thomas Wyatt's messenger.'

The woman, who was in fact Mistress Kat Ashley, turned white in the face and for a moment Francis Drake thought she was going to faint. 'Be gone,' she muttered. 'You lay a trap for my lady.'

'Nay,' Drake said. 'For she is already condemned.' He was amazed at the confidence his sense of purpose seemed to have given him. 'Not so. I cannot harm her—only help her.'

Kat Ashley looked at the boy, examined his level blue eyes, and seeing only sincerity in his face, pointed to one side of the courtyard, where a little door could be seen. 'Through there, boy, then over the wall.' Tis high. I fear you'll not be able to climb it. She is taking the air at the moment—' her face turned sad, desolate, '—fresh from receiving the Queen's commissioners.' Looking doubtfully at the sturdy young lad, she added 'Harm her not, for help is indeed what she now requires.'

But Drake was already gone. He was through the little door in a flash, unnoticed by the crowd of soldiers and women still milling around his patient donkey. His heart sank when he saw the wall: fifteen, no twenty, feet at least. No time to think. Start climbing. Luckily he was aided by a fine pear tree trained to the wall. For a boy accustomed to climbing a bucking, twisting mast in the steep, corkscrew chop of a North Sea gale, it was nothing. Sweating only slightly, Francis Drake made it to the top then looked down: a little piece of secluded garden not overlooked by any of the great oriole windows that were a feature of Ashridge. Good. Closing his eyes he jumped, landing with a dull thud in a deeply-dug flower-bed ready to receive next summer's gilly flowers.

Clambering to his feet he looked around him. Then he saw her for the first time, quite close, gazing calmly at him. His heart lurched sickeningly with excitement. He could get no clear impression of her: confronted by a brilliance more blinding than a noonday sun, his eyes lost the ability to focus and produced only a mere blur. Tawny hair of a golden lion and dark eyes set in unusually white skin; the interplay of colour giving the smooth youthfulness of her complexion a silky, olive look; the whole of her bathed in a pool of ethereal and unnatural brightness as though illuminated by means of some strange, nameless witchery.

Drake considered how he must appear to a surprised, defenceless girl: worn britches and a doublet of plain russet leather girded with a buff belt into which two great pistols and an ugly-looking cutlass had been jammed. Coming down like that from the top of a high wall, dirty, sweating, panting, he could only be a young cut-throat bent on robbery, plunder and murder. Before him was this glittering

Princess. Why does she not run, he asked himself desperately. If she were to do that, I would know she was human and could comfort her. By now, all girls would have run screaming for help, but she does not! He clenched and unclenched his fists in sheer frustration.

Are you then afraid of a girl? he asked himself. But girls do not usually have high nostrils proud enough to breath hot flame, or red-gold hair that glows like the northern sky on a high summer eve. He tried once more to examine her features. He could see she looked strained, tired, might even have been crying, yet the sheer intensity with which her face radiated inner fire, like some finely cut jewel, made him quite unable to look her in the eye. A feeling somewhat approaching terror possessed him. He began a weaving retreat to the wall, making strange gobbling noises from the back of his throat.

'Do not be frightened,' the girl said.

Ridiculous! He, a sturdy, pistoliered, dirty-faced vagabond dropping down into a lady's garden from nowhere and she tells him not to be frightened!

He groaned in a paroxysm of shame at his own awkward, tongue-tied, childish impotence. Miserably he wished the earth would rise up and swallow him, there and then.

'I am the Lady Elizabeth,' the girl said calmly, directly. 'As it is plain you are not here to rob me, you may speak. But first, you must go down on one knee. Then I will extend a hand and you shall kiss it.'

Francis Drake sank down as commanded, head to the ground, face burning, blushing a scarlet red. A hand came into view with slim fingers as white and pure as the first light kiss of winter's snow. Compulsively he grabbed it with all the eager clumsiness of someone who has just been admitted to a great secret, bruising the elegant, artistic fingers with his grubby mouth.

'Pray do not eat it, sirrah,' the Princess exclaimed, her mouth twitching dangerously near to a smile. She had tried to be stern, distant, but she was young, and whatever her troubles, could not help but give way to a smothered giggle. Somehow that little laugh made her seem human, no longer a being fashioned by divine hands and set apart from all others, and as a result, Drake slowly began to lose his awful paralysis of fear and regain his usual confidence.

'Your majesty,' he piped up. 'I come on urgent business.'

Again, that stifled giggle. 'Nay,' she said. 'Not "your majesty." Let anyone hear that and I'll warrant you'll join me at traitors' gate, soon enough! To commence an audience, first you must call me

39

"your grace" and after that, "madam", oft-repeated, should pleasantly suffice.'

'Yes, yor grace.'

'Well said, ragamuffin. Now state your business. What can a boy like you have to say to a princess?' Stern command crept into her voice. 'And by the holy cross of Abingdon, get off your knees and stand like a man.'

The Princess listened quietly as Francis recounted Wyatt's last message. Garbled though it might be, some of Wyatt's last desperate advice came burning through. 'You are the most popular and revered Princess Elizabeth. They will not, dare not, chop off your head without proof of treason. Proof: that is the important word. Others less popular will go easily to the block, the English common law fudged, stretched, ignored, circumvented, but Englishmen and women will never allow their beloved Princess to be beheaded unless solid, indisputable proof of high treason is first produced.' That was what this muddy-faced, pistol-carrying, burly lad was trying to say in his execrable Devonshire accent.

For days, weeks, she had let her fevered brain alternate from elation to low depression, spending hours alone in her room, as the strain of the last two years had taken its toll and reduced her to fit after fit of hysteria. Now, to survive, she would have to think clearly. Wyatt, of course, was right. Queen Mary would act only with carefully-planned justness and the appearance of legality. Why else had she sent two of her personal doctors to certify that she, Elizabeth, was well enough to be moved to London? Why had she chosen Lord William Howard, her own great-uncle, to escort her there, unless it was to demonstrate to a suspicious nation Mary's impeccable correctness? Yes, without proof, she was safe. Well, what proof of treason was there? Documents? Something written? Straightaway, deep, cold chill gripped her spine. Letters from Wyatt to her? He had been careful never to place any details of the plot on paper. From her to him then? No, he was always careful to destroy them, so he said, and she believed him. Now, however, she remembered something else. Something damning. Terrible. In his very last letter to her before the uprising, Wyatt had prefaced the contents with thanks for 'My lady's wonderful letter of good wishes and encouragement'. On its own innocuous, yet in the hands of a skilled state lawyer, that was proof. Cold damnable proof of previous conspiracy. It proved she had been writing to him immediately before the rebellion—and to what else could she have encouraged him, other than rebellion itself? Soon, they would search Ashridge from stem to stern for incriminating matter: and they would find that letter. Unless it could first be destroyed. Quickly, coldly, her mind reverted to the boy in front of her. By the mass, she thought, here is a bold, resolute boy. Perhaps I may still be saved. Hurry though. Soon, men would come to take her to her quarters. She would have liked to have dallied a little, enslaved and ensnared this lad—something so easily done with boldly subtle looks, a fine toss or two of that magnificent lion's mane of hair, framing the haughtiness of Tudor bone structure, but there was no time.

She spoke quickly, impulsively. 'Boy, you must do something for me.'

'My lady, whatever yew command.'

'In the long gallery—you cannot miss it, a great chamber running the length of the house—there is a reading table at the far end. On that table are placed two books, left there by me. Well boy, do you understand my directions so far?'

'Yes, yor grace.'

'In one of those books, and I recall not which, there is a letter from your recent master, Sir Thomas Wyatt. Soon, they,' she gestured eloquently, with long, supple fingers, 'will search my rooms for just such letters as this. So tonight you must break in there, and no matter what, destroy that letter. Do that for me, if you wish to save my life.'

'I will,' Francis said stoutly. 'I swear it.'

There was no time for goodbyes, for thanks even. 'Time's up, your grace,' grated a hoarse voice. The warning creak of a small door set into the far wall, opening on rusty hinges, gave Drake just enough time to leap behind a sheltering bush as the guards marched in, helmets, cuirasses and hauberks agleam in the faint winter sun, as they assembled round the slender figure of the young Princess.

The Princess Elizabeth turned and, head held haughtily erect, marched sharply away at the head of the escort of armed men, looking neither to left or right. Either he will succeed, in which case one day I shall rule England, Elizabeth thought to herself, or he will fail, in which case I shall be beheaded. It crossed her mind that she had given the boy an almost impossible task and if he were discovered, he would also certainly die. What matter? If a man would not risk his life for a beautiful princess, he deserved to die anyway.

She dismissed the point as one of no importance.

*'—and as for the traitor Wiat he migth paraventur writ me a letter but on my faithe I never received any from him'*

Extract from Elizabeth's famous 'tide letter' to Queen Mary.

# 5

The February night was cold and dark: moonless and still, with a mist rising quickly from the moat and outlying meadows, surging, eddying, and extending damp, grey entrails up the thick walls of Ashridge. Francis stood underneath the windows of the long gallery, higher than the wall he had already climbed to get there—far higher—and there were no projections, no pipes, just stonework and ivy. Well that would have to be enough. He was stiff and cold and what was worse, hungry.

That morning he had found his way back to his pony and jennet easily enough and had been careful not to trade all his goods, so as to provide himself with the excuse for staying in the manor grounds one more night. He had led his animals off to the stable-block, nobody giving a young pedlar lad a second glance, and had spent the rest of the day sleeping in deep straw, keeping himself out of everybody's way until nightfall. Now, not having eaten, his body craved the warming fuel of food to bring it alive. He put the thought out of his head and began silently flexing his muscles, making them supple and limber. Around him there was deep, blanketing silence, except for the eery call of nightjars and the occasional soft hoot of an owl.

He went up the wall, scrabbling for handholds in the thick ivy. He managed two, three feet, almost four, then his boots missed a toehold and he thumped softly back onto the ground, the noise of his fall masked by the soft, damp soil. Now try again, he told himself. Be more careful. Feeling delicately for cracks in the stonework where he could wedge the tip of his boot before reaching up again for another such crevice in which to insert his fingers, he climbed steadily upwards. Strong arms, accustomed to riding the bucking, frantically swaying masts and yard-arms of the wild Medway estuary, gradually hauled his body through the soft rustling ivy until, at length, his eyes drew level with the window. Inside there was a fire, softly flickering, throwing strange shadows on the shelves of finely-bound books. The ceiling was spendidly carved with intricate, geometric designs. He could see no one there, the fire lit to keep out the chill, that was all.

He drew back a fist and softly crunched delicate glass. The heavily-leaded window cracked with little noise, allowing Francis to turn the handle and open the window. He wriggled through and dropped onto soft Turkey carpeting, an island in a sea of finely-polished, planked, wooden flooring. In the far corner was a table, just as the Princess had said. He stole quickly over. The table was bare.

He felt a moment of panic. Quickly he looked around. Two books lay casually at the end of a book shelf, face down, put there perhaps by some cleaning wench. He examined them. The *Works of Cicero* in Latin and Melancthon's *Loci Communes*, a celebrated commentary on Protestant theology and statecraft. Amazing that anyone could understand these things, especially a young woman. He flicked over the pages of one of the books and a letter fell out. He didn't need to read it. The signature of Thomas Wyatt at the end was sufficient. A wonderful sense of elation gripped him. To aid her grace, the most beautiful Princess Elizabeth herself, was the heady stuff of any half-grown lad's dearest dreams. He turned, letter clasped in his hand, ready to burn it in the fire, but a hand seemed to snake out of the flickering semi-darkness, crystallising into iron-hard fingers that clamped down with savage force on his wrist.

'What have we here?' The voice was amused, bantering, self-satisfied, foreign. 'I expected some desperate, bloodthirsty bravo to try and burn her grace's incriminating letters, but what do I get? *Un muchacho*. A boy. That is all. *Es muy amusante*.'

Francis took in the man by the light of the fire: slim, thirtyish, a nobleman, by the finery of his slashed doublet and silken hose; dark, very dark, the skin smoothly fine from the grease of his native diet, yet crisped a deep brown by the Spanish sun. Slim, beardless, with a pencil-thin, carefully-groomed moustachio; eyes burningly cruel; hands and wrists as strong as iron from riding blood stallions; one hand holding a rapier, its diamond-hard point now pricking his throat, the weapon's beautiful Toledo, high tensile steel already flexing and dancing under the fire's flickering light, as pressure slowly built through the slender blade.

'The letter—give it to me. Now. *Immediatemente*.' A brown hand snaked out to take it from Drake's surprised grasp, but seafaring had taught the boy balance and the Upright Man had taught him to be as elusive as an eel. Drake threw himself, impossibly, backwards, into the roaring fire, bouncing off a half-consumed log in a flaring scatter of incandescent ashes, and free now of the dangerous rapier point, rolling over and over across the wooden floor, his rough britches smoking from his passage through the fire.

At the edge of the fire Wyatt's letter, which Francis had unsuccessfully contrived to throw into the heart of the flames, curled and smoked tantalisingly. The Spaniard now bent to pick it up, contemptuously ignoring young Francis. Suddenly a weight descended tigerishly on his back: a gouging, kicking, punching whirlwind of a boy, teeth seeking then finding his swordhand, fastening onto the meaty muscle of his thumb mound, then clamping home like the fangs of a hungry dog.

'*Hijo de Puta!*' The Spaniard cursed softly, sibilantly, springing backwards in pained surprise. Furiously he began to cuff the boy violently as he tried to free his hand, but though tears sprang into Francis' eyes, he would not let go.

Surprisingly, though locked together in a furious fog of combat, both of them were thinking clearly. If he should call for help, Drake thought, I am lost. Yet he does not. Why is this? Although I cause the Spaniard terrible pain, he remains as silent as a stalking cat.

The Spaniard knew the answer. He had even less right to be there than the boy. As the pain of his lacerated, imprisoned thumb coursed through his body, he discovered exactly how a heretic must feel when writhing and jumping at the first touch of the flame; the agony pear is popped into his mouth so that he may only moan, while eyes bulge clear from their sockets in agony. He, Juan Martinez de Recalde, illustrious knight of the order of Santiago, so tantalisingly near to an enormous coup that would ensure instant preferment at court, was held fast by the teeth of a dog, as though he were a bear being baited in a pit. Not one word did he shout: he did not dare. He had come over with the marriage commissioners, endured the insults of the hostile populace, happy that this nation of heretical savages would soon be brought to heel when his master, Philip, were made king. But first—Renard, that wily, cunning ambassador, had said—first, the Princess Elizabeth must die.

'You, Juan,' Renard had said. 'When she is confined to quarters, search her correspondence and what you find, give to me, then I will see *La Puta's* head chopped off.'

Yes. On the verge of complete triumph, he, Juan Martinez de

Recalde, head screwed up in agony, dare not utter a single sound, because Howard, Lord High Admiral, had been heard to threaten innumerable times that if he caught the Spanish interfering in domestic affairs, why he would take the fleet over to France. Yes. Body contorted, cuffing away at this impudent young puppy who was having such a *desayuno* on his thumb, he was completely and utterly impotent.

'All right,' he hissed. '*Muchacho*, release me and you may go free.'

Suddenly, quickly, Drake sprang back, picking up the rapier in one smooth movement and tossing it through the open window. With the other hand he slid the letter neatly into the fire. Breathing hard, the two late adversaries watched the all-important letter flare into bright flame before dissolving into ashes.

Drake grinned. 'I shall leave yew now,' he said. 'And I see that yew will not stop me, being as unwelcome here as myself.'

Looking at the boy, standing legs apart, face cheeky, mischievously disrespectful in his hellish, heretical religion, the Spaniard's eyes smouldered at the diabolical cruelties he would have liked to work on him. He recalled with pleasure the punishment meted out to lazy natives working the Peruvian silver mines. The whip? About as painful as a woman's kiss. No. He wanted to watch the boy flayed alive. Slowly. Very slowly. Eyes hard, he said 'Boy, *comè se llama*. What is your name?'

'I am called Francis Drake.'

'*Muy Buen*. Then we shall meet again,' the Spaniard whispered. '*Sin duda*—for I swear it on the holy *Virgen. Draque*. Yes, I will remember that name. *Francisco Draque*. It is burned on my heart for all time. One day, we will meet again, I assure you. *Adios, Francisco Draque. Hasta luego.*'

Juan Martinez de Recalde softly walked the length of the long gallery with all the slim, dark grace of a dancing master, closing the door behind him. Now it was time for young Francis Drake, elated beyond measure with his success, to slip out of the window and descend softly to the ground in a flurry of rustling ivy. His good fortune, however, had just come to an end. He had survived religious persecution; the awful cruelty of the Upright Man; had avoided injury in battle; the treachery of which everyone knew the gypsies were capable; the murderous rapier of a murderous Spaniard; but sooner or later, his luck had to run out.

The guard, disturbed on their rounds by a rapier clattering down the side of a wall under the long gallery, waited silently in the darkness. And the boy dropped safely and neatly right into their hands.

On 12 February Elizabeth, Princess of England, left Ashridge to travel towards her destiny. Certified fit to travel, albeit slowly, by Doctors Owen and Wendy, the Princess, thin-faced, eyes piercing bright from the fever that came from hysteria, weak in body and spirit, lay exhausted in her rolling, jarring litter with curtains tightly closed, as day after day the procession travelled a few more miles towards London and the grim fate she was sure awaited her.

When she had first been carried out, feeble from her weeping, not caring in her frantic, nameless fear how she looked, even to her own band of gentlemen-at-arms or devoted coterie of ladies, she had been taken past cart after cart laden with provisions, clothes and belongings of her household—for she was still Princess Elizabeth and must be allowed the courtesies of her rank—until she had been confronted, possibly on purpose, by the sight of the boy Drake, arms tightly bound, seated in an open cart. She was careful not to betray concern for him by any undue emotion. She could well imagine that the Queen's Council would have some very interesting questions to ask the boy; questions that might well be accompanied by torture; but she had been more worried about what the boy had achieved, than his probable fate. Had he destroyed the letter? Found it even? She burned to ask him, but Lord William Howard hovered near, watching her intently.

'This is the lad who broke into my house?' she had demanded.

'Yes, madam,' replied one of her ladies. 'It is he.'

She had gazed at him, levelling long, haughty nostrils like the twin barrels of some finely made, divinely-chased arquebus at the boy, hoping for a sign that would mean so much. And then the boy Drake had very deliberately winked; and she knew now that the letter had been destroyed!

Imperiously, finding new energy, she had waved her litter-bearers forward, and they, spurring their horses, began the devilish pitch and roll switchback of a journey towards London. Now she began to get better and when, five days later, the procession descended from Highgate into London, she had the curtains of her litter drawn back so that, to the amazement of her escort, she could be seen, face deathly pale, her thin, frail body magnificently clothed in an all-white dress shimmering and sparkling with jewels, as she basked in the open-mouthed admiration of the adoring populace. Even when the procession reached the City gates at Smithfield, where twenty gallows stood, the air still thick with the smell of blood from the butcher's work of drawing and disembowelling, the Princess's face did not change, though affronted by the meaty quarters and grim, ghastly, grinning heads spiked there of men who had fought for Wyatt. If anything, instead of softening into tears, her face hardened with purpose. She had not asked these men to rebel, or goaded them into becoming—traitors. She gazed at the filthy, blood-soaked heads oozing corrupt stink like freshly-punctured, overripe fruit will ooze juice, with no sign of tenderness, no sign of regret, and her keepers were impressed.

Despite the open litter, the magnificence of her dress and bearing, the finery of her gentlemen-at-arms in their velvet coats, the blue sur-coats and steel armour of the Queen's soldiers, the hundred men of the Queen's own personal guard clad in their brilliant scarlet and black livery, Elizabeth was very conscious that she was a prisoner. For a moment, she allowed her mind to dwell on the fate that awaited the lad, Drake. What would they do to him to make him confess? The rack had been much in use already, Wyatt mercilessly tortured, Sir James Crofts 'marvellously tossed' as the Council probed for evidence against her. Well, the boy would have to hold his tongue and take his chances. Let all men prove their devotion by dying for her. She was the jewel, the priceless, glittering heritage to be preserved for England's sake.

Confined to her apartments, she brazenly demanded an audience with her sister, the Queen. None was given. Slowly her disquiet grew. Had they found new evidence after all? Keep your nerve, she told herself. They have nothing. All you have to do, is keep your nerve. When Mary ordered her to the Tower, she knew terror once again. It held a fear for her that was beyond definition.

As the unreasoning and dizzy horror of heights is to one, and the inability to place his head under water is to another, so the fear of being shut up in the Tower was to her. For a moment she panicked, then the thought grew—no charges had been made. Keep calm. It is a cat and mouse game they play with you. To frighten. To terrify. So you must delay. That is the thing. Hours, minutes, even seconds. The longer you live brings in itself a greater chance of life. By hysteria mixed with entreaty, she delayed one day by missing one Thames tide, so that a letter of eloquence, wet with tears, might be sent to her sister. No good. Keep protesting your innocence. The Queen will assuredly hesitate. After all, she is only human.

This is how it should be, but it is not. Down river she went to the Tower, the state barge manned by watermen with gilded oars and in uniforms bearing the royal arms. Well that was a mistake. Should have sent her anonymously in some dirty old scow, but now—now she was encouraged to play the Royal Princess. Nostrils flaring ever higher, ever more proud, reddish-gold hair flaring defiantly in the wind coming off the damp river, she started on her journey from the steps of Whitehall Palace. Soon a cold rain began, making a dark occasion even more sombre. Down in the covered cabin of the barge sat her eight ladies-in-waiting, a gentleman and a gentleman usher, but the Princess would not go below. Instead she stood there, taking the last sweet breaths of freedom, day-dreaming of wild hunts on fast, galloping horses through woods heavy with the scent of spring flowers.

As the boatmen made fast by the grim archway with its overhanging grating, the Princess was aroused to fury. 'Why, this is traitors' gate! By whose command am I brought here?'

'Your grace, it is her majesty's direct order.'

'This place is not fitting for me and I shall not use it.'

Paget, the lieutenant of the tower, advanced down the steps. 'Madam. I fear the choice is not yours to make.' With a courteous gesture he offered her his cloak as protection against the pouring rain.

The Princess stepped out of the boat, oblivious to the water soaking through her thin shoes. Dashing fiercely aside the lieutenant's cloak, she said imperiously 'Here lands as true a subject as ever landed at these steps. Before thee, oh God, do I speak it, having no other friend than thee alone.' As the traitor's arch yawned above her head, she sat down on the top step, the merciless, drenching rain quickly soaking her to the skin. 'I will go no further,' she announced firmly. 'I am no traitor.'

The lieutenant became confused. He could not use force on a daughter of Henry VIII, while behind him, causing an ever greater problem, the honour guard of yeomen warders, instead of presenting a grim façade, had for some reason sunk to their knees and were now shouting at the top of their voices 'God preserve your grace'.

Elizabeth, realizing that there was no possibility of those particular yeomen warders ever picking her up and carrying her forcibly inside, squared her shoulders and straightened her back in obstinate defiance.

'You had best come in, madam,' the lieutenant said, his voice pleading, 'for here, you sit unwholesomely.'

'I shall not enter,' the Princess said, slanting her high-bridged nose at him.

A still life: picture the scene if you can. Elizabeth sitting there, the yeomen kneeling, the lieutenant bewildered, not knowing what to do next, while the rain sluiced down impersonally on the shoulders of the immobile figures before cascading away down the steps and merging with the muddly swirl of the river, glad to be free of such a place. At this moment, Elizabeth achieved what she had set out to do: create a legend to be passed by word of mouth, through the length and breadth of England.

Suddenly, unable to stand the tension and the sight of the Princess's defiant distress, the gentleman usher broke down and began to sob aloud. Now she could end it: here was her cue to round off gracefully this memorable tableau. She rose and said with enormous poise, 'Tush, man. I need no friends to weep for me.' Turning, she swept gracefully into the Tower with all the upright arrogance of a Queen.

So it was that a medium-tallish young girl of fragile but erect figure around whom shone, some said, a light of unearthly luminosity, took possession of the Tower not as a captive, but more as a triumphant general. And all, apparently, because she could not stand to see a grown man weep for her! Lodged there on the second floor of the belltower, pale-skinned, nerves as tightly drawn as lute strings, she turned at bay, a slender, tawny-haired, infinitely cunning, infinitely clever, she-cat: challenging her sister, the Queen, to find sufficient courage to execute her.

*'Much suspected, of me*
*Nothing proved can be.*
*Queen Elizabeth, prisoner.'*

Scratched on a window pane at Woodstock by Elizabeth.

# 6

From March to May she stayed there, constantly interrogated by the Council in their dark robes of death, led by the insensately hostile Gardiner. Many were tortured. No one talked. Crofts, dragged from the rigours of the rack to confront the Princess, flatly refused to give evidence against her. Elizabeth, encouraged by Drake's wink that had told her such volumes, knew that Gardiner lacked proof of treason and accordingly no progress at all was made in her questioning. Pale-faced, exuding a strange, high-tensioned, straight-backed, girlish vitality that made her different from all other women Gardiner had ever known, she had asked him in her scornful, Tudor drawl for his evidence. 'Where,' she demanded scornfully, 'are the letters from Wyatt to me? Where are those from me to him?' And Gardiner could not produce them because he did not have them.

So stalemate. Yet Gardiner had a way of breaking it: by applying torture to the youthful person of Francis Drake. Elizabeth, not lacking friends, got wind of his intentions and knew exactly how to cope with that particular gambit. Through the Council, she appealed to the Queen for mercy to be shown the boy, not, let it at once be said, out of the slightest concern that a young fellow might be hideously disabled or suffer unimaginable pain, but with the cold agile mind of a woman who would always have a steely flair for self-preservation.

'How haps it,' she asked, aquiline-nosed and haughty, 'that a young lad is to be tortured to obtain statements against me? Pray ask my sister the Queen to pillory him, hang him if she will, but not to torture a young imp who indeed, had no part in any treasonable design.'

And the Queen, as quirkishly humane in things temporal, as she could be hideously cruel in things spiritual, had listened. Gardiner, denied the use of the rack, or the interesting rigours of the 'iron

50

maiden', fumed with frustration and planned a different way to get at Drake's person for the evidence he was sure the boy possessed.

Mary could not keep her sister in the Tower for ever. The situation, somewhat like a powder keg, must either be defused or explode. She sent Henry Bedingfield, pompous and pedestrian, to escort the Princess to Woodstock. No sooner on the river, than the gunners of the steelyard, thinking she was free, fired an enormous salute. Like some glorious state occasion, all London turned out to greet her. At Whitehall a secret landing intended to be followed by a furtive journey into Oxfordshire now became a royal progress. Village after village set the church bells a-ringing despite Bedingfield, like some flushed, fussy old beldame, promptly placing the ringers in the stocks. At Rycote, where the prisoner was to have passed a miserable, solitary night, Lord Williams of Thame had convened all the local gentry to do Elizabeth honour. In Bedfordshire and Buckinghamshire peasants lined the road calling 'God save your grace', and at High Wycombe it is recorded that cakes and biscuits were thrown into the Princess's litter in prodigious quantities. Mary was furious and the more liberal regime planned for her magnetic, red-headed sister was quickly converted into strict house arrest.

Weeks went by. To the jeers of all true Englishmen, Mary married Philip of Spain in huge pomp. And with the Spaniards insisting on Elizabeth's death, her life hung once again in the balance, literally by a thread. And now Gardiner, who had quietly, through the year 1554, worked a fine anti-heresy bill through parliament, giving him the inalienable right to burn heretics, played his trump card. He summoned before him a lad whom he had kept rotting in prison for just this precise moment. A lad who had a father who was a well-known Protestant teacher, stubbornly and proudly heretical. To this boy, who was Francis Drake, the Lord Chancellor now proceeded to put several simple, but highly-charged questions. 'Believest thou, Master Drake,' he had asked him first, 'that the bread and wine of the sacrament is substantiated into the very blood and body of Christ?'

'The text saith,' the boy answered back sturdily, unmoved by Gardiner's rich robes, 'that Christ took bread. Not that he changed it into another substance.'

'In the 22nd of Luke,' Gardiner retorted, 'does not Christ plainly say that the bread is his body? Deny that and thou will call our Lord Jesus a liar.'

51

"'Tis my belief,' Drake answered, 'that we take these things in remembrance only, of our Lord Jesus Christ.'

Now Gardiner pounced on him with the sharp claws and cruel, satisfied face of a tiger. 'Then thou art condemned to heresy out of thy own mouth, as well as thy father's,' he said. Then added with enormous meaning 'Before I order thee to be burnt, I would have thee inspect, first, the formalities.'

Lord Chancellor Gardiner had indeed been diabolically clever. To obtain Drake's confession of guilt in Wyatt's plot, he could take the lad right into the searing agony of the very flames themselves and Queen Mary, in the raging morbidity of her religious zeal, was not likely to interfere.

Next day Drake was taken to Brentwood to see the suffering of a youth named William Hunter who, for reading the English Bible and then hurling abuse at a succession of Catholic churchmen including Bonner, Bishop of London, himself, had been condemned to be burned at the stake. Chancellor Gardiner, to ensure Drake's ultimate terror, had seen to it that the burning would be hideously and agonisingly protracted. He had ordered that none of the usual gunpowder bags be slung about the victim's body so as to despatch him quickly to eternity and that only such green faggots might be used in the burning, as could be carried on the backs of two horses.

Accordingly, when the fire was lit, Hunter suffered terrible, long drawn-out pain, the flames only burning his feet and the thick smoke doing little more than scorching his hair and charring his face. Wiping his streaming eyes with his hands, Hunter said quietly, 'For God's sake, good people, let me have more fire.'

More logs were now brought, in defiance of Gardiner's edict, but this, of course, took time. By now Hunter was black in the face, his tongue so swollen that he could not speak, yet his lips moved continuously in prayer. To the crowd's amazement, he began now to stroke himself all over with his blazing fingers, just as though he were bathing himself gently in the fire. Suddenly he turned towards Drake and his mouth, already shrunk to the gums, parted in a ghastly smile. Incredibly, he kept knocking his breast with both hands, while fat, water and blood poured from his finger ends, continuing to do so until both forearms broke off and fell into the fire. At the last moment, just before death, Hunter somehow jerked himself upright, clapping the mangled stumps of his roasted arms triumphantly together in a shower of brilliant sparks and Francis Drake knew the gesture had been for him and him alone, proving that with the right spirit, any pain can be bearable. Drake had just received a lesson in courage that he would never forget.

Next day Gardiner had the boy brought before him and, awesome in his fur tippets and full-length sable gown, asked in his high churchman's voice 'Well, boy, do you talk now, or are you to be burnt?'

To his amazement, instead of being terrified as he should have been, the boy looked right back at him through the iciest of blue eyes and said indifferently, 'Burn me.'

Suddenly now, at the darkest moment, the gloom lightened. The Queen, relenting in her behaviour towards her sister, finally granted an audience to Elizabeth. When the Princess entered the bed chamber, Mary, her body swollen, her face pale with cold sweat, sat limply propped up in the great bed, shadowed by rich hangings of crimson and gold. The arras hangings of old Flemish work depicting scenes from the life of the Virgin moved ever so slightly. Elizabeth noticed this and fought down an incipient little giggle. Philip, of the cane-coloured moustache and lecherous eyes, had a well-known habit of hiding behind many an arras when the plump behind of a maid-of-honour might be conveniently spied on, undressing. The habit, it seemed, died hard, even extending now, to affairs of state.

Elizabeth sank to her knees. The room was stifling hot. She tried not to notice it: tried hard not to notice anything; tried not to smile; show her contempt for this old lady pretending to have a child, this pathetic sister of hers with her dainty little kindnesses and great, morbid, religious cruelties. She eyed the inscription on the cradle near the bed:

'The child which thou, O Lord of might, has sent
To England's joy in health preserve, keep and defend.'

What appalling verse, she thought. At my court, men shall compose verse better than that, or be sent packing for it.

Without rising or waiting for the Queen to speak first, she said 'God preserve your majesty. You will find me as true a subject to your majesty as any. Whatever has been reported to you, you will not find otherwise.'

'Then you will not confess?' asked Mary.

53

That was how the audience went: Elizabeth affirming her loyalty, not asking for forgiveness because she had, she kept pointing out, done nothing wrong; the Queen, suspicious to the last, demanding an admission of guilt as a price for a pardon. Elizabeth's tongue was spun gold that day. The Queen, exhausted, ill, waved her away, saying in a tired voice, 'Very well. You have won your freedom, but what am I to believe?'

'There is another matter,' Elizabeth said. 'For a full year a lad has been straitly kept in prison on my account. Francis Drake by name. If it pleases your majesty to free me, I beseech you to free him as well, for he was never in my service and has suffered handsomely this past year, for breaking into my house at Ashridge.'

'So be it,' the Queen muttered. She turned her ageing, swollen body away from her beautiful sister. 'So be it.'

As Elizabeth sank into a low, swooping curtsy of grace and thanks, Mary suddenly said in a deep, harsh, agonising voice, looking straight at her husband hidden behind the arras, '*Sabe Dios*'—'God knows.'

It is doubtful if God himself knew whether she was guilty. The only person who knew for certain was the Princess Elizabeth, and she was not telling anybody. Smiling like a cat that has just drunk a bowl of cream, the tawny-haired Elizabeth walked lithe, straight-backed and free into the glorious spring air.

Her first act was to summon Cecil, her man. 'Find the boy,' she commanded.

'Bring him to you, madam?' Cecil asked.

'What for? A lad whose speech is so thick in the Devon dialect that I can scarce understand a word he says? No, give him rewards and send him on his way.'

'What rewards?' Cecil asked, always careful. 'You have little enough money to call your own.'

'Tush, tush, man. Away with your objections. Good Robin Dudley will lend me all that is meet for my needs until I gain the throne.'

'The throne?' Cecil could scarcely bring himself to whisper the words.

'My sister is not made for old bones,' Elizabeth said contemptuously. 'Soon, I shall be Queen of England.'

Cecil, white in the face, shaken by his mistress's sheer directness, managed to ask 'And the boy Drake—what am I to do for him?'

'You are stupid today, Cecil,' she flashed. She flicked those slender, twining, velvety-white fingers that he knew so well at him. 'By the blood and wounds of Christ, away with you, man! Find out what calling the boy wishes to follow and why, you must assist him in it.'

'It is said he likes the sea,' Cecil ventured.

'Then bother me no more. 'Prentice him to a good man—perhaps the skipper of some sailing bark—and pay the fee.'

And so through the strange patronage of a grateful Princess, Francis Drake was launched into the career at sea that he had always dreamed of.

# Part Two

*'Have a care to my people.—Every man oppresseth and spoileth them without mercy. They cannot avenge themselves, nor help themselves. See unto them. See unto them, for they are my charge.'*

Elizabeth to her Judges, when
assuming office at the beginning of
her reign.

# 7

Cecil, as usual, carried out the commands of his mistress with efficiency and Drake duly found himself apprenticed to one Nathaniel Dyer, master of a small sailing bark. Life, although hard, was exciting enough. Manning a small coaster of 'ten tons burthen' in the short, steep chop of a channel gale was dangerous work, but Drake, used to the treacherous shallows of the Thames and Medway estuaries, took to the narrow seas in manner born. To come bursting into some foreign harbour, nimbly furling the great lateen sail that enabled the bark to sail so close to the wind, was work for an agile youth with strong legs and a stronger stomach. Then nothing could ever compare with the thrill of laying alongside in some foreign port: the bewildering hurly-burly of merchants; of unloading cloth, leatherware, old shoes in which there was a bustling trade with the French; and filling the hold with wine and canvas on the return journey. There were voyages to the great Netherlands ports that served the whole of Europe, Antwerp, Flushing, Dordrecht, to be laden with more exotic cargo: packs of taffeta and damask for the backs of gentlefolk, hops, sugar, Burgundy glass, straw hats and even Venetian lutes. In a few short years Drake learned something of international trade: the cunning needed to match the rapacity of customs men; the many thieves of all kinds that hang around a dockside.

And in those years he grew into a man. Into a burly, muscular mariner with a fine chest and the great legs that a man needs to balance on a steeply canting deck: not tall, short if anything, with a slight rolling gait, perhaps assumed in the pride he felt for his profession. Sure of himself now, he no longer smiled the way he had

59

when he was a little boy. The world had taught him much that was sad and painful, and it showed in the bright blue eyes that would look right through a man, as if trying to lay bare his innermost thoughts, before he would nod quietly and break into his broad Devonshire speech, as soft as the West country rains.

One thing stayed with him all this time: his vivid memory of the Princess Elizabeth. Exposed to the white heat, the especially luminous brilliance of the young Elizabeth, the effect, as can be imagined, on the mind of a mere lad, had been gigantic. Often, when there was a lull in the blow of the Channel winds and he could idle, with just a corner of his eye on the sail, he would remember an imperiously beautiful girl with long hands and smooth, white skin, with hair like some fierce, tawny, magnificent lioness: and he would dream a young man's dream of chivalry and knightly service. Sadly, he knew that he would never have a chance to be close to her again. The Princess Elizabeth was the most beloved person in the whole kingdom and everybody was waiting with bated breath for the dumpy, tired old Mary to die and take her frightful religious tortures with her to the grave. When Elizabeth became Queen, she would have no inclination to honour the unknown youngster who had once climbed up the side of her manor house of Ashridge and done her the service of destroying a certain letter, especially when he turned out be be a burly mariner who smelt of tar and caulking, with calluses from rope-burn on his palms that were the size of cart tracks!

Then for Francis Drake life changed with amazing speed. Old Nathaniel took ill and died from a flux, and the kind-hearted old man left Drake his bark in his will. From being penniless, Drake now found himself solvent, with a vessel of his own. More important, he was no longer shackled in the semi-bondage of apprenticeship, but his own master now, free to go wherever he wished.

Within the month poor tearful, prayerful Mary died unlamented and Elizabeth became Queen in such a hysterical outburst of rejoicing as had never before been witnessed in England. As the coronation approached, Drake knew he must go to London. He wanted no rewards. His heart was bursting with affection and loyalty and like most other lusty young lads that the Queen newly counted as her subjects he was, perhaps, a little in love with her too. If, however, he had quietly analysed his thoughts, he would have realised something else: that his interest in Elizabeth was also proprietorial. After all, not many young boys had dropped down off a high wall and calmly engaged this magnificent Princess in conversation at the tender age of thirteen.

Yes, there were many reasons why Francis Drake knew he must go to London and see the Queen crowned. So, with a gold coin thrown to a boy to keep his eye on his precious bark, a stout jerkin overlaid with a little lace in keeping with his new status and a pair of soft doeskin riding boots, newly bought, Francis Drake mounted his horse and, one hand never straying far from the sharp dagger on his hip, he rode to London.

In a few short weeks a nation captured. A long, slender, slimly-fingered hand placed firmly on the tiller of state. England weak and impoverished, menaced from the south and the north, with Mary Queen of Scots about to be declared lawful Queen of England by a hostile, irascible Pope the moment he could detect the slightest weakness by this pitiful little country of no more than three million people.

There was none: no weakness. The Queen and Cecil saw to that. A whole set of decrees prepared and set before her slim, determined hand for signature. No funds to be transferred out of the country. Gresham appointed to reform the currency and negotiate loans. The defences looked to.

Up and down the Thames the Queen progressed, showing herself with much trumpet-playing, singing and playing of regals, and such shooting of guns as was never heard before. The message was simple: 'I am your Queen. Love me as I love you.' Some of her subjects she charmed, some she pitied: with some she jested and to others she gave a quiet ear of sympathy. As coronation day approached, tiny little England rose to her in a surging, swelling bear-hug of affection. All Europe, which had sneered, now paused then drew back, like a hungry beast with respect for its prey.

The coronation was a two-day, unbelievable, spectacular explosion of joy. On Saturday 14 January it snowed just a little, adding a fine white sparkle to the glittering, jewelled and golden collars of the court, assembled at the Tower for the start of the procession. With a great clatter of drums and the squeal of fifes, the thousand strong court began a slow, stately procession through the streets of Westminster. It was a magnificence beyond belief: the yeoman of the guard in new scarlet coats with silver and gold spangles; the officers of state in crimson velvet; privy councillors in crimson satin; even

Henry VIII's poor, withered old jesters, Will and Jane Somers, given a new set of clothes for the occasion!

The Queen sat in a travelling litter decked in yellow cloth of gold and with eight huge cushions lined in white satin. What of her? A sight to make men shade their eyes and fall to their knees. A clear-skinned, flame-haired beauty of five and twenty with a flaunting, high-bridged nose, cosseted in twenty-three yards of gold and silver with ermine trimmings and silver and gold lace coverings. On either side of her walked the gentlemen pensioners, the distillation of blue-blood aristocratic maleness in their peacock finery of crimson damask, bearing gilt battleaxes; while all around, a multitude of footmen in crimson velvet jerkins studded with massive gilt silver, and ornamented front and back with a white and red rose and with the letters 'ER'.

From Fenchurch Street to Cheapside the streets were lined with wooden rails made of Windsor Forest timber and hung with tapestries, velvet, damask and silks, behind which stood the members of the City liveries in all their fine pomposity of costly, furred robes. Everywhere a riot of banners and streamers. People who had been waiting in the cold with inexhaustible patience. At one place, Elizabeth spotted a man sobbing, who had turned his back for shame. The Queen stayed her litter. 'Why do you weep, sirrah?' she demanded in a cool voice, clearly heard over the burgeoning scream of the crowd.

'For gladness.'

'We'll warrant it is so.'

A little further on, an old grey beard nodded admiringly and said 'Remember old King Harry VIII.' And at this, she was seen to smile more broadly than she ever did the rest of that day.

They welcomed her with pageant after pageant: allegory after magnificent allegory. Oh yes. The people knew. With that hair and that face. She was King Harry's daughter. This was a real monarch again. Not to be trifled with by Frenchman or Spaniard.

And in the shadows, partly hidden by the waving throng of people lining the route, she kept on seeing him. A burly, well set-up, brown-haired fellow with a jaunty, slightly rolling, sailor's walk, with a look—was it—could it be? Somebody familiar? And the Queen's memory was jogged. At one time she half made a gesture to this man, whose shadowy figure somehow managed to melt through the crowds and be close at hand, watching her whenever she stayed her litter. No good. The roars of the crowd and great jangling of the bells were too loud, too confusing.

At Fleet Bridge, a ragged old beggar-lady stood with a single branch of rosemary. The Queen ordered the whole vast procession halted and beckoned the woman forward. ''Tis for us, lady? We'll warrant that's the prettiest flower we've seen this morning.' Reaching out a hand, she took the nosegay.

'God bless you. God bless your majesty,' the petrified old woman stammered.

'May he bless us all. For you are our people.' There it was again. The message hammered home. You are our people, our charges. You have our love.

When the city recorder presented her with a thousand marks in a richly wrought purse of crimson satin, she said 'We will be as good to you as ever a Queen was to her people. And we will not spare, if need be, to spend our blood. God thank you all.' At this, there arose such a marvellous shout of rejoicing, that the very close-built, timber jumbled buildings of Fleet Street seemed to shake to their foundations.

And there again, she made out the figure of this short, compact man with strong shoulders and chest, who, although his eyes were bright and blue enough to burn a hole through tempered steel, observed her with a quiet, satisfied admiration. Impatiently she shrilled a command to a nearby gentleman pensioner to fetch him over, but the young man, bowing humbly, turned and disappeared into the crowd with a jaunty walk that was somehow familiar, although not quite identifiable.

Passing through Ludgate, she reached Temple Bar. Here, yet another long and complicated allegory awaited her. Patiently, attentively, she watched it unfold, her mind all the time trying to remember where she had seen that young man before, a fellow who bore the bronzed, weatherbeaten complexion of a sailor, who walked with a strut and about whom, despite his lack of height, there was something remarkably striking. With a start she realised that the allegory had finished and that she was expected to say something. Desperately she searched her mind for an appropriate line with which to feed the crowd's maudlin sentimentality. 'We,' she let her long Tudor drawl linger over the words, 'are plain English and you may be assured that we will always stand your good Queen.'

Surrounded by an ocean of love, waves of emotion pressing in against her temples, she passed on now, to her palace of Westminster. She needed time to rest and prepare for the morrow, her mind still occupied by that jaunty fellow with blue eyes and tanned face, who had so strangely melted away when she had come within hailing distance of him.

When the Queen halted at the Palace, she artfully drew attention to the fact that the tiny nosegay of rosemary given to her by the beggar lady was still held carefully in her hand. By afternoon, all London would know and marvel. By evening, the story would have passed into legend. Laughing deliciously in her girlish triumph, she turned and gazed on sweet Robin Dudley. Now there was a man to really admire, tall and straight-backed in the saddle, in the prime of his handsome, florid youth. A magnificent rider herself, she noted the indolent ease with which Dudley controlled his fiery stallion, using only one hand on the reins, whilst the other led the Queen's gold-draped hackney. Educated together as children, there had long been a strong bond between them. Conceited, self-centred, drivingly ambitious, Elizabeth still managed to adore sweet Robin with rampantly girlish abandon. Let all my men at court be as dashing, graceful and stylish as my Master of Horse, she thought. Let my gentlemen pensioners be tall, strong and straight: no small fellows that nobody will take seriously! Yet her mind kept going back to that small, square-shouldered man who had watched every phase of her procession through careful blue eyes. Tomorrow she would tell Robin about it. She was always amused to see how darkly jealous he became, the moment she talked about another man.

Next evening, after the coronation, when the slight, upright figure of the Queen, bearing sceptre and orb, swept regally into Westminster Hall and took her place at the high table, the flicker of a thousand torches seemed to catch the magnolia texture of her flawless skin, making it glow with a smoky, unearthly radiance against the backcloth of her blue-velvet costume. Such was the cheering, the noise of organs, fifes, trumpets and kettledrums, that it seemed to the bemused Francis Drake, watching outside, that the world must be coming to an end.

At one in the morning, towards the end of this great feast, Sir Edward Dymoke, her champion, rode into the hall mounted on a huge charger, with a fine clatter. In full burnished armour, he roared the challenge of single combat to all who disputed Elizabeth's right to be Queen of England.

No one disputed him. There was not a man there, who would not now have died for her. Which was, of course, precisely as Elizabeth had intended.

*'The Queen poor, the realm exhausted, the nobility poor and decayed. Want of good captains and soldiers, the people out of order. Justice not executed.'*

Government memorandum assessing England's condition at the time of Elizabeth's accession.

# 8

Crouched in a filthy ale-house near Smithfield, young Francis dozed over an empty pot as the first thin rays of the winter sun picked out the mass of befuddled humanity around him. He had celebrated the Queen's accession only too well. His tongue was thick and his eyes almost glued together. He shook himself awake, looking around him with distaste. Normally he did not drink to excess, but this had admittedly been a special occasion. He pulled himself to his feet, tripping over the outstretched boots of an old man snoring and dribbling horribly on the bare floor, mute witness to the extraordinary carousal that had taken place. Shakily he went out of the door, glad to breathe fresh air again. He began to walk down the cobbled way, knitting his thoughts together. Suddenly he clutched at his purse. Not there! Just a tattered remnant of leather dangled from where it had once hung on his doublet. 'God's teeth,' he swore. How would he pay for the stabling of his horse, get back to his bark, when he had not a groat with which to buy so much as a loaf of bread?

As he stood there, furious with himself for allowing his purse to be cut, strange sounds intruded upon his ears. A mass of women came round the corner, clattering and banging with wooden spoons on pudding bowls, shouting scorn at an unfortunate young girl who had been stripped to the waist and tied to the tail of a slow-moving cart. A beadle was following behind, whipping the girl with even, powerful strokes, grinning evilly at the answering scream of agony brought by every cut of the lash. At the sight of such cruelty, Francis could not help himself. He leapt across the cobblestones, confronting the man, pinning his arm with his own.

'Rascally beadle,' he roared, his voice high with youthful fury.

'Hold thy bloody hand.'

The beadle breathed hard. He was, had he chosen to admit it, slightly out of breath. Wielding the whip was apt to be tiring work. 'Well now,' he said eventually. 'What have we here? Some fresh-faced stripling up from the country, I trow, who has never seen a strumpet lashed at the cart's arse. Stand away, fellow. This doxy comes fresh from a trugging house, condemned by order of the court.'

'Lash that whore no more,' Francis said calmly, 'or I shall dot you one athwart the pate.'

'Be gone,' roared the beadle, who had now regained his full voice. 'Or 'ere she reaches the Bridewell this doxy shall receive double measure.'

For an answer, Drake snatched the whip from the beadle's hand and brought it down across the man's ugly face. The beadle screamed for help and behind the knot of women following the procession, three stout constables emerged, carrying staves. Drake defended himself as well as he could: to have drawn a dagger against Queen's officers was a hanging matter. For full five minutes there was a fine fight, with fists and oaths flying and blood scattering in all directions, but three grown men armed with cudgels proved too much in the end for Francis, burly and muscled as he was. They fetched him up against a wall, dazed from a clout on the head, and tied his hands securely.

One searched him for money. 'He carries not a groat,' he said.

'A vagrant,' said another, thoughtfully.

'And he assaulted three of the Queen's men,' said a third. They grinned and nodded at each other. A lengthy sojourn in the counter seemed the best possible cure for such a lusty vagabond as this.

In due course they brought him up before the prison sergeant, a man with one fierce eye, wearing a dirty leather jerkin secured by a strong, linked chain on which many huge keys clashed and jangled together. The sergeant eyed the burly, tightly-bound figure of Francis Drake speculatively. 'Well boy,' he growled. 'Here you may lodge well or ill, according to your purse. What say you?'

'My purse was cut,' Drake said shortly. 'I have nothing.'

'Think again,' the sergeant said in a wheedling voice. 'For a little garnish you may sleep on the master's side with meat at every meal, claret to wash it down and a whore sent in to soften your pallet.'

'I tell you again, I have nothing.'

'What?' shouted the sergeant in rage. 'Then how may I make a living? I'll warrant there's a gold piece or two sewn in your doublet: for that you may still have the knight's ward, tolerable enough for a youngster.'

'There is no money for yew, master warder,' Drake ground out between his teeth. 'So dew what yew will with me.'

The sergeant grinned evilly at this, showing broken yellow teeth. 'There's a touch of Devon in that voice, I trow. Then for your miserable Devon poverty, 'twill be the hole for you.' The hole was the bottom of the scale: a fetid, verminous, damp, overcrowded cell in the counter prison, filled with humanity's dregs who could not afford to bribe the sergeant for better accommodation.

'Here, it is said thou art buried before thou art dead,' roared the sergeant, shoving Drake into the gloomy darkness. He slammed the cell door shut and walked away laughing, the crashing, clanging sound of the great keys secured to his chained jerkin dying away into the distance.

For two days and nights Drake endured the company of those miserable souls in hell, coughing their life away in the semi-darkness. He ate the thin gruel provided once a day, shivered with cold and grimly fought off the rats that came squeaking hungrily round his warm-fleshed legs. He would have to get out of there quickly if he was not to rot into an early grave. Who could help him? All it would take was a royal or two with which to grease the sergeant's palm and he could walk out a free man. Impossible. In the whole of London he had not one single friend to help him. Again he racked his brains, hunger forcing his brain to work with crystal clarity.

Carefully he thought back. There was a man who had rescued him from prison before: a gloomy, long-faced man in the dark robes of learning who had apprenticed him to old Nathaniel. Would he help again? Unlikely, Drake thought. A person of his rank would not wish to be involved with a beggar lodged in the counter for attacking three of the Queen's constables. Then he remembered something the man had said at the time, words that had had no meaning to a lad of thirteen and which he had put away at the back of his brain until such time as he might understand them. 'I have need of a man such as you,' Cecil had said. 'One day, when you are full-grown, you shall come to me and I shall accept you into my service.' Yes. Those were his words. Drake recalled them clearly.

Drake now waited for the coming of dusk with barely-concealed impatience. By reason of his superior strength he was easily able to push and thrust aside the half-starved wretches from the favoured position under the gratings, where there was air and light. Soon, Bow Bells would sound, signalling the advent of the bellman, who would set out to patrol the streets, calling the hour and guarding the citizens against fire and robbery. Somehow, Drake knew, he must persuade him to do an important errand. It was not long before Drake heard the man's measured tread.

'Remember your clocks,' the bellman was singing in a deep, bass voice. 'Look well to your locks. Fire and light—and God give you a good night—for now the bell ringeth.' In a second, to the accompaniment of a loud clanging, the bellman came into view. Under his arm he carried a stout stave for protection, a lantern in one hand, his bell in the other. Behind him a large mastiff walked obediently to heel.

'Hist, bellman,' Drake whispered. 'Do you wish to earn a nice fat purse?'

The dog set up a furious growling, which its master quickly quelled with a blow from his stave. Halting in his tracks, he gazed down into the darkness of the gratings and said scornfully, 'And how might a penniless rogue rotting in the counter assist me to such matter?'

'Go you to Master William Cecil at his town house,' Drake whispered. 'Tell him that Francis Drake, whom he 'prenticed to a sea captain four years ago, lies in the counter and craves his help. He will reward you. Never fear.'

'It is you who will fear, sirrah, if he does not,' the bellman said grumpily. He shuffled off, still singing his cry into the dark reaches of the night, leaving Drake in terrible doubt as to whether he would carry out the errand.

At dawn four retainers, identically dressed in gilt-buttoned doublets of sober, black cloth and carrying sputtering torches, marched up to the counter and waking the sergeant, demanded, and promptly obtained, Drake's release. They took him with them and with quiet, silent efficiency, burned his clothes, made him bath in a steaming hot tub to kill the vermin, stood patiently by while he dressed in clean doublet and hose, and then took him before their master.

Cecil, with his mighty capacity for work, had already been at his papers for a couple of hours. A black bonnet pulled down over his

69

ears to keep out the draughts, he listened to the young man's explanation, now and then cocking sideways his stern, careworn face so as to hear the lad more clearly.

'Know you that I am the Queen's chief minister now?' he said gently, after Drake had finished.

'No sir,' Drake looked at him in amazement. 'Then I dew humbly thank yew for what yew have done.'

A small smile hovered at the corners of Cecil's shrewd, sternly-set lips. Not for a moment would he betray the fact that he had discovered the identity of that familiar-looking lad who had dogged every step of the Queen's coronation procession and had aroused Elizabeth's burning curiosity. Cecil was starkly aware of certain matters. The Queen was young and susceptible to men. Very susceptible. It was therefore important in the turbulent politics and shifting jealousies of the court, that the men she should have around her should be his men.

'Once,' he said, 'I made you a promise. That when you were grown, I would take you into my service. How say you to this?'

'I would be honoured indeed, sir.'

'And how shall you serve me?'

'I am only a humble seaman, Mister Secretary. I know nought else.'

'Perhaps so, perhaps not.' Cecil's shrewd eyes brooded intently on the burly, uncompromising figure of Francis Drake: the youth's honest face, the blue eyes that were able to bore with such unconscious, uncommon strength into a man. 'Yet time spent at court in the presence of the Queen would not come amiss.'

'Court?' Drake exclaimed, excited beyond measure at the thought of seeing again the beautiful Elizabeth. 'Indeed sir, I would like that. When may I go. Tomorrow?'

'Nay lad.' Cecil fought away a sad smile at the youth's enthusiasm. 'First you must be made presentable. The attributes and manners of a gentleman are many and varied and to learn them will take much time. Yet,' he considered for a moment, tapping his quill pen on his writing-desk in careful thought, 'I would not have you lose the skills of a seaman, for I trow the future destiny of this realm may well lie on the broad oceans.' Once more he stopped and thought, before arriving at a typical Cecil compromise. 'I have it. Of every two weeks, you will spend one under the tutorship of my good friend Master Ascham of Cambridge—I warrant he'll turn you from a yokel into a courtier if anyone can. The other week you will spend plying your seaman's trade at sea. Will you agree to that?'

'Yes sir.'

A frown knitted momentarily on Cecil's high, condemning forehead. 'I shall expect from you that which I expect from my own sons: that you will be obedient and refrain from all lechery, and that you will fear God.'

'I am strong in the Protestant faith, sir.'

Cecil nodded, but as Francis, taking this as his cue to leave the great man's presence, turned to go, Cecil called him back. 'Remember Francis, you are always my man first. Not the Queen's.'

Drake, bewildered, asked 'And dew we not all serve the Queen?'

'I serve England,' Cecil said quietly.

'Is that not the same thing?'

'At this moment, yes. And pray God it shall remain so. Yet the Queen is a woman and has a woman's weaknesses. One day, she may wish to serve herself.'

'Well, and should that happen, then I shall have to choose,' Drake said gaily.

As he bowed himself out, Cecil bent back to his papers, not allowing the set gravity of his features to be disturbed by the immense surprise he had received at Drake's remark. There was, it seemed, a distinctly piratical edge to the youth's character that he, a student of human nature, had at first entirely failed to suspect.

Lessons then, with Roger Ascham, lately tutor to the Queen and none better. For many months, Ascham was to instruct Francis painstakingly in the mysteries of Latin and Greek: of Horace, Demosthenes, Sophocles and Livy. Ascham's pleasure in finding Drake literate, thanks to the efforts of his father, turned to displeasure when he realised the boy's complete lack of interest and failure to make any progress. He switched, seeking to arouse a spark of enthusiasm, to modern languages and the mysteries of the italic script which Ascham was then engaged in pioneering, but in none of these did Francis Drake shine, with the exception of Spanish, in which he made rapid progress, thus causing Ascham to revise his opinion that the youth was a mere clod.

'Why?' he asked one day. 'Why is it that Spanish interests you?'

'Because,' Drake answered, treating him to a cool glance from his level blue eyes, 'it is my ambition one day to fight the Spaniards.'

'But Master Francis, they are our friends. Is that really your intention?'

Drake's eyes burned at the still vivid memory of the cruel, moustachioed Recalde. 'No,' he said. 'It is not my intention. It is my mission. If the Queen wishes to make herself mistress of the oceans, one day she will have to fight the Spaniards.'

So, Ascham thought: at lessons only a lad, but of war he talks like a grizzled campaigner! Very well. A gentleman must learn something of the martial arts, so let us stimulate him in this department. Accordingly he had a fencing master brought in, also a riding instructor complete with English great horse rudely wrenched away from a peaceful retirement in a field close to Westminster tiltyard. In these things Drake did only moderately. He was, Ascham had to face it, clumsy; the subtle deadliness of the rapier never mastered, the lithe movements of *attaque* and *riposte* wasted on the fellow, although his wild, brawny sweeps with the broad-sword could be effective enough. As to the tilt, despite no lack of courage, even a moderate lance would fell him to the ground.

Ascham began to despair of turning Drake into a gentleman fit for court. True, he had begun to absorb some of the elementary points of courteous etiquette with the help of Castiglione's *Book of the Courtier* and Tusser's *Five Hundred Points of Good Husbandry*, both books a 'must' for any man with pretensions to gentility, but the going had been hard. Even after six whole months of tuition the best Ascham could claim was that Drake now spoke a little Spanish and that his ripe Devon accent had been demolished into an acceptably pleasant, regional burr. There was something special about the youth that intrigued Ascham: a strange quietness cloaking a hint of steel underneath. Such a man, when aroused, could be a killer, Ascham thought. There was also the amazing fact that Drake, while normally dense at mathematics, became positively brilliant as soon as the subject was expressed in terms of navigation, of cross-staff and astrolabe, in matters of latitude and the possibility of one day calculating longitude.

Ascham, with the passing of time, dropped his guard, revealing in the process a previously well-hidden side of his personality that brought a slow, thoughtful smile to Drake's round, tanned, seaman's face. Ascham, it seemed, was a man of parts. He enjoyed hunting and cockfighting, and was so fascinated by the science of archery that he had once written a tome on the subject called *Toxophilus*. He was also, as Drake was soon to find out, a wild and absolutely compulsive gambler. Drake only learned this by accident when at the butts, having been instructed in the principles of archery, Ascham could not help giving him two free shots in every five and wagering with him at level chances. When, for the first time, Ascham lost a royal, he immediately asked to double up. Now, a window of blue ice masked Drake's face. Now he would reap a sweet revenge for all that dusty studying that he had been made to undergo! Although clumsy as a yokel, leaning into the huge longbow at the vast range of two hundred and forty yards, his handling of tutor Ascham was expert. Using his money as a tool, like some broad, bloody hammer, he was merciless, always obtaining, it seemed, the edge to the odds. In desperation Ascham tried him at dice, and then at cards, Spanish Primero, English Trumps. Losing at that too, he confessed to being crazy about cockfighting and now a smile of wicked satisfaction spread over Drake's face. Having protested that this was not an activity for a God-fearing man strong in the Protestant faith, Drake allowed himself to be initiated into the mystery of this bloody sport. Ascham, instead of winning back his money, found that Drake appeared able to read the characters of the fighting-cocks like open books, judging from some hidden perception which one would be bold, which one was a coward, and so on. Ascham continued to lose a fortune. Drake had studied his man as he had studied those fighting-cocks. He had noted the twinkle in Ascham's eyes, the merry, upturned nose that exactly matched the curve of his out-thrust beard, and knew that this tutor of his had certain, grave, personality weaknesses. He had merely waited, exposed them, and used them.

Stripped of every penny he had in the world, Ascham stumbled, not to his employer, Cecil, but to the Queen, whose tutor he had once been and with whom his relationship was the close and happy one of intimate friends.

'Well, my Ascham,' said the Queen, who had covertly been following the development of Cecil's protégé with considerable interest. 'How fares young Drake at his studies?'

'Badly, your grace.'

'Badly? Surely he can tickle a lute, stroke a viol, sing a partsong by now?'

'No, your majesty.'

'His dancing then? Surely with those strong sailor's legs he can spring into a gay galliard near enough to polish the very stars?'

73

'Execrable, your grace.'

'Languages then?'

'No progress, your majesty, except in Spanish.'

'And the martial arts, what of those? We like a man to be a man, not some simpering fop to sit among the cinders.'

'He is,' Asham paused, 'clumsy, your grace.'

'By the blood and wounds of Christ,' Elizabeth shouted. 'Which of you is the biggest simpleton? In six months he must have learned something! What has he been doing all this time?'

'He has been ruining me,' Ascham said in his blunt, Yorkshire, honest way. 'Yes, your grace. That is what he has been doing all this time.' To the Queen's immense surprise, Ascham, a man now into his forties, burst into floods of tears and the Queen found herself laying his head in her lap, comforting him like some child, while Ascham endeavoured to compose himself.

'How?' Elizabeth asked in a wondering voice. 'In God's name, how has he managed to ruin you?'

'He was always telling me how God-fearing he was,' blubbed Ascham, 'how he prized sobriety and pure-living, how strong and secure he was in the Protestant faith. When I suggested a little wager at archery I was not to know that his nerves were of ice, that his morals were as pliant as a spring sapling. I lost more and more money, then went to moneylenders to raise more, your grace. It was terrible. Terrible, what this young lad did to me. When we got to dice and cards, he flayed me, stripped me as bare as a sheep in shearing time.'

'Then he is not such a fool,' the Queen said thoughtfully. Although she might have forgotten him, despite his previous services to her, she was quick to realise that a man of Drake's exceptional qualities might be even more useful in the future, when it came to dealing with the hard, hostile world that menaced her crown. Besides which there was another matter, far more important. Drake, an adoring lad now, would soon be an adoring man, and in spite of herself, the wild, rampant, romantic vanity that lurked so girlishly only just beneath her regal mask had been aroused by this strange youth who could not stay out of her life. 'And what is your further judgment of him, my Ascham?' she asked, intrigued by what she had heard so far.

'He could be a useful servant, your grace.'

'Nay,' said the Queen. 'You underestimate him. A man who uses nerve to conquer knowledge has courage of a special kind; the ever-present sort, rather than the kind generated by strong ale. He did not

74

dice with you for the love of a wager, my Ascham. He set out to destroy you. That quality is as rare as it is terrifying.'

'Y—yes, your grace,' stammered Ascham, amazed at the Queen's percipience.

'Let him be brought to court,' she said. 'We shall call him "my corsair".' A small quirk of interest imprinted itself on the sharp oval of her face, her reddish-coloured eyebrows arching faintly across the glowing paleness of her skin at the thought of another male, another slave, safely twisted round her little finger.

'Madam,' ventured Ascham, bringing the Queen back to the present as he intruded into her pleasant fantasy, 'his manners remain rough. Some months are needed yet to fit him for court. Besides, he is Cecil's own man.'

'God's death,' spat the Queen in a ringing voice. 'Are we not mistress of this place?' She thought for a moment, then went on more calmly, 'Perhaps you are right, Ascham. It would be better to let Cecil present Drake at court when he thinks it meet. I'll warrant he'll decide soon enough for himself, whose man he is.'

'And me, your majesty?' Ascham said piteously. 'What of me?' He began to weep again. 'I am a ruined man. From being a prosperous scholar I have not a groat to my name. This fellow has stripped me bare with his wagering and dicing.'

'Rest easy, Ascham,' said the Queen, laughing. 'Continue with your teaching, for even such a rough diamond as this Drake may still be polished with some advantage. As for money, we plan to further your career.'

'My thanks to your grace.'

'Oh yes,' said the Queen, her mouth twisting in gentle mockery, 'such a God-fearing man as yourself, who abstains from gambling and watching cockfights in cheap ale-houses, must certainly deserve speedy preferment in the Church.' There and then, in the wet and windy month of October 1559, her golden-black eyes twinkling with a terrible glee, she graciously raised him to the post of Prebend of York.

Sunday: the Queen, tall and slender in a modest, fitted bodice with long sleeves and a full skirt, went to Windsor chapel, her sober clothes only sparsely adorned with jewellery, so as to emphasise the spectacle of a God-fearing virgin attending prayers. That was the impression that the gaping onlookers, crowded into her great

75

presence-chamber, received. In reality, she stalked past the worshipping figures of her handsomest courtiers, inspecting them like some beautiful, possessive, bird of prey.

Further down the line Francis Drake, newly brought to court by his patron, Cecil, slowly sank to his knees as the Queen approached. Although he was well-dressed enough in a soft, slanting cap with a burst of downy feathers over one ear, a long, high-collared doublet, short hose, a rakish crimson cloak ornamented with lace and embroidery, his apparel was modest compared to all the finery of the gentlemen courtiers, the puffed sleeves, the pomaded beards, the taffetas, the damasks. Cecil, recognising that the youth must be allowed a certain dash, had grumblingly handed over a finely-pared purse, telling Drake that he must be content with only one such outfit until the Queen gave some definite indication that he might be allowed to stay at court.

Pale-skinned, imperious, the young Queen swept down the line of courtiers and allowed her bold, darkly golden eyes to alight on the bent, abased figure of Drake. 'God's death,' she said, producing her usual oath, 'and who is this?'

Forbidden by protocol to answer directly, until he was presented, young Francis could only feast his eyes silently on the magical figure of his Queen. She could not help but notice the steadiness with which he held her gaze, and that whilst there was no arrogance there, a quiet self-confidence was not lacking either. The Queen, who knew perfectly well, from Cecil, who Drake was, did not move on. Instead, she exclaimed impatiently, 'Well by Christ's bones, is there no one here who will present this lad?' At this, Sir James Crofts, a gentleman pensioner now, his limbs still sore from his racking at the time of the Wyatt rebellion, limped forth and made the necessary presentation.

For Drake, the moment his lips touched the magnolia flesh of the Queen's exquisite and slender hand, the years rolled back. It was as if that desperate, gasping conversation in the walled garden of Ashridge had been only yesterday. He allowed himself to show a little emotion, running his tongue over his lips and grinning faintly.

'Ah,' the Queen said loftily, discreetly veiling merriment from her pale, oval face, 'Drake. We remember you now. Do not think we have forgotten that little service you once did us. When we are back from chapel anon, Cecil will present you afresh in our privy chamber. Then we will talk further.' Turning to Crofts, she said airily 'Quarters must be found for this man. He stays at court for a while.' She passed on, the huge farthingales of her maids-of-honour swishing against each other like softly-blown grass in a summer meadow.

Now with her gone, there was a feverish buzz of conversation. The court at this time was in a singularly excited state and sensitive to the slightest changes of favour shown by the Queen. The reason for this was the wild passion Elizabeth had lately shown for sweet Robin Dudley. For months now, while stern, father-figure Cecil had gone to Scotland to negotiate a French withdrawal there, to the greater security of his mistress, the Queen herself seemed on the point of surrendering in a far more important direction! Taking advantage of Cecil's absence she had gone out day after endless day with sweet Robin, galloping her wild stallions until they nearly foundered, her hair loose and flaming in the wind, eyes sparkling, pale cheeks alive with the sheer joy of being young and in love. With all duties of monarchy forgotten, she had given up the summer to dalliance with Robin, while England began to despair and ugly rumours reached the unhappy Cecil of their impending marriage.

If the mice played while the cat was away, then the cat must come home as soon as possible, and so Cecil did, with a magnificent treaty under his belt, only to receive the full blast of his imperious mistress's shrill displeasure for interrupting her dream of love, for recalling her to duties long ignored. Cecil then was in disgrace: yet young Drake was known to be Cecil's man, and the Queen had singled him out, dallied with him, even flirted openly with him under the smouldering eyes of Robin Dudley. Why? The court buzzed and throbbed with speculation. The boy—why, he was nothing. A stripling some seven years younger than the Queen and certainly not tall and beautifully-made the way she liked her men to be. Still, her affection for Drake had been made palpably obvious. Was it, perhaps, meant as a deliberate slap in the face to her adoring favourite Robin, who liked at all times to stand beside the Queen? It was more than possible. One thing was certain. Robin Dudley, possessive, jealous and arrogant, was not the kind of man to stand idly by, at such a time. All eyes, therefore, turned upon him.

The court went silent as Dudley, twirling the waxed tips of his fine, down-turned moustachios as if in deep thought, detached himself from the crowd of courtiers and walked slowly over towards Drake. Tall and well-made, with a somewhat cruel and fleshy face and the muscled, stoutly-fashioned calves that made the Queen's heart bound, his magnificent figure walked with a natural grace. To

77

everybody's amazement, he placed his arm genially around Francis Drake's shoulders and said casually 'There is little to see here at Windsor unless old castles are of interest to you. Come, I will show you the stables.'

With extraordinary affability he escorted Francis across the grounds until they came to the stalls where the horses were quartered. 'As you know, lad,' he said smiling, 'I am Master of the Horse to the Queen's grace.' Carefully, he pointed out various animals, all glossy from good feeding and currying. 'Looking after her beasts is difficult. She will prove them to the utmost, you know. Here is Bay Arundel whom she has foundered in the forefeet, Bay Killigrew whose hinder leg is swollen, Bay Hunsdon with a sore shoulder from too long at the gallop. It is droll the way she names her horses after the court, is it not? Here is Great Savoy with the huge cod, all asweat after coming from the mares.'

'With due respect, my lord, I am not overfond of horses.'

Dudley grinned, quick to seize his cue. 'However that may be,' he said, 'the Queen seems overfond of you. Can you explain that?'

'No, my lord. I cannot.'

'I would advise you,' Dudley went on, 'to remember that there are those well able to serve her grace better than you.'

'More fitted, but less able,' Drake replied calmly.

'Have a care,' grated Dudley, his face darkening into black displeasure. 'In one year of her reign, her majesty has favoured me with honour and privileges far too many to mention, including the glorious Order of the Garter conferred in this very place. Think you that she cares for the silly goose glances of mere striplings?'

'No, my lord.'

'Then leave while you may.'

'I am the Queen's to command,' Francis said calmly, eyeing the great lord directly in the face. 'When she wishes me out of her presence, only then shall I leave.'

Dudley's face mottled with fury and his fingers made a straying movement to a jewel-encrusted poignard at his belt; but realising that he dare not draw steel against Drake for fear of the Queen's wrath, he quickly stifled the gesture. There is more than one way to kill a cat, he thought to himself.

'Come then, we shall dispute no further.' He led Drake slowly back to the castle, through the beautiful grounds.

Francis Drake noticed a covert wink given by Robin Dudley to a nearby gardener, but thought nothing of it until, while admiring a great sundial that could, it was said, tell the time in thirty different ways, a great jet of water burst from a hidden fountain and soaked him from head to foot. Drake reeled back, hastily trying to brush water off his only suit, but it was ruined. There was no doubt about that. Soon, it would be a mass of crumpled wrinkles.

'Well sir,' Dudley said, his fleshy mouth broadening into a grin. 'You see now, how you must be careful. The court can be a dangerous place, you know, strewn with pitfalls for one so young.'

Drake did not reply. For a moment his blue eyes went as icy as the water that now soaked him to the skin, but in a moment, relaxed. He walked away and asked a servant to conduct him to his quarters.

*'I will have but one mistress in this realm and no master.'*

Queen Elizabeth.

# 9

That evening the Queen sat in her privy chamber, bejewelled, girlish, vibrantly provocative, her gown an open rabatine of lace and cut-work to show the glowing, magnolia texture of her slim neck. Close by her side, in his accustomed place, magnificent as a peacock in padded, stiffened, short doublet, French hose and bright garters, sat Robin Dudley. On one knee in front of her, in the grave, dark stuff of a man of learning, was secretary Cecil.

'And where is the young man?' the Queen demanded. 'We are not accustomed to being kept waiting.'

'Unfortunately, madam, Francis Drake has met with an accident,' Cecil murmured. 'My lord Dudley was pleased, by way of a jest, to have your hidden fountain soak him to the skin. Alas, being a lad but of slender means, he has no other clothes fit for court. I beg your majesty to receive him another day.'

The Queen smiled. While annoyed at what Dudley had done, she was secretly delighted at the childish jealousy her sweet Robin had shown. 'Well you should not have done it, Robin,' she murmured. 'The deed was unkind and we are displeased.'

It was Dudley's turn to come round and drop to one knee. 'To displease your grace makes me as miserable as a Levantine galley slave,' he announced formally. The Queen, somewhat mollified, stretched out a slim, white hand, which Dudley proceeded to kiss reverently.

Now, eyes glittering, the Queen rounded on Cecil. 'One suit of clothes?' she said, her haughty nostrils pinching with contempt. 'Surely a protégé of yours is entitled to more than that, master secretary? Perhaps you should loosen your purse a little. We cannot abide a man who counts pennies.'

A great sadness settled on Cecil's face. Already, in one year of office, he seemed to have aged ten. His eyes looked weary and care-worn and grey streaks were appearing in his grave, scholar's beard.

Despite his brilliant treaty with the French, the Queen, in her rage at Cecil rushing back to disturb her lovemaking, had made him defray the whole staggering cost of his trip to Scotland himself: and now, she was accusing him of penny-pinching! At times, his mistress was a terrible burden to him. Bowing low, he said with some feeling. 'We are all your majesty's devoted slaves.'

'Then see he is dressed properly,' she commanded. Relenting, she added 'On this occasion, you may charge the tailor's fee to our purse. Tomorrow even then, we shall see this Drake.'

Dudley reddened, furious at the Queen's determination to give this unknown fellow the extraordinary privilege of an audience. The boy will be lucky to be still alive by tomorrow night, he thought darkly to himself. I will see to that.

Both men, bowing, now backed out of the Queen's presence, but the Queen had caught the murderous look on her favourite's face. She turned to a maid-of-honour, her eyes glowing pools of thoughtful blackness, set in beds of soft gold. 'Dudley means to prove the boy,' she said softly, 'and that is well, for we too must know his mettle. However, he is young and we do not want him harmed. See the servants keep you well informed of what passes.'

'Yes, your grace,' the maid-of-honour curtsied deeply.

'Shall we tilt together?' asked Dudley, forcing pleasantness onto the sulky arrogance of his ruddy face.

'My lord,' Drake said, 'you know this may not be done. I am not of knightly degree.'

'You have learned something of the art?'

'Yes, my lord.'

'And I must needs keep in practice, because I am to meet Her Grace's Master of the Tilt in full combat, before many days are gone. Of course—if you are frightened?' His eyes gored into Francis Drake's face, leering, openly insulting. The remark was dreadful. Quite unforgiveable. Dudley had hoped to provoke Drake into drawing cold steel, knowing that the certain punishment for duelling at court was the striking off of the hand at the wrist.

Drake said nothing. The great dangers he had already suffered in his short life, not to speak of the sudden, explosive emergency of a rip-tide or channel squall, had taught him the advantage of remaining ice-cool at all times. That Dudley meant either to cripple or to kill him, he had not the slightest doubt. There was, he knew, no other course than to meet the challenge head-on. Cecil, perhaps even the Queen, might intercede to save him, but his career would be finished and he would ever afterwards be branded as a coward. So he must face Lord Robin Dudley at the tilt, and the man's skills were known to be as redoubtable as they were lethal.

'As your Lordship pleases,' he said, forcing fine indifference into his soft, Devon burr.

'Follow me, then,' Dudley's voice was as mocking as his low, courtly bow. Dudley led the way over to where a long stretch of sand had been laid out, bisected by a continuous wooden barrier. 'Of course at Westminster,' he said carelessly, 'there is a proper tiltyard with a gallery from where her Majesty may watch. Now that the peasants have been deprived of all their Saints Days,' he laughed in somewhat of a sneering way, 'we have to give them something in its place. Each year, therefore, there'll be a great tournament to mark the date of her Majesty's accession, and it is but weeks now, 'till the first. That is why I crave the favour of some practice.'

'Of course,' Drake said quietly, who knew exactly what Dudley was planning for him.

Dudley shouted orders to a throng of ostlers and servants, and in seconds all was activity and bustle as two great war-horses were hurriedly bridled and accoutred. Close by the stables was a long, timber-built armoury and changing-room. As they went inside, they were greeted by body-servants, bowing low. 'You come to tilt, my lord?' one of them asked in a tone of the deepest respect. 'Which armour will you have, the Missaglia, just arrived from Milan, the Helmsch-mied or your favourite Lochner?' He gestured at three suits of elegant armour: one with the flat, steely brilliance of the Italian school; another with the spiky, intricate fluting of German design; and finally at the breathtaking magnificence of a suit entirely overlaid with brilliant, multi-coloured enamel—and worth a King's ransom. Dudley allowed Drake to take in the opulence with which the Queen liked to maintain her Master of the Horse, before replying casually 'Two old working suits will be meet enough, I want no advantage over my friend here. And the lances are to be blunt. Nothing *a outrance*. We chance to pastime here for only a few minutes.'

As a servant checked through the many suits, sucking his teeth in concentration, and finally selected one roughly approximate to Drake's size and began the complicated job of strapping him in, Francis Drake had time to appreciate the subtlety of Dudley's plan.

Had he taken advantage of a better armour, a faster horse, he would have risked being shunned by the court as an unchivalrous bully, but by using only basic equipment he had relegated the whole thing to an idle, unimportant practice between friends. Drake grinned wryly to himself as he was winched up into the saddle by means of a hook suspended from a chain. The damage Dudley planned to inflict upon him, would be no less deadly.

'You see?' Dudley shouted at him, his voice mocking. 'Ordinary saddles for us both, no aids to hold me in place. You may tumble me just as I intend to tumble you. And don't forget to close your visor.' He crashed his own down in front of his handsome, florid face, wheeled his horse and galloped away down the yard.

Slowly, Drake took up starting position at the end of the sanded course. Despite Dudley's orders, the servants had given him an ill-fitting suit that pinched the flesh cruelly and which had little of the linen lining left inside to absorb the crashing falls he knew he must endure. He tried to forget such worries and concentrate on just one thing: survival.

'Ready?' Dudley shouted, voice muffled by his helm.

'Ready,' Drake answered.

A servant put a trumpet to his mouth and blew a piercing blast. Motion: the thunder of a great animal. No stopping now. Move into a full gallop, lance secure in its rest just under the right armpit and canted over the barrier at an angle of fifteen degrees. Don't watch the other's weapon, aim for the centre of his chest, impulsion—speed. 'Yah,' Drake shouted at his horse and dug in his spurs. Now a racing, full gallop: two men hurtling towards each other at a combined speed of fifty miles an hour. Off he went, cleanly out of the stirrups, the colossal, backward impact of Dudley's lance turning him in a violent somersault: a quick flash of sun and sky through the visor, then a juddering, bone-smashing crash onto the sand, all breath knocked out of him.

He blinked, opened his eyes. His visor was swung open by a servant. He wanted to stay down there, not move. The servant helped him to his feet, assuming he would wish to make another tilt. A wrong assumption, he thought ruefully. A leg felt numb; never mind. They placed him on the hook and hoisted him back in the saddle. Concentrate on that grinning, florid face at the other end of the yard.

The trumpet blasted harshly. 'Have at you,' Drake cursed. Charge home. No quitting. No bending low in the saddle or your lance lies

wrongly. Sit up straight. Lord, for what we are about to recei . . .
'Uuugh!' Again he was swept clean off by Dudley's science and skill,
half a hundredweight of man and armour plucked into the air, then
hitting sand with enough force to make the very ground shake.

Visor back. Blood on the mouth. This time, Dudley grinning at
him, his triumphant, moustachioed face sweaty, enjoying the thing.
'Enough boy? Do you yield?' Every bone in your body crying out for
relief. Body seemingly paralysed. Who knows what is broken? Shake
your head and spit in his eye. Francis Drake yields to nobody.

Again, the hook transferred him to horse. Dizzy now, hardly able
to sit the saddle. What was that knot of girls doing there, wearing fine
lace shawls encrusted with pretty jewels? Must be imagination.
Never mind. Charge. Harder. This time try to get in quicker, more
directly. Eyes a red glare of concentration, wanting only to wipe that
handsome sneering figure from his horse.

The same moment of suspension in a pool of utter silence before
hitting the ground, then the crash of your body wounding itself, the
breath entirely gone and now, a desperate, gasping, throat-rattling,
wheezing race against time for a feather of air to sustain your tortured lungs. Flesh cut to ribbons between pauldron and gorget, vam-
brace and gauntlet, where cloth piccadills should have masked the
abrasive action of the articulated joints; the poor, sweat-rotted lin-
ings of your armour seeping hot; wet blood. You fell on your left
arm. Broken? Probably. But you still have your right arm.

'Again,' he croaked to the servant. 'One more course.'

'Yield sir,' the man whispered. 'In truth you have done enough to
deserve all honour.'

'Hoist me again.' The servant caught a glare from those unblinking blue eyes and knew this man would never surrender. Reluctantly
he coupled Drake to the chain, ready to hoist him back onto his
horse.

A girl detached herself from the others. Face averted in her shawl,
she came closer. 'Come here, honeydugs,' Dudley bawled, 'and tell
me. Did you ever see three prettier lances?'

Drake watched as if in a dream, his brain dulled and semi-
conscious, only hook and chain restraining him from falling to the
ground again. Was the girl real or some fantasy caused by his injuries? He had no way of knowing. The girl threw back her shawl to
reveal flaming hair, a high-bridged nose and a pale, challenging face.
'So "honeydugs", is it, my lord?'

Dudley, tall, indolent, graceful, uninjured, slid from his saddle and in an instant was down on one adoring, submissive knee. 'Your grace. Forgive me, pray. I did not recognise you.'

'This contest must cease. How came you nearly to kill the lad?'

'Oh, an idle pass or two for practice, and he would not yield.' Dudley laughed. 'It seems his legs are so short that he flies off like any cannonball, when touched with the lance!'

'God's death, my lord. With such legs I vow he'd stand fast on a ship's deck in a tempest while Master Dudley lies puking down below.' Having administered this stinging rebuke to Dudley in front of her favourite's ostlers and armourers, Elizabeth added in a sharp voice to one of her maids-of-honour. 'Have Drake released from his armour and conducted to a comfortable chamber, there to wait upon my doctor.'

The Queen stalked off, eyes glittering. She found her breath was beginning to come in short pants from emotion. It always did, at times like this. Because she was Gloriana: the glittering maypole around which all life danced. Let men continue to fight each other for her favour, divided, jealous, uniting together only when necessary for her protection. Only in such a way could a woman hope to govern a kingdom.

Next morning the Queen held a privy council. Cecil, majestic in black silk, his beard resting soberly on a high, starched ruff; Bacon, his brother-in-law, the Lord Keeper, whose features had the rare combination of being both fat and shrewd; Clinton, Lord High Admiral; and Lord Howard of Effingham, a sailor of repute and adored by the fleet, now holding the post of Lord Chamberlain for helping to save Elizabeth's life under Mary, were all there. The Council had a nautical look indeed this morning, and for reasons that all would soon understand.

As the Queen entered, all stood, except for the aged Marquess of Winchester, who had special dispensation to remain seated. Even then, he shuffled his thin, aged shanks in an effort to get to his feet. Elizabeth flashed him a brilliant smile, motioned him back to his velvet cushions—a movement which allowed her to show off one divinely slim, white hand. The Queen was magnificent in white velvet, a coruscating riot of pearls and jewels. The Council did not fail to notice the perfumed gloves, newly imported from Italy, and the daring new fashion of silk hose peeping out under her billowing farthingale. That she meant to play the feeble woman today was obvious: the damsel in distress appealing for protection from her gallant knights. In other words, she was short of money.

The Queen sat, everybody following suit in a fine rustle of silks and taffetas. 'My Lord Treasurer,' the Queen addressed Winchester, 'pray read us your estimates for the late war in Scotland.'

In a wavering voice, Winchester read out a set of figures that made the Queen's face go pale with worry.

'God 'a mercy, gentlemen,' she said theatrically. 'The treasury is exhausted. How then are we to defend ourselves if we have no funds?'

Cecil hid a smile. The Queen was playing brilliantly on the heart-strings of the Council, using all her fine command of woman's wiles. 'Madam,' he said gently, 'why, you must ask Parliament to vote you moneys. That is the proper place.'

'Pooh!' the Queen said with a great sniff, forgetting all her daintiness for a second. 'All they can think of is marrying us off to some mountebank.'

The Council chuckled, enjoying the Queen's derisive reference to some of the greatest princes in Christendom as mountebanks.

'Nevertheless, madam,' Cecil said. 'They think only of your welfare and your kingdom's prosperity.'

'The way to this country's prosperity,' said Elizabeth thoughtfully, 'is through trade. Now then, Clinton,' she turned to her Lord High Admiral. 'We understand you have a matter of interest to raise on this subject?'

'Indeed, madam,' Clinton rose to his feet. 'Does your grace recall the name of Hawkins, a Plymouth family of ship owners?'

'The name is well-known,' said the Queen. 'Sir William Hawkins was a great explorer and trader under our late father's patronage.' Her face alive with interest, she added 'Does Sir William still live?'

'I regret not, madam,' Clinton said, 'but his two sons carry on the tradition of their father. Young John Hawkins in particular has come to my notice by reason of his marriage to the daughter of Master Ben Gonson.'

'What! Treasurer to our navy?' The Queen raised the lightest of tawny-coloured eyebrows in a fine arch. 'By Christ's bones, that should prove a useful marriage for a mariner.'

'Indeed so, your grace.' Clinton permitted himself a slight grin at the Queen's cynicism. 'And now this John Hawkins fancies much to undertake a certain trading venture, a round trip. Slaves from the

Guinea coast, for sale to the Spaniards in their New World possessions.'

Elizabeth frowned. 'Is not this rich trade in the New World forbidden to us by Spain?'

'That is unfortunately true, madam.'

'By God's death,' the Queen said, emphatically thumping the table with a slim hand, all girlish pretensions of the damsel in distress now quite forgotten. 'What we might do for this realm of ours if we could cut ourselves a piece of Philip's pie!'

Winchester, the old man, suddenly let out a raucous, half-senile cackle. 'Piracy, she talks,' he said. 'Why I warrant 'tis the very person of old King Harry himself who sits at the head of the table.'

The Queen, who adored the man, was not in the least offended. On the contrary, she now allowed herself to flirt with him outrageously. Fluttering her eyelids, she purred, 'If only our Lord Treasurer were but a younger man, we might well find it in our heart to have him as a husband!'

The Council, relieved that the Queen had not been angry, and that all was still sweetness and light, laughed with a certain degree of nervous relief.

'Now then Cecil, what think you of all this?' The Queen turned yet again to her chief adviser.

'The commercial risk is so large, that Hawkins must indeed have your grace's support.' Cecil was blunt.

There was silence while the Queen thought deeply. 'Very well,' she said at last. 'You, Cecil, must arrange a backing for Hawkins with some rich merchants in the City of London, and invest some of your own money in the voyage. When your plans are complete, we shall see then how best we can help.'

'As your grace pleases.'

The Queen allowed the Privy Council to bathe in the warmth of her girlish smile. 'We have commanded a bear-baiting to take place within the hour,' she said. 'So, if there is no further business . . .'

'None, your grace.'

As the Queen rose to her feet and the Council stood in humble respect, a terrible scuffle started up outside the council chamber. The ripe oaths of guards could be heard as they tried to restrain someone demanding immediate access to the Queen. The doors flew open and a messenger burst in, prostrating himself at the Queen's feet. 'Your majesty, your majesty,' the man sobbed with exhaustion. 'I have dreadful news. The wife of Lord Dudley has been found with her neck broken.'

All colour drained from Elizabeth's face and with it, all dignity, all queenly grace. Instead, there was just the terror-stricken look of a young girl in her mid-twenties, fearing for her lover, fearing what her lover might have done for love . . . With enormous effort she managed to mask most of her emotion, squash the insidious onset of hysteria. 'Sit down, gentlemen,' she ordered in a shrill voice. 'It would seem there is further business.'

There was business indeed. Only the day before, the Spanish ambassador had, according to court rumour, informed his master that Robert Dudley had sent to kill his wife in order to marry the Queen. And within twenty-four hours, Amy Dudley had been found dead. In her own little kingdom, the Queen was about to be damnably tainted as an accomplice to murder.

As the true gravity of the situation slowly saturated the thoughts of the Council members, their faces became grave and dark over the pretty tracery of lace-work decorating their throats. No monarch could survive scandal of that sort, and if the Queen were deposed, so would they be. They were all literally in the same boat.

Right through that day until late into the night they debated, their muttered consultations broken only by some nourishing broth or the occasional stimulation of a strong aqua-vitae. At the end of that time, only one man was still thinking clearly. As usual, it was Cecil.

'Madam,' he said, addressing the tired, haggard Queen. 'Madam, even if a coroner's jury should clear Lord Robert, it will not be enough to acquit him of the deed.'

'Is this not all that the law requires?'

'In this case you must do somewhat more than the law requires.'

'In what way?'

'You must send a reliable man to investigate on your behalf, at first hand. Only by such means can you show clearly that you are no accomplice.'

'But Lord Robert is a powerful man. If the report favours him, the world will only say that he bought the agent who made it.'

'True enough, madam,' Cecil said patiently. 'But not if the agent is a proven enemy of my lord. The report would be believed then.'

Elizabeth looked at Cecil and colour returned to her pale cheeks. Never had she admired him more. His thinking had, as usual, been simple but also brilliant. An investigation would only be believed if carried out by someone well-known to have little love for Dudley. 'You will have to choose your man well, Master Cecil,' she said at length. 'He will have to be experienced.'

'I have a certain fellow in mind,' Cecil replied smoothly, 'though he is but no more than twenty.'

'Twenty?' the Queen said aghast. 'His youth is such that he will discover nothing. And if he does, it will not be believed.'

'With respect, madam,' Cecil said, his grave eyes twinkling for a second while he smoothed the hairs of his glossy beard, 'that is not so. Not only is young Francis Drake a lad of intrepid quality, but he lies upstairs, soundly battered at the hands of Lord Robert Dudley, for all to see. Is this not just what we require?'

Suddenly the Queen laughed, not the pretty little titter of a girl daintily brought up, but an outright guffaw, loud and indecently irreverent. 'Yes, my lord,' she said. 'That your choice is a good one, we cannot deny, but we wager by the great cod hanging from our best stallion that when the time comes, Drake will be neither your man nor ours.' She drummed her slim white fingers thoughtfully on the Council table. 'To bell the cat is no difficult matter, but what if the cat turns out to be a tiger?'

Upstairs, lying bruised and dazed in his bed, Francis Drake gave Cecil a surly reception when the mission was explained to him. With little else to think of, other than the raw cuts and weals liberally adorning his body, he had come to realise that he had not been sponsored at court through any act of kindness, but only as a reliable pawn to be used in the endless game of court chess played by competing factions. Quickly, he had grown resentful of Cecil for using him in this way. 'I am a sailor,' he had muttered. 'No foppish courtier useful only for his dance steps or graceful intrigues.'

Gravely, Cecil lectured the boy. 'Francis, do you not know that the court is the only place in the country where great careers can be made? Know you not of your immense good fortune in being called by your first name by Elizabeth Tudor? Leave here and you are nothing. But stay and serve the Queen and the whole world can be yours.'

Reluctantly, Drake agreed to accept the mission marked out for him and promised to leave early next morning. In the meantime he lay in bed, his bruises liberally smeared with goose grease by one of

Cecil's servants, and drinking many a draught of hippocras brought by one of the Queen's pretty maids-of-honour, serving adoringly this stoutly-built lad who had faced the great Dudley with such bravery in three consecutive tilts. Drake, reading his Bible as was meet in a man of strong religion, had seemed uninterested in all this attention until one especially pert maid-of-honour, whilst bending to collect a bed-vessel, found herself unexpectedly smacked in a tenderly soft place. Straightening up indignantly, she saw a pair of bright blue eyes set in a round, merry face gazing at her fixedly and with a strange intent-ness of purpose. Letting out a shriek, she fled the room. From then on there was no more spiced wine, no finely-cooked victuals, but only a vile-tasting electuary of sweet roses in wormwood water, to cool his blood.

Next morning, therefore, Drake was quite glad to set off. Although his body was stiff and protested with every movement of his galloping horse, his youth and strength quickly enabled him to recover and with the sun shining brightly through leaves tinged with the first creeping brown of autumn, he knew himself, despite his wish to get back to sea, glad to be serving the Queen once again.

When the village of Abingdon finally came into view, he took ac-commodation at the local inn and at once set out for Cumnor Hall, where Amy Dudley had been living before her death. The house was covered with a profusion of dark ivy and gave out such an air of dark-ness and misery as to fill Drake's normally happy nature with de-pression. He tolled the bell and a maid appeared at the door, her face red and flushed with much crying. She answered to the name of Pirto. Although she could not read, one glance at the ornate seal on the document in Drake's hand convinced her that he had the right to question her.

Slowly, patiently, Drake was able to build up a picture of Lady Dudley. Simply brought-up and of good station, she was the daugh-ter of a rustic knight, Sir Hugh Robsart by name. She had married young in a love-match with Dudley. But his career had risen with meteoric speed and as courtiers' wives were discouraged at court, she had been left increasingly alone and in a miserably depressed state. Despite this, Lady Dudley had, it seemed, accepted her lot bravely enough, giving way to her emotions only by the occasional wildly extravagant buying of clothes and desperate trips to London, dis-couraged, but tolerated by my lord of Dudley.

How had she died? She had been found at the foot of the stairs with

90

her neck broken. Drake went and examined the staircase. It was squarely built of dark oak, the slope of the stairs was gentle and turned at right angles every ten feet or so, hardly steep enough to cause death by a fall. However, if Amy Dudley had dropped from the top of the stairs through the central well, it would have served well enough to kill her. By now, Drake was sure of something. Amy Dudley's death had been no accident. She had thrown herself to her death down the well of the stairs, or she had been pushed.

He went back to the inn, showed his Queen's commission to mine host and began questioning him closely. 'Had any stranger stayed at the inn the night before Lady Dudley's death?'

'I cannot say,' the landlord replied. 'We have many strangers staying here all the time.' Try as he could, Drake could obtain no more information.

Later, having dined, he lay on his bed thinking. There was no real clue as to what had happened. The jury would deliberate and, finding no firm evidence, would clear Dudley; or half clear him, rather, leaving him with the taint of murder and the Queen tainted with him— and that certainly would not do.

Now, as Francis Drake lay on his narrow bed in a country inn, a sudden thought came to him. The assassin would not have been a local man, but more likely plucked out of the London stews for the purpose. Such a fellow, not wishing to be caught, must needs come and then return to London very quickly, and for this he would require an especially fine horse, one possessing exceptional speed and stamina. Such an animal, Drake thought, must certainly be known amongst the great sub-culture of grooms, coachmen and ostlers who served in the great, sprawling establishments kept by the nobles alongside the river Thames. All he would need to find out was the horse's name.

To his great joy, young Will the Ostler, sitting by the kitchen table shining bits and spurs and cleaning mud off dirty saddles, remembered such a horse well, at the tavern on the night of Amy Dudley's death. In exchange for a shining new royal, he gave its name—Bay Marianne—although he could recall nothing of its rider, other than that he had been a rude fellow who had kept his face averted under a high cloak and paid him meanly for rubbing down the horse's steaming flanks.

First thing in the morning Drake packed his things and left the inn at great speed, a distinct gleam in his eye. Back in London he began frequenting those ale-houses in the Strand patronised by the hordes of grooms employed at the great noblemen's houses lining the river. Inevitably the conversation would turn, as it always did, to the subject of fast horses, great gallopers they had known, each groom, ostler and blacksmith vying with the others to show the excellence of his knowledge. It was easy enough to loosen mouths by many a pot of strong ale and to introduce into the conversation, the name of Bay Marianne. Sure enough, someone knew of the horse and Drake had little trouble finding out where it was stabled. Always a man for quick action, Drake immediately left the ale-house and went round to the stables. Seeing the head groom, he proceeded to offer a large sum of money for the horse's purchase. The horse was out, the groom told him, but he might wait in the stableyard, if it pleased him, to inspect the horse when its owner brought it back.

Wait, is exactly what he did, until London town grew dark behind locked doors and the stables fell cold and silent as Drake lurked invisibly in the shadows. Around midnight his keen ears picked out the soft click of approaching horse's hooves and in seconds a rider had dismounted from an animal answering Bay Marianne's description and had led it into an empty box. Lighting a candle, the man began to unsaddle and unbridle the mare. Silently Drake padded in after him. By the guttering candlelight he could make out a lean, sinewy bravo of about forty, with a curved poignard of the Turkish style stuck in his belt. 'How now, sirrah,' Drake said softly. 'Hast undertaken any fast journeys to Cumnor Hall in recent times?'

The man turned, a lithe whirlpool of darkness in his black cloak. Drake sensed, rather than saw, the glint of cold steel as the man drew his curved dagger with snake-like speed. Only by leaping acrobatically backwards did he save his life, the keen blade ripping a great tear across the front of his doublet. The man snarled and deftly backhanded the razor-sharp weapon into a trajectory designed to sever Drake's head from his muscular shoulders, but by using all the springy strength of his sailor's muscles, Drake leapt high into the air and kicked the man strongly in the chest.

The knife went flying away and then they were both on the ground, wrestling at close quarters. For seconds, nothing could be heard but the muffled grunts of each man trying to overcome the other. The bravo was still the stronger, just, with Drake not quite grown into full manhood, but as muscle cracked with strain while each man sought a more lethal handhold, youth began to tell against age and the older man was soon panting hard. Drake suddenly pulled the man into a sitting position and dealt him a smashing blow across the mouth with a fist pickled by salt walter into the consistency of iron. The man's mouth foamed with an awful spray of frothy blood. One more pile-driving punch into the upper belly was enough to lay him, retching and choking, in the straw.

Drake stood back and listened. All was quiet. He straddled the moaning, bleeding man. 'Talk,' he said. 'Talk quickly and talk for your very life.'

What the man told him was so appalling, so terrifying, that he knew the Queen could never be told. Nor could this bravo lying in front of him be allowed to live, possessing such a secret. Yet Francis Drake did not kill defenceless men. He would kill this fellow in self-defence, or not kill him at all. Drake got to his feet and deliberately turned his back. He began to walk away, his skin prickling and burning as it awaited the first stinging pain of a dagger driven home between his shoulder blades. He walked softly, forcing himself to make a tempting target. Would it never come?

Then he heard it. The soft, tell-tale rustle of straw, the indrawn rasp of breath which the other man could not quite hide. Drake went down on one knee, half-turning at the waist as he reached for his own dagger. Many times had he practised the move, fingers going for the knife with the speed of light, whipping the blade out in a lethal arc that could kill a man or, in such treacherous times, save a man's life. Now it came as fast as silk, as smooth as quicksilver, a mere blur of the wrist as the knife's upthrusting point sought the other man's tripes, cutting home through gristle and blood.

Drake clambered to his feet, an unholy smile on his lips. Coldly, he contemplated the awkward heap of what had once been a man, ripped from crotch to neck in horrifying dissection. He wiped his blade in the straw, padded across the silent stableyard, climbed the nearest wall and melted into the darkness of the night. He needed to think, to consider, to analyse. The secret of who had ordered Amy Dudley's murder was safe with him—as long as he chose to keep it.

The Queen was in a towering rage and she looked, Drake thought, quite magnificent. At times like this it was her invariable custom to place herself under Holbein's portrait of Henry VIII, so as to remind her subjects whose daughter she was. Drake examined the portrait: yes, the same imperious cast of feature, the same angle of proud jaw.

Even if femininity forbade that arrogantly masculine legs-apart and hand-on-dagger stance, the comparison was well enough made. He looked up at the Queen in admiration. From his position on his knees, he thought that in anger her beauty became positively bewitching, with the red-gold hair of her Yorkist ancestors matching the temper flushing her cheeks.

She had listened to his story and had found it quite plainly unsatisfactory. Cecil looked on, an impressive black-robed shadow standing silently in a corner, while the Queen mercilessly interrogated Francis Drake. Again and again, she took him through his story. 'And so, sirrah. This man you captured. What did he tell you?'

'Madam, that he had killed Lady Dudley by hurling her down the well of the stairway.'

'And of he who sent him?'

'He would admit nothing.'

'My Court of Star Chamber would have made him less taciturn. You say he sprang upon you as you were about to manacle him and you had to kill him?'

'Unfortunately so, madam.'

The Queen began to walk agitatedly backwards and forwards across the chamber. 'This man,' she whispered, her high-bridged nose arching and quivering in frustration, 'was sent by whom? Who sent him? Do you not see, sirrah, how important it is for us to know?'

Drake hung his head for a moment, then looked again at the Queen. The pulse beating strongly under the soft whiteness of her neck really was most delicate. He found himself having to steal glances at her as if a man's very thoughts of love had to be rationed. 'Madam,' he said, 'this man was not in the employ of Lord Robert Dudley. For this I will publicly vouch.' He glanced at Cecil, quiet, silent and grave, in a corner. 'Surely that is enough?'

'No sir, it is not enough,' the Queen screeched. She was silent for a moment and nothing could be heard except her quick pants of breath as she fought to regain her temper. 'Now, Master Drake,' she said with a strange quietness, 'you will swear on the Holy Bible and on the suffering body of our Lord Jesu, that this fellow did not name he, who employed him to do this murder.' She thrust a Bible in his hand. 'Now swear it.'

There was silence. Drake could do nothing but hang his head.

'Swear it. I command you. Or else name the author of the deed.'

'I must not.'

94

'Must?' the Queen hissed at him venemously. '"Must" is not a word to use to princes!'

'Madam.' For what seemed an eternity, Francis Drake struggled to phrase what he had to say, with a cushioning of tact sufficient to avoid giving mortal offence to the Queen. In the event, being young, he failed miserably and just blurted out the truth. 'Madam, it were better for you not to know and for your own sweet sake, I shall never tell you.'

The Queen, furious, rushed forward as if to strike him across the face with her fan, then checked herself. 'A monarch who sentences a subject in rage, is no sort of monarch,' she said. 'That you must be punished, is obvious. Tonight, you will come here and make your "adieus" and we will decide what is to be done with you.' She turned to Cecil and flashed, 'Get out. I don't doubt that the two of you are in league together.' Imperiously, she flicked her fan to indicate the audience was ended.

Cecil and Drake trod the corridors of Windsor in silence until they reached the open, formal gardens where fountains played and birds sang and they could at last talk unheard. Cecil was the first to speak, choosing what appeared to be a most surprising subject. 'Your family,' he said abruptly. 'I have had my intelligencers seek them out. It was difficult, but in the end they were successful, finding them in hardship and obscurity, living on the charity of some distant parish. Through my personal recommendation, the Queen's grace has raised your father to the living of Upchurch. 'Tis a right comfortable one, I believe, with a fine house. Their worries should be over.'

Drake, instead of thanking him, said abruptly, 'I am not a man to be bribed.' There was an awkward silence while they trod crazy paving, ducked under the bowers of scented autumn roses, sniffed the fragrance of the last waving gillyflowers.

'So you know,' Cecil said flatly.

'That you had Amy Dudley killed. Oh yes.'

'And you would not tell the Queen? That was sensible.'

'On this point I still have to make up my mind. So pray tell me why I should not.'

Cecil looked at Drake keenly. The boy had become a man, no longer rash, but mature beyond his years and careful in his decisions. He must deal with him diplomatically, cleverly. 'The answer is simple enough,' Cecil said. 'The Queen and Lord Robert are exonerated from the deed, but only as long as they do not marry, when heavy suspicion would once again fall on them.'

'If I told them what you say, you think that would prevent them marrying?'

'That is why you must never tell what you know. At all costs the Queen must stay single. As a Virgin Queen she will be the greatest monarch England has ever seen, but if she becomes wife to an unworthy master, this country will know only anarchy.'

'Pretty reasoning for cold-blooded murder!'

'Nay,' said Cecil smiling, not in the least offended. 'Say not that. Say rather, I spared poor Amy Dudley weeks of agony. She had a malady fast growing in her breast. She would have been dead in six months anyway.' Suddenly he gripped Drake's arm with enormous strength, his veiled statesman's eyes widening with inner conviction. 'Don't you see?' he said fiercely. 'As long as she was healthy, there was never any problem. Only because she was dying was it necessary to kill her at all!'

Taken past a bewildering collection of gentlemen esquires of the body, maids-in-waiting and chamberers, Drake was received by the Queen in a withdrawing chamber favoured by her for the quiet playing of music. Seated at a virginal made entirely of glass, the Queen wore a simple dress with her silky red hair pinned neatly back behind her ears, as if to bring back the memory of when, as a young girl, she had first met Francis Drake in a secret garden at Ashridge.

She was playing with considerable spirit a variation of an old air—'Bonny Sweet Robin'—her slim fingers flowing almost savagely over the keyboard and the significance was not lost on Drake. It was the Queen's way of telling him that thanks to his obstinate silence, she would be prevented forever from marrying her own Sweet Robin.

Abruptly, Elizabeth stopped and gazed at the man kneeling in front of her. 'You are banished from court,' she said coldly. 'Say what you wish to say, then go.'

Now was the time for which Drake had secretly practised, slaved: when all the rest of his life would hang in the balance, depending on what he might now do. Glancing at a bandore, a richly ornamented, twelve-stringed lute standing in a corner, he said 'Would your Grace pray allow me to say goodbye in my own way?'

The Queen, intrigued, nodded. Drake struck a chord, rich and heavy in a minor key, tinged with all the youthful passion he felt for

Elizabeth. Still on his knees, he sang in a tenor voice, trained, cossetted, moulded and trained again by the patient, gentle Ascham, a poem
to the Queen that he had for many months been composing into the
small hours:

'Those eyes that set my fancie on a fire'

he sang, looking into the cold fathoms of her expressionless face—

'those crisped haires which hold my hart in chaines
Those dainty hands which conquered my desire
that which of my thoughts doth hold the raines
Then love be Judge what hart may therewith stand
such eyes, such head, such wit and such a hand.'

He stole another look: was there perchance a softening in the
angry rigidity of her features? There was. The Queen's lips seemed to
be trembling, fluttering, then compressing back to their previous
severity, as though she were in the grip of some powerful emotion
that she did not want Francis Drake to discover. Encouraged, he
sang on.

'Those eyes for clearness doth the starres surpasse
Those haires obscure the brightness of the sonne
those hands even more white than ever Ivorie was
That wit even to the skies hath glory wonne.'

The Queen's hand was bent now, her shoulders shaking.
Amazed at his ability to affect Elizabeth's mind by musical arts so
painfully learned at Ascham's hands, Drake struck another rich
chord, but as he did so his fingers seemed to get tangled up, and
what should have been a resonant, tinglingly mellifluous shaft of
harmony dropped from his lute with all the aesthetic beauty of a
half-brick.
The Queen now quite literally exploded from held-in, pent-up
laughter, bellowing openly in Drake's face like some stampeding
mare. Well, he would finish the song anyway. Red-faced, he forced
himself to complete the verse. 'Such eyes,' he repeated, obstinately

97

drawing each word out to its proper length, 'such wit—and such a hand.'

Elizabeth came towards him, tears rolling down her cheeks, literally weeping with laughter. 'By God's wounds,' she said, 'you play that thing as though you are firing an arquebus.' As she dissolved once more into almost maniacal laughter, Drake could only wait on one knee, head down, flushed and embarrassed, for the Queen's parting dismissal.

Eventually the Queen brought herself under some sort of control. 'Well, Master Drake,' she said, between guffaws, 'you saved our life once and for this we are in your debt. We are equally in your debt for making us laugh as we have never laughed before. For these reasons we shall see you preferred as a mariner. Yes, take your voice to sea where 'twill be more effective than singing love songs to ladies, for I swear, a courtier's arts do not become you. The banishment remains. Now be gone.'

More like a whipped cur than a man, young Drake bowed his way out of the Queen's presence.

Elizabeth's fingers glided effortlessly over the keyboard of the virginal, stopping now and again to dab her still streaming eyes with a lace 'kerchief. How to prefer Drake? That was simple. John Hawkins of Plymouth needed the favour of her backing. Well, she would ask a favour in return, that Drake be taken into the firm of Hawkins brothers.

As she played on, her mind reverted to Robin Dudley. The uncontrollable laughter generated by Drake's appalling musical talent had quite changed her mood and she no longer experienced a feeling of sombre martyrdom. How stupid she had been, she thought, to fall so nearly into the clutches of one lusty adventurer. Had she not made herself a promise, long ago, that all men must be made to fall in love with her, but none must ever be allowed to love? Yes, she would favour first one, then the other. A word here, a present there, a gracious preferment, a bright smile, and they would all soon learn to adore her. And then, when she was no longer a girl, then they would worship still, her lovely hands and her hair, and her face too: there were tricks to preserve such things.

Yet the Queen had not foreseen one thing: that as the years passed and the wrinkles began to spread insidiously across her features like the first winter snowflakes on a frozen meadow, she would, in the loneliness of her angular spinsterhood and with all the hysterical, unstable power of her approaching climacteric, blame Francis Drake and Francis Drake alone, for her condition. And she would learn to hate Drake as she had never hated any other man.

*'She is a great woman; and were she only a Catholic she would be without her match.'*

Pope Sixtus describing Elizabeth.

# 10

Yes, two wonderful things had happened. The first was that Drake now had the direct patronage of the Queen, something for which every ambitious young man in the country would have given his soul. The second was that Cecil's intelligencers had gone out and miraculously found his family, plucking Edmund Drake, the preacher, straight from obscure poverty into the prosperous living of Upchurch. From Cecil, Drake learned that the Queen had commanded John Hawkins to ship his distant kinsman Francis Drake on his next expedition, and it now seemed a splendid idea to stay with his family until news of Hawkins' compliance with the Queen's wishes was received.

As he went through the vicarage gates, a packhorse laden with presents clopping placidly along behind the spirited horse that Francis had piratically 'inherited' from Amy Dudley's murderer, he found to his amusement the family assembled in a respectful line as they waited to welcome this brother of theirs, who, it was said, was actually on speaking terms with the Queen. Had they not been expecting him, they would never have recognised this strong young fellow with wide shoulders and unblinking blue eyes, above whose determined mouth a lustily twirling moustache with finely waxed-up ends had lately bushed out. Clad in a rich cloak with a taffeta doublet underneath, finely raked with an extravagant line of gold buttons, and an expensively chased dagger at his belt, Drake vaulted off his horse, grinning at the way they all stood there in rigid unease, shy, in the face of all his sartorial magnificence.

Twelve long years had passed since Drake had been parted from his family and many of the children standing there had been born during that time. Accordingly, he embraced all his many brothers and sisters in strictly descending order, enquiring everybody's name in turn, although his two brothers closest to him in seniority, Joseph and John, he had just been able to recognise. When the greetings were done they took Francis inside the house, where his father Edmund stood in front of a roaring inglenook fire, the Bible, as usual, clasped in one hand. His father, Drake found, had changed little over the years, but his hair was grey now, his back a little more bent and bowed with age and the cares of bringing up his brood of eleven children.

When Francis came up to him he held out his hand and shook it with little enthusiasm, saying in his ripe Devonshire accent, with more than a touch of sarcasm 'The Lawd is marvellous in all his deeds and we dew give thanks to him for returning to our fold a lost sheep.' Only then did Francis realise why Edmund had not come out and made him more welcome. His father had still not forgotten that Francis had been the only one of his children to rebel against his iron hand by running off to sea.

'Where is mother?' he asked. 'Baking in the kitchen?'

'She has not been spared to us,' Edmund replied. 'The Lawd was pleased to take her in her last childbearing. As yew were not present at the funeral, I will hold a special prayer meeting this night, directly after evensong, when yew may pay yor respects.' He turned away bitter-eyed, not hiding his dislike for his oldest and most rebellious son, who had turned up dressed in extravagant courtier's clothes that were a blasphemy in the eyes of the Lord.

After prayers in church, private prayers in the vicarage later, all the time prayer upon more prayer, Francis Drake began to experience, in the days that followed, the same restlessness that had led him to go to sea when a lad, directly against his father's wishes. He found himself spending more and more time with his two nearly full-grown brothers, Joseph and John, who would follow tales of his roistering coasting trips across the English channel with excited, wide-eyed interest. He started taking them out in a hired boat on the Medway and teaching them the rudiments of seamanship and was amazed how quickly they took to the sea, how pathetically eager they were to please. Under his eyes, their bodies, more accustomed to Bible reading than heavy exercise, began to grow muscle and sinew. John, the closest to him in age, was far more thickset and promised to grow into a formidable barrel of a man; while Joseph, slimmer and taller than his brothers, was the silent one, a slight stammer in his speech, which tended to become worse when he was excited, resulting in him

101

talking only when absolutely necessary.

When a courier brought the expected letter from Hawkins, Drake ripped it open with excited anticipation. There would definitely be a place for Francis, Hawkins wrote, as ship's officer, but it would be a good year and a half before the vessels could be properly fitted out for the next venture. 'Go back to your coasting,' Hawkin's precise handwriting was easy to read, 'be assured, dearest coz, that when my expedition is ready, I shall inform you.' With that, Drake had to be content. Meanwhile he was wasting his time at Upchurch, while his own sturdy ten-tonner rotted on the slipway. Accordingly, after prayers one night, he announced his intention of leaving, only to find to his amazement John and Joseph on their knees with tears pouring down their cheeks as they begged him to take them with him. Drake considered: well why not? He needed help in his boat and one day, when he was a famous seaman—and he never doubted for a moment that he would be famous—loyal ships' captains with the same blood running through their veins would be useful. So he accepted them gladly and the three men made haste to pack their belongings and say their goodbyes.

Edmund, who had not been there to welcome Drake, did not see him off either, attributing his present good fortune to God rather than to his son.

And so the three brothers plied their trade on the narrow waters of the channel and the East coast, in happy companionship, John and Joseph filling out amazingly and becoming experienced sailors under the able tuition of their eldest brother. However, months slid by without Drake hearing from John Hawkins, and months grew into first one year and then two years. Worried and impatient, Drake determined to go to Plymouth and see Hawkins. Accordingly, he left his boat in the able care of Joseph and John and one sparkling day in the autumn of 1562 found him standing on the wind-blown promontory of Plymouth Hoe, staring out to sea, his hand shading his eyes.

There was no pleasure in Francis Drake's face: his whole body was hot with fury. Bitterly, he watched Hawkins' three ships, the *Salomon*, the *Swallow* and the *Jonas* beating out of Plymouth Sound, the sun dancing on the water as they set out on their voyage to Africa and the Indies. Even as he stood there, drums began to beat and the ships dipped their royals smartly and in turn, as if in derisive salute to him. Francis Drake turned on his heel, his face working with emotion. He

102

knew now that Hawkins' soft words had meant nothing: that the man he dimly remembered as a sly, foxy-faced boy really did hate him, as rumour had so often said, and had indeed left without him.

Very well. He would now go to court again whether banned from Elizabeth's presence or not. He would petition the Queen for redress and if that did not work he would storm in on fat William Hawkins sitting chubby and prosperous in his fine Plymouth office, counting the profits of his brother's near-piratical ventures, and shake him 'till his flesh wobbled like jelly and threaten to slit his throat unless he received the employment promised by Queen Elizabeth. He had heard there was illness in London, sweeping the court, but neither plague nor the pox would deter him. A crazy rage possessed him, lying thick and heavy, tightening and choking in his throat, as with fists clenched, he impotently watched John Hawkins' ships disappear over the horizon. Eyes glittering with purpose, Drake wheeled his horse and galloped away from the Hoe.

The Queen, meanwhile, had deliberately thrown herself into a whirl of activity. Aware that Hawkins would soon descend, with all his sly glibness, on the Spanish Main and attempt to trade there in defiance of Philip's laws; aware also that her French adventure to help the Huguenots was going badly; she had judged it expedient to be graceful to as many of her European neighbours as possible.

Accordingly, she gave audiences in the great Paradise Chamber of Hampton Court for many hours at a time, a magnificent tour-de-force, according to those privileged to watch it: the Queen rising from her brown velvet throne to acknowledge, with a graceful gesture of a slim white hand, every single high-flown compliment that she received, and incredibly addressing one ambassador after another first in word perfect Spanish, then in elegant French, Italian and Latin, as though it were the most natural thing in the world. There were those who said she was on her mettle because the newly-returned Queen of Scots considered herself more beautiful than Elizabeth, but of course they were only being spiteful. A Queen of England would surely not allow such considerations to enter her head.

That evening the throne room was hung with huge drapes of gold and silver brocade and after a great banquet, the gentlemen of the Inner Temple performed for their distinguished guests a court masque entitled *Gorbuduc*. In such masques the script would be suddenly departed from and guests invited to participate by dancing with members of the cast. To the Queen's pleasure, she found herself dancing with a lithely handsome young man who could, without doubt, dance a fantastic galliard. Always difficult to master, with its five steps, its mandatory leap and a beating of the feet together in mid-air, it was mainly left to young men to attempt at all, but this fellow knew wheels and springs and lifts and turns that had Elizabeth floating and swooping spellbound in his strong arms and which made your neat cinque-pace and pretty-pretty capriole look as old as March-brewed beer!

The Queen retired that night with her ears still ringing with the sound of curtal, sackbut and viol, and her face flushed and bright, as much from the impact of this new fellow, one Christopher Hatton, as it was from the reflected brilliance of her jewels.

Next morning, to work again: an hour's close study of a book by the eminent Doctor Dee on the science of astrology, followed by a slow, meditative read of *Demosthenes* in its original Greek, for the good of the soul. Then take that bold new Irish hobby on a wild gallop through the waving meadow grass that still grew rich and long at the water's edge, with all the time a smile and a glance for poor Robert Dudley riding at her side, and still scowling with jealousy at Hatton's triumph the night before. A woman of many, many parts. Such parts as the rest of the world would one day find out—mostly to its own cost and England's benefit.

Later that afternoon the Queen began to feel unwell. A body bath was deemed advisable and the basins in the Queen's bathing-room were accordingly filled. For once the Queen took no satisfaction from eyeing the smooth whiteness of her body in the mirrors hung everywhere to satisfy her vanity. She was feeling worse by the minute. Dr Burcot, eminent German physician, was sent for and arrived in the full doctor's panoply of scholastic gown with long, hanging sleeves, square-cornered black hat that he did not deign to doff, and an ebony staff engraved with the Aesculapian symbol, that he did not even trouble to put down.

One look at her was more than enough. 'My liege,' he said, in his ungraceful German way, 'thou shalt have the pox.'

'Take the knave out of our sight,' the Queen screamed, quite unnerved by such a dreadful remark.

Burcot stumped away in a fury and although in five days' time there were still no spots, the Queen's illness had plainly got worse. That night, she began to ramble in semi-conscious fever and the

Council, gathered round her bed, became starkly aware of two things: the strain under which the Queen must have been labouring, and the grim, near-certainty of her imminent death.

'Who is to succeed us?' the Queen began to moan. 'My sweet Robin must be appointed Lord Protector and his body servant Tamworth, who sleeps in his chamber, given five hundred pounds a year.' At this, Cecil and the Privy Council exchanged meaning looks with each other.

Now, despite the fact that she was plainly delirious, her voice went suddenly flat and hard with hate. 'And if the Queen of Scots be taller than me then she is too tall, and if we are both musicians then I am the better, and I warrant she could never leap a galliard the way I ruffled it with that rascal Hatton.' Exhausted, she lay back, eyes glazed with tears from silent weeping, only the rasping moan of her hot, shallow breathing audible in the packed, hushed chamber.

When Drake arrived, he was met by the nearly-frantic Cecil, who for once was at a loss what to do. Not so Drake. Always a man for violent, direct action, he was round at Burcot's house within minutes of matters being explaind to him. Ignoring all the usual courtesies, Drake crashed the door open with his heavy riding-boot and Burcot, in the middle of dinner, found himself fetched up against a wall, the point of Drake's jewelled dagger scratching pretty patterns on his thick neck. 'You must come. The Queen dies.'

'By God's pestilence,' Burcot cursed. 'If she be ill, let her die. Call me a knave will she for my goodwill?'

For an answer, Drake smiled. It was a smile a lot of men would die watching: a fixed, jolly uplift of the mouth at the corners like the snarl of a wolf, accentuated in its silent menace by the line of his curled moustache and the hard, manic, unblinking glare of ice-blue eyes. Burcot, gazing into that murderous smile, knew without any doubt that the man holding the dagger would slit his throat as easily as he might slice a piece of bread.

'Very well,' Burcot said with an oath, 'I will go.' In a furious passion he tore down the stairs and thundered away to Hampton Court.

Brought to the Queen's bedside, he said 'Almost too late, my liege.' He ordered a mattress to be put down in front of the fire, and sending for a length of scarlet cloth, he wrapped her in it, leaving one hand out, and then had her carried to the mattress. He put a bottle to her lips and told her to drink as much as she liked and presently, red spots began to appear on her hands, at which the Queen began to moan and lament. 'God's pestilence,' Burcot swore again. 'Is it better to have the pox in the hands, or in the heart and kill the whole body?'

This bringing out of the eruptions saved Elizabeth's life and she was soon up and about, keeping to her chamber until the marks on her face should heal. She had escaped permanent blemish, although Lady Mary Sydney, Robert Dudley's sister, who had nursed the Queen devotedly through the illness, took horrible disfigurement.

Days later, Burcot and Cecil were granted audience. For Burcot, there was a fat grant of land from a grateful Queen and a pair of gold spurs that had once belonged to Henry VIII. For Cecil, there was something different: a closely-reasoned enquiry into the state of the kingdom. Halfway through, Elizabeth changed the subject and enquired blandly how Burcot had been made to come.

'Madam,' Cecil said, 'he was brought here by Drake. At point of a knife.'

'Drake? What was he doing here? Did we not banish him from Court?'

'Your grace, the fault is mine. I permitted him to come.'

The Queen, very pale and emaciated from her fever, stormed up and down the chamber, working herself into a fine rage. 'You did what?' she shrilled. 'The court has enough swaggering ruffians without this disobedient mariner. See him gone from court this instant. Only by bringing Burcot does he escape punishment.'

'As your grace wishes.'

'And you,' the Queen flashed, 'look at this mess in which you have embroiled us. At Le Havre our men die like flies from the plague and we spend sackfuls of treasure for nothing. Go now, make peace with the French,' her voice rose into a scream, 'before we are reduced to begging in our petticoat in the streets.'

Watching her high-beaked nose levelled accusingly at him from a face made thin by illness, Cecil was reminded of some lean imperial eagle fluffing its aureate feathers: deadly, dangerous and unpredictable. With the tongue-lashing over, he was glad to leave the withdrawing chamber, relief showing on his grave, set features. At his next audience, she would, he knew, be all charm, all courtesy and radiance, her vituperative hysteria completely forgotten. The storm had blown itself out and he would once again bask in the warmth of the Queen's affection, until the next time. Does she do it on purpose? Cecil asked himself. Lately the Queen's rages had seemed to be taking on a deliberately pre-planned edge, as though

106

she were producing them to order. Little remained now of that sweet, proud girl he had promised to serve. She was fast becoming a cruel and demanding mistress, a woman both formidable and cunning.

As he left court, something else struck him. The Queen's wish, expressed in her delirium, that Tamworth, Dudley's servant of the bedchamber, be given five hundred pounds a year. And what, he thought, had the so-called Virgin Queen been doing in Dudley's bedchamber at all? He tried to put the matter out of his mind.

Drake, sent packing with a terse message from Cecil, had only one card to play in his fight to force the Hawkins family to employ him as ship's officer: direct, violent, forceful action of the swaggering kind in which he excelled, and which had made the obstinate Burcot see reason so quickly. Accordingly, it was now the turn of fat William Hawkins to end up writhing against the wall at the end of a sharp dagger; and on a fish day too, just when his mouth was watering at a table groaning with ling, pike, salmon, haddock, whiting, gurnards, tench, birts and sturgeon.

'My post at sea, Master William,' Drake said in a soft, coaxing voice. 'Prithee, where is it? The Queen herself has so commanded, as you know.'

'There is nothing at present,' William spluttered.

'Stuff a turd in thy teeth for the liar thou art. I mean to have such work.' Drake pushed the knife-point through the fine lacework of William's ruff until it pricked the soft reaches of his flabby throat. 'Think again.'

'My brother John will not suffer it.'

'Why not?'

'He says you are suited for a common seaman only, and must touch your forelock to all of Hawkins stock, like your family have always done. Not,' he added hastily as he felt the sudden press of the knife-point, 'that I agree.'

Now, once again, Drake smiled: that lazy, piratical, upturned, easy-going, happy, buccaneering, pre-murder, wolfish grin; and William Hawkins knew real terror. 'You may go,' he trembled, 'as third officer. Purser. To San Sebastian.'

'When?'

'The vessel sails next week. God willing.'

'Under whom?'

'Captain Lovell is the master.'

'An old fool and a drunkard to boot,' Drake said contemptuously. ' 'Tis precious little glory I'll reap there.'

'There's nought else and when John finds out he'll be full enough of choler, I'll warrant.'

'Then I accept,' Drake said with a sudden, soft laugh. Turning on his heel, he made for the door and collided with a tray of hot carp, lamprey and eel, fetching a frightened squeak from the dark-haired wench carrying the tray. Spearing a large, juicy steak of conger eel onto his still unsheathed knife, Drake swaggered off into Kinterby Street, where William's fine house stood cheek by jowl with that of his brother John, close by their firm's fine boatyard at Sutton Pool, Plymouth's inner port.

It was only on the way back to his own lodgings that Drake knew he had seen the wench before. For the life of him though, he could not remember where.

# 11

Drake sat in a low-beamed ale-house close by the Hawkins boatyard, gazing gloomily into his amber-coloured beer. The work of ticking off hard tack, salt pork and water casks, of poring over endless cargo manifests of wool bales and hides, had depressed him. He was not cut out for purser's work, there was no doubt about it, but there was, it seemed, no alternative. Not if he wished to ship in a Hawkins vessel.

'You go to San Sebastian, zorr?' A voice cut into his confused, depressed thoughts.

'I do.'

'Then we'll be shipmates then.'

Drake turned and saw a gloomy-faced man as bald as a coot with a bony, highly-polished head, who had taken a chair opposite him at the wooden, planked table. Muddy-eyed, he had the pasty skin of a man who had suffered a lifetime of constipation. 'I am Thomas Moone, ship's carpenter, zorr.' Although unsmiling, his Devon accent was pleasant and when Drake extended an arm to shake hands, he was surprised at the sinewy strength of the grip.

''Twill be a tame voyage, right enough,' Moone said thoughtfully.

'There seems little choice,' Drake tried, but failed, to keep the awful depression out of his voice.

''Tis a pity we cannot liven things up, you and I,' Moone's voice dropped into a note of conspiracy. 'Now the war's over with the Frenchies, we must fashion a new kind of—' he paused to emphasise the word—'privateering.'

'Privateering?' Drake said softly. The magic word conjured up the boarding of fat treasure ships and the ripping of fine jewels off protesting Spaniards. 'You have been doing that? I envy you, Master

109

Moone.'

'Ay,' Moone said smugly. ''Tis known I can work as well with a cutlass as a saw.' Drake smiled and signalled the potman to bring over a flagon of ale for his companion. There was more to this Moone, it seemed, than met the eye.

'Thank 'ee, zorr. Thank 'ee.' His voice had the same Devon softness as Drake's, nothing blowhard, nothing raucous, and as each of them carefully blew the froth off his ale, he looked into the other man's eyes and knew him to be a pirate.

'Know you, zorr,' Moone added, after a few seconds meditative thought, 'that the Inquisition is loose in San Sebastian? They'll never let us land. Make us unload by tender, more likely. Won't risk Englishmen running through their port at a time like this.'

'Why is that?' Drake asked, interested.

'When we was blockading the Frenchies, we lifted some of their cargoes although they was neutral. Now the Dons, zorr, are proud men and don't take lightly to this treatment, so what did they do? Why, they arrested crews of English seamen and threw them into San Sebastian jail by way of revenge.'

'But the war,' Drake said, 'is over. Surely now they'll release them?'

Moone said meaningly 'The Inquisition goes about to examine them for heresy.'

'And the Spaniards won't let them go?'

'Don't dare to,' Moone said. 'The Don's a decent enough fellow, given a chance, but the Inquisition is a mad dog that knows no master.'

Drake's blue eyes gleamed. 'Those seamen are likely to die cruelly,' he said. 'If only we could rescue them. Now that indeed would be a task well done.'

To his amazement, Moone stood up, hands on hips, eyes bright with eagerness. Drake now realised that because of his grey, gloomy face, he had tended to underestimate Tom Moone. Although short, the man had great, rippling, veiny biceps on his upper arms and had freebooter stamped all over him. 'Can be done, zorr,' he whispered. 'A crazy scheme, but can be done with a Queen's gentleman to lead us and save our hides from an English jail afterwards.'

Suddenly it dawned on Drake just why Moone had engaged him in conversation and so cleverly worked the topic round to that of rescuing English seamen. With a shock, he realised that his stocky, opulently-dressed figure had become quite famous in the small, closely-knit parochial atmosphere of Plymouth. Local gossip had marked him down as a hard-bitten young roisterer with elegant court manners, friend alike of the Queen, her chief minister and her favourite, Dudley. That kind of reputation set him apart from the smug, bourgeois, Plymouth merchant society, and in an age when a man's destiny was judged by the power and wealth of his patrons, had made a proposition of the kind he had received from Thomas Moone inevitable. A man like Drake would not only lead well, but also have the influence at court to save their skins from diplomatic protest afterwards, perhaps even, secure a discreet reward from the Queen.

'Well Moone,' Drake said, smiling broadly, the flesh of his tanned mariner's face crinkling round his blue eyes, his moustachios climbing bravely into a broad smile, 'if you're looking for a man who hates Dons, I'll warrant you've come to the right place, and if your plan is crazy enough, count me in, for only the crazy ones ever succeed. Now then, tell me how we shall rescue those seamen.'

The two men bent forward until their heads were almost together and remained locked in whispered conversation through the small hours of the night, their eyes glowing in the smoky light of the ale-house fire.

The *William and John*, one hundred and fifty tons, new, carvel built, with a full course of sail on main and foremast, lateen rigged at the stern, butted down through the Bay of Biscay, a gentle nor-westerly breeze speeding her on her way. William Hawkins would certainly not have entrusted such a fine ship to a man like Captain Lovell where any kind of risk might be involved, but the voyage was a short one and the danger of pirates small, in those waters. The Spanish had lifted their embargo on trade with the English and San Sebastian was only one of many ports in Spain where the Hawkins brothers had connections. True, an Atlantic gale smashing against the continental shelf could throw up terrible seas in the Bay of Biscay on a long, lee shore, but Lovell, though a drunkard, could be relied upon to give himself plenty of sea-room and had a lifetime of deep-sea navigating behind him. Ships had to be used and if skippers drank, that was one of the risks shipowners had to take.

The voyage was uneventful, the wind holding favourable and light the whole way. Lovell, thickset and grizzled, with the blackened teeth of a drinker of ardent spirits, had locked himself in his cabin, content to let the mate, Holderness, sail the ship. Drake had slept on his straw palliasse in his cupboard-sized cabin, while down below the twelve men of the crew drank their gallon of beer a day and quarrelled, cursed and diced the voyage away. Dawn broke to show the distant peaks of the Pyrenees silhouetted sharp and black against the rays of the rising sun, while ahead of them, protected from all weather by the verdant hills of Northern Spain, the quaint, picturesque little harbour of San Sebastian lay snugly tucked away in a corner of the shell-shaped Bay de la Concha.

As they entered the roadsteads with merely a ripple of a bow-wave, main and foresails furled as they headed towards harbour, a big galley flying the flag of the Biscayan squadron detached itself from the quayside, its oars opening and closing fan-like at increasing speed, as it rapidly built up way in the calm water. With extraordinary efficiency the galley laid itself alongside, to cries of revulsion from the English seamen at the 'zoo' stench of the miserable captives chained to the oars. Their cries quickly muted to a whisper, however, when it was noticed how big and formidable the galley was, with its ugly, brass six-pounder mounted on a platform in the bows—the vessel's bronze ram that could tear a hole in the stoutest planks, the silent knot of pikemen and arquebusiers gathered menacingly in the waist.

In contrast to the ragged breeches and welted backs of the galley slaves, the small man who came aboard the *William and John* had the rumpy self-importance of a jumped-up official. Glistening in steel morion and breastplate, a feather in his helmet and a crimson sash across his plump stomach, he bowed low to Lovell, who had staggered up onto the poop deck, bewhiskered and unshaven.

'It eez with much regret,' the official began peremptorily, 'that as capitan of this port, I have to tell you that you may not come alongside. I assure you, Señor, that I am quite desolated.'

'And how am I to unload then?' Lovell spluttered.

'I shall send tenders to take off your cargo. Believe me, every facility will be supplied, food, water . . .'

'Some of your Indies rum would not come amiss,' grumbled Lovell, teetering slightly.

The Port Captain hid a grimace of disgust at the sour breath on this Anglo-Saxon pig, bowed from the waist and said courteously, 'It shall be supplied, sir, of course.' He walked across the steeply-canted deck and peered over the *William and John*'s tumble-home. 'I see, sir,

112

you have a ship's boat in tow. *Yo siento mucho*—I regret very much—
I moz take possession of it temporarily. I have strict instructions that
no—' he knitted his brows, searching for a word that did not convey
insult 'Lutherans—may be allowed on shore whilst the Holy Inquisition remains in San Sebastian.'

As Lovell, in a gentle, alcoholic haze, shrugged his shoulders in
acquiescence, the Port Captain delivered him a flowery salute, then
transferred himself back into the galley. With a crack of his whip, the
galleymaster jerked his crew into a neatly-synchronised, much-
practised manoeuvre which enabled the big galley to turn in its own
length and surge smartly back towards the quay, the *William and
John*'s pinnace bobbing merrily along in its wake.

From noon onwards tenders came alongside and Drake, in charge
of cargo manifests, was kept very busy. He could not help, however,
becoming increasingly conscious of the activity that was coming
from the Plaza Guipuzcoa, the main square in the centre of the city.
Very plainly, a large crowd had assembled there to watch a ceremony
of some kind. Moone, who knew about such things, explained that
the prisoners, bearing green candles and clad in saffron-coloured,
penitential tabards, were now being put through an elaborate ceremony of recantation and repentance, only to find, to their unspeakable terror, that although their souls had been saved, their bodies had
not. That night, they would die in agony.

As dusk fell, it was time to move. With Lovell snoring like a pig,
dead drunk on Spanish rum in his cabin, four men, sweating,
grunting, heaved up from the hold a carefully concealed piece of
extra cargo: Moone's pinnace, made in three collapsible sections
that he had spent many years in perfecting. Drake, noting the way
the pinnace fitted together like some well-contrived jigsaw puzzle,
could hardly hold back a whistle of admiration at Moone's skill in
the art of carpentry. Moone now rammed caulking into the already
tight joins, then using a cloth-covered hammer, nailed a stretch of
skin tightly over their tops, all the time having the men sing lustily
to cover the noise. The boat was lowered away over the bows with
scarcely a splash and four men climbed aboard. Drake, Moone and
the brothers John and Thomas Martyn, whose soft grins and
rounded, apple cheeks belied their fearsome reputation for braw-
ling and lethal cutlass work in the stews of Plymouth Catwater.

His crew deliberately kept small so that the number of people
rescued might be as large as possible and the element of surprise

preserved until the last moment, Drake took the pinnace away from the port, heading past the dark shape of the Isla de Santa Clara towards the open sea. Now, with muffled oars, they crept quietly round the lofty promontory of Monte Urgull, aiming to ground on the beach that lay on the other side of the mountain, close to where the jail, thoughtfully placed by the Spaniards away from the town, was situated.

The night was quiet, a moon rising on the horizon and bathing the four men in eery half-light. Drake searched for any sign of discovery, but there was, in fact, no activity by the Spaniards at all. There had earlier been three fishing boats bobbing placidly at the entrance to the harbour, a lantern flickering at each bow to attract the fish, but the fishermen, attracted more, perhaps, by the thought of free wine than the sight of heretics frying in bubbling agony, had soon put into port.

The moment the pinnace shivered to a halt in the soft sand, the four bent to with a will, hauling it on shore and hiding it in some large tussocks of rough grass amidst sand dunes. They then marched inland as silently as possible, guided by Moone, who had a fair knowledge of the town gained from previous voyages. Suddenly Moone stopped and pointed at a line of torches winding down serpentine, towards the town. 'The jail is up there on that hill,' Moone whispered. 'They bring the prisoners now, for punishment.'

'There are many torches,' a seaman whispered.

'They'll be well escorted, never fear,' Moone answered. 'The Papists like a fine procession on such occasions.'

Quietly crouching in a dark ditch at the side of the dusty track, they watched the mass of humanity come closer. Soon the excited chatter of the bawling, drunken crowd eddying round the procession could be heard, then the solemn chanting of the monks and finally, the rhythmic creak of leather and clink of metal as the glittering line of halberdiers came into view, holding their blazing torches.

'Listen,' Drake said, fighting down the excitement in his voice. 'We will join them. Split up, mix with the crowds. Only when it has had its fill of blood, will this mob ever go to bed. Mark this place well, for we meet here an hour before dawn and then when all are asleep, we will attack the jail and rescue such prisoners as remain alive. Be careful. If challenged, pretend to be Flemish seamen. Show no English coin. Speak to no one. If there is free wine,' he grinned at them in the darkness, 'drink only a little. There is man's work to be done, 'ere this dawn.' Silently the four men shook hands. Then splitting into pairs, dispersed into the darkness; casually joining the ever-growing maelstrom of humanity escorting the procession into the Plaza.

As the procession poured into the wide, handsome main square, the sweating crowd, restored to strength by the welcoming cool breeze of evening, roared their anticipation. The scene, Drake thought, was like the very hell from which the Papists had laboured so long to save the souls of the obstinate English seamen. Everywhere braziers full of coals and huge torches flared and flamed, filling the huge, raised, wooden dais with brilliant light and throwing the close-packed four-storey houses that surrounded the square into sharply-flickering, smoke-filled shadow.

First into the Plaza were serried ranks of massed monks and Capuchin friars in their distinctive habits chanting in slow, solemn Latin, heads bent under their thick cowls in prayer; then, escorted by two ranks of halberdiers and arquebusiers, polished helmets and breastplates gleaming in the bright light, came the prisoners.

Preceded by a man mounted on a magnificent white stallion, carrying the standard of the Holy Office, red with a silver sword in a crown of laurel, closely followed by three men bent under the burden of a huge crucifix wrapped entirely in black crepe, the prisoners shuffled into view, accompanied by a great roar from the crowd. Quickly they were hustled into a great cage built on the raised wooden dais and then, with standard and crucifix attached to the altar, the Grand Inquisitor, the elderly, angelic-looking Doctor Moya de Contreras, rose to his feet and celebrated mass, his voice vibrant from the strength of his emotions.

Drake's heart went out to that pitiful group of English seamen herded into that cage. Here were no churchmen, bred to iron discipline, determined to suffer for their faith. Instead, clad in their brilliant yellow sanbenitos, marked front and back with a vivid red St Andrew's Cross, their faces white and pinched from torture, confinement and the rack, they huddled together waiting for their torment to begin like a flock of frightened sheep which first smells the blood of the slaughterhouse. The crowd shared no such emotion: as the Grand Inquisitor prayed, bags of wine were freely passed around and a splendid stink of garlic filled the smokey air as people munched bread rolls, happily anticipating the delicious cruelties to come.

To a great roar of excitement, the first batch of prisoners were dragged forward and the Inquisitor confirmed their sentences: '100 lashes'; '200 lashes and ten years in the galleys'; 150 lashes followed by religious instruction'.

One after another the prisoners were stripped of their sanbenitos and triced up to posts; then burly men in black jerkins laid into their naked backs. Blood and flesh flew into the air as the cruel, black whips cracked with staccato-crisp explosion on cringing shoulder blades, literally slicing strips of skin from the suffering seamen as though they were cutting butter. Drake ground nails into his hands until his palms bled, and found difficulty in restraining himself from rushing to the dais and stabbing the merciless men who raised their whips with slow, majestic curl then brought them down in a huge arc contrived to obtain the maximum impact. Next to him, Moone's eyes bulged with terrible emotion and he began to moan so loudly that Drake had to nudge him. Drinking, heads tilted back from wineskins passed from hand to hand through the happy, friendly crowd, the two men forced themselves to smile and laugh at the sight of their countrymen being flayed alive. There was one moment of anxiety when a drunken, flushed-faced Spaniard placed his arm round Drake's shoulder and started jabbering in Catalan, but Drake, grinning, replied in his sharply-accented Spanish, explaining that he was a seaman from the Spanish Netherlands, and the incident passed off happily.

Now was the moment when, with the showmanship born of years of experience, the Inquisition would produce the grandest and grisliest of its hellish spectacles. The deaths by garrotting, awarded as a merciful death in exchange for the earnestness of a heretic's recantation, Drake was able to watch; the feeble waving of the victims' limbs as the wire was tightened round their throats, ending in one final, shuddering convulsion, had the one merit of being over quickly. Burning was another matter. He had never forgotten being made to watch one when still a boy, and even now woke up at night sweating from the imagined smell of roasting, crisping flesh.

Summoning up all his self-control, he braced himself for that awful scream made by every victim when the first heat of the flames singed naked flesh. Soon, as the fire heated up, would come the bull-like bellowings of agony as fat merged with blood into a living, yellow fry of blistering, bubbling human tissue; and after that, he knew, there would be even worse to follow, with smoking human limbs falling out of the fire like so many pine logs rolling off a

116

household grate. Somehow, he managed to swallow the vomit surging into his throat and staggered off arm-in-arm with Moone, the two of them giving the impression of two harmless drunks staggering away to sleep off their debauch.

Safely cloaked by the darkness of their roadside ditch, they waited for the other two men to rendezvous, each man silent, alone with his thoughts. In spite of a damp mist that had got up, Drake could feel the need for revenge settling hotly on his sword arm. Somehow he fought down the pounding urge to shed Spanish blood and forced himself to be patient. Soon, with a soft whisper of recognition, the two others joined them, miraculously sober from the sight of their countrymen being tortured. They settled down to doze as best they could, only to be nudged suddenly awake by Drake, as a cart carrying those prisoners who had been punished and were now being returned to jail rumbled past, escorted by a line of halberdiers.

Before long the halberdiers returned down the road to town, no longer marching in step, but with their duty done, laughing, yawning, arms trailing, as they looked forward to sleep after a long night's duty.

In the cold eery light of a half-dawn, four determined Englishmen swooped on the sleeping jail like avenging angels: Moone with two others bursting straight through the door of the adobe guard house, Drake diving cat-like through the window of the upstairs bedroom where the *Comandante* slept naked beside his fat, blowsy *mujer*.

Down below, a short savage fight took place, those Spaniards who had blearily dived for their weapons, spitted on English cutlasses, the other two guards who had found the sense to raise their arms, quickly gagged and trussed like chickens.

Upstairs, Drake's jewelled dagger balanced on a pinpoint over the palpitating heart of the Comandante, while his wife, corpulent in her nightdress, heaved air into her great, hanging bosoms and prepared to unleash a shattering scream. 'Madam,' Drake said calmly, 'I regret to advise you that the health of his honour the Comandante, rests in your hands. Have the favour—*haga el favor*—to restrain yourself, if you wish him to stay alive.' The woman, amazed by this stocky, moustachioed Englishman, gulped hard and the scream died stillborn.

'I beg you not to disturb yourself, Señora,' Drake went on, smiling gently at her, 'for Francis Drake does not war on women. You are as safe with me as you are with your confessor. I am desolated by the

117

necessity to tie you both up. I am sure you will understand.' The woman nodded dumbly, eyes riveted on Drake's dagger, still only a mere finger pressure away from depatching her husband into eternity.

When Moone and his companions came bounding up the stairs, he had them bind the Comandante and his wife securely, but when the woman whimpered at the tightness of her bonds, Drake ordered them loosened, smiling gently at her until she assured him she was comfortable. As they left, Drake executed a deep bow, saying as he did so 'Allow me to compliment the Señora on her great beauty. A skinny girl is plainly of no use to anyone, whilst a fully-fleshed woman is the finest treasure a man may possess.' The woman, formless, fat and flabby, flushed with pleasure, never for many years having received any compliments or courtesy from anybody.

Downstairs, in the cells, they gathered up with incredible tenderness the moaning human jetsam of what had once been men. Weakened previously by interrogation and starvation, their backs no longer had a covering of skin and resembled more underdone joints of roast beef. Working with calm efficiency they loaded the moaning men into the cart, then hitching up the horse set off down the hill.

To reach the place where the boat was hidden the rescued men would need to be carried, but Moone and the others had strong shoulders and two short trips were all that was necessary to deposit them on the beach while they relaunched the pinnace. As the sun rose fiery red over the foothills of the Pyrenees, giving promise of a hot day, the pinnace swept quietly round the little spit of land, carrying four of the English seamen, Drake staying on shore with the other three. Soon, the pinnace could be seen on its return journey, the sun much higher now. Shortly it would be broad daylight and it could only be minutes before sharp eyes detected them.

Suddenly, church bells began to toll. No sonorous summons to worship, but a mad, crazy jangle of alarm. The pinnace came grinding up on the shore and cursing, working madly, they loaded the remaining men then unbeached the pinnace, turning its bows out to sea. Now, rowing for their lives, they rounded the small Cape once again and laid alongside their ship, willing hands reaching down to haul the weakened seamen to safety.

The margin of success or failure, of life or death, had now become desperately close. Already, to a summoning riffle of kettle-drums, pikemen could be seen galloping down the stone jetty into

118

the waiting galley. Seconds later, oars flashed in the sun as the galley got under way and headed towards the English vessel. No time for explanations, to ask for orders; even before Captain Lovell staggered up on deck, eyes blinking myopically in the bright sunshine, Holderness, the mate, had the anchor taken in and all possible sail set. Clumsily the *William and John* wallowed in the oily sea, whatever breath of wind there was coming in foul, off the bows. Meanwhile the galley was closing fast, oars flashing in mighty unison as the galley master had the stroke set by the deep beat of a drum.

A flash, followed almost together by the thud of the gun and the shattering crash of impact, as a stout cannonball fired with a fair degree of accuracy from the galley's six-pounder made the hull shiver. Soon the galley could either ram, come alongside and pour pikemen into the waist, or just stand off and pound them into bloody wreckage. 'Go for the oarsmen,' Moone roared. Even before his shout had died away, the two of them were running to rip the tarpaulin off the gun mounted in the bows.

As the next flukey breeze fanned their cheeks, he screamed to Holderness, who spun the wheel over. Slowly the galley grew into solid shape in the vee of the gunsight: only a bowchaser, yet properly aimed at one of the banks of oarsmen, it might well do its work.

Now the galley master made his mistake. Seeing the *William and John* make its turn, he altered course to anticipate its probable direction, and in so doing laid the flank of the galley open to the bowchaser. Drake was sorry for the slaves he was now going to maim or kill, but there was no alternative. Snarling, he pulled the lanyard. The gun barked, recoiled, sending a swathe of chainshot winging towards the galley. Only now did the galley's great weakness become apparent. It took only two injured slaves to slump over their oars to cripple a powerful, formidable, engine of war. Until those two slaves had been unchained and replaced, the galley could only advance in some bizarre, sideways, crabwise motion. By then, they would have gained the open sea and put themselves beyond the galley's reach.

As the *William and John* caught a freshening breeze, turning its inperceptible bow-wave into a pleasant musical chuckle, Captain Lovell was still too drunk to care that members of his crew had raided the Spaniards, showing contemptuous disregard for his own authority. The more sober members of the ship's crew were, however, worried men. They had been involved in hostile action against a country with which their own was at peace, killed Spaniards and

119

damaged a Spanish man 'o war. With no commission from the Queen, without Letters of Marque, they could all be hanged as pirates, at the very least imprisoned, if it served the Queen's whim to placate such a powerful monarch as King Philip. All their fates depended now on Drake: the stocky, chunky Devonshire boy who had carried out this insane foray into a foreign country with such incredible and icy audacity.

Did he really have that all-important property, that unbelievable advantage, that marvellous, much-coveted, incredibly-prized patronage that every subject of Elizabeth dreamed about, would have gladly sold his soul for? Did he really have the personal ear of the Queen?

Well, what the Queen might do, nobody could guess, but what another woman did, fat and ugly, bosoms wobbling with emotion, was to bore all the citizens of San Sebastian who would listen with a tale of the courtly chivalry she had received at the hands of a charming, blue-eyed Englishman.

And so began a legend about a man whom some would call—El Draco.

# 12

When the Queen read the Spanish note, a fast ship having been despatched with a formal protest from Philip, she did so with a distinct air of annoyance. Her large, dark pupils wide with ill-temper, she roved quickly through the flowery, ornate writing, then catching the line of a frown in a nearby mirror, brushed it quickly away with a jerky stroke of her long, tapering fingers. Why did they persist in making a statesman out of her, she thought pettishly. Had she not ministers to handle such matters? Then she remembered how, on an outburst of selfish egotism, she had insisted on making herself absolute mistress of her country's affairs, and had so made a rod for her own back.

Well, it would have to wait: something far, far more important awaited immediate attention. Lately she had been hearing more and more of the beauty of Queen Mary of the Scots; her dancing, her dainty skills in all things from needlework to music. Melville, Mary's plenipotentiary, happened to be at court and when he had casually told her maids-of-honour that the Queen of Scots was the taller of the two, her jealousy had known no bounds. Unaware of how childishly she was behaving, she stalked the chamber in frustration. The matter must be corrected immediately. Melville must be sent home with a proper appreciation of her superiority in all things. Snapping slim fingers, she came to a decision. In three quick strides she grasped the bell-rope then pulled on it savagely until maids-of-honour and body servants skipped all a-dither into the chamber, and sinking to their knees, listened as the Queen spat curt instructions.

After dinner that evening, Lord Hunsdon asked Melville if he would like to hear a little music. The answer in the affirmative, Hunsdon conducted him to a door of a gallery. Inside someone was playing the virginals remarkably well; a complicated piece by that young fellow William Byrd, who was beginning to make a name for himself.

121

Melville pulled aside the portière and went in. The Queen was playing, her back to him. 'Excellent, excellent,' Melville was compelled to murmur. At this, the Queen broke off the complicated procession of twangling notes, and affecting perfect surprise, turned round. Melville, lost in admiration, noted how perfectly Elizabeth's fair skin was set off against black velvet, how elegantly her reddish-yellow hair had been drawn back into a gold net sewn with pearls and precious stones.

'Why, Sir James,' the Queen cooed. 'We did not know you were listening. You took us quite by surprise.'

'Madam,' Melville replied, 'no master in Europe could play a piece such as that with under a month's practise. In this, you are indeed greatly superior to my own mistress, Queen Mary.'

Smiling like a feasted tigress, the Queen dallied graciously with the Scotsman for a while, before gently dismissing him. The perfect success of her little trick had put her into a remarkably good temper. Her first reaction on hearing of Drake's raid had been to disown the whole operation and throw the ringleaders, Drake included, into prison; but happy now with her petty triumph over Mary, she allowed her mind to veer towards generosity. After all, she thought, Drake had carried out a remarkably successful operation and if she quickly claimed some part in it, she had the chance of reaping fantastic adulation for only tiny outlay.

She summoned a secretary to take down a letter: 'My corsair,' she started. 'Everywhere our subjects are exploited and ground down. In rescuing these good men you have done no more than act as your Queen's own sword arm. Dispose, therefore, these two bags of gold among our loyal seamen as you think fit, but for you, Francis, apart from a small gift, your Queen's good graces and the right to visit us here at court must be sufficient.'

Such a letter, so noble, so generous, would be sure to be read out aloud, and in days the whole of the West Country would be cheering her to the echo. Equally pleasurable was the thought of this stocky, sturdy Drake kneeling at her feet, expressing admiration and devotion in his soft, Devon burr, all the time raking her body with bold eyes. The thought of this fine flirtation to come was exciting. She felt herself shiver very slightly, in anticipation.

In the six years since she had become Queen, Elizabeth had shown herself to be vain, conceited, bullying, arrogant, inconsistent to a degree; yet incredibly, by using a measure of perceptive intuition unknown to mere men, she was continuing to reign brilliantly, doing all the right things—and mainly for all the wrong reasons.

Standing on a wooden stool in an ale-house, Drake read the Queen's letter to the assembled seamen. As Elizabeth had so cunningly contrived, the letter gave some credit to them, more to Drake, and most of all to the Queen herself. The low, oaken rafters of the tavern, from which hung many a side of bacon cured to a dark, tacky black from the smoke of the log fire, rang to three hearty cheers that Drake raised for Her Majesty. One by one, the crew of the *William and John* stepped forward to receive their reward: Holderness, Tregarron, Trewithick, Harkness, honest seamen these, with good West Country names. For Tom Moone, the ferocious little carpenter, and the two apple-cheeked Martyn boys who had shown a remarkable penchant for piracy, there were especially fat purses of gold. It was strange how these men, many of them experienced old salts who had sailed with William Hawkins to the Brazils in days long past, lurched forward to receive their gold in the strange swaggering roll affected by mariners, happily knuckling their seamed foreheads to this stocky young man in dandified dress with twirling, upturned moustachios and blue eyes that could bore a hole through a ship's hull. Quite plainly, the eery, semi-divine light of Queen's favour beating down on Francis Drake's stout shoulders had caused them to treat him with the kind of reverence due to God.

Drake looked down on the men fondly. Normally he was quietly-spoken, yet when the time came he could shout and plead as eloquently as anyone, and because such a thing was so unexpected, its effect was that much more dramatic. 'Remember me,' he bawled at them. 'Remember my name, Francis Drake. I have plans to squeeze gold out of the Dons that you would not believe. One day, when the Queen gives me ships. Will you come?'

'Yes,' they roared. 'Us'll come, zorr. Just let 'un know and us'll come.'

For a moment Drake's blue eyes seemed to glow and redden in colour as if in a wild rage for more adventure, then they were soft and composed again, as stepping down from his stool, he walked out of the tavern, nodding and smiling, shaking a hand here and there. Quickly he walked the short cobbled way to William Hawkins' house in Kinterbury Street. John Hawkins, recently returned

123

from his slaving voyage to the Indies, had left his grand house in London to see how brother William had been running the Plymouth business in his absence, and to have words with Francis Drake. The summons that Francis had received from his employers had been peremptory and curt.

While fat William wobbled his flaccid chins and rubbed his hands in anguish, John received Drake with icy hostility. It was the first time Drake had seen John Hawkins since that grand time so long ago, when he had succeeded in rolling the foxy-faced boy in a drain full of stinking turds. Over the years, Hawkins' features had changed little and he was still narrow-chinned, thin-lipped, with a mouth full, as such kind of face so often is, of small, sharp, vulpine teeth. As the two men faced up to each other, it became plain to fat William, still trembling from the tongue-lashing he had received for permitting Drake to sail with Lovell, that the two men had been, and would always be, enemies.

'Hazard my ship, will you sirrah?' John Hawkins practically snarled. 'Since all turned out well, there is little I can do, but I'll have no more murdering pirates aboard my ships. Your villainy, sirrah, was inexcusable and no more than I might expect from a mongrel nipping at his betters' heels.' He went on for many minutes in such fashion, dredging from the bitterness of his soul the worst, the most insulting, venom of which he was capable, hoping to provoke the young man standing in front of him to a duel and then dispatch him with his sword-play, well-known to be brilliant.

To his amazement, however, Drake stood there, stocky legs spread easily apart, placidly smiling at him and quite undisturbed at the insults flying round his ears. Slowly the realisation came to John Hawkins that this broad-chested young man, with the lazily smiling blue eyes, was perfectly well aware of the power the Queen's friendship gave him and that if he were not careful he would be saddled with Drake's services, soon to have Drake equal and then eclipse him in the brilliance of services rendered to the Queen. Hawkins groaned with inner fury. He had made a splendid trip and amassed a great deal of wealth, some of it, so the rumour went, for the Queen. He had even persuaded the Spanish colonists to trade with him in stark defiance of Philip's laws. Well, persuasiveness had always been John Hawkins' stock in trade, but in the end, Hawkins knew with heavy, leaden bitterness that he did not have that one priceless commodity that Francis Drake possessed to such large degree: the commodity of charm.

'Well sirrah, I have decided nevertheless to retain your services.' Hawkins felt the gall rise, stinging and bitter in his mouth, as he bowed to the inevitable, but he was not finished yet. 'However, I regret you may not accompany me on my next voyage. I go with Queen's ships, flying the royal standard as Queen's Admiral and in this venture, men of diplomacy will be needed, not—' he paused, 'men of violence. Far better that you should go with your friend Lovell in '66. By then, I fancy, we shall be needing fighters rather than traders.'

The look of easy contempt faded from Drake's eyes. He took in the thin smile of Hawkins' foxy face and realised at last, the true depths of the man's cunning. The Dons had left Hawkins alone, the first time. Coming as master of a powerful fleet, they might bend a second time, but what would happen when a leaky old tub or two, commanded by a drunken, useless captain, reached the Spanish colonies and attempted to trade yet a third time? The answer to that was simple. The Spaniards would kill them; and if they did not, the sea would. Should they, by some miracle, return, then their certain lack of success would be compared unfavourably to Hawkins' fat profits from his previous voyage; and Drake's star would fall and Hawkins' would rise. At small loss and without incurring the Queen's displeasure, Hawkins was contriving Drake's ruin.

Not allowing for a moment the smile to leave his face, Drake made a graceful bow to the two brothers then turned on his heel and made for the door. On the way, he met William Hawkins' wife. Remembering meeting a young maidservant in much the same place, on his last visit, Drake was prompted to ask a question. 'Mistress Hawkins,' he asked, 'where is that black-haired young serving wench of yours? I vow that I have met her before.'

'I think, boy, with the company you keep, that is most likely,' Mistress Hawkins replied acidly. 'As for Mary Newman, since a few good smacks across the face did not cure her habit of breaking my plates, I disposed of her services.'

Drake left the house, heart pounding. Now he knew. Knew for certain. Mary Newman, that sweet young girl who had cossetted him, cuddled him, protected him, when as a young boy he had languished so miserably as a captive of the Upright man; that same girl who had given him hope to live when he had been miserable enough to die, was in trouble, probably starving. After his voyage, he had leave

125

coming. Now he would use it: to find Mary Newman.

Many years ago he had sworn a great oath to protect her when he grew into a man. In the surging, youthful optimism caused by his chance meeting with Sir Thomas Wyatt, which had led in turn to the glittering privilege of the Queen's personal patronage, he had quite forgotten his solemn obligation. Now, with a fresh sight of that pinched, undernourished face, his mind full of wide, lustrous eyes made cavernous and strangely beautiful from abuse and starvation, he knew where his duty lay. So, for well over a year, while Hawkins, secure in the Queen's favour, first fitted out a prestigious fleet and then departed on his autumn voyage to the Indies; Drake, instead of himself courting Elizabeth and pandering to her compulsive need for flattery, proceeded to forsake his mistress and range like a wild man over south-western England, searching for Mary Newman. Day after day he rode, following the vaguest rumour, stopping all he met for news of any girl answering Mary's description, combing the elemental and largely untouched patchwork of green, gold, brown and grey that was Elizabethan England. Through vast, primeval forest darkly flanking sleek strips of farm and grassy meadow, over desolate moorland sharing horizons with the shaggy, windswept grazing of hills and saltmarshes, he travelled: and all to no avail.

Drake returned to Plymouth at the beginning of July 1565, depressed and desperate. Strangely enough it was fat William Hawkins, to whom he had needed to go for permission to extend further his leave of absence, who eventually provided the clue to Mary's whereabouts. 'Know you Francis,' he said kindly, his chins wobbling in plump, comfortable unison. 'Know you that only last year her Majesty, in her concern over the starving beggars and vagabonds who range so freely over our countryside, was pleased to enact a new statute.'

Drake shrugged. 'And how, prithee, does this affect Mary?'

'The law says this: that no man or woman out of work may obtain poor relief from any parish other than their home. I doubt the girl will find ready employment in these dark times, so provided she shall not have fallen into the hands of villains you will find her in only one place, Honiton. And if you hurry, you will arrive there in time for the great fair, where those who are unemployed must, by the very same statute, solicit employment or be whipped for idleness.'

Thanking him, Drake at once set out for the beautiful town of Honiton, long prosperous from its fine lace industry, arriving there on the morning of 20 July, precisely, as to archaic and quaintly time-

126

honoured ceremonial, the fair duly opened.

'Oyez, oyez,' shouted the town crier. He looked up at the gilt glove carried on the top of his decorated staff and proclaimed at the top of his voice 'The glove is up, the glove is up. The fair is open and God save the Queen.'

Now, in wonderful, bustling tumult, as hot pennies were thrown to shrieking children from the windows of the main inns, the fair began in all its populous, many-sided activity. Braving the careful stare of constable and suspicious beadle, Drake swaggered past stalls where pigs were roasting whole; where horse-dealers bragged and their patient charges—which had submitted to varied and painful tricks to cover their defects, such as garlic and mustard sharply squirted up their nostrils to hide the glanders, black marks burned on their teeth to simulate youth—now stood in head-down resignation awaiting new masters. Through the huge crowd Francis walked square-shouldered, jostling and being jostled in turn, one careful hand on purse, one on dagger: past dancing dogs, a black wolf, and a hare that played the tabor; past a trained ape that would leap over his chain at the mention of the Queen and yet lie marvellously sullen at the mention of Philip or the Pope!

Soon he came to that section of the festivities that had stimulated his journey to Honiton: the mop fair, so called because those wanting work displayed a badge of their trade; a shepherd, a lock of wool in his hat; a milkmaid, a tuft of cowhair; but for all those poor drudges of house wenches far too numerous to describe, only one thing that instantly identified their calling—a mop. Drake ranged down the line of curtseying girls: some blowsy; some still with the pretty bloom of youth that would disappear soon enough after labouring fifteen hours a day and then being dragged off to play doxy to a lustful master; some retired whores with features twisted by the French Disease; others prematurely old and crabbed from the pitted, moonlike craters left by the virulent outbreak of smallpox that had recently swept the country. There, in this pitiful, straggling, pathetic line he found Mary Newman.

Head downcast, she did not even know he was there. Used to rough hands pinching her arms to feel the work in her, raising her chin to see whether health or illness shone out of her eyes, she stood there lack-lustre, half-starved, uninterested in this latest inspection.

'I trow this wench could do a day's work.' The cheerfulness of Drake's voice, allied to the hint of gentility Ascham had somehow

127

managed to graft onto his rich Devonshire burr, made her look up. She knew him at once. Had she not had one fleeting glimpse of Francis when he had collided with her at William Hawkins' house? Her fright at breaking a dish had prevented her looking too closely, but her first impression had been overpowering. Now, her senses reeled with pleasure at seeing Francis Drake again. His magnificent clothes, that fine moustache, those clear blue eyes, the sheer over-powering vitality of the man, left her practically devoid of speech. She knew only, that she loved him dearly. Such fierce emotion coming on top of months of privation were too much for her. Slowly, she corkscrewed to the ground in a dead faint. Drake picked her up and tramped away. The girl, worn down by poverty, was a mere insubstantial wraith, a shadow made of skin and bone. He was not conscious of the weight of her on his shoulder.

When she recovered consciousness, she was sitting in a warm, smoky tavern, a glass of good ale and a huge dish of venison pie in front of her. She wanted to talk, to apologise, to somehow please with pretty conversation this fine man who had befriended her, but hunger was stronger. She attacked the venison pie with such a vora-cious appetite that Drake felt compelled to place a restraining hand on her thin arm. 'Gently girl,' he chided. 'If thy stomach be as empty as it seems, then thou goest about to do thyself an injury.'

Soon, the strange sensation of a full belly attacked her with insi-dious strength. Once again she felt her eyes burning with fatigue. How terrible. How rude! No gentlewoman would ever behave in such fashion. She cried a little, tears streaming from the corners of her hollow, dark-smudged eyes; but sleep she did, nevertheless, her hair cascading in thick, black waves across the table's rough tim-bers as her head slumped forward onto her bosom. She never felt those same gentle hands lift her up and carry her effortlessly away. For an eternity, it seemed, she slept, waking just enough to savour and enjoy the delicious sensation of warmth, clean white sheets and soft feather pillows before drifting back yet again into drugged slumber.

A week later, when Mary was fit to travel, Francis Drake left for the village of Stoke Gabriel, where, with the reward given him by the Queen, he had been able to take a lease on a pretty cottage close by the beautiful River Dart. He had already installed his two younger brothers, Joseph and John, there, having realised that the centre of gravity for all sailors in search of wealth and glory was with little doubt, the County of Devon. Now, they fished the local waters, rubbing shoulders with neighbours bearing such names as Davis, Gilbert and Raleigh, all of whom, destined to be great sailors and explorers, would one day adorn the pages of history books to the glory of all English speaking nations.

To this idyllic place, where steep, wooded hills sweep down to the water's edge, where at low tide herons stand and fish and men net salmon, where a little creek runs up to the lovely village of Stoke Gabriel through the soft Devon greenness, he came at the turn of the year, Mary still pinched and drawn, mounted on a sway-backed palfrey as gentle and as fat as butter. Here, Drake hoped, his two brothers, aided by the kindly fisherfolk who dwelt nearby, would soon nurse Mary back to health and in turn, when she was well, she could sew and cook for them, until Francis returned from his voyage to the Indies.

It had never occurred to Francis that he should not marry the girl. Had he not sworn a great oath and made a solemn promise to Mary, all those years ago? Francis Drake was never a man to bend an oath or break a promise. As he left to join Captain Lovell, he and Mary were already engaged to be married.

# 13

Sailing with four ships in November 1566, Lovell had, on the face of it, been given a perfectly easy job by John Hawkins: to supply the crooked and venal treasurer of Rio de la Hacha, Miguel de Castellanos, with some ninety or so slaves he had ordered from Hawkins the year before. Lovell, however, on arriving at the Spanish Main, found the corrupt Castellanos under the lash of a terrifying new governor sent out by Philip to make strict enquiry into the colonist's illegal trading with Hawkins the year before. Accordingly, while the four ships quivered and danced in the torrid Caribbean heat, and down below the negroes suffered agonies of torment, Castellanos refused point blank to accept the slaves he had ordered and in the end, to avoid them perishing in his holds, Lovell had to give them ignominiously away.

The voyage, with a drunken captain, possessing neither the prestige bestowed by wearing the Queen's colours, nor the dignity of being carried out in Queen's ships, had turned into complete disaster. Hawkins, with amazing skill, had succeeded in placing a permanent blight on Francis Drake's career. No wonder Drake sat, only a few weeks after his return, legs dangling over the slimy, seaweed-encrusted sea wall hard by the Cat-water, miserably throwing stones into the turgid water.

All around him were the sounds of creaking spars, of gently groaning timbers, as ships heaved gently to the rhythm of the ever-changing tide. Other sounds, too, invaded his senses, combining to feed his mood of black depression: the slap-slap of paint brushes as men suspended in cradles decked out two great Queen's ships, that had lately sailed into Plymouth, in the brilliant green and white of her Majesty's personal colours. Drake looked in awe at the huge *Jesus of Lubeck*. She represented seven hundred tons of impressive power, even if she was old-fashioned with an appallingly high top hamper. The *Minion*, too, was impressive: four-masted and almost as highly-charged as the *Jesus*. It was a symbol of the Queen's faith in John Hawkins that she was now furnishing a pair of her great ships for such a mysterious, secrecy-cloaked voyage.

What he would not do to be going on that expedition. Drake bit his lip with frustration, listening to the banging of hammers, as copper sheathing was checked to lie snug against the hull and standing rigging made strong and tight: and to the rumbling their trucks made as guns were run out and back again, while alert eyes checked the ships' armament for faults. Nothing but the best would do for Hawkins. The Queen would see to that.

As horse-drawn drays clattered along the cobbles, delivering barrel after barrel of ship's stores, Drake could feel the blood pound in his veins, pressing darkly against his brain in the heady excitement of all these marvellous preparations, yet at the same time he felt a terrible sadness at not being part of them. The Queen, it was rumoured, was sending Hawkins off on some fantastic quest for gold in Africa and was sparing no expense to see that Hawkins was properly equipped. But for him, Francis Drake, there would be no more adventuring, for in the course of only two years his career had collapsed about him like a pack of cards. Again and again Francis despairingly reviewed the ruin of his life. First, his father had died and yet another brother, Thomas, slender and finely-made, had come to join the others at the Stoke Gabriel cottage, the sea-lust shining eagerly in his gentle face. Three hungry brothers to share the humble profits of one little fishing-boat while they waited confidently for their big hero, Francis, to carve out a future for them. The bitterness of his misery overwhelmed him. He had been able to do nothing for them.

Another problem also sat heavily on his shoulders: Mary Newman. The girl had not made the expected swift recovery back to health. Instead, she had developed a troublesome cough and although she tried desperately to cope with the household chores, she tired with terrible ease, her face remaining thin and wan, those large and strangely lustrous eyes shining with even more brilliance from their sombre frame of darkened, fatigued lids.

In his desperation, Drake thought once again of turning to the Queen herself, but that was impossible. Even the very thought shrivelled him with fear. Only two years ago she had asked him back to court and he had, quite plainly, ignored her. Had Lovell's voyage been successful, he might still have been able to work his way back into the Queen's favour, but the expedition had been a disaster. If he

131

so much as showed his face at court, he risked being clapped in the Tower.

All these thoughts clouded darkly the brain of Francis Drake, as he sat blinking in the autumn sun. Suddenly, he froze. A shadow, no, seven shadows smudged the horizon. Quickly he shaded his eyes and looked again. Imagination? No. Ships, all of them with towering forecastles. Idly he examined them again, their shape becoming clearer by the second as, fully-rigged, they drove towards Plymouth on a brisk south-westerly wind. He had seen ships like that before. Where? He scratched his head, then suddenly remembered. San Sebastian. Galleons. Yes, that was what they were, galleons, swarming with Spanish soldiers able in minutes to overwhelm a fleet lying at anchor.

He rose, turned. A man was standing near him. 'Spaniards!' Drake cried. 'Raise the alarum!' The man smiled faintly and just strolled away. He would have to do something himself. In seconds he was racing down the quay steps, half-falling, skidding on the slime-encrusted stone in his tearing urgency. Tumbling into a rowing boat he began to row strongly towards the steep sides of the *Jesus*, roaring all the time 'Spaniards! The Dons are upon us!'

Hawkins came out on deck to find out what all the noise was about and was galvanised into instant action. His look-outs might have been asleep, but Hawkins was not so easily caught napping. To the mad shrill of pipes and whistles, men were called to action stations, the anchor cables shortened, and men sent aloft to man the fighting tops and yards, so that if necessary the fleet could get under way. Hawkins ordered the magazines to be opened and the guns run out and loaded. Drake, mad from excitement, could only rest on his oars and watch.

The Flemish Squadron—for that was what it was, the pride of the Spanish Netherlands fleet—came storming on, taking the customary channel, leaving St Nicholas Island to port. When the lead ship came abreast of the fort there, without pausing, her topsails still set, her ensign brazenly undipped, Hawkins' suspicions were confirmed. On they came, driving straight for the Hoe; anyone, Drake thought, who says the Spaniard cannot handle ships, should see this! Clearing How Start, the huge warships turned towards the inner harbour, making audaciously straight for Hawkins' vessels. Hawkins watched the distance narrow, the Spanish flag still insolently undipped. As the Spaniards came within range of his big cannon, Hawkins gave the order to

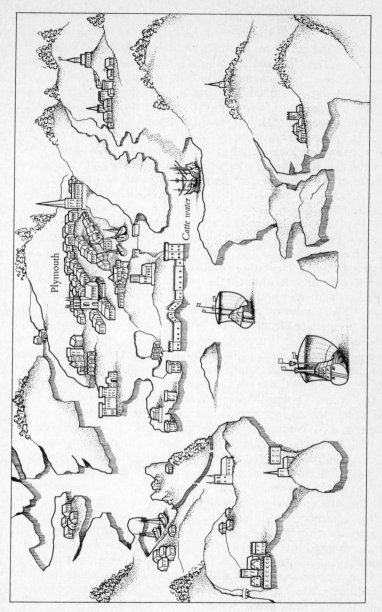

Old Plymouth in Tudor times.

fire, aiming high at the ensign. Incredibly, the Spaniards kept coming. In the acrid smoke haze, the crews madly rammed home fresh charges and hauled the heavy gun carriages back into the firing position. 'Give it to them, men!' Hawkins screamed.

The fleet was enveloped in a cloud of billowing smoke, but it was the leading Spaniard, commanded by the wily old Admiral De Wachen, that caught fair and square the great swirling broadside of the *Jesus*. Stroking his pomaded beard in annoyance, he knew that, thanks to an alert look-out, the element of surprise had been lost and that he must anchor and afterwards, complain, lie and bluster himself out of the affair as best he could. And so, as protests, counter-protests, courtesies and discourtesies flowed between the two fleets and messengers from both Hawkins and De Wachen galloped up to the Queen at Greenwich, each hoping that his version would be believed, Drake still remained idle at Plymouth, a seething powder keg of frustration.

Until a new dimension was suddenly added: a Spanish ship full of Flemish prisoners destined for the living hell of the galleys sailed into Plymouth Catwater and dropped anchor close by the other Spaniards. Now, Drake rubbed his chin with his hand and slowly the gloom disappeared from his face to be replaced, at the prospect of a good fight, by that broad, happy smile of old and eyes that had become as blue as polar ice. Swiftly he set off for the nearby village of Stonehouse, stepping carefully over the open drain that ran down the cobbled street into the sea in his search for the crooked, smokey little cottage where Thomas Moone lived. He found Moone, grey-faced and as morose as ever, recently returned from cod-fishing off the grand banks of Newfoundland. When Drake explained what he had in mind, Moone's dull eyes gleamed with life and the whipcord veins of his arm muscles bulged and burgeoned at the thought of a murderous boarding action. 'Can us do it on our own?' he asked.

'Why not?' Drake said. 'They're only Spaniards.' Both men roared with laughter and hugged each other in delighted anticipation.

Next afternoon in full daylight, while the guards, replete from a large lunch, drowsed in the pleasant autumn warmth, two very determined, masked men swarmed silently over the side of the Spanish vessel, cutting down several of the crew before their surprised and terrified comrades surrendered. The captives, pale and blinking from perpetual darkness, allowed themselves to be lifted from the pools of filth-encrusted urine in which they sat and, massaging their manacle-chafed limbs in disbelief, staggered into the bright sunshine of the upper deck. In no time at all they were ferried to shore by several cheerful Plymouth boatmen, who, hearing the sound of steel clashing on steel, had come rowing out to see what was happening. The Flemish prisoners magically disappeared into thin air and De Wachen, in absolute fury, could do nothing other than depart with his fleet from such unhospitable, piratical and heretical waters. Months later he would learn of the great part played in the whole débâcle by a certain Francis Drake and would make this matter the subject of a personal report to his master, King Philip.

The sight of the Spanish fleet boldly sailing into Plymouth Catwater, with all the contempt for poor little England that the action implied, had roused Francis Drake into a slowly-mounting fury. The fight to rescue the Flemish prisoners with the small but ferocious Tom Moone by his side, had done something to assuage his sense of rage and frustration, but his mood at seeing the pitiable condition into which the Dons had reduced their human cargo had become one of deep and bitter hatred of the Spaniard and all things Spanish.

Suddenly, he was able to shake off the dreadful gloom and despondency that had paralysed him over so many months. He would screw up his courage and face the ultimate hazard of an interview with a furious Queen. Better to risk a spell in the Tower than the certainty of standing on Plymouth Hoe and watching once again, Hawkins sail out of Plymouth without him.

Everywhere, the Spaniards were supreme, ruthlessly exterminating all those who wished to trade peacefully within their vast dominions, destroying with fiendish and agonising torture all those who dared to oppose them and now, they had sailed arrogantly into Plymouth to inflict correction and punishment as if, as if—he could feel his face flush hot with red rage—Devon men were no-account, fawning lackeys of King Philip ready to cringe at the first sound of Spanish gunshot! Inside him, this strange sense of God-given mission, that he was the one to curb these fiendish Dons, grew and burgeoned, burning and blocking all other thought, all other matter from his fevered brain.

When Hawkins sailed, he, Francis Drake must go with him: that was all that mattered. He would summon up his last ounce of courage and lay his submissive neck under the lashing gale of fury, the shrewish and terrible anger of a Queen whose invitation to court he had blatantly ignored, a Queen whom it was known did not exactly take kindly to being scorned.

But if he was ever to get into her presence, there was something that he must first do. Something that he vastly disliked. Borrow money. Fat William Hawkins, who was sentimental enough to honour his father's wishes that his kinsman Drake should be provided for, even if brother John was not, duly obliged. Drake, who would need to cut a figure half-way between roistering adventurer and elegantly-educated gentleman, if he were ever to attract the Queen's favour once again, was accordingly able to fold in his saddle-bags, in addition to his already fine wardrobe, a rakishly cut, embroidered, white satin doublet. If that was not enough, fat William Hawkins also managed to sneak from one of his wife's jewel cases a splendid row of flawless, dazzling pearls to flash around his neck—on Drake's solemn promise to return them once the Queen's attention had been duly directed to its wearer.

Handsomely provided for, Drake post-horsed rapidly out of the West Country in search of the Queen. He found his heart pounding with trepidation. He would rather have faced a regiment of Spanish arquebusiers, he thought, than his formidable mistress, but there was no choice. If he was to sail in Hawkins' fine expedition, the Queen was his only hope. And time was growing perilously short.

'Beans!' cried the object of Drake's attentions, in a fury of scorn and disgust, stamping a satin-slippered foot.

'Beans?' echoed Leicester in amazement, who, now the Spanish ambassador, De Silva, had departed from court to a fine flourish of regals, trumpets and kettledrums, had resumed his accustomed place close to Elizabeth. 'Beans, you say. Pray kindly explain, madam.'

'Not now, Robin. Not now,' the Queen muttered. Savagely she turned her neck this way and that, and felt that awful neuralgic, stabbing pain again. It had been with her, that savage crick in the neck, for the whole summer of '67, forcing her, in sudden hysteria, to cancel the royal progress scheduled for that year. The pain, although she did not know it, had been caused by tension and worry. She had received enough of both over the last few years, and the strain which she had been under would show in the way that she would take suddenly to her sick bed for days, pallid and wasted, then with a remarkable resurgence of nervous energy take up the reins of state with bizarre vitality, only to sink once again into one of her troughs of nervous despair. It was not the regime of a woman entirely well either in body or mind and Leicester, looking at her, was concerned.

Although hollow-eyed from carrying burdens that no woman should be made to carry, at thirty-four she was still a slim, beautiful woman and Leicester continued to adore her. Still the most unpopular man in the kingdom, after Cecil's cunningly-contrived murder of his wife Amy, he knew he could be destroyed with a wave of the Queen's slim hand any time she wished; and Leicester, formerly plain Dudley, but now created Earl, tried hard to know his place. Superb in the saddle, whether at hunt or joust, poet, linguist, letter-writer of note, conversationalist of wit, effortless architect of glorious progresses and processions, he was the only man in the kingdom fit for the Queen's side. Only three years before, full of arrogant self-confidence, he had, his body servant sworn to eternal secrecy, climbed into bed with Gloriana and borne down on her with all the strength of his lusty thighs and stout calves, only to find himself astonishingly rejected in an inexplicable welter of high-pitched hysteria. Not one to give up without a fight though, Leicester still kept the Queen's company, constantly.

'Madam,' he said patiently, still puzzled about the beans and accustomed to being taken into the Queen's closest confidence. 'De Silva seems highly discommoded. Is there some way that I may be of help?'

'Yes, by leaving us alone,' the Queen replied testily. 'Peace is what we require more than anything. We will have you paged, Robin, when your presence is again required.' Leicester gave her a long, graceful, somewhat ironic bow, a thing full of rich wavers and pleasantly swooping bends, then backed out through the long, gaily-painted state room that the Queen used for granting audiences to ambassadors.

Alone at last, Elizabeth, gazing out of an upstairs window, began to feel immediately more tranquil. Richmond had always been her favourite place. None of her other palaces could ever compare to the beauty of Richmond with its towers and pinnacles, each one crowned with an onion dome on which gold and silver vanes sang in the wind like so many harps. Then there were the fruit trees, two hundred and twenty-three of them in all. One autumn day she had counted every single one of them, groaning with magnificent peaches, apples, filberts and damsons. The Queen, never a great eater of meat, loved her fruit. Other reasons had been added for her frequent stays: over the last few years her nervous complaints had suddenly expanded and flowered into terrible obsessions; Elizabeth now absolutely abhorred draughts, smells or bad tastes of any sort—and Richmond had no draughts at all, splendid drainage and pure spring water to drink.

But why all these nervous obsessions, accompanied frequently by terrible temper and increasing hysteria? The answer was simple. She, a vital, intelligent and feminine woman, had found herself no longer able to make love, and the knowledge and the awful frustration was eating into her mind from within, like a worm in a juicy apple. From her earliest days, the sending of first her mother then her stepmother to the block for sins of the flesh, had instilled in her a terrible fear of sexual emotion. With Seymour, long ago, in a welter of girlish enthusiasm, she had tried to shake off this miasma of terror that threatened to close her loins tighter than the shell of a frightened oyster; was succeeding too, until he, unbelievably, was despatched to the block for the very same offence. So one of the human race's most agreeable pastimes had become for her a nightmare, and the Queen had only learned what she had hitherto dreaded to accept when stout, sweating Dudley, clamping his big, muscular thighs on top of hers, had galloped happily into the tilt, lance held high, only to receive a truly shattering rebuff. How to keep her shame a secret when half Europe was seeking her hand? Easy, because the need of every frigid woman is to flirt floridly and continually with every man she sees, as if the very concentration on the preambles of mating will make up for the loss of the mating act itself: and this happened to coincide exactly with how the Queen found it necessary to rule, in a male-dominated society.

Now, as she lay on her bed, scrabbling irritably at that needle-point of pain that refused to go away from her neck, she was miserably conscious that a truly grave matter of state beset her. In Plymouth a great fleet waited to sail and the Spanish had been fooled into believing it was just a harmless gold-prospecting expedition to Africa. Then De Silva's spies, lurking at Greenwich, had discovered tons and tons of damning beans being loaded into the capacious holds of the *Jesus* and the *Minion*. Beans, as everybody knew, were the staple food of slaves. So the Queen's clever little game had been found out. The cat was out of the bag with a vengeance. Desperate for money after Parliament's defiance, the Queen was brazenly participating in a slaving expedition that would directly invade King Philip's dominions. For somehow, she knew, she must find the money to build a fleet. Her kingdom, ridiculously poor, tiny and under-populated, was gravely menaced by Spain, rich, hugely-powerful and vengefully anti-protestant. Would, she thought, the studious Philip ever be capable of open hostility?

Already she knew the answer to that. Ruefully she thought of the great Netherlands squadron that had swooped down out of the chan-nel mists and attacked her ships as they lay riding in Plymouth Cat-water. What must she do? Everywhere she was confronted by a thousand perils and there was no one to whom she could turn for advice, for Cecil would never condone the semi-piracy she had plotted with Hawkins. So she lay on her couch, suffering agonies of frightened indecision.

Fitfully, she managed to sleep for an hour or two: the peace and fragrant air of Richmond allowed her at least that; until, unable to rest further, she rose and paced endlessly back and forth, stark naked in front of a full-length mirror. She found herself running her hands over the unbelievably soft, whiteness of her shoulders and breasts—at least she might grant herself a pleasure that she would never grant a man. Tiring of the action, she went on to admire the pulsating slim-ness of her legs and body; not an ounce of fat over the rump, the vio-lent exercise of daily horse-riding had seen to that. She stopped, went closer, and peered into the mirror. Was there a certain dullness to one of her cheeks? A slight marring, a tiny diminution to that velvety, milk-white complexion romanticised by poet and musician through-out the length and breadth of Europe? Heaven forbid. She must use her cosmetic toilet water at once. She had had it made up six months ago, from a recipe that included new-laid eggs, powdered egg-shell, burnt alum, powdered sugar and seeds of the white poppy. The whole mixture would need to be shaken unconscionably into a froth three fingers high.

Wan and hollow-eyed, she tugged at her bellrope. She would take her daily bath now, and meanwhile her maids-of-honour could start beating the liquid. She must, she knew, look superb for the evening audience. As always for Gloriana, the Virgin Queen, nothing short of perfection would do.

Suddenly she balled slim fingers into small, white fists of frus-tration and savagely snarled the word 'beans' under her breath, caus-ing her maids bringing hot water for her tub, unaware of their mistress's awful isolation, to titter in sudden surprise.

139

*'Though I be a woman, yet I have as good courage—as ever my
father had. I am your anointed Queen. I will never be by violence
constrained to do anything. I thank God I am endued with such
qualities that if I were turned out of my realm in my petticoat, I
were able to live in any place in Christendom.'*

Queen Elizabeth lecturing an
intransigent Parliament, October 1566

# 14

Pomaded, ruffed, accoutred, dressed and glitteringly bejewelled in
the height of absurd magnificence, the stocky figure of Francis
Drake, walking through endless ante-chambers, shown past lines of
sputtering torches held by Yeomen of the Guard, was finally
escorted by two elegant gentlemen pensioners into the presence of
the Queen of England. There, on his knees, he was made to endure a
shrill weight of invective and endless insult that made the back of his
submissive neck gently turn a glowing red. 'So, Master Drake,' the
Queen finished. 'In our generosity we invite you back to court and
for two years you do not come near. Yet you have no excuse, it seems.
We have waited in vain for an answer. We have listened, yet you say
nothing.'

Aware that he had not yet been given the slightest chance to speak,
Drake began haltingly 'O glorious lady, O divine bloom, O flower of
all England . . .'

'Stay sirrah,' the Queen spat shrewishly. 'Spare us your poetry,
which we dare say is no less cloddish than your lute playing. If you have
nothing else to say, then be gone.'

'Your grace,' Drake said miserably, 'to serve you as a mariner, is
all I crave. One chance—'

'You have had your chance with Captain Lovell,' the Queen
sniffed. 'And was that not a disaster? It seems we were mistaken
about you, Drake. There is not the capacity there that we thought.
You have been amply rewarded for past services, now take your soft
Devon speech out of our sight, never to visit here again.'

'Madam, do not inflict such pain on your adoring subject,' Drake implored.

'You have suffered little such pain, it doth appear, in the last two years. No doubt some troll, some doxy, has taken up your time well enough, while your Queen had prior claim.' Elizabeth managed to put into the remark all the terrible, wounded jealousy she had experienced at the thought of any of her courtiers associating with other women.

'Cut me off then from your gracious presence, madam, so that I wither and die like a tree without soil . . .' Drake, who had been practising for days this final flight of imploring eloquence, was suddenly interrupted by the sound of enormous scuffling outside the presence chamber. A few seconds later, the great doors burst open and Leicester came in, breathing hard, his thick dark hair in disarray across his forehead.

'What means this saucy intrusion?' the Queen demanded angrily.

As if in answer to her question, Thomas Bowyer, Gentleman of the Black Rod, the ultimate guardian of the Queen's privacy, rushed in, placed himself in front of Leicester and knelt. 'Gracious and mighty madam,' he began. 'My Lord of Leicester would not wait and I could not stay him, save with cold steel. Is, then, my Lord of Leicester King, or is your majesty Queen?'

Nothing was more calculated to rouse Elizabeth into transports of fury and Leicester bowed his head while a storm of torrential eloquence beat around his ears like angry hailstones. '—S'death!' The Queen spat, the nostrils of her high-bridged nose pinching with rage. 'God's death, my Lord, we have wished you well, but our favour is not so locked up in you that others shall not participate thereof, for we have many servants unto whom we have, and will at our pleasure, confer our favour. If you think to rule here you are much mistaken, because we will have here but one mistress and no master.' Her eyes moved from the tall, muscularly-erect figure of Leicester to the kneeling Bowyer and thoughts flashed through her mind of Leicester's reputation for violence: the tilt in which he had nearly killed Drake; the death of his wife Amy, about which she and her subjects still had their suspicions. 'And look,' she added with a final jet of threatening venom, 'that no ill happen to Master Bowyer here, lest it be severely required at your hands.'

The Queen now waved Bowyer imperiously from the chamber, while Leicester sank slowly to his knees in feigned humility. 'Most high and magnificent lady,' he whispered. 'Most splendid majesty.

141

Let not thy bosoms, more exquisite than globes of purest alabaster, heave with hatred at this thy poor subject, who could not bear to be parted from his most fair mistress one minute longer lest he die of loneliness.'

The Queen's delicately-spanned eyebrows slowly arranged themselves into reddish-gold arches of amused pleasure. She had long ago made her subjects aware of her unassuagable appetite for men's compliments, knowing that in the end her authority depended absolutely on the tenuous line of myth and chivalry flowing from powerful nobles towards the godhead of her beauty. 'Well then,' she said, her voice a little softer, 'since you are here, what then, is your excuse?'

'Madam, it is only this,' Leicester said. He pointed to a parchment clutched in his right hand. 'I have a report direct from my Plymouth agent, who says that the alarm at the Spanish attack was raised by none other than Francis Drake here, and if it were not given, why your majesty's ships were probably lost.'

Drake, motionless on his knees, suddenly remembered the stranger to whom he had spoken when he had first seen De Wachen's galleons storming over the horizon and knew now who it was.

' 'Tis true, Francis?' the Queen demanded.

'Madam,' Drake modestly replied, 'your commander is Hawkins, and as the responsibility is his, so the credit must be his also.'

'We will decide who shall have the credit,' the Queen said, smiling. She turned to Leicester. 'Is that all? I vow it is still not sufficient to justify your invasion of our privacy.'

'Most elegant lady, it was Drake, also, who almost single-handed boarded the Spanish prison ship and made off with those poor fellows bound for King Philip's galleys.'

'Drake!' Up went her eyebrows like little jets of red flame. 'Again?'

'Indeed, madam.'

'Why were we not told?'

'There is often jealousy, madam, between kinsfolk.' Leicester diplomatically avoided mentioning Hawkins by name.

'I see,' Elizabeth said, her smile becoming slightly mocking. Shrewdly, she let her mind search for the reason for Leicester's sudden championing of Francis Drake. They had not in the past been exactly friends. Then suddenly she knew. Leicester himself had invested heavily in the Indies voyage and a fighting devil like young Francis, passionately devoted to preserving Leicester's profits, would be no bad thing. Satisfied that once again she had continued to

142

master the treacherous tricks and turns of her courtiers, the Queen smiled, then said, 'We will consider these matters further. Tomorrow we go down river to visit an old friend and you and Drake shall both accompany us.' She waved a slim, bejewelled hand in graceful dismissal, indicating the audience was at an end. 'Now leave us, for we are much fatigued.'

Neither man, seeing her slim, erect figure, the luminous, pale skin of her graceful neck, realised the mental anguish and pain the Queen had been recently undergoing. Nor had they realised that in the terrible stress of her indecision over Hawkins' voyage, she had fallen back on one last desperate measure. She would consult a strange but brilliant man, deeply skilled in the magical science of astrology: the eminent Doctor Dee.

Next morning, as trumpets shrilled a morning greeting to the Queen on a bright, fine autumn day, Elizabeth stepped into the state barge for the journey to Mortlake. Following her in close attendance was Leicester, amazingly elegant in a black doublet trimmed with the finest cambric at neck and wrist with britches of the same colour, padded with bombast, and stockings of silk. His buttons and buckles were all of gold and pearl, carefully wrought, whilst a short sword hung handsomely at his hip in a velvet scabbard. Not to be outdone, Drake had donned his dazzling white satin doublet. With Mistress Hawkins' fine rope of pearls swinging round his stout sailor's chest, his curling, upturned moustachios freshly trimmed and waxed at the tips, he walked with a distinctly piratical air.

The Queen, perhaps stimulated by the close attention of two such splendid men, had thrown off the despondency and depression of the day before, and took her place in the barge, eyes shining, her magnificent mane of pale red hair blowing silky and free in the wind, the magnolia-pale skin of her cheeks incredibly translucent in the morning sun.

To a gleaming flourish of painted oars, the barge drew away from the quay, the Queen sitting in an open red satin awning, behind which a cabin decorated with the royal coat-of-arms and a floor strewn with flowers awaited her should she wish to retire. When she reached Mortlake, twenty of her most handsome gentlemen pensioners were ready to carry her in a splendid open litter along the few hundred yards of cobbled way that led to Dr Dee's house, while the Queen responded to her subjects' loyal cheers by

143

superb, gracefully-flowing gestures of her white gloved hands.

Dr Dee was waiting to greet the Queen. Even if he had not been, she would not have berated him, for Dee was one of the most learned men in the kingdom: a fellow of Trinity College, Cambridge, a distinguished scientist, mathematician and astronomer; but it was for his skill in more mysterious arts that the Queen had come to visit him today.

Dee was a tall man with, despite hours of daily study in his darkly occult garret, a very fair, almost rosy complexion. He wore a long beard that reached clear down to the silken girdle that spanned his waist. For clothes, he affected a strange black garment somewhat like an artist's gown with loose, hanging sleeves that gave him a proper aura of gravity and mystery. It was plain to see, with the speed that Elizabeth commanded him off his knees, the respect in which she held him.

'Well-a-day, good doctor,' she said with a ringing confidence that she certainly did not feel, as Dee escorted her inside his house. 'We are come to consult you on certain grave matters pertaining to our reign.'

'Madam, I am content that you have,' Dee answered, his voice soft with kindness, 'for I see from the hurt in your eyes that a painful matter sore besets your majesty. Let us now climb into my turret, where we may talk alone.'

As Dee began to climb the winding stairs, the Queen turned and said in a commanding voice to Leicester and Drake 'Wait here.' Then following the learned doctor, she entered a small, darkened room.

By the light of flickering candles, she could see a chart of the constellations on the ceiling, and pentangles and mysterious symbols taken from the Hebrew *Cabbala* on the walls. On a table covered with black drapes there was a large crystal ball. Dee, throwing protocol to the winds, sat down on one side, motioning Elizabeth to be seated on the other. 'Now, my dear,' he said, his voice gentle and encouraging. 'You are in much distress, so I am going to help you.'

Anybody listening to their conversation would have been amazed at the liberties taken by Dee, but for many years now he had been playing the role of a wise and respected father comforting a frequently-distraught daughter.

Predictably in a welter of womanly sobs and tears, all the Queen's miseries came flooding out. 'Dee, we are desperate for money, menaced without and within. Please advise us.' Her voice was imploring.

'Madam, my art has always been at your command.' Dee bent to his almanacs, astrological tables and a great parchment scroll containing Elizabeth's original horoscope cast by him at the beginning of her reign. He looked up, inclining his head wisely. 'Nothing has changed, great Princess. Venus, ascendant in the house of life, promises power and success. Has not your reign been so far brilliant? Was not the date of your coronation well cast by me?'

'You do not understand. Our only recourse is to send Hawkins slaving in our cousin of Spain's dominions. Such a measure is desperately dangerous.'

'The stars have always said you shall reign well only if you reign with boldness.'

'Then Hawkins will succeed?'

Dee peered into his crystal ball, hands cradling the top of the sphere into a fine, light mist. He shook his head as if the mist was forming some kind of barrier, then said cryptically, 'The stars say only that Hawkins must go.'

The Queen breathed hard. 'Tell us this. Will Philip ever attack our realm from across the seas?'

'I have long ago cast the King of Spain's horoscope. Saturn, being in the sixth house in opposition to Mars, is retrograde in the house of life. I see only drowning men with white faces round your Majesty's shores.'

At this the Queen smiled and a pulse seemed to beat for one brief moment under the fair skin of her high temples. 'If you are wrong,' she said, 'Philip will be glad to burn us both on a slow fire at his next auto-da-fé!'

Dee stood up. He had decided to give her an expert political judgment, clothed with all the dread authority of a famous seer. 'Madam, the stars that run their courses in the heavens do not lie. Their advice is plain. Queen Mary of the Scots lies imprisoned at Lochleven, the French are weakened by civil war. Your enemy, Spain, is fully engaged by the Flemish rebels. All this will change, but now, be bold. I say no more than this.'

'And Hawkins will bring us money?'

Dee, who knew Philip's excellent intelligence system and how ferociously he would be preparing to receive the planned expedition, did not want to answer that. His answer was repetitive. 'Madam, the stars give no precise indication. They say merely that Hawkins must go.'

145

The Queen, who had fully recovered her poise and was much heartened by her consultation with Dee, now stood and announced that pressure of state business made it necessary to leave. Thanking Dee and promising him generous reward, she went back down the steep, winding stairs. There, Leicester and Drake awaited her on their knees. As both men, commanded to rise by the Queen, straightened, Dee with the strange sixth sense peculiar to a seer, found himself bounding forward, compulsively affected by a most unusual magnetism he could feel radiating from the short, stocky, finely-dressed blue-eyed man in front of him.

'Give me your hand, sir,' Dee said, excitement in his voice.

When he looked at Drake's extended palm and saw the horny rope marks, then, transferring his gaze, saw the tan on Drake's face that could only be incised by wind and sea, his excitement grew even more intense. 'Why you must prefer this man greatly in his profession, madam,' he said in amazement. 'For a silver light of destiny doth brightly shine all around him!'

The Queen looked sharply at Doctor Dee. Her feelings towards Drake could only be described as latently hostile. It was many years since he had saved her life, yet she remembered only too clearly how Drake, by his obstinate silence, had prevented her marriage to her one true love, Robin Dudley. Now, in her middle thirties, with spinsterhood stretching ahead, the hostility was becoming less latent: more pronounced. Yet Dee had clearly divined some great task, some special destiny for the fellow, and for his astrological skills she had complete and unreserved respect. 'Very well,' she said abruptly. 'We shall see Hawkins gives him a command in his forthcoming expedition.'

A strangely-knit web of chance and circumstance had conspired to grant a young Devon seaman the unique patronage of a great Queen, a web knit with suddenly renewed strength by the weighty prophecy of a man, half-charlatan, yet wholly wise.

For Francis Drake destiny beckoned. Now, he would need to go out and grasp his opportunities with both hands before the Queen's latent grudge towards him flowered in the first chill of middle-age, making her deaf to her astrologers and the entreaties of her ministers, knowing from then onwards only hatred.

# 15

Juan Martinez de Recalde, grandee of Spain, still slim and hard as he entered his middle years, had not forgotten the boy Francisco Draque, who had bitten his hand clear to the bone in the long room at Ashridge, and had thereby deprived him of the honour of doing a famous service to his king by ridding the world of Elizabeth. For over ten years the name had remained as clear in his head as the scar of Drake's teeth on his hand. Yes, Draque. Francisco Draque. They would meet again, and soon. That was why he was out here in this steamy, fever-ridden outpost of his most Catholic Majesty's dominions.

Now, carefully mounted on his shivering, nervous horse, he watched the bull. Small, without the murderous bulk of your *pablo romero*, and lacking the ferocious cunning of the *miura*, these local scrub cattle could still be mean and vicious and had the frightening capacity to turn in their own length. Blood was coursing down the animal's shoulders in great, rhythmic jets and it was bellowing profusely, always the sign of a coward—a *manso*. It had taken up its *querencia* in a corner of the makeshift ring set up in the plaza of Margerita and there, in its safe place, it would be mean and dangerous. It would have to be dislodged. He motioned to a *mozo* to lean over the pile of timbers acting as a barrier and plant a *banderilla* with a firecracker attached in the animal's rump. As the firework exploded with a loud crack, the bull shot straight for Recalde's stallion and he could hear the horse groan with the expected pain of the rowels that would plant bloody tracks along its flanks, knowing that it must now erupt into instant motion so as to provide man with yet further proof that a ridden horse can turn faster than a baited bull. Unlike most noblemen, who trained their horses in the art of *rejon* with love and care, Recalde enjoyed the instant, heart-jumping panic

147

of a muscled, silky-skinned horse that had been trained with the whip. He liked his women like that too: young Indian girls of the Arawak tribe, noted for their gentleness and docility, unlike the wild gypsy girls on his Andalucian estates who would spit in his face and reach for his eyes with their long nails whenever he tried to assert the rights to which his feudal position undoubtedly entitled him.

Recalde swayed slightly in the saddle. In the tropical humidity of Nueva Andalucia a man, weakened by women, sweated easily and lost condition. How then did he, a most noble knight of the Order of Santiago, come to be providing such a brave spectacle for this bunch of fat, unspeakable bourgeouisie who formed the ruling officialdom of this broken-down New World colony?

For a few moments, while his assistants occupied themselves with weakening the bull sufficiently for the final sword thrust, Recalde remembered. Out of the blue, the summons had come, rousing him from discontented domesticity with a nobly beautiful wife who had turned out to have the obstinate, tightly-closed legs of a novitiate devoted to the Church: a summons straight from the King. Scenting a chance to do his majesty some distinguished service and at the same time absent himself from the frigid Doña Isabel, he had gone, but quickly. Up into the torrid summer heat of Central Spain he had travelled until he had come to a village high on the south-western slopes of the Guadarrama mountains, where the brief flush of spring flowers had only recently withered into the tinder-hot dust. There, in a darkened room, while all around could be heard the sound of thousands of workmen labouring to finish the great, gaunt, magnificence of the escorial palace-monastery that was to serve as Philip's last resting place, the monarch with a Hapsburg lip and cane-coloured hair received him.

Recalde, bidden to sit down, found himself eyeing with enormous sympathy this supposedly grand monarch, turned into the biggest clerk in the world by a mountain of parchment reports from all over his empire that cascaded freely across his desk and demanded his meticulous attention. Quiet, dignified, conscientious, no longer a lustful peeker behind curtains at the soft backsides of maids-of-honour, Philip had become as loved in Spain as Elizabeth was in England, despite the reputation some gave him for a certain cunning. Watching the hollow-eyed King shuffle his paperwork wearily aside, Recalde burned to serve him.

148

'Recalde,' Philip said in the chiding voice that could not understand anybody beyond the seas coveting Spain's treasure. 'Elizabeth is my enemy. Not satisfied with sparing Hawkins, she has now financed him for another and bigger expedition to my colonies. He, and the bunch of corsairs with him, must be taught a great lesson. He must be cured once and for all of his heretical piracy. We have selected you for an important mission: to arrange the destruction of the English fleet.'

'*A sus ordenes*—at your orders, majesty.'

'Soon, Hawkins will sail for Africa, expecting to arrive in our dominions next spring, his holds full of negroes for illegal trading. What he does not know is that the flota will leave for Mexico several weeks early, in the hope of catching the pirate unawares. Your mission is to ensure the rendezvous of the two fleets, and to achieve this, you will be given the highest authority.'

'I understand, majesty.'

'Ensure Hawkins does not leave our waters 'till the flota arrives. Do you understand? This must be arranged at all costs.'

'*Entendido*.'

'Your mission being secret, you shall tell your wife that you are going to Nueva Andalucia to inspect pearl fisheries. Doña Isabel owns such fisheries there, does she not?' The King's voice was dry and incisive.

Recalde blinked at Philip's disconcertingly minute knowledge of his wife's wealth, but the question being rhetorical, decided that no answer was necessary.

'You shall leave immediately in a fast mail packet,' the King went on. He paused for a moment, then added thoughtfully, 'There is a man sailing with Hawkins who is . . . of interest. On two occasions already he has conducted bold and successful raids on our property to free prisoners. His name is Francisco Draque. Have you heard of him?'

Even as Recalde eyed the bull, standing head down, close to exhaustion and ready to be dispatched, he remembered minutely the sensations he had experienced at the King's remarks: the involuntary shiver he had given, despite the heat; the sweat that had beaded his thin, elegant moustache; the killing lust, then as now, that had come to clog his throat. 'Yes, majesty,' he had whispered. 'I know this man.'

'Kill him,' Philip said. 'He is more dangerous than an army.' He

149

bent back to his papers. Realising that the King had just terminated the audience, Recalde had backed away, ushering himself reverently out of the royal presence.

Now, lurking in the coolness of the shade, he could see the King's courier, and knew that this could only mean important news. He would have to finish the bull quickly. He leapt off his horse and gazed at the bull, snorting, pawing sand, blood pumping rhythmically down its sides. With its tossing muscle wearied, there was now for the first time an area about the size of a Venetian ducat through which a good swordsman might thrust good and true for the heart. '*Venga*,' Recalde called softly. '*Venga, torito.* Come little bull.'

Across the whole length of the ring the animal thundered towards him, lowering its head in one final, brave effort to gore this man who had so baited and hurt it. The crowd screamed with anticipation as they watched Recalde posture with indolent grace in unmistakeable profile towards the bull, sword gracefully extended in front of him. This was something they had heard about, but never seen. Recalde, enveloped by the bull's horns, raised himself gracefully on to his toes, allowing the bull literally to eat up the sword, so that without any effort on his part the blade slid deeply between the animal's shoulders until it was buried to the hilt. Recalde raised his hand in one arrogant, commanding sweep and the bull coughed once then obediently fell down dead at his feet, all four legs pointing stiffly skywards. Why had he done it, Recalde asked himself: exposed his body to extreme danger so that a bunch of jumped-up customs officials might experience, just once in their lives, the sight of a nobleman killing *recibiendo*? He knew the answer. For weeks now he had been honing and sharpening his sword play for just one man: El Draco.

Languidly acknowledging the storm of applause with a wave of one hand, Recalde strode away, mopping his smooth, tanned face with a towel that a slave had handed to him. In the shadows the courier, grey-faced from his privations, travel-worn, awaited him respectfully. Without a word Recalde ripped the seals off the despatches the courier had brought. The message was curt and to the point: the flota had left its moorings in the Guadalquivir river and was cramming on all sail for Mexico. This year it would arrive early and with any luck catch Hawkins napping.

Now Recalde, travelling by coaster, on horseback, by laborious mule train over the mountains, visited one after the other, the Governors of Rio de la Hacha, Borburata, Cartagena, even the high and mighty Bishop of Valencia, and unfolded to them his meticulously worked-out plan. All of them accepted him with the unquestioning deference due to a direct emissary of the King and agreed to do exactly as he wanted. Some, it was agreed, would pretend to accept Hawkins' facile pretence to be their protector against pirates; others would delay him by well-timed, but not over-spirited resistance, yet others would involve the unsuspecting Hawkins in protracted negotiations over the right to trade. Only one thing was certain: by a nicely-blended mixture of provocation and welcome, Hawkins would be made to stay until the flota destroyed him. And if that didn't, the end of season hurricanes would.

When at last the sails of Hawkins's ships appeared over the deep blue of the horizon and made for the first landfall of Margarita, Recalde, forewarned by watchful coasters and fishing boats, was exactly in the right place to join the welcoming committee. At the thought of meeting his enemy Draque once again his palms itched for the feeling of a sword's hilt. In turn, he found himself reminded of someone else who had found the courage and temerity to oppose his will: the young slave girl, Aruba.

In the rocky bay that sheltered the Port of Asuncion, capital of Margarita, Hawkins' fine fleet rattled down their anchor chains and awaited their first contact with the Spanish colonists. Hawkins had the captains of all his ships assemble on the poop deck of the *Jesus*, and as a pinnace shot out from the port, each man wondered what kind of welcome they would receive. True, Hawkins had done great business with the mayor, three years before, but Philip had now threatened grave punishment for anyone who traded, or showed even the barest courtesy to the English pirates.

Piped aboard to the shrill twitter of bosun's whistles, the Spanish officials, sweating in full armour and helmets, assembled opposite Hawkins' captains, placing themselves behind their spokesman Recalde. Slim and elegant in a beautifully-chased, handmade cuirass, over which his silk sash of nobility had been draped, Recalde suggested himself as a figure of considerable importance.

Despite having been out of their home port for half a year, and with conditions on board ship pitiable after the long Atlantic crossing, Hawkins had insisted on all the formality and pomp appropriate to a royal ship. Sailors having deck duties stood rigidly to attention in tunics of the royal colours and Hawkins himself, dressed in his finest clothes, paced between his personal guard of foot soldiers, hand resting on the pommel of his sword. As Recalde stepped forward in formal greeting, Hawkins' trumpeter, Jean Turren, clad in a brilliant tabard, blew a great fanfare that echoed round the bay, sending flocks of gulls and booby birds wheeling across the water in frightened flight. Hawkins and Recalde exchanged bows and compliments and Recalde introduced himself as the governor's personal envoy sent to welcome the Englishmen. Invited to meet Hawkins' captains, Recalde's slim figure walked down the assembled line of men, his teeth white against the smooth tan of his face as he welcomed them with great courtesy. As he came level with Drake, he stopped. 'Your face is familiar, sir,' he said in fluent English. 'Pray tell me. What is your name?'

'I am called Francis Drake, and I think we met many years ago when I was but a lad. Did we not have some struggle over a letter?' Drake's eyes crinkled with hidden mischief.

'Ah, Draque.' Recalde's face remained an olive mask of courtesy, despite the bitter memories Drake's remark had evoked. 'I remember you well now. We must celebrate the fact that old enemies have become new friends. Your Admiral will be entertained personally by the Governor, but you, I insist, shall dine with me.'

Drake, fearing treachery, would have made flowery excuses, but catching a nod from Hawkins that was impossible to ignore, accepted the invitation instead.

'Gentlemen,' Recalde said, smiling broadly at the assembled captains. 'As you know there are certain difficulties placed between us on the question of trade. However, I am a great believer in the English expression "where there is a will, there's a way". You are welcome here and all your ships' wonts shall be attended to.' Touching his hand to his helmet by way of salute, Recalde descended athletically down the rope-ladder to the waiting pinnace, followed by the plump, puffing local officialdom.

That evening Drake dined by candle-light with Recalde in his simple house by the beach, which had been constructed so as to be practically open to the elements. To start with, both men eyed each other warily, but several strong rums soon had them chatting pleasantly together.

'Your house surprises me,' Drake said. 'I expected with your position and rank, to find a large stuffy place, encumbered with many servants.'

Recalde grinned. 'It is useless to build anything substantial here. What the hurricanes do not destroy, the corsairs will.'

Sitting there in the soft, tropical darkness, the mosquitoes kept at bay by the coolness of the ocean spray, with no noise other than the boom of the breakers and a furious grunting and hooting that had suddenly broken out, as troops of grey-faced and black, woolly monkeys contested a nearby piece of jungle, Drake found himself at ease. 'It is indeed pleasant here,' he said, stretching out his stocky legs luxuriously.

'I will drink to your Queen if you drink to my King,' Recalde said, 'to show we are friends.'

'Very well,' Drake said indifferently.

'To his most Catholic Majesty, Philip of Spain.' Recalde lifted a tumbler made of delicate, glitteringly blue Venetian glass.

Drake drank, although the toast nearly choked him, and he could feel a flush mounting to his cheeks. 'To Bess,' he said mischievously, unable to help it. 'Our beautiful heretic Queen.'

It was Recalde's turn to try and quell the tick of murderous hatred that had developed on the left side of his smooth, olive face. Well, he remembered the King's orders. 'Kill him,' Philip had said. 'The man is more dangerous than an army.' Yes, Recalde thought, eyeing the stocky, grinning Englishman, you are a pirate and a corsair and one day I will kill you with the rest of your heretic brood. But not now. Almost subconsciously he felt the scar on his hand where Drake had bitten to the bone all those years ago. Soon, El Draco would die. But not yet. With infinite politeness he bowed and raised his glass to drink the toast. 'Let us eat,' he said cheerfully.

To Drake's surprise, Recalde went off to fetch the food, returning with an enormous platter on which all manner of steaming delicacies had been heaped, hot and savoury, on top of a mountain of yellow rice.

'You cook yourself then?' Drake said, surprised. 'For a Spanish nobleman that is indeed unusual.'

'A hobby of mine,' Recalde replied languidly. 'The natives may be relied on only to poison or ruin one's food.'

Drake waded in with tremendous energy. All manner of meat and fish seemed to emerge, spiced and savoury, as he speared into the mass of yellow rice with his fork, and his stocky figure and cheerful, fleshy face seemed to swell visibly after the rigours of the ocean voyage. Before long, morsels of spiced goat, *lenguado, langostina* and

153

garlicked chicken jostled beans and pimento for a resting-place on his fine, upturned moustachios. 'Delicious,' he said. 'What manner of food is this?'

'But a simple dish from the area of Valencia,' Recalde said modestly, refilling Drake's tumbler with a light dry wine to set off the taste. 'I am indeed glad, Draque, that I did not kill you at Ashridge, for I like to see a man enjoy his food.' Suddenly he snapped his fingers and called out sharply in Spanish.

A girl came into the room, tall and graceful, with long black hair. Her skin, lighter than the average Indian's, glowed palely in the candle-light and Drake could see her small, firm breasts quiver minutely as she bent to offer him more food. '*Quiere mas, señor?*' she asked in awkward, accented Spanish, her voice low and husky. Drake put her at no more than fifteen. Enveloped by her bare-fleshed smell and aware that in this climate she was already a woman, he felt desire rise strongly. 'For you Dons,' he said thickly, 'fornication is as necessary as idolatry.'

'Hah!' Recalde laughed delightedly, ignoring Drake's little outburst of Puritanism. 'I can see you like her, Draque, and that is good, for having noted your appetite for well-spiced things, I plan to loan her to you as a servant.'

Drake looked again at the girl's face. Her cheek bones were high and fine and he could see she was touched by noble Spanish blood, with flaring eyes and an erotic, over-full mouth that spoke of many other exotic admixtures.

There was a sharp slapping sound of flesh on flesh, as Recalde sank strong fingers into the softness of the girl's thigh and spun her abruptly around. Despite the pain, she made no sound, but Drake could see her eyes were full of hate. 'Now you can see why she dislikes me,' Recalde said, grinning, as he pointed to her back.

Drake, for the first time, seeing the raised whipmarks which had been masked by the high bronze of the girl's skin, felt the sweat rise to his forehead. The sweat of disgust and distress that he always experienced on seeing women ill-treated. 'You are a cruel people,' he said harshly.

Recalde shrugged. 'We have a problem here. Once there were many Indians, meek and industrious, but we killed them off in only a few short years, making them dive for pearls. It was little enough sacrifice: have you not seen the wonderful products from the oyster beds of Margarita, the *Ave Marias* and *Pater Nosters*, heavy and translucent, glowing with white fire? However, now we are short of labour and have to rely on Guaiquerias and Caribs and other doubtful breeds, equally savage and intractable. Hence the need, despite our King's prohibition, for the negroes between the decks of your ships.' He grinned, white even teeth showing between his lips, as he pointed at the girl's blemished back. 'Hence, also, the need for frequent doses of the whip.'

Drake stood up. For him, midway between disgust at Recalde and desire for the girl, the evening was ruined. 'I must go now,' he announced.

Recalde raised a languid eyebrow. 'I shall send the girl over tomorrow,' he said. '*Yo siento mucho*, I regret very much, I cannot give her to you, only loan her for the rest of your stay. Although I shall drown her sons at birth, her daughters, possessed of their mother's fiery and untameable beauty, should be much in demand. You will understand that she is of some value to me and I must have your word as a gentleman to hand her back when you leave.' He paused, then smiling openly, said 'Of course, I have no objection to you planting a little heretic in her belly, if she will let you.'

Now was when the devil came to tempt Drake: a devil of lust and fornication, of warm, smoky flesh on steaming equatorial nights quite alien to a clean-living, religious and God-fearing man. Easily, he could have declined and walked off into the night. Instead he found himself saying, to his own horror, the words 'I accept.'

'I shall have her sent over in the morning,' Recalde said smoothly.

As Drake disappeared into the darkness, the Spaniard could not help laughing. His contempt for the English heretics was enormous. It was well-known that hypocrisy was their besetting sin: to criticise him for thrashing a slave, while between decks they held hundreds of sweating, tortured Africans, was amusing in the extreme. Bible in hand, these preaching, prating Lutherans were also the plundering pirates that cursed and bedevilled the civilised world. Yet they had a weak spot. Under all their godly cant they were as lustful as other men and by beguiling Drake with the slave girl Aruba, Recalde knew he had taken the first step in springing the trap that would keep these English pigs in happy drink and fornication until it was too late. Then, by means of storm or the Spanish flota, they would all die. Recalde hoped it would be the latter. The thought of a single, savage

155

sword thrust bursting Drake's guts in a thick splatter all over his own decks sat heavy and pleasant in his mind. He would be avenged and the King would be obeyed.

*'If you find your enemy in the water up to his waist help him out; if it's up to his neck, push him under.'*

Duke of Alva, most notable of
Philip's generals.

# 16

Drake's ship was the *Judith*, fifty tons, a command given to him by Hawkins on the death, off Africa, of the previous skipper. Had Hawkins passed Drake over yet again he would have incurred the Queen's wrath and Hawkins, not wishing to suffer in person or in pocket, had reluctantly bowed to the inevitable. Well, it was a command if you could call it that: more a grand rowing boat, a jumped-up pinnace, with two pitiable cabins, one tiny, for the captain and another small, for the crew of seven men. Bobbing there in the sheltered bay off the island of Margarita, Aruba, manacled at hands and feet, was passed aboard ship by Recalde's servants, to a chorus of whistling and jeering from the English seamen, part-lustful, part-sympathetic.

Drake had her carried down to his cabin then personally struck off her manacles. He straightened, roaring a curse as the knife the girl had grabbed off a table carved meat from his ear, just missing his eyeball in its ferocious course. Her full, generous mouth twisted in a snarl, the girl retreated into a corner. Knife held in front of her, naked except for a tiny cloth over her genitals, her perspiration-beaded breasts jutting forward into hard, ochre-tipped nipples, she waited for the man to come at her.

Drake opened his hands in mock surrender and speaking in Spanish, told her that he meant no harm. He soon realised, however, that the girl's grasp of the language was far more limited than his own. Putting on that open, cheerful smile that could charm a bird off a tree, he advanced on her, but the girl, spitting like a civet cat, delivered a lightning fast slice with the knife that only just missed cutting off the tip of one of Francis Drake's fine moustachios. '*Para usted, nada,*' she hissed in bad Spanish. 'For you, there is nothing.'

Drake, beaten, retired to the crew's quarters, locking the cabin door, if only to ensure that neither he nor his men became sudden casualties. Mostly caught by the press gang, the crew had accepted Drake with the open dislike accorded to any captain who, according to rumour, had gained promotion through merely pandering to the Queen. Their jealousy over the captain indulging his lustful fancy with a young slave girl, while their lot was to caulk seams and stitch sails, had quickly turned to scorn, however, when Drake announced that having abandoned his cabin to the girl he was moving in with them.

Very soon the *Judith* was the laughing stock of the fleet, her sailors coming in for a string of ribald remarks from the crews of the other ships. The men of the *Judith*, with the fierce loyalty sailors have for their own ship, quickly found these conditions unendurable. With barriers of rank broken down as much by their captain's close proximity as his abject defeat by a mere slave girl, they began treating their stocky, blue-eyed commander with scant respect, failing to touch their forelocks or call him 'sir', or even to step out of his way whenever their paths crossed on deck. All this, Drake strangely endured. Each morning, like some shamefully nagged husband, he would take a tray of food to the girl's cabin, invite her to eat and then smilingly duck his head at the storm of missiles the girl would send his way. After a week, the cabin began to smell like a farmyard and the slave-girl took on the filthy aspect of a wild beast.

One morning Drake heard a wild scream and went down to find the cabin door hanging open and the girl writhing and spitting in the burly arms of Oxenham, the ship's mate. 'I'll show 'un ow to dew it, me andsome, I'll show 'un,' Oxenham roared in a ripe Devonshire accent. Drake blinked in surprise. John Oxenham had always struck him as being a grave and sober man, correctly spoken, his behaviour, if anything, excessively proper for a sailor. Now, for the first time, he took in the pendulously drooping beer-belly hanging over a wide, notched leather belt, the ring in one ear, the over-powering smell of strong ale, and realised that when drunk the grave Oxenham was transformed into a roaring plundering devil with a love of piracy equalling that of his own.

'Put her down,' he commanded. In a second, his rapier was bending its point against Oxenham's bulging guts. 'Drop her.'

Oxenham did so, then crouched into a fighting stance. Brave as a bull, he disregarded the rapier and moved in with a soft-footed speed incredible for such a great cliff of a man, only to recoil, not from the thrust of Drake's blade, but a punch under the heart that momentarily paralysed him and made him gasp for breath. The blow carried no real weight, but was enough to make Oxenham pause and in so doing, remember that to offer injury to his captain was a hanging matter. Disappointed at having to pass up a good fight, he grinned and swaggered away.

Next morning, for the first time, the girl was calm and listless and did not throw things at Drake when he brought her food. Distressed at her deteriorating condition, Drake impulsively offered her freedom. Instantly understanding the sweep of his arm, the girl raced up on deck and went straight over the side in a graceful, swooping dive, then swam for shore in a natural racing crawl. She was almost there, when to Drake's amazement she turned and swam back to the ship, hauling her slim body dripping onto the deck, shaking water from her long, jet black hair to the groans of lust coming from the watching sailors.

'Free!' Drake said. 'You are free. Why come back?'

'*Libre*?' She echoed softly, then shook her head, allowing her finger to trace the pattern of a large, raised, lividly-coloured letter 'C' branded on her thigh, the terrifying stamp of the infamous slave market of Cubagua. 'No. *Nunca*.' Knowing well the awful mutilations practised by the Spaniards on escaped slaves, she had preferred this blue-eyed young corsair captain as the lesser of two evils.

From that moment, there was trust between them. Conversation was difficult with her limited Spanish, but as the days went by, Drake was able to learn something of her background. She was, it seemed, a Cimarron from the area of Panama, where escaped negro slaves already carrying the Hidalgo blood of their late masters had joined together with Indians in the interior, making for themselves a new tribe. The hybrid vigour of their mixed blood-lines had succeeded in producing people of magnificent physique as well as unsurpassed ferocity, and Drake had already found for himself that the girl lacked neither of these qualities.

Not once during four long months did he touch her. The ingrained Puritanism of his strict upbringing, which taught that fornication was wicked, allied to his own extraordinary courtesy to all women, forbad it. Then, in the strange magic softness of a high summer night, as he sat under the stars whittling a piece of wood and listening to the cacophony of hoots and growls coming over the water from the nearby jungle, she had stolen over and kissed him with her full, slightly negroid lips, and stroked his neck tenderly with

159

slim, sensuous fingers descended, on one side, from generations of decadent Spanish aristocrats.

Now, all Drake's pent-up desire surged through his body. All his stocky strength, all his youthful vitality, exploded in his need for her. He kissed her back with enormous passion, the musky smell of her light-brown skin driving him almost crazy. She led him down to the cabin. Silently, she pointed to the palliasse, indicating that they were to share it together. As they lay there in each other's arms and Drake, inexperienced in the arts of love, hesitated, Aruba breathed hot flame in his ear and said '*Yo te quiero.*'

In Spanish '*Yo te quiero*' means either 'I like you' or 'I want you'. Quickly, Aruba clarified her meaning. And Drake would need to spend many hours in secret prayer in order to purge such terrible, but delicious, sin.

From April to August, Hawkins and his ships ranged up and down the coast, meeting differing reactions and welcomes, but always managing to do business, taking in a fortune in gold and hides in exchange for slaves and good English cloth. True, the Spanish seemed to trade with agonising slowness, but there was no need to worry, they assured him: the hurricane season would be late this year. And so, as the Spanish kept up their lavish hospitality, the summer wore on, dreamy and endless, and a sense of timelessness and lassitude stole over everyone, Hawkins and Drake included.

Suddenly Hawkins woke up to the fact that it was almost September and that he must be gone. He had asked for food and water, but Recalde had shown his beautiful white teeth in a grin and assured Hawkins that he would get far better supplies, far fresher water, in the port of Cartagena, further along the Spanish Main. Hawkins had duly arrived at Cartagena, only to find big guns mounted on formidable defences, belching shot at the English ships. He had had no alternative but to turn away, short of all kinds of essentials.

Drake had taken the girl, Aruba, with him in the end, despite his promise to Recalde. Not a man to break his word lightly, he had felt justified in his course by reason of Recalde's treacherous betrayal of the English fleet. He welcomed the chance to save Aruba from more of her master's awful cruelties and planned, if opportunity presented, to set her on shore at some place where she could rejoin her people. Surprisingly, Hawkins, as Puritan in background as Drake himself, had tolerated one of his captains taking a nubile bed-wench along on

160

the voyage. Not one to do Francis Drake any favours, Hawkins, in reality, was merely paying out enough rope for his kinsman to hang himself with. When the Queen heard how one of her favourite courtiers had been making passionate love to a younger and more beautiful girl, her fury and her jealousy would know no bounds and Drake's goose would be nicely cooked! Such pleasant thoughts, though, were to vanish quickly from Hawkins' mind in the face of grave and terrifying problems.

In all the vast Caribbean there was, given the prevailing trade winds, only one way to go home—by passing through the narrow Florida channel. This late in the season the winds, even there, were likely to be contrary. Hawkins' only hope, therefore, was to enter the Yucatan channel and sail round Cape San Antonio at the western extremity of Cuba and then, clawing to windward and aided by the current, beat a laborious passage through the Florida channel into the open sea and the zone of favourable westerlies.

He was, however, as Recalde had so astutely and treacherously planned, far too late. As he reached the Cape, the sky changed from serene to brassy blue and then through various shades of grey before reaching a uniform and ominous black. Without warning the sullen, oily sea, hit by the first shrieking hurricane of autumn, exploded into huge and terrifying chasms of sea-green, churning water and the wind whistled and whined with unbelievable frenzy through the yard-arms as Hawkins' eight ships fled under bare, foam-lashed poles before the wrath of the storm.

Night after storm-wracked night, following as best they could the faint loom of Hawkins' lantern hung on the stern of the *Jesus*, the ships plunged back into the open gulf, hurled chaotically ever southwestwards by this terrible wind, like the first, confused, whirling leaves of autumn. With masts and spars gone, top hamper carried away, pitiably short of provisions and the rotten timbers of the *Jesus* beginning to burst open like so many corks, Hawkins knew that he must find shelter, yet all along this vast and wild coast of Mexico there was only one such place suitable to the wind-driven course of his crippled fleet: San Juan de Ulua, chief port for collection of the annual treasure of gold and silver.

As Hawkins made his landfall, he was not to know that only just over the horizon the formidable Spanish flota, pledged to destroy the Protestant corsairs before it collected the treasure, lay hull down on a converging course. Recalde, handsome, devious, treacherous, had, it seemed, got his calculations right.

Well almost right, because Hawkins, using superb seamanship, was in first by a whisker, and with the garrison mistaking him for the flota, was able to storm and occupy the strategic fort on the island of Arrecife de la Galleaga. The island was everything, for the port was in reality not a port at all and was useable only by reason of this island which constituted a breakwater some two hundred and fifty yards long, with deep water on its lee side. Here, in the teeth of the storm, Hawkins secured his ships, lying close in, moored by head-ropes to the island and prevented from swinging by means of stern anchors. From that awful wind there was no shelter, but the bank of shingle broke the biggest seas screaming out of the Caribbean under the mighty lash of the winter northers, and although the island might seem awash with the waves breaking over it, Hawkins was, for the time being, safe.

Not so the flota. Deprived of shelter, it could be driven to total disaster on a lee shore, and Hawkins had a terrible decision to make: let the Spaniards founder and guarantee all-out war between England and Spain, or share the shelter with the Dons and risk being overwhelmed. In the end, he chose the latter course, having no other real choice. Negotiations, therefore, took place in the airy, scent-charged cabin of Don Martin Enriquez de Almansa, Viceroy of Mexico, newly come to assume his powers. With many pleasant bows and much exchanging of compliments, all was easily arranged. The Spanish ships would lie alongside the English in all friendship and harmony until Hawkins, properly provisioned and re-equipped, left for home.

Later that day, Don Martin, exhausted from the rigours of his journey and the strain of negotiating with such a slippery, persuasive customer as Hawkins, had a visitor. At first, he refused to grant him an audience, but on the visitor's credentials being presented to him, made haste to receive his caller. It was Juan de Recalde. Swaggering slimly in, the nobleman did not bother to bow. His position as the King's direct emissary was all-powerful and he wished Don Martin to receive the correct impressions.

'Don Martin,' Recalde began coldly, 'do I understand you have concluded negotiations with the Lutherans?'

'That is so, Don Juan. We will share this port in peace, until they go.'

'Are you not aware that His Majesty has charged you with the

162

destruction of the heretic corsairs?'

Don Martin smiled a weary smile. He was a peaceable man, well-liked by all, with open, honest features. Although affecting the drab, clerical robe and close-fitting black hat befitting a High Catholic grandee of Spain, there was a distinctly humorous turn to his mouth. 'It is a pity,' he said, 'that His Majesty did not arrange with the Almighty for that extra puff of wind to waft us home, before Master Hawkins. In the circumstances I have made the best bargain I can.'

'There is a better bargain to be had,' Recalde said grimly.

'And what, sir, is that?'

'We have overwhelming power. The English must be exterminated.'

'I have given my word to Hawkins that he is safe. The word of a Spanish gentleman is solemn and binding.'

'The commands of your King are more binding,' Recalde said bitingly. 'Besides, such an oath as yours, given to Lutheran corsairs, is not valid before God.' He paused. 'Am I to record your refusal to carry out this great task given to us by our King, our Saviour Jesus Christ and His Holiness, our Lord's vicar on earth?'

'Oh well,' Don Martin said fatalistically. 'Put that way, I have no choice but to agree.'

The two men called for a plan of the island and summoning their commanders, began to discuss the necessary logistics for an overwhelming attack.

Later that day, the English commander also had a visitor: Drake.

Hawkins, in his cramped cabin, in sharp contrast to that enjoyed by the viceroy in his great galleon, looked up from maps and inventories of stores and said irritably 'Yes?' The knowledge of the Queen's increasing trust in Drake had, if anything, increased Hawkins' hatred for his jaunty, disrespectful kinsman.

'You have exchanged hostages?' Drake asked.

Hawkins clamped his thin lips together in rage at the way Drake had failed to address him either as 'Sir' or 'Captain', but with superhuman control managed to keep his temper. 'That is so. Ten English gentlemen, against ten Spaniards of knightly degree.'

'Their hostages are neither gentlemen nor knights. They are common seamen masquerading as their betters and commanded if necessary, to die.'

'Die?' Hawkins said sharply. 'What are you suggesting?'

163

'The Dons are treacherous. Their oaths to Protestants are regarded as no oaths at all. Unless we take precautions, we will be massacred to the last man.'

At this, all Hawkins' ingrained arrogance and condescension came out, bubbling acidly through the rising bile of his temper: his pride at being granted a coat-of-arms, the inordinate dislike of inferiors who try to climb the social ladder, could no longer be suppressed. 'Leave me sirrah,' he shouted angrily. 'For when I require advice on the behaviour of gentlemen, I shall seek it elsewhere than from some upstart yeoman.'

Drake did not allow himself the luxury of taking offence. Roused, his compact stockiness became only too easily a formidable, murderously dangerous, fighting machine and he would save that for the Spaniards. His eyes very blue, very thoughtful, he left Hawkins' cabin.

A day duly passed without bloodshed; then a night, with Spanish timbers uneasily rubbing stout English oak; then another whole day, and the watchful English began to relax; then next evening, at half-past nine, it happened. As Hawkins and his captains dined with their Spanish hostages, a watchful serving steward, John Chamberlain by name, stopped the splendid clatter of fine silverware by shouting at the top of his voice 'A dagger! A dagger!' Courageously falling on the arm of one Augustin de Villanueva, he just managed to prevent the lethal thrust that Villanueva had vowed solemnly two days before to plant into Hawkins' guts.

From that moment, all chaos broke loose: a loud trumpet call blasted out from the deck of the *Almirante*, the Spanish flagship, and, as the English officers scattered from the dining-table, fleeing to rejoin their ships, Spanish guns began to belch dark smoke and fire.

'Come with me,' Drake shouted. As always, he had an eye for a good man. Grabbing Chamberlain by the arm, the two of them emerged on deck as a storm of shot ploughed the timbered decks of the *Jesus* into a million murderously sharp splinters. Heads down, running at full speed, by some strange miracle only superficially bleeding and scratched, they leapt onto the firm sand of the island and made for the *Judith*.

Behind them, the Spaniards would pay now for their treachery. Never mastering the art of ship gunnery, treating their vessels only as springboards from which to launch superbly-equipped infantry, they had lashed the towering deck of the *Jesus* with a hail of small-arms' fire from close range slings, versos, bases and fowlers, but the English sailors were mostly below in safety, manning their great cannon. With a deep boom , the huge cannon of the *Jesus* opened up, smashing heavy metal into the side of the *Almirante* until her powder magazine ignited with a huge roar and she went sky-high, to triumphant English cheers.

As the *Minion* was warped out of the line of fire of the *Jesus*, Hawkins' two flagships were able to pour their fire into the *Capitana*, breaking her timbers at the water-line, smashing her gilded upperworks and ornate superstructure until she, too, sank low in the water, a shattered, burning hulk.

Two great Spanish ships of war destroyed. Hawkins and his men were fighting bravely, gloriously, but was it victory? Not a hope. Even as Drake and Chamberlain ran headlong across the shingle towards the little *Judith*, Drake knew the odds against the English were impossible. Already the Spanish, in a single charge, had overcome the unsuspecting garrison manning the fort strategically governing the island and now, slowly, so slowly, the Spanish were turning the big guns on the *Jesus* and the *Minion*. Within a minute or two both ships were under a storm of shot and shell, and with blood running out of the open gunports, disappeared into a smoky, hellish gloom, reeling under the weight of Spanish cannonballs.

By the time the two men leapt onto the *Judith*, it was almost too late. Recalde had swarmed aboard with a picked contingent of thirty men and had rapidly pushed the seven-man crew back into the stern where, heavily outnumbered, they were making one last desperate stand, the Spaniards milling around in gleeful competition to dispatch the Lutheran corsairs. 'For God and Saint George,' Drake roared in a tremendous foghorn voice that carried high above the sounds of battle, his chest heaving with the joyful prospect of combat, his blue eyes wide with a homicidal, almost happy, frenzy as he shouted, 'now let us conquer these traiterous villains.'

With one mighty stroke of the axe left beside the *Judith*'s head warp for just such an emergency, Drake severed the rope so that the vessel, as if secured by a spring to its rear anchor, shot straight out into open water. Now, nine men against thirty, they would settle it. To Drake, anxious not to spoil a good fight, the odds seemed just about right. An oar was lying in front of him. He picked it up.

'Give us 'un,' bellowed Oxenham, powder-grimed, blood trickling down his jerkin onto his massive stomach from a glancing rapier thrust. A compact bunching of stout shoulders and Drake threw it.

Grunting like a wild boar in rut, Oxenham laid the oar horizontal and slammed into a file of Spaniards, sweeping them off the deck, tumbling the armoured soldiers into the water, where they screamed and thrashed, sinking under the weight of their armour. It was an amazing feat of strength, something Drake would never forget. With a roar of triumph, the axe still in his hand, Drake plunged into the fight. No sword for him. He had never conquered the gentleman's art of swordplay anyway, but with a heavy axe wielded effortlessly by his immensely powerful arms in a two-handed action, he carved a wicked, scything path towards his shipmates. Nobody else mattered; it seemed to be just the two of them now: Oxenham and Drake, roaring and cursing, both with that awful grinning bloodlust on their faces that marks the difference between just a soldier and a fighter, to whom battle is just a game.

To awful shrieks and groans, Spaniard after Spaniard fell to the ground, limbs shattered by the dreadful swing of Drake's axe, or spitted on the sharp point of the pike that Oxenham had picked off the deck. Together, each man cut a gore-ridden, crimson trail towards the other, slipping and sliding on broken flesh and the viscous slime of slit intestines. Then, in the middle of the *Judith*'s deck, they met, and for a moment the mad heat of killing-lust stole from their eyes and, recognising each other, they nodded and grinned for one crazy second, their approval.

'Watch 'un, zorr,' Oxenham's voice was soft but urgent. Instinctively, Drake ducked and a pistol ball ruffled his curly brown hair. He turned. It was Recalde, who, dropping his pistol, rapidly changed rapier from left to right hand and now advanced towards Drake, a thin, savage smile on his tanned face. That he was a superbly-dangerous swordsman was obvious from a heap of Drake's shipmates lying bloodily at his feet, while Recalde was unhurt and as immaculate as ever.

'Protestant corsair, prepare to rot in hell,' Recalde spat.

Oxenham swore mightily and would have closed with him, but Drake, laying a hand on his arm, said 'Leave him. This man is mine.'

The two men came together; suddenly Drake hurled the axe towards him on the upswing and Recalde, taken aback, raised his sword-hand in reflex action. In a flash, Drake was upon him, inside the certain death of Recalde's glittering rapier point. They grappled: one, thin, full of tensile arrogance; the other stocky, well-fleshed from Devon cream and beef; both with the strength that only hatred can give. Not a word was uttered as they sought for a killing hold or a place to cripple or maim, each man trying to blind the other or ruin his manhood. Soon, sweat began to run down each man's face in hot rivers as they groaned under the muscle-cracking strain, neither willing to give way. For an eternity, it seemed, they remained there in this appalling, murderous embrace, as if in the act of dealing death, they found it necessary as two old friends to make some bizarre, loving farewell.

Then Drake ended it. Stepping back, he planted an explosive left hook into Recalde's guts: a blow delivered with hammer violence and at a polecat's speed; a blow that was as Anglo-Saxon as a spring-time maypole on a village green. As Recalde writhed on the deck a ragged cheer went up behind him, pitiful in its dimensions. Drake turned and could not believe it. Only two other Englishmen left: Oxenham and the lad Chamberlain, blond-haired and green-eyed, still with no more than fuzz on his chin, yet with a bloodied point to his sword that bore witness to his part in the fight. 'Tie him up,' Drake commanded, indicating Recalde.

The storm of shot and shell whistling about him dragged his mind back to the larger battle. With one bound he axed the rear cable around which the *Judith* had been slowly swinging and set the fores'l. He looked around, trying to take in the state of the fighting. What to do? What help to give? The English were in desperate straits now. The *Jesus*, which under Hawkins had fought with amazing, stubborn bravery and was by reason of its size unable to maneouvre, was doomed and sinking. As the *Judith* closed, Drake could see the figure of Hawkins, distinct in his ornately-silvered armour, beckoning to him.

As he made fast to the *Jesus*'s stern, survivors began to leap aboard, carrying bags of coin and treasure in accordance with Hawkins' orders. With his ship bulging at the seams with humanity, Drake sheered off and allowed the *Minion* to take his place. Protected by the towering sides of the *Jesus* from the storm of chain and dice shot coming now from the red-hot barrels of the Spanish guns as they aimed to cripple the English ships and prevent all escape, the *Minion* was able to take on more survivors and yet more treasure. Suddenly, a shout of panic went up. 'Fireships!' Sure enough, through the smoke and gloom, two fast-moving ships alight from stem to stern from tinder-dry brushwood slung onto their decks were

167

bearing down rapidly on the stricken *Jesus*. Hawkins could be seen motioning the sailors desperately over the side. 'Jump!' somebody yelled, but Hawkins stayed, looking desperately into the hellish gloom for Paul, his nephew, who had sailed as his page. In the end he jumped aboard the *Minion*, convinced that the boy had already left the *Jesus*. The fire ships passed harmlessly by and Hawkins' nephew, who had not jumped, would become a Spanish prisoner.

Out into a night of storm Drake took the *Judith*, battered, loaded so heavily that she wallowed dangerously in the rough sea. Hawkins had signalled him from the *Minion* to anchor and keep station, but Drake, in the murk of conflict, had no way of seeing the signal. Hit by the incessant winter norther that would now blow for many months, the *Judith*, with only stumps for masts, could only go one way, south-wards. During this time, Aruba, who had sheltered from the battle deep in the ship's hold, came into her own. She was everywhere, moving among the overcrowded mass of wounded men comforting, stroking foreheads, peeling off strips of cloth to make bandages. Somehow, she endured the hell of dysentery, the bloody flux that took off most of those who did not succumb to infections of their wounds, tranquilly, a look of compassion in those dark flaring eyes.

Fourteen days later, after drifting further and further southwards, land came into view again. As it did so the wind dropped, which was fortunate because it had not been possible to navigate the vessel without a mast, and drifting at the mercy of the elements they had been in great danger of shipwreck. Now Aruba came up on deck, and with the wind ruffling her jet-black hair, gazed intently at the shore, where lush green foliage came right down to the shimmering white sand. Looking at Francis Drake, she said simply, '*Eso es la tierra de las Cimarrones.*'

At this moment Drake realised that he loved Aruba; he also knew that he could not keep the girl, that their spontaneous, torrid love affair had no place in real life and that both of them must return to live among their own people. Launching his tiny pinnace, he rowed with Oxenham to the shore. There, while the burly Oxenham cut down a stout tree and attached it to the stern of the pinnace ready for towing back to the *Judith*, where it might serve as some sort of mast, Drake took a passionate farewell of the delightful Cimarron girl who had so charmed him.

'*Nunca, yo olividare. Nunca,*' she said, her broken Spanish husky from emotion. 'Never will I forget.' One last kiss planted on Drake's lips, then turning on slim legs, she disappeared into the jungle. Drake stayed only long enough to refill his water barrels from a nearby stream. He had been tempted to seek provisions from the local natives, but with little guarantee of meeting Aruba's tribe, they would undoubtedly be taken for Spaniards and risk mass slaughter.

Before setting sail, Drake struck the chains off Juan de Recalde and invited him, with an elaborate bow, to make his escape. With a large Spanish garrison nearby, at Nombre de Dios, Recalde should soon be safe. Honour had impelled Drake to free the treacherous Spanish nobleman, in view of breaking his own word over Aruba. It was the nature of the man.

Loaded down to the gunwales with sick and dying, the sea washing over the decks, the timbers leaking like sieves from the tempest of gunfire she had endured, and with no food at all on board, Drake pointed the tiny *Judith* out into the wintry vastness of the ocean. Anyone privileged to observe this stocky, brown-haired man nursing the tiller might have been amazed to see a cheerful smile crinkling his bright-blue eyes. The sea was his friend and would not let him down. Now there was only one thing left to do: go home.

> '*When she smiled, it was pure sunshine that every one did choose to bask in if they could; but anon came a sudden gathering of clouds, and the thunder fell in wondrous manner on all alike.*'

Sir John Harington describing the Queen.

# 17

January '69. Drake, still in his faded, travel-stained clothes after post-horsing to London, quaked on one knee before the Queen. A little paint on that long, pale face? Surely not. A great jewel swinging on a high forehead, framed by tiny, silky cocoons of flaming red hair. Sharp, piercing black eyes that saw everything and missed nothing, impassive, while he told his story.

How, with a boat filled with groaning, dying men, a pathetic jury-rig lashed to the stump of the shattered mast, they had butted their way northwards. Against wind and weather three days of painful progress could be wiped out in an hour, as the screaming winter northers swept them implacably back to the south. Eating only the rats and mice that had drowned in the bilges, they had known that they would all perish unless food was somehow found. Then they'd seen the porpoise. Launching the pinnace, Oxenham, with all the strength of his rippling thews, had managed to cast a sharp pike with a length of rope secured to its end into the animal's side and a bucketing, corkscrewing chase had begun, with the bowsprit of the pinnace rearing high into the sky, then burying itself deep into green foam as they'd pursued the stricken beast. Eventually, exhausted and soaked to the skin, they'd killed the porpoise and hauled it aboard. Then they'd kindled a fire in the galley and roasted the flesh. The taste was delicious, just like mutton.

Drake heard the Queen's sharp intake of breath, of interest. Encouraged, he told her how, using the pinnace again, they had taken the *Judith* in tow. Together, Drake sweating, Chamberlain's young, fair-skinned body trembling, Oxenham's great beer-belly heaving from the strain, they'd rowed the *Judith* through the treacherous Florida channel and out into the region of favourable westerlies. As Drake, quite carried away, continued to extol the excellence of his

170

shipmates, the Queen gave a sharp slap-slap of impatience with her fan. She was easily bored with tales of little men. The fate of a whole kingdom was at stake. 'What about our ships? Our treasure?' she demanded.

Drake told her in detail about the great battle. When she heard that most of Hawkins' craft had been lost, including the towering *Jesus*, the Queen hissed something under her breath and her breasts began to rise and fall sharply. Quickly, Drake averted his eyes, waiting in trepidation for his mistress's onslaught of fury. Everyone knew that the *Jesus* had been a worthless deathtrap of a rotting hulk, but the Queen, no doubt, would place a huge value on it. To Drake's surprise, though great pearls rattled softly and the snakes embroidered on her bodice glared at him with cruel, unwinking, sequinned eyes, no outburst came. Judgment suspended. 'Go on. Go on,' she snapped.

'There is at least some treasure, madam.' Drake explained how, even in the last desperate minutes, Hawkins had insisted that plate and coin be transferred to the *Minion* and the *Judith*.

'And of Hawkins. What news? Is he lost?'

'In troth, madam, I do not know, for in the heat and storm of battle, we parted company.'

Again, that rap, rap, of her fan against long white fingers as the court held its breath, waiting for the great explosion, the venomous accusations of blame that must surely follow. In the silence the moan of an easterly gale roaring down the River Thames rose to an eery howl as it curled freezing tentacles of sleet round the weathered stone of Whitehall Palace. 'By the faith,' the Queen snarled in sudden, febrile petulance, drawing a rich, velvet cloak around her slim shoulders as flaming cressets clamped to the walls smoke and spat in the icy draught, 'is there no warm nest anywhere in our realm where we may be spared this hellish tempest?'

Behind her, Leicester, flushed and jowled from good living, bit back a smile, while Cecil, darkly-robed and solemn-faced, his features rapt with concentration, came forward and bending, whispered for a long time in the Queen's ear. To the amazement of the court, the Queen began to snigger thinly. Her sailors slaughtered, her fleet treacherously attacked, an expedition into which she had sunk a great deal of money ruined and the Queen, never a good loser, was actually purring like a kitten! Those courtiers who were gathered round the throne could believe neither their eyes nor their ears.

171

'Well, good Francis,' the Queen said gently. 'These are grave matters on which we must weightily consult. Now get thee home where thy brothers await thee.' She paused, her eyes unusually and suspiciously soft. 'Hast thou money?'

'All lost, your grace. Lost or spent.'

'A purse of royals shall be sent to compensate you.' Another barely stifled groan escaped those around Elizabeth. Cheese-paring, some would say—even mean—she had never been known actually to offer money. Unable to credit his welcome, relieved that he had not been made the object of the Queen's frustrated and shrill vituperation, Drake thanked his mistress and bowed his way out of the great audience chamber.

Outside the huge oak doors, Christopher Hatton, recently appointed one of the Queen's gentlemen pensioners, was standing doing honour duty, the gilded letters 'ER' stamped on his finery adding even greater stature to his already impressive build. Hatton smiled gently down at the stocky seaman and Drake, in his turn instinctively liking him, smiled back. A man to watch, he thought idly, and no conspirator, like all the others gathered round the Queen, with their bland, treacherous faces. Drake, not one to curry favour deliberately, did not linger to gossip, although he sensed Hatton would have welcomed conversation.

Days later, Drake was to learn the true reason for the Queen's exceptionally good humour. Three great ships laden with pay for the Duke of Alva's army in the Netherlands had come to shelter in English ports from Huguenot privateers. Desperate for money as usual, by reason of Parliament's continued refusal to vote supplies until she married, the Queen, at Cecil's whispered suggestion, had found in Hawkins' débâcle, a perfect excuse for sheltering the Spanish treasure indefinitely. Drake's news had been timed to sheer perfection and the Queen would come out of the disaster with a handsome profit.

Back at Stoke Gabriel they welcomed him with cries of joy: John, bull-necked and brawny; Joseph, who stammered much and said little, except with the point of his sword; and Thomas, still a slender, growing lad. Mary, above all, had anxiously awaited his homecoming. When his ship had become overdue, she had suffered tortures of misery. She wept, hugging him tightly and Drake, picking her up in his arms, could not fail to notice how thin she was, her body almost wasting away and feather-light to hold.

For days all was laughter and pleasure and great were the plans the three brothers now made for the future. With Hawkins apparently lost at sea, splendid opportunities for advancement might now be safely expected. Queen's ships would be made available to wreak revenge on the Dons, and good men would be needed to skipper them.

Then suddenly, out of the blue, the letter had arrived from Cecil, numbing in the paralysing effect of its shock. Hawkins, it seemed, had just brought the *Minion* limping into Mounts Bay and his first action had been to curse Francis Drake, accusing him of desertion in his hour of need. Such accusation, Cecil wrote drily, would require searching examination by the Council. Nor, Cecil went on, had Hawkins neglected to tell the Queen of his dalliance with the beautiful slave girl Aruba and his acquisition, without informing Elizabeth, of a fiancée. Drake, the letter suggested, would do well to stay away from court 'until further advised'. Beneath Cecil's neat, legible, emotionless writing, Drake could only guess at the Queen's tearful hysteria. She had always had this grudge against him for refusing to tell what he knew of the Amy Dudley murder and it was painfully evident that these accusations had fallen on terrifyingly fertile ground.

As Francis Drake furiously dashed the letter to the ground, he realised that his hostile, jealous kinsman of the thin lips and narrow teeth had finally succeeded in dealing his career a mortal blow. Mary, although pretending to share Francis' sadness, was in fact delighted. Now, with no chance of her man being sent off to hazard his life at the Queen's whim, on distant oceans, they could marry. And there would be children, at least five. She would prattle on about them in her high servant's chitter as, arm-in-arm, Drake would patiently walk her, day after interminable day, along the wooded banks of the swirling River Dart, where in the soft Devon climate the first primroses were already peeping through. Excited and happy about her forthcoming marriage, Mary seemed to lose some of her awful, skeletal thinness and her cough, if not getting better, at least grew no worse.

As the year wore on into summer, Drake, occupying himself with the humdrum tasks of mending the nets and caulking the fishing boat, resigned himself to his inevitable fate. On 4 July 1569, he was joined in marriage to Mary Newman in the ancient church of St Budeaux. Watching them walk down the aisle to the organ strains of a lively wedding march, brother Joseph could not forbear to play a lively

173

rat-a-tat on Drake's drum, that he used aboard ship for the giving of commands. Bending to sign the register, with that fine sound echoing off the mellow, brown stone of the church walls, Drake was reminded sharply of stirring voyages made and splendid battles won, and for a moment his broad chest expanded and the blood began to race in his veins. Then, Mary's ripe, servant-wench voice, shrill and intrusive, shattered his thoughts and he knew, sadly, that married to such a woman he would always be banned from court, excluded from all gentlemanly social activities and, worst of all, forever banned from personal access to his true mistress, the Queen.

By marrying this stupid, artless girl, by paying off a debt that he had always sworn to pay, he himself had hammered the final nail in the coffin of his career. As his quill pen squealed briefly across the parchment, Francis Drake had to bend his head, so that Mary should not see the pain in his eyes.

Out of the blue, the letter came, handed to him by a supercilious court courier, who, by the pained twitching of his nose, was obviously not accustomed to the smell of common fishermen. The text of the letter, written in neat, copperplate handwriting and signed by some anonymous clerk, read:

> To Fra Drake Esquire:
> It would give great pleasure to your friends C Hatton and Fra Walsingham if you would join them in the box they have reserved at the Tabor Inn, Southwark on the fifth of Jan, next, on the occasion of a great bear-baiting to take place there.
> Your obed't servant,
> Etc, etc.

Hatton—Walsingham—stars rising swiftly in Gloriana's magnificent universe. What could it mean? No time to delay. There was no arguing with a summons like that. Brush the moth out of your best doublet, have Mary run a smoothing iron over crushed velvet and wrinkled taffeta and gallop post-haste for London.

Through the cold damp stews of Southwark, ducking from the slops and turds flung down from the overhanging, timbered houses, Drake galloped into the crowded courtyard of the Tabor Inn, there to be greeted by attendants and escorted into a private box. Both Hatton and Walsingham stood to greet him. Hatton, of course, he

174

already knew slightly, but Walsingham was an enigma. Only a year before, he had emerged as Cecil's favourite aide, entrusted, it was rumoured, with a network of spies and intelligencers without parallel in all Europe. A brilliant linguist and a polished diplomat, educated, like Hatton, as a lawyer, Walsingham had already shown himself as a manipulator of men, of kingdoms even. If anybody could anticipate the secret machinations twisting and turning in the Queen's devious brain, it was Walsingham. Dressed from head to toe in black, as befitted a high-protestant gentleman, with eyebrows and beard even darker than his clothes, the Queen, who liked nicknames, was already addressing him affectionately as 'My Moor'.

Hatton, in contrast, was a peacock of a man, outdoing even Leicester in his liking for fine clothes. His figure was every bit as tall and impressive as Leicester's—the Queen only liked big men around her. He was pleasant where Leicester was arrogant, and lacking Leicester's animal charisma, endeared himself to the Queen more by the superb grace of his dancing, his depth of wit and knowledge, and, most of all, by the simple fact that he could be trusted. Hatton then, in a short peascod belly, wearing French hose with parti-coloured garters that elegantly set off leg and knee, pearl earrings dangling from the lobes of his ears, formally welcomed Drake with a hard, dry handclasp and bade him sit down between himself and Walsingham. None of them said anything. The spectacle was just beginning and a good bear-baiting was not to be ignored.

Tom O'Lincoln, nearly seven feet high from the tips of his battle-torn ears to his savage back claws, sat shackled to a great iron post in the centre of the courtyard, lolling sullenly on his chain. A bear famous for his courage, he was covered with half-healed scars from previous combats and adored by the common people. 'Aye there, Tom O'Lincoln,' cried the children, hurling nuts and sweetmeats in front of his enormous claws, but attendants with long rakes nervously edged the food away from the bear's reach. He would not fight well on a full stomach.

Now, to a huge roar, came the mastiffs, four to a leash, short-nosed with powerful jaws bred for gripping, slathering with anticipation for the fight: eight in all. Released, they sank onto their bellies, glaring with intent red eyes, watching, waiting for an opening. The bear snarled and backed against his pole. Urged on by the crowd's curses and their master's whip, the dogs charged. Black fur exploded into savage action and the first mastiff, reaching for the bear's throat, was caught squarely by a great cuff of a front paw that sent it flying into a far corner of the pit, there to lie whining and scratching in the agony of a ruptured gut. In seconds, another, ripped from throat to crotch, lay twitching in the dust, seeping crimson blood from the tracks made by the bear's huge claws. Now though, attacking from all sides, the mastiffs were all over him and for many minutes it was all Tom O'Lincoln could do, just to hold his own. Eventually, bleeding profusely, minus some large patches of fur and hide, he managed to dislodge all the mastiffs except one, which had succeeded in clamping its great yellow fangs tightly to one tattered ear. Growling in triumph, powerful jaws locked solidly home, the animal would be impossible to dislodge.

'Well sir,' Hatton exclaimed, waving his jewelled cane in the air with emotion, 'what will Sir Bruin do now, pray tell me that?'

' 'Tis a well known brute, going by the name of Brown Boxer,' Walsingham murmured, eyeing the hound expertly, noting its huge, angry hackle, swollen into a great ball of fur. 'Sir Talbot here will never be satisfied with just an ear, mark my words.'

Even as he spoke, the mastiff, profiting from the bear's furious struggle against the pack of hounds which had rushed in anew, tearing and worrying at its flanks, suddenly shifted its grip to the bear's sensitive muzzle. The bear let out a strident howl of agony and with its little pink eyes glaring in homicidal fury, now went berserk. Rolling his enormous bulk over and over, like some out-of-control, rogue beer-barrel fallen off a brewer's dray, he left a trail of broken bodies, squashed and jerking, behind him. Fetching up at the end of his chain, there was only this savage, rangy mastiff holding fast to the bear's bloodied muzzle.

'Ten royals, sir, that hound is as good as dead,' Hatton said, but Walsingham, with the puritan's dislike of gambling, smiled and shook his head, watching the climax of the frenzied struggle with shrewd, penetrating eyes.

Now the bear literally began to embrace the mastiff. Placing forepaws around its adversary, it pressed; then it pressed harder; then it squeezed; then it crunched; and like so many pistolets discharging, the hound's ribs cracked, distinctly, one after another, the sound sharp and brittle, carrying over the crowd's roar. The hound let out a deep, mournful howl and dropped like a sack of empty fur, dead at the bear's feet.

'Interesting,' Walsingham remarked. To huge applause, Tom

O'Lincoln was led from the arena, snuffling at the end of his chain after the nuts and fruit thrown at him by his cheering admirers. 'In concert, the dogs must win, but with no hand to guide them, they are destroyed.' He looked at Drake, a slight smile hovering at the edges of his normally grim mouth. 'In war, the quality of leadership is all-important.'

The remark, so obviously made as a compliment to Drake, dragged Hatton's thoughts successfully away from the excitement of the fight. 'Sit down then, gentlemen,' he exclaimed, 'for we have much to discuss.'

The three men retreated back into their box, insulating themselves from the cries and oaths of the populace, as the bear-baiting, with animals less famous than Tom O'Lincoln, continued unabated. 'Master Drake.' Walsingham did not waste time or mince words. 'We are here on a matter of high policy and great secrecy.'

Drake's blue eyes crinkled into an incredulous smile. 'Secrecy—here?'

'In my business you learn quickly that the most open places are usually the most secret,' Walsingham said. 'You would agree that any spy of the Dons would, in this tumult, be hard put to overhear our conversation?'

Half-bowing in courteous acquiescence, Drake asked 'Tell me then, sir, how may I help you?'

'Not us,' Hatton cut in, unsmiling, 'but our lady, the Queen.'

Drake's ruddy face grew rapt with attention. 'The Queen? How may I be of service to her?'

Walsingham brooded at him for a moment with dark solemn eyes. 'I will be frank,' he said, his voice expressionless, dry as dust. 'With Hawkins in high favour and you, sir, in plain disgrace, the Dons cannot complain if you were to commit certain—depredations—in their territories. A sovereign cannot be held responsible for the actions of a pirate.'

Drake, to Walsingham's surprise, laughed out loud. 'Why sir,' he said 'the name "pirate" sits well enough on my shoulders. Given a sound ship and a chance at Spanish treasure, I vow I would continue to merit such a name.'

Hatton and Walsingham glanced at each other. This young fellow seemed to be every inch the man they wanted. Now to try him further. 'All could be easily arranged,' Walsingham said, 'but I remind you of the meaning of the word "pirate". Caught by the Dons,

177

you will be tortured, then hanged. For reasons of state your own country could disown you quite readily. I would be the first to hand you over to the Dons, or send you to the block, if the interests of my liege lady the Queen, would be so served.' He paused, eyeing Drake narrowly through his shrewd, dark face. 'What say you to all this, Master Drake, for to die anonymously or to grow poor and old in lonely disgrace is always the nature of all intelligence work.'

Accustomed to interrogating terrified traitors, Walsingham was vastly surprised to find himself practically incinerated by a blazing glance from two of the bluest, widest and most murderous eyes he had ever seen. 'Doubt me in all things but one, sirrah,' Drake whispered, on his feet now, fingers very close to the jewelled hilt of a dagger caught at his waist. 'Doubt not my loyalty to the Queen's grace until death, or I'll spit your fries to the wall and hang them there, like a haunch of venison.'

'Easy, easy,' Hatton said hastily, with a gentle smile that came pleasantly from such a large man. 'Let us come straitly to the matter in hand, as I see you grow impatient. The fact is, the Queen must build a fleet to defend her realm from the Spaniards, yet lacks any money with which to do it. We propose that you should now remedy this.'

Drake looked sharply at Hatton. He had been wrong, he now realised, to assess the man as just a large, pleasant, amiable fellow. He was now showing himself as an acute and plainly trusted adviser to the Queen. 'What then is my task?' he roared, twirling his fine, bristling moustachios in frustration. 'For I can bear to wait no longer to hear it.'

'The Spanish scour every ocean for "El Draco,"' Walsingham spat, his face suddenly brutal, his voice hard and blunt. 'So go then and smite them by land. Capture a whole year's Spanish treasure-train at Nombre de Dios, and bring it back safely to England.'

A year's treasure train! What an idea! What a thought! Crazy. Impossible. Only the devil's cunning of Walsingham, sitting in a closed, dark room in the security of Her Majesty's court, could have hatched such a plot. But to whom should the task be entrusted? The Queen had known. In disgrace or not, there was only one man in the whole kingdom capable of carrying out such a dare-devil, suicidal act of piracy. Francis Drake. Galloping home, changing from one post-horse to another, defying the need for sleep in his eagerness to tell his

178

brothers the news, Drake, for the first time in his life, felt a sensation of fulfilment.

Soon, back at Stoke Gabriel, what a fine hive of humming industry there now was. In no time at all two little ships, neat, well-found and seaworthy, were lying at anchor in the estuary and within days all manner of stores began to arrive. For once, nothing was stinted: barrels of beef, properly salted too; hogsheads of prime beer; ropes, tar, caulking, new rigging; and wonder of wonders, money with which to pay a crew.

The smack of firm action this. Funds were earmarked through the privy purse to escape scrutiny either by Parliament or Spanish spy, and if that were not enough, Hatton had been fed lucrative monopoly after monopoly by the Queen, precisely so that he might disburse monies on her behalf for secret ventures. A good team, Drake thought. None better. Hatton, Walsingham and Drake. 'We'll do great things together,' he'd confided to Mary one night, snug in the marital bed. But the girl, instead of smiling, had turned her frail body to the wall and sobbed. The thought of losing her husband so soon had reduced her to a state of misery. She relied on him. Needed him. Surely he knew that. On the marriage night, the memory of her hideous rape by the Upright Man had welled up suddenly in her mind, paralysing her body, making her shrink away from her husband's hearty caresses. In all the months before Francis' departure, they never succeeded in consummating the marriage and blaming herself, Mary began to blame him as well, turning inwards, shrewish, hysterical.

The Queen, it is true, suffered from much the same malaise, but whereas the Queen could throw all her energies into the demanding role of a powerful monarch, things for little Mary were different. Terrible now were the reproaches, the shrill tongue-lashings, the hysteria. Many men would have reached for the sure medicine of switch or scold's bridle, but Francis Drake, gentle as a lamb to all women, had merely bowed his curly head to the storm of abuse and thought with longing in his eyes of embracing his one true love: the sea.

One dark night in 1570 two small ships slipped away westward. Because of their size, indeed they were no bigger than many fishing-boats riding hove-to around the Devon coast, the Spanish, preoccupied with the depredations of the Huguenot sea-beggars, knew nothing of their departure. Before long the *Swan*, twenty-five tons, and the *Dragon*, little bigger, manned by a bunch of lads drawn from every ale-house from Sutton Pool to St Budeaux, from every tavern between Stonehouse and the Catwater itself, altered course to the south-west, dipping eagerly towards blue water and the fabulous flying fish.

And Francis Drake swaggered on his poop deck, sheer contentment showing in his wide, blue eyes. Should the Dons catch and hang him, then he'd die with a curse on his lips for King Philip and a compliment to his mistress the Queen. And there was no better way for any man to die, than that.

*'More than a man and, in troth, sometimes less than a woman.'*

Robert Cecil describing the Queen.

# 18

So for two years Drake roamed the Spanish Main, reconnoitring, carefully planning his intended assault on the Dons' treasure, with only a short visit in between to see his miserable, ailing wife, report to Walsingham and Hatton, and unload a fat parcel of ducats, velvets and taffetas gleaned from several unlucky and unsuspecting coasters.

The year's treasure-train and the bulging, burgeoning treasure-house of Nombre De Dios itself: Drake's blue eyes burned at the very thought. But to ensure surprise and secrecy, his expedition would have to be tiny and what were sixty or seventy seamen against a large garrison guarding a town the size of Plymouth? Impossible, even if they were Devon seamen, each man worth three of the Dons. No. An extra ingredient was needed to nourish such a devilish brew: the Cimarrons.

Drake remembered all he had heard about them: their hatred of the Spaniards, their reputation for unsurpassed ferocity. Nor had he forgotten Aruba of the long slim legs, jutting, darkly-nippled breasts and silky black hair, who had taught an English pirate, unschooled in the arts of love, many things. In his quest for the Cimarron tribe, however, Drake was doomed to be disappointed. Whenever he chanced to anchor at some isolated Indian settlement, he would ask *'Conocen ustedes los Cimarrones?'*, only to meet, should they understand his Spanish, either ignorance of their exact whereabouts, or raw fear at the Cimarron reputation for fearsome savagery. Only one other thing remained to be done before going home: he must find a base where stores could be accumulated, secure from wind, weather or Spaniard.

One day he chanced to put in at a small cove, screened by a narrow entrance and protected by two small headlands. There were no rocks, and a sandy bottom against which fish of infinite variety and colour could be seen swimming in great numbers. Only when he stepped

181

ashore did Drake realise that owing to some trick of topography, the harbour and ships lying there were practically invisible from the sea. Now, while his men took their ease, swimming in the silky clear water, lazing or playing at bowls on the shimmering white sands, Drake went inland a little, accompanied by his brothers John and Joseph. It seemed an excellent site for a base, with hills rising high and jagged on all sides beyond the dense, steaming jungle, likely to prevent discovery by marauding Spaniards.

'Well?' asked Francis of his brother John, eyeing his thick-set, bull-necked figure with affection. 'What think you of this place?'

'Oh, 'tis proper,' exclaimed John in broad Devonshire. ' 'Tis certainly proper. And the beach is a fine one for careening.'

'And you?' Francis asked Joseph.

' 'T-t-t-is m-m-m-eet,' Joseph admitted.

Looking at his two brothers, Drake was seized with a feeling of pride and love: John, with much the same stocky frame as himself, but with his coarse shoulders and tree-trunk of a neck, built on a much larger scale; and Joseph, who spoke very little because of his stammer, but could say all he needed with a rapier. Never once did they question his orders, trusting implicitly their flamboyant elder brother who had somehow swum into the exalted favour of the Queen.

That night, after they had unloaded stores to await their visit with the expedition proper, they chanced to come across a great wild fowl, twice the size of a domestic fowl, caught in a noose set by some wandering Indian and shrieking loud enough to wake the dead. Endlessly reminded by the rigours of their voyage home, of the splendidly succulent meal the fowl had provided, they decided to call their new base —Port Pheasant.

Back in England, with the passing of time, the Queen's bouts of vituperative near-hysteria seemed to grow worse, to the discomfort of her ministers and those near to her. By contrast, however, her common touch with humble folk had long ago turned into a life-time love affair and was a marvellous thing to watch. Now, in July '72, the Queen about to go on progress, a humble carter waited under a palace window as she scurried and hurried about, deliberating and then deciding and then rejecting which costume to take, which piece of jewellery to wear. 'The Queen is like my wife,' cursed the carter, sweating in the summer heat. 'Can she not stop changing her mind?'

A flash of vivid hair at the window: 'Get thee gone, knave,' the Queen hissed loudly. 'Thy insolence is insufferable.' At the same time, a golden royal floated down and landed—plunk—on the ground in front of the astounded carter. Legend.

See her now, at prayer, the vast line of carts packed up, ready to go. Racked by strain and nervous fancies, she is pale and frail, hair strained back from the temples and pushed into a net with garlands around it, a small pie-dish of a ruff on a white, slender neck, a narrow bodice holding her waist. Elbows extended, hands palm to palm, she is in repose, beautiful still. It is true that at nearly forty her girlish slenderness is giving way to a certain angularity and that a cosmetician's brush has skilfully sealed off the lines of passing time with a special white paste, yet at twenty paces she still retains the radiantly ethereal youth of maidenly Gloriana. To Warwick she will go this year, but first to Theobalds to see poor Cecil, whom she has recently made Baron Burghley for his ceaseless, grinding work and who, worn out in her demanding service, lies ill in bed.

'Stoop madam, I pray you,' squeaked a maid in panic, as the slim Queen strode towards the low-beamed door of Burghley's bed-chamber.

'We will stoop for your master's sake,' the Queen said stridently, 'but not for the King of Spain's.' Legend.

Back in her coach, she preened and polished herself, her bodice low-cut and daring now, the whiteness of her bosoms obscured with gold net to glitter and dazzle; and pearls, enormous pearls caressing her slender neck like black, muscat grapes clinging to a vine, that she had bought cheaply from those who had seized the jewels of Mary Queen of Scots. Having just crushed two plots, both aimed at placing the treacherous, dissembling Mary on her throne, it would please her to bask in the sunshine of her subjects' loyalty wearing Mary's pearls.

Last year, she had progressed in state to Hunsdon House in Hertfordshire, to thank her kinsman for crushing the rebels. Born in a litter by her tall, strong gentlemen pensioners all in black cloaks and gold chains, what a spectacle she had made, dressed from head to foot in shimmering white, with her nobles gathered round her, Hunsdon holding the sword of state, Hatton, Burleigh, Leicester all there, with Effingham, Oxford and Clinton.

Now, a year later, she would repeat the spectacle, at Warwick. Just outside the town, at Forde Mill, the burghers came to welcome her, but the recorder, dumpy little Master Aglionby, who was to make the speech of welcome, found himself so overcome by the Queen's magnetic, pulsating radiance, that he buried his head in his arms and wept with fear. Restored by a nip of ardent spirits, Aglionby launched into his speech, which turned out to be of interminable length, at once thanking the Queen for doing her duty and a-spelling out what such duties were. Those around the Queen caught their breath and waited for a curt dismissal, a shrill oath of impatience, but the Queen, through the years, had learned disciplines.

Eventually, when Aglionby had finished, she crooked a long, slim finger and said 'Come here, little recorder.'

As Aglionby, much trembling, knelt by the litter, the Queen, dark eyes glittering with mischief, said boldly, ' 'Twas said that you would be afraid of me, but in the end, you were not so 'fraid of me as I was of you.'

A huge shout of laughter, a thunderclap of adulation and predictably, more legend. Well pleased with herself, the Queen held council that night at Warwick castle with Walsingham, Hatton and Leicester.

'Now Walsingham,' she said. 'You are just back from France. What news of Alençon?'

'He is small and young, 'tis true, madam,' Walsingham said with some nervousness, 'but comely.'

The Queen rapped her jewel-encrusted fan sharply against the table, not entirely managing to hide her irritation. Alençon, she knew, was little more than a child, runt-sized and badly pockmarked into the bargain, yet she was forced into these farcical courtships one after another, in order to prise any funds at all out of those stupid dolts who sat in Parliament.

'And Drake?' she inquired, changing the subject. 'He is equipped and ready?'

'He goes next week, madam, from Plymouth. I understand all is prepared.'

'Without our protection,' Elizabeth rasped. 'That has been made clear?'

'It has, madam.'

For a moment there was silence, then Leicester said, 'My liege. This question of Drake's voyage, prompts me to pose a question.' He paused. 'Have I leave?'

'Our Eyes (her nickname for him) hast our permission,' the Queen purred.

184

'Madam, should the King of Spain one day offer you peace and fair trade in exchange for the person of Francis Drake, what would your majesty's policy be?'

The Queen's black eyes gleamed. She had long suspected that Leicester was in receipt of a Spanish pension, and whilst she did not doubt that he would be loyal enough in time of war, knew that her answer was likely to be repeated verbatim by sweet Robin to the Spanish ambassador. The question might even have been prompted by King Philip himself.

'Our kingdom is poor compared to the King of Spain's,' said Elizabeth, biting her lip in thought. 'Were a handsome enough offer made, we would have to sacrifice Francis Drake in the greater interest of our people.' There was silence while they digested what the Queen had just said, and in that moment, by some trick of memory, something happened to make her remember with peculiarly vivid clarity, the refusal of Francis Drake to give her the name of the man who had engineered Amy Dudley's murder. It was many years ago now, but that moment was etched as clear and sharp on her mind as if it were yesterday. Yes, there was no doubt: had she been able to marry Dudley when she was young and twenty-six, none of her nerves, her hysteria, her terrible, secret frigidity would have come to plague her. In her need to find a scapegoat, a whipping boy, she had discovered with a dreadfully mistaken percipience where the blame must lie. In her venemous bitterness, all her grudges, all her fury, came welling up, to be placed squarely on the stocky shoulders of Francis Drake. Hot rage gripped her, unreasoning and cruel, as sudden and stormy as it was unrehearsed. 'Nay,' she spat. 'There's more. We will make our meaning yet clearer still. Should Philip offer peace and trade, why, we'll send the pirate's head to him in Spain on a golden tray, like any John the Baptist!'

Leicester, concerned with the expense of entertaining the Queen at Kenilworth for the next three days, was delighted. Philip would pay a large cash reward for learning how easily and quickly the Queen had taken the lure.

Together they walked up and down on the Hoe, taking care not to injure the closely-mown turf of the bowling-green on which local merchants were apt to play on a summer's evening. The sun glittered on the water, making Hatton shade his eyes, as he took in the fine sweep of the Sound, St Nicholas Island, the cruelly-fanged

185

Mewstone and Rame Head in the misty distance. 'It is better that we should not see too much of each other,' he said abruptly.

'Why is that?' Drake asked.

'One day, the Queen will sacrifice you to the Dons in exchange for peace. As her trusted servant I may be the one to place your head on the block. How can we be friends?'

'You have already warned me,' Drake grinned. 'Besides, my mistress has a liking for me and in the end methinks I will be preferred to the Dons.'

'You are wrong.' The normally kind, courteous Hatton was being unusually blunt. 'Now you are a minnow, not worth the catching, but come back with golden treasure in your holds and you become something else.'

'What is that?'

'A piece on the chessboard of politics, one day to be expended to the greater advantage of your Queen.'

'She would not do it.'

'She will. She can,' Hatton said grimly. 'Some grudge stemming from her youth festers and plainly grows in her mind. She has set her face against you.'

Drake was silent. He adored his Queen; had always served her well. And this was how she would repay him. By death? He did not ask for gratitude, but surely his loyalty, the desperate danger of the trip he was now to undertake, deserved better than that.

Sensing the misery of his companion, Hatton tried to take his mind off the Queen's ill-will. 'Your stores—they are stowed?'

'Indeed. All is ready. We wait only for the tide.'

'Powder and shot?'

'Chain-shot only.'

'What is that pray?'

'Two round shot chained together. Even of small calibre it will destroy rigging and prevent pursuit.'

'I can see you are well-prepared and so wish you good luck and bid you adieu,' Hatton said. Awkward from embarrassment, he turned and walked slowly away.

Drake watched him go before eyeing the sky and sniffing the air. Yes, a fresh northerly breeze was springing up. He went quickly down the hill to the Catwater and expertly eyed the water, rising now against the slimy, seaweed-encrusted harbour wall. He would leave within the hour. He blew sharply on his silver whistle and as his

186

bosuns came running, rapped sharp instructions for the crews to be rounded up from the nearby taverns.

What a bunch of men they were, the West Country's finest: Tom Moone, bald-headed and pockmarked, true, yet with the small man's explosive, killer speed in a fight; big-bellied Oxenham, so amazingly grave and respectable, 'till you put a sword or a bottle or ardent spirits into his hand; brother John, burly and bull-necked; brother Joseph, silent as the grave into which he was wont to despatch any Don within reach of his lethal, flashing rapier; young Chamberlain, fair-haired, with a slender body as tough as wire; all of them expendable, at the Queen's whim, through a grudge-hate of Francis Drake growing irrationally stronger, day by day. The thought was terrible to contemplate. Seventy mad pirates crammed into two ships, the *Pasco*, seventy tons, and the *Swan*, twenty-five tons, commanded by brother John, all of them volunteers. Seventy men to assault a town the size of Plymouth? The odds were crazy, impossible.

But Drake had advantages. The Spanish Army, mostly little more than third-rate native levies, was strung out protecting the mule-born treasure that had been disembarked on the Pacific coast and was now winding its way across the Isthmus of Panama. Then there was the element of terror and surprise. Drake had never forgotten Moone's collapsible pinnace, which had enabled him to raid San Sebastian with such success. Now he would repeat the operation, but on a more ambitious scale. His men would attack by night, from the sea, with muffled oars, as silent as jungle cats. Then in the darkness they would be gone again before the Spaniards recovered from their first panic-stricken paralysis.

As soon as his ships arrived at Port Pheasant, Drake spread a map of Nombre de Dios out on the hot sand and called his men together for a conference. 'Lads,' he said. 'Our first task is to destroy the heavy guns, cannon of great power. One battery is mounted on the heights of Nombre Point and there are yet two others protecting the arms of the harbour mole. While Captain John lands down coast and, marching inland, attacks from the rear, Tom Moone will go for the sea emplacement and Oxenham and Chamberlain the harbour guns. As for me, I will take my men and head for the town centre, there to spread terror and confusion.'

'And there'll be gold?' growled John, his burly, red-necked features alive at the thought of the action to come. 'There'll be gold, Cap'n?'

All the men laughed, with the exception of Oxenham, who stood there gazing gravely over the top of his great, hanging paunch, looking with terrible disapproval, it seemed, at this bunch of villainous cut-throats gathered round him. Oxenham, when sober, was well-known to be a most respectable and God-fearing man to whom the thought of looting and pillage, was diagraceful—when sober!

Drake, in answer to his brother's question, stabbed at the map, his eyes blue and wide with the thought of treasure. 'Here. The Governor's house in the main square. By now it should be stacked to the ceiling with gold. Lads, I've brought you to the treasure-house of the world. All you have to do is go in and take it.'

As his men cheered, Drake just as quickly stilled them. 'Now,' he roared, 'let us pray to Almighty God to grant us success.'

Taking from his pocket a copy of Foxe's *Acts and Monument*, he proceeded to read with great solemnity of the terrible martyrdoms inflicted by the late Queen Mary on simple Protestant people. He finished with the Lord's Prayer.

Many of the seamen were hard put to muffle their laughter or hide their grins at this strange habit of their commander to play the simple minister of religion. A cleric's cloth sat strangely on a thieving, plundering corsair.

*'These startling developments have agitated and alarmed this Kingdom.'*

Dispatch to the King of Spain from his New World colonies.

# 19

De Recalde reached out a brown hand and smartly smacked the woman lying beside him on her naked behind, bringing a surprised squeak in response. '*Fuera*,' he said curtly. 'Get out.' The flesh of the auburn-haired Conchita, wife of the local and rather elderly butcher, at first so white and desirable after a continuous diet of native girls, now, after he had made love to her, seemed sickly and flaccid by contrast.

He lay there, wondering why the King had called him back for urgent consultations. Not that he would be sorry to leave this festering outpost of the Spanish Empire, but in his time there he had transformed the defences, erected huge gun emplacements to command the harbour mole and had trained a small but élite force that would be directly under his command in the event of attack—and El Draco, his spies had told him, was coming! He hoped he would be given time to deal with the corsair, his arch-enemy, who had plagued his mind for so long.

As the woman flounced sulkily off the bed and reached for her petticoats, her milky, blue-veined, over-ripe bosoms quivering like newly-set blancmange, the door burst violently open and Antonio, her portly butcher of a husband, rushed in. He stopped, took in the scene and eyes popping from his crimson, corpulent face with rage, unsheathed his sword, mouthing terrible curses.

Recalde moved fast; it was plain that the butcher's honour had been impugned and the fat little fellow intended to run him through. He leapt out of bed, slid his sword from its scabbard, where it lay on top of his clothes on a nearby chair, and grinning widely, oblivious to his complete nakedness, prepared to have some sport. 'Hey Carnicerito,' he said. 'You should keep your blade for slicing lamb chops, not for noblemen.'

189

'*Hijo de puta*,' the butcher cursed. '*Yo quiero sputar en sus cojones.*' 'Son of a whore, I wish to spit on your eggs.' Purple-faced, his sword fanned air as Recalde, nimble and lean, contemptuously danced out of his way. Suddenly, there came the sound of church bells. Not a solemn call to worship, but the wild, furious, cacaphonous jangling that Recalde had ordered in the event of attack. Now, he would have to move very fast.

'Little butcher,' he said casually, white teeth gleaming through thin lips. 'Normally I might have let you live, but it seems quicker to kill you. *Vaya con Dios.*' As fast as a snake's tongue, his sword buried itself in the butcher's stomach. Moving with the speed and thought of an alley cat, Recalde managed to leap down the stairs and dress himself, in one continuous fluid movement, leaving behind him the woman Conchita, screaming at the sight of her husband's guts boiling out on the floor, her naked bosoms flopping whitely and fatly over his moaning face as though she were trying to give him suck.

Recalde blew three quick, shrill blasts on the silver whistle that he had taken from some captured English sea captain, and from nowhere thirty men quietly appeared, wearing full armour, carrying either caliver or primed arquebus. Trained to a hair over many months, to remain disciplined in face of panic and confusion, they were Recalde's élite guard, his guarantee that all corsairs would be repelled. Crouching over the stocks of their weapons, they waited in two rows, calmly peering in the direction of the darkened market-place, ready to deal with any attack.

Drake and his men, in three of Moone's pinnaces, lay under the shelter of the eastern point of Nombre Bay, pitching in the uneasy sea, waiting for the first streaks of dawn to dilute the pitch blackness of the night. Soon, Moone and his crew would have to climb that rocky, surf-pounded promontory and destroy the huge guns that were mounted there, commanding the entrance to the bay. If they failed, and they stood a good chance of being mown down like flies as they clambered up the steep boulders, the pinnaces returning from assaulting Nombre de Dios would be sunk like sitting-ducks when they passed under the point. Ferocious little Tom Moone was highly conscious of his vital part in the whole operation, and despite the chill of the perpetual sea spray, the surface of his polished bald head shone with perspiration.

Imperceptibly, a glimmer of grey crept into the sky. 'Good luck, men.' Drake whispered. 'Good luck to us all.'

The three pinnaces now moved gently forward, water chuckling from their bows, the path of each boat diverging, like the spines of a lady's fan: Drake heading for the quayside and the town's very vitals; Chamberlain and Oxenham each pulling strongly for one of the twin harbour moles where murderous, large calibre cannon had been mounted to command and enfilade the busy shipping roadsteads. Unless those guns were neutralised, Drake's three pinnaces would stand little chance of ever leaving that harbour.

Two long minutes, the longest he had ever known, and a row of steps grew into solid shape in front of Chamberlain. Young and lithe, he leapt ashore and led his men in a tremendous rush up the steps, the horny soles of the men's bare feet making only a slight pattering noise despite their headlong rush. Two hundred yards to the end of the mole and the men, following Chamberlain's terrific sprint, thought their lungs would burst. All for nothing: the guns were silent and deserted, the guards carousing in some harbour tavern. Laughing hysterically, the slender, fair-haired Chamberlain hammered home the spikes.

Oxenham was much slower than Chamberlain. He was, after all, a much-respected man, who liked to conduct himself with gravity. Therefore, having hoisted his huge belly up the steps on the other side of the mole, he made a point of walking very deliberately, panting laboriously, to the end of the mole where the guns were installed. Running does not come easily to a big man with a large stomach and behind him, men swore harshly, expecting at any moment a hail of fire from the waiting Dons that would sweep them off the wall like crumbs from a table. Only one more yard, then Oxenham stepped unhurriedly down into the pit where the guns' crews might be. Just one scared white face peered up at him: an ammunition boy, that was all. Looking back, Oxenham heard faint shouts and the distant gleam of armour winking under hastily-lit torches, as soldiers began surging along the mole from the direction of town. They too, lax in discipline, had stolen away from their duties to drink with their comrades, and had left their guns unprotected.

With several mighty blows, Oxenham drove marlin spikes into the gun breeches with a heavy hammer, making them useless, and the men, seeing they had ample time to reach their pinnace before the soldiers arrived, clustered round the shaking, terrified boy, swigging wine that the gun crews kept there.

When he had drunk almost a full bottle of wine, Oxenham laid hold of the trembling lad and made ready to drop him gently into the sea. Guffawing hugely, he explained, 'Us only kills the big fishes. Us always throws the small ones back!'

'Give way with a will,' Drake roared. No need for surprise any more. The need now was only for speed. With Drake crouched over the tiller, blue eyes killer-clear, the old battle-smile curled wide across his lips, the pinnace shot right through the centre of the harbour, grounding with a distinct shudder close to the busiest part of the fort.

The boat quickly secured, they scrambled ashore and within seconds were surging up the main street towards the Governor's house at the far side of the plaza, where part of the treasure was known to be always stacked.

'All right lads, you know what to do,' Drake laughed insanely.

A flash of fire and pikes tipped with tow exploded into brilliant flame. A twang of bow-strings and small, lethal, roving arrows, also spurting flame, hissed terrifyingly in all directions. A splendid innovator, Drake was now employing weapons brought solely for the purpose of spreading terror. He was not finished yet. Three of his men he had armed not with pikes, but with drums! Added to the strident blasts blown by Drake's personal trumpet boy, young Sam Higgins, the enormous thunder of the drums' rat-a-tat reverberating off the walls suggested not twenty or so crazy corsairs, but an invading army. Screaming with fear, their houses catching fire on all sides, the population exploded into the streets and surged up in the direction of the main plaza with only one objective: to flee the stricken city.

In the sombre half-light of dawn, Drake and his men reached the plaza. Here for the first time was open ground, but with the population running panic-stricken in all directions, Drake did not anticipate the slightest trouble. In front of him, ornate and apparently undefended, lay the Governor's house.

'Remember men, take only what you can carry away,' Drake shouted, his moustachios bristling at the thought of loot. 'Look for the jewels—and wait now, for my signal.'

Watching their commander's hand, poised to come flashing down, the men dreamt only of fat pearls, necklaces of thick chain-gold, coruscating Peruvian emeralds that were the wonder of the civilised world, as they prepared for their triumphant, headlong rush across the deserted square. In front of them lay priceless treasure. All they had to do was carry it away.

With the crowd stumbling past in a wild, blind stampede, crashing into them in a crazy urge to escape, some of Recalde's arquebusiers became infected with the same unreasoning terror and began to moan and whimper, only seconds away from abandoning their weapons.

'Stop that!' Recalde's voice was harsh. 'The first man to run will be crucified over a slow fire. Break ranks, backs to the wall. Let the crowd through and then reform on my whistle.'

After the mob had passed by, the market-square became strangely silent, then in the semi-darkness, Recalde saw a string of needle-point lights appear on the other side of the plaza; slow-matches that could only mean a large army of musketeers. All at once, he began to laugh. A feeling of happiness, of perfect contentment rose up and pervaded the soul of Juan de Recalde. All those things, the drums, the flaming pikes and arrows, then the slow-matches, could only have been dreamt up by one man: Francis Drake.

'It's a trick,' he whispered to his men clustered in the darkness under the wall of the Governor's house. 'There are only a few of them. When they charge, wait for my signal. One volley and why we'll sweep these devilish Lutherans all the way to hell.'

The soldiers, reassured, caressed the comforting weight of their weapons and waited. Slaughtering heretics was well-known to be a task much approved of by the church, and they were all religious men.

'Come on lads,' pleaded Tom Moone, in his soft Devon burr. ''Andsomely now.'

Desperately his men leapt for the wet, treacherously-jagged rocks. With the pinnace corkscrewing in the wild, surging eddy of the sea, they would often miss their footing and fall straight into the water, to be pulled out gasping and half-drowned; while others would take crashing, bruising falls as they missed the few footholds available on the slippery, slime-encrusted boulders. Eventually, with all the men ashore, they managed to wedge the pinnace in a cleft between two huge rocks, securing it with ropes so that it would not be pounded into matchwork by the lumpy waves ceaselessly booming in from the open ocean.

They started the long climb towards the top of the promontory. The rocks were steep, jagged and apt to break loose under the pull of a man's hand. Grimly, they worked their way higher, then two men, unused to mast work, suddenly terrified by the height, froze.

'Don't look down!' someone shouted.

'Curb your tongue,' Moone hissed venomously, but it was too late. Up here, high above the roar of the sea, their voices would be easily heard and all surprise had been lost. Anxiously, Moone peered upwards. He was close enough now to see the slits in the embrasures, but he detected no activity. In the gloom he could discern no heads peering over the high defensive wall. The guns continued to point menacingly out to sea, their barrels gaping black holes ready to launch fire and ruin on the pinnaces the moment they re-entered the channel under Nombre Point. They are just waiting, he thought, until we show ourselves, then they'll blow us to kingdom come.

Up onto the last slope. No more than a short stretch of flat, shingle-strewn turf. In the quickly-lifting darkness, Moone identified his men and detailed them off into two parties. One would be led by him, the other he had deemed it politic to place under the command of their leader's tall, taciturn, younger brother, Joseph Drake.

Quietly, Moone led his men along the slope, to make a second angle of approach. He dare not delay any longer. He took hold of the bosun's whistle hanging by a cord around his neck. When he gave the signal, they would attack at once, from both directions, hoping to split the baptism of fire that must surely come, now they had lost the element of surprise. While some men cursed and others prayed, Moone, his bald head gleaming from a mixture of sweat and sea-spray, poised himself to blow the whistle.

'Charge!' The roar of a man's voice could be plainly heard from the other side of the square. Around him, Recalde's men tensed, waiting for their commander's signal.

Out into the plaza came the heretic corsairs, twenty or thirty of them, moving at a fast lope. Eyes twitching with hatred, Recalde waited with iron self-control until they were within killing range. In the lead was a broad-shouldered, stocky man who could only be Francis Drake. Lovingly, Recalde sighted down the barrel of his weapon, aligning it dead centre on the Englishman's heart. A moment to cherish. A moment to remember. '*Ahora!*' he said sharply. 'Now!'

There was a blinding flash of fire and through the eddying, drifting smoke it could plainly be seen that the Lutherans had been

194

decimated. True, a soldier had discharged his weapon a split second before Recalde, jogging his aim at the vital moment, but Recalde was sure he had got his man, There, unmistakably, was Drake, writhing on the ground with the others.

Grinning, Recalde gave the order to reload. With arquebus and caliver, the process would be long drawn-out and tedious, but why risk defeat by closing and fighting it out with cold steel, something for which his native levies had little relish? After all, those English who had survived were marooned in the Governor's house and with soldiers recovering their wits and pouring back into the town from all directions, time must be on his side.

Suddenly he heard appalling screams behind him, then men came rushing past, blood pouring from their heads. From entirely the wrong direction, more Englishmen had amazingly materialised. John Drake had made his detour round the town and was now charging home at the head of his men, hefting a great stonemason's hammer in his awesome thews. As Recalde watched, a soldier rash enough to level a pistol at the solid mass of John Drake took the huge weight of the hammer directly on his head, his skull cracking like an eggshell, brains spilling out onto the *calle* in a warm, grey, bubbling mass.

One moment Recalde had men under his command, next, he had none, as terrified they fled blindly down a side street. Recalde, cursing, just had time to melt into the darkness of an alley as John Drake and his men swept past into the square, while at the same time Oxenham and Chamberlain's men, following up from the harbour, joined their shipmates in the ransacking of the Governor's house.

Recalde was not completely dissatisfied however; the pirates were a long way from their boats and he would soon have the house surrounded by a mass of soldiers, once he had rallied them under the threat of blood-curdling punishment. Besides, he was quite certain that he had killed Drake. At that range it would have been impossible to miss.

Cursing, stumbling, high on the promontory overlooking Nombre Bay, Moone's men picked their way over the broken boulders lying in the short turf towards the fort housing the great cannon. A few yards more and they would be within range of the lethal scatter-shot of caliver fire. 'At a run, me hearties,' Moone shouted. 'At a run—if you ever wish to see old Dartymoor again.'

Amazed at their luck in not being spotted, they reached a stout wooden door at the side of the block house. A few well-directed blows and the timbers splintered, then gave. Bursting in at the head of his men, Moone realised with sudden hair-raising horror why, although the fort had been fully garrisoned, not a shot had been fired, not a man injured. In fearful, dread perspective, Moone took in a truly terrrifying scene. Lying twisted, contorted, in groaning, vomiting heaps, were the soldiers of the garrison, their heads resting in their own sick and blood-encrusted excreta, their faces yellow with approaching death, while Joseph Drake's men, who had got there first, walked among them with dazed looks, filling their pockets with loot.

'Back!' Moone screamed, recoiling from the appalling stench. 'Get out! 'Tis the "Bloody Flux".' Arms flailing, he drove his men from the filthy, nauseous place. As they retreated at a dead run down the slope, to await Drake's return, Moone knew that while his own lads had suffered only a few seconds' exposure to the dying men, young Joseph, Drake's stammering brother, and his men, were likely to pay a dreadful price for their headlong rush into that dreadful charnel house. Bitterly, he reflected that while no guns would belch shot and fire at the retreating Englishmen, the Spaniards had unwittingly found a far more dangerous weapon with which to eliminate the Lutheran corsairs—disease.

In the smoky inferno of the terrible volley of gunfire that had torn such a gaping hole in his ranks, Drake stumbled to his feet, more in reflex action than in any clearness of thought. He was wounded, he knew that, but the crazy exaltation of battle was upon him and he felt no pain. Looking down at the shattered body of young Higgins, his boy trumpeter, lying outstretched on the cobbles, he experienced no emotion, so dazed was he from the suddenness of the onslaught. 'Into the house,' he roared, slowly gathering his wits. 'On into the house.'

Crashing through door after door, followed by the sound of horny feet and hard breathing as Chamberlain's and Oxenham's men came up to join the remnants of his own group, Drake reached the store-rooms. By the light of flickering cressets they saw the tantalising sight of a fortune in silver stacked in thick, heavy, gleaming ingots from floor to ceiling.

'Too heavy to carry,' Drake roared furiously. 'Back to the

harbour.'

Only then did Drake's men realise, looking through the windows, that the square, previously deserted of all but dead and wounded, now contained a solid mass of soldiers rallied by Recalde, their weapons levelled and covering every possible exit point from the Governor's house.

'Us be lost,' Oxenham shouted hoarsely. 'Us be surrounded on all sides.'

Convinced they were doomed, the seamen, staring at their commander, were amazed to see that he was actually smiling. 'A little patience, my lover-r-rs,' he said softly, matching Oxenham's broad Devonshire with his own, 'and we shall walk straight through them.' Even as he spoke, a clap of thunder shook the buildings and torrential rain started sheeting down on the town of Nombre de Dios.

Slowly the men took in the situation and, nudging each other, began to smile lovingly at Francis Drake as though he were God himself. No guns, Drake had said, bow and arrow only. They had thought him mad, but Drake had not forgotten the sudden tropical downpours that were apt to drench Nombre De Dios before the sun came up and burned the clouds away. Arrows could be fired for a few minutes at least, in the rain, while at the first drop in their touchholes, caliver and arquebus became quickly useless.

'Give 'em a touch of old English, boys,' Drake said quietly.

The hardened, boiled leather cuirasses of the soldiers could not withstand the hail of arrows that now whistled towards them with the extraordinary power produced by expertly-drawn longbows, and at the sight of their comrades falling like ninepins, the native levies broke and ran.

'Back to the treasure house on the quay,' Drake ordered.

Stumbling down the narrow streets with their walking wounded, Drake's men retreated back through the town until they reached the water's edge. There, they broke into the treasure-house and hunted feverishly for jewels and movable valuables, conscious that their immunity from attack would last only as long as the rain.

Nothing. Until they discovered a secret strong-room next to the cellars. There . . . the treasure must be there. There was no doubt. And at the very moment of their joy as they realised that chestfuls of glittering loot were actually within their grasp, Francis Drake gave a loud groan and spiralled forward onto the ground in a dead faint. 'Capn's wounded. The commander's hit.' The dread words carried round the men in an awed whisper.

Shocked by the river of blood coming from Drake's foot, they debated swiftly what to do. He must have been hit at the first volley, yet all the time he had said nothing, given no sign. Francis Drake must have the strength of ten men, but now . . . but now . . .

'He must be treated or he will perish,' Chamberlain said.

The others agreed. All thought of treasure banished from their minds, they backed off to their pinnace, and joined by Moone's boat, rowed away as fast as the strength of their arms would allow them. They took refuge on a small island used for victualling, just a few miles to the west of the town, and there, nursing their wounds and their injured commander, they went to ground, smarting at their defeat.

Next day Recalde, curious to learn the fate of his arch-enemy, Francisco Draque, had himself rowed over to the island under flag of truce. There, his pinnace rocking gently just out of musket range, he shouted across to the men on the island. 'My compliments, gentlemen, on your bravery.' His English, from his stay at court in England at the time of his master's marriage to Queen Mary, was colloquial as well as perfect. Correctly suspecting a spying expedition, the English made no reply.

Recalde tried again. 'Pray tell me, my masters,' he called, 'with what poison you tipped your arrows, so that I may seek the remedy?'

'Englishmen do not use poisoned arrows,' came the surly reply.

'That is good. Now permit me to ask you, gentlemen, is there anything you need? And how is the condition of your famous commader, El Draco?'

A voice brayed back at him, tinged with a pleasant Devon burr: Drake's voice, surprisingly strong and resolute for a badly wounded man. 'Why I am already much recovered sirrah, and as to your other question, all we require is some of that special commodity which you get out of the earth and send into Spain to trouble all the earth.'

So Drake was alive and still insolently searching for treasure! The news, for Recalde, was infuriating. Very well, he thought to himself, the battle is only half over and I have a little time yet before I have to take ship for Spain. Before I go, I shall destroy once and for all this nest of corsairs and their accursed leader who so sadly plagues my master. Already a plan had taken shape in his mind, as brilliant and as devious as only a man like Recalde could devise. There was, as the saying went, more than one way to kill a cat!

He spoke sharply to his oarsmen, promising them twenty lashes apiece if they did not row faster. He could not wait to fit together all the pieces of his beautiful and murderous design.

*'Drake . . . was so vehemently transported with desire to navigate that sea, that falling down there upon his knees, he implored the Divine assistance that he might, at some time or other, sail thither and make a perfect discovery of the same.'*

Camden, describing Drake's first view of the Pacific Ocean.

# 20

They returned to Port Pheasant only long enough to pack belongings and burn the *Swan*, hoping that the Spaniards would believe they were ridding themselves of excess stores and shipping before scuttling home tails between their legs. In reality, they surfaced on the western shore of the Gulf of Darien, virgin jungle awakening to the sound of ripe Devon oaths, the busy wheeze of bellows, the ring of an anvil and the snap-snap of axes lustily wielded. Monkeys, watching from the dank green foliage, gibbered in open amazement at the mysteries of quoits, bowls and archery, all the pastimes of an English mayday fair.

In the hot steamy climate Drake's foot, which had begun to mend so well, became swollen and plainly infected, throbbed agonisingly. Everything seemed to be going wrong. Drake knew that unless he could find allies to supplement his numbers and show him the country, he would almost certainly fail to wrest any treasure from the Spaniards: and his fate, from a plainly hostile Queen, would not be difficult to guess at. Accordingly, suffering in both body and mind, his normally cheerful, ruddy face grew sombre and morose and his crinkling, blue eyes, slack and miserable. His men, grumbling openly, began to lose faith in their leader.

One night, Drake was jerked out of a feverish, restless sleep by a fearful commotion. Throwing on his clothes, he limped out of his crude hut to find most of his men already pinioned by savage-looking natives who must have sneaked into the camp with the silence of leopards and overcome the lookouts. With his bad leg there was no chance of running away, and in seconds the natives had rushed him and begun tying his hands.

Pushed and shoved at the end of sharp spears, Drake and his men were sent stumbling along a jungle trail, until after a few miles they came to a native village standing in a clearing. Quickly the natives tied them to stakes, and piling a mass of vegetation at the base of each one, set fire to them, all the time capering with joy, pointing scornful fingers at their victims and shouting *'Espanoles, Espanoles!'* It took little intelligence to realise that the natives had taken the seamen for Spaniards and now intended to take pleasant revenge for cruelties they had suffered at the Spaniards' hands.

So this is the end, Drake thought. He remembered the burnings he had been made to witness, the terrible agonies he had seen men suffer. Coughing, retching from the smoke, he wondered with extraordinary calmness how severe the pain would be. As the whole wretched scene began to swim before his watering eyes and his brain clouded, his last thought was that the natives did not have the Spaniards' dedication to the art of causing exquisite pain and were choking their victims to death before the flames had even touched them. He found the thought vaguely amusing and as his head slumped forward on his chest, a slight grin touched his lips.

Strangely, he soon regained some sort of consciousness. Wheezing horribly, lungs struggling for a whisper of air to sustain the last defences of an asphyxiated body, he opened his eyes again. He seemed to be lying on his back, but the scene was quite unreal. In his delirium he dreamt that a beautiful girl was bending over him, nuzzling his ears, nibbling his mouth with her soft lips. A dream of love. A man often dreamt of erotic fancies in the last moment before death. Then his head cleared.

Unbelievingly, he looked at the girl: took in her light copper skin; the flared eyes and high cheek bones; the long hair, plaited now, that hung halfway down her back; those high, jutting breasts with their ochre-tipped nipples; and what was she saying—was it possible? *'Mi amor, mi amor. Francisco, te amo mucho.'*

Coughing, spitting, blue eyes crinkling, round, ruddy face alive with pleasure, Drake sat up.

Aruba.

Later Drake, limping heavily at the head of his men, was motioned into the biggest hut in the village. There, at the far end, stood a man dominating with effortless arrogance all the other natives kneeling in front of him. His skin was dark, almost Nubian in its polished blackness, yet his features bore the extraordinary light bones of a pure

Castilian aristocrat, with a slender, delicate nose and clear grey eyes. Drake did not kneel. He had long ago made it a rule to kneel to no man. Only to God.

The native, tall, with the indolent, self-confidence of authority, was obviously the chief. Looking directly at Drake, he made an all-embracing sweep of the village with one muscled arm and said 'Cimarrones.'

Drake smiled and nodded. '*Ingles*,' he said.

Seeing the blank look on the chief's face, Drake had a sudden idea. 'Fletcher,' he bawled, 'come here.' Fletcher, the parson, was a small rotund man, quiet enough when he wasn't sermonising, with round, button eyes. Without any training, he had learned to draw and paint beautifully. 'Show him where we come from,' Drake said.

With the aid of a stick, Fletcher drew a rough map of Europe in the red dust. Pointing to England, Drake extended his arm to embrace his men. Then pointing to the outline of Spain, he said '*Espanoles*', and snatching the stick, thrashed the dusty contour of that country into oblivion, a savage scowl on his face. The chief's face parted in a wide smile, understanding at once. He turned now and began talking furiously to Aruba, who had been standing behind him with some other women and was, Drake feared, one of the chief's most valued wives.

Eventually, the chief came forward and kissed Drake on both sides of his sweat-flushed, moustachioed face, much to his embarrassment in front of his own shipmates. Then, taking a knife, he placed Drake's index finger next to his own and made two small cuts so that their blood intermingled. Beckoning Aruba forward, he indicated that she should try and interpret.

'*Es su compadre de sangre*,' Aruba managed to convey in a low voice. 'You are blood brothers.' In her stumbling Spanish she managed to convey to Drake the chief's gratitude for Aruba's rescue from the hell of Spanish slavery. Although she was his wife, she explained, the chief was returning her to Drake as a present. From the emotion in the eyes of the assembled natives, it was plain that a Cimarron could make no more generous gesture than to give his wife to another man.

As the chief, coming forward, put his arm round Drake's shoulder and kissed him again the men, seamen and Cimarron alike, happy to be allies, clapped each other on the back then poured out into a clearing where a great feast had been prepared by the Cimarron women.

202

The succulent aroma of roast sea-turtle soon began to mingle enticingly with the deliciously bready smell of maize cakes as a monumental banquet now ensued.

Next morning Drake awoke flushed and weak, with a high fever.
One look at him was enough for Aruba to know what had to be done.
With great care she took hold of his injured foot and slowly cleaned
the swollen, purple-flushed wound with cool sea water. Not resting
until it was clean, she began to squeeze the wound harder and harder,
until most of the evil-looking pus had been drained away, while
Drake gritted his teeth from the pain. Quite plainly still not satisfied,
and with Drake eyeing her anxiously, she took a sharp piece of iron
and with one sharp stroke widened the wound, making it bleed copi-
ously. Then she took seaweed and wrapped the foot inside the slippery, foul-smelling strands until they had soaked up all the blood.
Finally, to Drake's surprise, she went to a corner of the compound
and scooped up some ordinary red dirt and smothered it liberally
over the wound. Nodding with satisfaction, she bound the wound up
with strips taken from Drake's britches.

He lay back. Already the wound felt much calmer. Although the
ball would stay in his foot and he would always limp a little, the
wound, Drake felt, would now heal. Aruba put soft arms around his
shoulders and began kissing and nibbling him all over with her pout-
ing, sensuous mouth, so incongruously negroid against her high
cheek-bones and skin of the lightest, velvety copper.

Thus, in adulterous fornication and considerable sin, standing—
or perhaps rather, lying—in the shadow of eternal damnation,
Francis Drake, as Aruba wound her long, slimly-muscled,
pearl-diver's body around him like some clinging tropical creeper,
savagely, furiously, ecstatically, gently and also somewhat fearfully—made love.


Every three days she would inspect the wound. Meantime in between
love-making, she would bring him delicacies to eat: whole fish, tan-
gily charred in embers and served on a banana leaf; the soft white
flesh of the green lizard, which, when roasted to a turn, tasted like delicious roast chicken. Drake, as his foot healed, would limp down to
the seashore and watch her dive for pearls, going deep, then with a
watchful eye for sharks, race her lean, copper body back towards the
man she loved in a natural racing crawl, there to dry in the warmth of
the sun, while they sucked oysters still fresh in their seawater. A

dream of paradise. Few words passed between them. With true love there is no need.

No dream lasts forever, and when at last Drake could once again walk and run soundly, he told her one morning that he would soon be gone, with a party of Cimarrons and seamen, to raid the Spaniards. In her misery she took herself off to a quiet corner of the jungle and there, squatting on her haunches, burst into a flood of desperate tears. Fearing the inevitable, she had, only days before, gone to the village wise man and asked him to cast the bones. The bones did not lie, and they said that she would never see Drake again.

The cellar was gloomy and dank, the clang of leg-irons and the drone of men's voices magnified and distorted, the slightest sound echoing cavernously off the cold stone walls.

The Indian was quite naked, a river of sweat dribbling down the smooth, hairless pit of his stomach, joining an estuary of yellow liquid where he had urinated in his terrible fear and pain.

'Give him a little more,' Recalde said idly. As the gaoler took another turn on the thumbscrew, Recalde moved away and took a delicate phial from his breast pocket. He extracted the dipper, its handle exquisitely worked in rock crystal set in gold, and touched a trace of scent all along the line of his thin, hair-line moustache. Useful things these. It had been a present from the captain of a Mediterranean galley. The scent of men being tortured or whipped was well-known to have a peculiarly acrid stench.

'Repeat your story,' Recalde said curtly, as the Indian's agonised howl died away.

The native was only one of Recalde's many spies sent out to glean hard news of Drake's whereabouts. Finding nothing, he might have been tempted into invention. Hence the need for interrogation. In between his weeping and sobbing, the native tried hard to explain the strange game of bowls and quoits he had seen the Englishmen playing on the beach and now Recalde's mobile, olive face grew intent with concentration. The native had to be telling the truth. Without a doubt he had found Drake's lair.

Recalde turned to his captain of the guard. 'Now then,' he said. 'You must requisition me a fat, defenceless merchant ship, then you must stuff it, not with cargo, but with soldiers. Then we will dance her along the coast as enticingly as a young gypsy *puta* from Seville and Francis Drake will attack and be destroyed. By interrogating the prisoners that we take,' he let his teeth shine whitely in the dungeon's gloom as he inclined his head towards the weeping native, 'we shall also learn the site of the Cimarron camp and the rebels shall be duly punished.'

The captain of the guard, who knew of his commander's formidable reputation, found himself lost in admiration at the murderous skill of Recalde's planning. '*Si, mi general,*' he said softly, promoting him as much as he dare. 'It shall be done.' He turned towards the twisted, contorted body of the native spy. 'And him?'

'Release him,' Recalde said kindly. 'Such loyalty on the part of his most-catholic Majesty's subjects must always be rewarded.'

The gaolers, laughing amongst themselves, struck off the man's fetters. Stumbling up the stone steps that led out of the dungeon, the native looked dumbly at the crushed bone and mangled flesh that had once been a thumb.

Inexpressibly exciting to Drake's men hidden on both sides of the tortuous mountain trail, the clank of mule bells came clearly up from the valley below. Soon, the long *recua*, the treasure-train, would be their's for the taking. All they needed now was patience. The fabulous treasure of Peru was almost in their grasp.

As the first gleaming helmets of the Spanish cavalry guarding the convoy came into view round a steep bend, one John Pike, a famous frequenter of Stonehouse taverns, stumbled out onto the trail, whooping at the top of his voice, drunk as a lord on the Cimarron's hellish, home-brewed fire-water. Warned of the ambush, the cavalry men wheeled their horses and galloped back to the mule train. With all surprise lost, the chance of taking the treasure had completely vanished.

All this planning; the long wearisome journey; all for nothing. Tears of rage filled Drake's blue eyes. Was his run of failure and bad luck never going to end? He had a brief conference with the Cimarrons. 'We shall plunder Venta Cruz,' the chief said. Drake, having deprived them of their revenge against the mule train, had no option but to agree.

Quickly, they descended on nearby Venta Cruz in a sudden, savage attack, the Cimarrons soon rounding up the small garrison and capering happily around the soldiers as they made ready to burn them. From inside one of the larger houses, Drake caught the pitiful sound of many women screaming and wailing. Forcing the heavy bolts on the door, he saw an extraordinary sight. He had found a hospital for expectant mothers and there, huddled together, were at least ten Spanish women, all with swollen bellies and in the final stages of pregnancy.

Incredibly the light of battle faded from Drake's icy blue eyes, to be replaced by a look of amused mischief. 'Ladies,' he said, bowing low from the waist, as he dredged up his most flowery Spanish, 'such beauty in such an interesting condition, requires the pleasantest of treatment. You shall be kept safe and so shall your menfolk. *El Capitan Francisco Draque* does not make war on women.' Quickly, he sent word to Oxenham and Moone to prevent the massacre of the garrison. Remembering the kind words of this stocky little man with a brown beard and twirling moustachios, those expectant Señoras would live to perpetuate a magnificent legend: of El Draco's kindness and chivalry to all women.

Cimarron and corsair trudged the long trail home in two distinctly hostile and sullen bands, but when they reached the Cimarron village, all quarrels were promptly forgotten. For unspeakable horror awaited them.

Recalde's plan had worked perfectly. Burly John Drake, storming aboard the tubby merchant ship at the head of a raiding-party, had died with his men in a hail of arquebus and caliver fire. Recalde had managed to 'question' a few of the seamen before they breathed their last, and as a result Recalde had learned the whereabouts of the Cimarron camp. Now, as a result of Recalde's punitive action, women lay in screaming heaps around the bewildered warriors, violated, mutilated and defiled in a way that defied description.

For Aruba, however, a particularly-hideous fate had been reserved. Pegged out on the ground, close by a nest of flesh-eating ants, where her chest had been was now a cavernously gaping hole filled with a writhing mass of blood-crazed insects. Recalde had extracted a malevolently ingenious revenge on his old enemy.

Grief-stricken, Francis Drake returned to his own village, only to find the rest of his seamen lying in the final, contorted agony of the bloody flux. A foul, fetid miasma of corruption hung in the air in a thick, stale, stinking mist that defied description. Many a brave lad was already gone, eyes staring, bloody vomit drooling from his mouth as though frozen in the last agonised spasm of life. Cradled in Drake's arms, brother Joseph lay writhing as the black gates of death

206

opened before him, managing somehow to break the terrible news that brother John had already perished, blown to bits in the attack on the disguised Spanish merchantman.

Somehow the survivors stumbled away, erecting a few pitiful shelters of palmito boughs and plantain leaves to ward off the worst of the rainy season that had just begun. During this time, lashed by one drenching downpour after another, with mosquitoes rising in droves in the humid heat and man after man perishing from dysentery or yellow fever, Drake brooded, a broken man, hunched over a smoking fire, nursing a private and terrible grief, speaking to nobody.

Aruba, who had loved him, had died in terrible agony. His brothers, John and Joseph, who had trusted him, were dead also. He had failed everybody. The depression that he had experienced on leaving England, with the Queen turning against him, his wife nagging and ill, was nothing to the burden of suffering, of self-blame that now lay with unbearable weight on his bowed shoulders. Somehow he lived with his terrible misery, hugging his private grief to himself. In all this time, dirty, unwashed and a recluse, his loyal friends Moone and Oxenham watched over him, so that while the darkness of madness temporarily touched the brain of Francis Drake, there was always food and drink for their beloved commander.

In January, as the steamy, incessant rain slackened, then ceased, they had visitors: the chief of the Cimarron people at the head of a band of warriors. Tall and straight, the chief looked down his fine Castilian nose at the wreck of a man he saw before him, his grey eyes kind with understanding. He had lost only women, whereas this Englishman had lost brothers. 'Come,' he said through the interpreter Pedro. 'The rainy season is over. The treasure-trains move again. Come. We must put the past behind us.'

Drake made no answer.

'What?' the chief said sarcastically, 'is the famous Drake no longer interested in treasure? What then has happened to the greatest pirate in the world?'

At this, a slight smile touched the features of Francis Drake. Rising, he put his hand on the shoulder of the Cimarron chief, then the two men embraced closely, all previous quarrels forgotten. And behind him a bunch of desperate seamen who had given themselves up for lost, began to grin happily and exchange knowing winks. Their Captain was a well man again and this time there would be no mistakes. This time, there would be loot.

207

'Why do we go this way?' Drake asked the chief through the interpreter for the tenth time. For days now, instead of winding down through the hills to lay ambushes close to Nombre De Dios, the Cimarrons had led the way inland, taking a tortuous, switchback route, but higher, ever higher into the Cordilleras, so that Drake, suspecting treachery, had cautioned his men to be on their guard.

'There is something the chief wishes you to see,' came the answer, evasive, meaning nothing. Always the same. What was there to see that they had not already seen? Steaming jungles, full of colourful, screaming birds; great waterfalls thundering through riven rocks; waving savannah grasslands; and now, precipitous trails winding along the thickly-forested sides of high mountains. All these wonders they had gazed upon. There could be nothing else. When pressed, the chief would allow a mysterious grin to appear on his sensitive, finely-boned face, but would say nothing.

Eventually, at the summit of the ridge they had been climbing for four days, they came to a tree, by the span of its trunk bigger, higher that the others. Up—the chief motioned to Drake with his hand. There were steps cut into both sides of the vast trunk and it was obviously a landmark of some sort. Drake shrugged. 'Who wishes to try it with me?' he asked.

'I'll come with 'ee, cap'n.' John Oxenham waddled forward. Conscious of the crazy, marauding piracy with which he was consumed when the worse for liquor, Oxenham, when sober, always hastened to show his captain what a grave, respectable and thoroughly responsible man he was.

The two of them went up the trunk hand over hand, Oxenham incredibly nimble, despite the size of his beery paunch. As they approached the top, where the foliage crowned, their comrades on the ground appeared now as no more than large dots, while all around them a magnificent vista opened up, of sierras and vast, distant ranges of mountains smudged darkly against the horizon.

'Look there, cap'n,' Oxenham said. Pointing to the north, the Caribbean could be plainly seen, distinct, blue and coralline.

Drake nodded, bored. He was satiated with sightseeing and wished to get on with the serious business of extracting treasure from fat Spaniards. Peering to the south, his eye caught for a moment a distant gleam of water, no more than a vague sheen, caught by the sun and distorted by the heat from a blue into a wavering green colour. He looked again. A lake? Certainly it must be a vast one. Then by some trick of wind and temperature a window opened suddenly through the shimmering haze, magnifying for a few seconds the distant view, and he saw for the first time the great Pacific ocean, endless, enormous, boundless, stretching to Cathay, the Spice Islands, reaching to infinity, perhaps to the very edge of the world, for nobody really knew its limits. Words caught in his throat, such was his emotion. Soundlessly, he tapped Oxenham on the shoulder and pointed.

'Oh cap'n,' Oxenham breathed. 'Oh cap'n. We be the first Englishmen to gaze upon the great South Sea. We be the first. Does 'ee know that?'

Drake said nothing. He looked again, shading his eyes with a hand. A Spanish preserve. Not a man 'o war in the whole vast waste of water because none was needed. Galleons and stately treasure ships sailing placidly north with the uncountable wealth of Peru, the mines of Nicaragua, the silver mountain of Potosi. It was all there, waiting to be taken. He knew now, that this was his destiny: that all his life had been just preparation for this task that lay before him. When eventually he did speak, it was with a voice trembling from emotion. 'I pray God,' he said, 'to spare me long enough to sail an English ship on that sea.'

'Amen to that,' said Oxenham. Still shaken from the amazing sight, the two men climbed down.

No mistakes. No drunkenness. Cimarron and Englishman descended on the clanking, laden, mule-born *recua* bearing treasure to the port of Nombre de Dios with the fast, deadly accuracy of lean and hungry birds of prey. In minutes dead Spaniards and panniers full of silver and gold ingots, ripped open, lay across the track, only the mules, glad to be rid of their burden, cantering up the road until the Englishmen, needing them to carry away the vast haul of plate, caught them again.

'Thank God,' Drake breathed, his hands stroking the smooth, heavy metal. 'Thank God. Now our voyage is made.'

Clasping the chief, kissing him on both cheeks, swearing eternal friendship, it was soon time to be saying farewell. Drake took his leave of his brave Cimarron allies, knowing that his memory of Aruba would always stay locked in a corner of his mind, clinging there like the smell of sweet fragrance in a scent cupboard. The treasure, he knew, would go for defence, for some secret purpose known only to Walsingham, and no doubt he would be allowed some small percentage for his trouble. One question, therefore, burned continuously on his mind during the long voyage home. As the scapegoat, the pirate answerable to an irate and threatening Spain, how long would the Queen let him live to enjoy the proceeds?

*'The Queen had a hard time of her progress in the Wild of Kent
. . . where surely there were more dangerous rocks and valleys . . .
than in the peak.'*

Lord Burghley writing of the 1573
progress to the Earl of Shrewsbury.

*'Thence to Mr Tufton's at Hothfield, where she continued two
days and some of her courtiers were entertained at Surrenden, the
hospitable mansion of the ancient family of Dering.'*

Nichols' *Progresses of Queen
Elizabeth* for the year 1573.

*'What Mendoza bringeth is yet unknown, but men of judgment
think that the chief end to his coming is to entertain us with Spanish compliments to lull us asleep for a time until their secret prac-
tices be grown to their new and full ripeness.'*

Walsingham writing to Burghley, 13 July 1574.

# 21

On 9 April 1573, Drake dropped anchor in Plymouth Sound, and
entrusting his considerable treasure to the care of fat William Hawkins, now the Queen's governor in Plymouth, made haste back to
Stoke Gabriel.

His reunion with Mary could not be called pleasant; she had
plainly gone downhill during his fifteen months' absence and was as
thin as a shadow, her eyes dark, cavernous saucers and her face pale
and drawn. Her cough, like the dreadful croaking sound of an
injured jackdaw, would jerk him awake in the middle of the night and
keep him sweating abed through the small hours, alone with his dark,
troubled thoughts. Nor was it easy to live alongside young Thomas,
while all the time bitterly blaming himself for the deaths of John and

Joseph.

The arrival of a messenger one night, on a foaming, blown horse, had come as a relief, especially when Drake found the man bore orders for him to report to Walsingham. 'Come to Surrenden in Kent, cloaked, masked and in darkness,' the message had said: curt, blunt, almost brutal, typical of the Queen's chief intelligencer, as ready to hang a man as shake his hand. Well, Drake thought, he had been told the rules of the game and must now accept the cards as they fell.

So post haste to Surrenden, an honest house surrounded by a fine deer park and clipped yew hedges. Inside, Master Richard Dering, freckled, his nose close-veined from too close an acquaintance with hippocras and canary, could be depended on to provide a merry table groaning with fish and fowl for the entertainment of courtiers, while the Queen on her royal progress lay close by at Hothfield.

Drake was shown into a study, close-panelled in oak, private, secretly reached. Inside were Walsingham and Hatton. 'Gentlemen.' Drake executed a stiff bow.

'I congratulate you on the success of your voyage,' Walsingham said, stone-faced.

'And the Queen?' Drake said, a trace of mockery in his voice. 'Does she congratulate me also?'

'The Queen's grace,' Walsingham's voice was wary, 'must needs twist and turn to save her little kingdom.'

In the corner Hatton stirred, showing French corked slippers, elegant hose and short breeches in the latest fashion which set off pleasantly, his muscled, dancers legs. 'Francis,' he said, smiling, 'what news we have for you is not good. By the Convention of Nighmegen, signed this very spring, all differences with the Spaniards are forgotten. Next year the Spanish fleet comes to visit us and Mendoza also, to seal the bargain.'

'And me?' Drake's voice was hard. 'What shall become of me?'

'You were told what to expect,' Walsingham said brutally. 'You are a corsair, protected by no privateer's commission, with no Letters of Marque behind which you may hide. The Queen has no option but to punish you as mercifully as possible. By exile.'

Drake stood up, his ruddy face flushed with rage. 'You may do with me as you please,' he roared, 'but I remind you that good Devon lads sweated and died to bring home that treasure.'

'You shall receive a fair share of the value,' Walsingham said

212

urbanely, 'and so shall your seamen. Pirate you may be, but you shall be a rich pirate.'

Gazing at his blunt, obstinate nose, dark-jowled face, the gloomy forehead balding into a widow's peak, Drake knew Walsingham to be merciless, unscrupulous, yet not without a certain honesty. 'And the future?' he asked.

Walsingham shrugged. 'You shall go to Ireland where my lord of Essex has need of your kind. The treasure shall go to build Queen's ships.'

Once again Drake managed to ignore the insult. 'Our ships,' he replied mildly, 'will need to be much improved. Who shall design them?'

Hatton laughed, genial, unfailingly pleasant. 'That, good Francis, you shall find out for yourself. Go to Appledore in Devon and all shall be soon revealed. My personal secretary, Doughty, shall escort you there and thence to Ireland.'

Walsingham stood up. 'Come Hatton,' he said harshly. 'The Queen awaits us. You are only newly appointed captain of Her Majesty's bodyguard and you should not be seen talking too long with a pirate.'

The two men bowed and departed, leaving a furious Francis Drake. Both the Queen and Walsingham were treating him now as little more than a vagabond and a cut-throat.


On the journey, Drake found Doughty an amiable companion, sympathetic and humorous, yet such was his fury at the plain contempt in which he was now held by most of the court, including, it seemed, the Queen herself, that he did not talk much with Hatton's young secretary, preferring to keep his own company.

At Appledore, an isolated hamlet on the North Devon coast, Drake met with paralysing surprise. There, bending under the quaintly low beams of the village tavern, was a man who had always hated him and whom he had every reason to consider his chief enemy—John Hawkins.

'There are matters we must needs discuss,' Hawkins said, smiling through thin lips, his hand outstretched.

'I will not talk with you,' Drake said and turned his back.

'Stay cousin, for these are matters of moment.'

'I will stay sirrah, if you insist. But I warn you, our conversation shall be at sword point.'

Hawkins' smile grew wider. 'As to a duel, nay to that, for I have work to carry out for the Queen's grace. Instead, I make you a proposition. Only hear me out and then if you need my apology, you shall have it, gladly given.'

The two men locked eyes as they had done so many times in the past, then Drake, his voice full of suspicion, eyes blue as frost, said abruptly. 'Very well. So be it.'

'Oxenham has told me of the great South Sea that you espied from the top of a tree. I am convinced that to keep Philip of Spain from our throats, Englishmen must sail that sea to show him that the treasure route is no longer a Spanish lake. Magellan found the seas there monstrous, higher even than my four-storey house in Kinterbury Street. This task needs a mariner of great experience and with the Queen requiring my presence here to serve her to better advantage, you must go instead.'

'I am in plain disgrace with her Majesty.'

'Never mind about that,' said Hawkins grinning. 'Come over here. He beckoned Drake over to the window. There, displayed on a table, was the gleaming model of a ship. Grudges forgotten, enmities temporarily placed to one side, the two men bent over the model, their eyes gleaming as though they were little boys.

Drake ran his finger along the varnish that glistened slickly on the vessel's rakish lines. 'She is indeed handsome,' he said. 'Pray tell me, which ship is this?'

'The *Foresight*, three hundred tons. Built for the Queen by the Navy Board to my design. I trow it may be many years before another like her is built.'

'Why is that?'

'The Navy Board are fools and thieves. Fools, because sooner or later we must fight Spain and they favour unhandy, highly-charged ships, crowded with soldiers, whereas we need ships that may keep the seas for weeks at a time and if necessary, cannonade the enemy in his home ports.'

'If that makes them fools, what makes them thieves?'

'The Winters control the Navy Board.' Hawkins' face became set and grim. 'Gonson, my wife's father, knows all yet can do nothing. They are a powerful family, these Winters. For all the Navy Board builds, the Queen's grace is charged double.' He sighed. 'One day, perhaps, I will be placed in charge. I pray God it will not be too late.'

'Tell me more of this.' Drake pointed to the model, shining slickly under the dancing sunbeams of the tavern window. Disinterested in politics, he was fascinated by the strangely radical lines on which the ship appeared to have been constructed.

'Ah, 'tis plain enough that you like her,' Hawkins said, grinning. 'Built to my specification: length between keel and beam increased to a proportion of at least three to one, set low in the water with her waist decked over, the forecastle reduced and placed aft of the stem-head instead of overhanging it. As you know, the higher the ship, the more she strains and the faster her seams break apart in a tempest. I' faith, we both remember the *Jesus*.'

Drake grinned. This was a new Hawkins, differences of rank forgotten, both men united, however temporarily, by their consuming love for the sea. 'Ay,' he said. ' 'Tis true. For narrow seas she was meet enough, but for deep sea sailing—' He left the rest of the sentence unsaid.

'They will not listen,' Hawkins said, his thin lips compressing together in anger, as he tugged his pointed, reddish-coloured beard in frustration. 'Now this beauty here is fast, able to sail close to the wind and keep the sea in any weather. With the high overhang reduced to a quarter, by such an amount will the action of sea and wind also be reduced.'

Suddenly, Drake realised the direction in which Hawkins was steering the conversation. 'For me?' he exclaimed, breaking in on John Hawkins' train of thought. 'You plan that I should take her to the great South Sea?'

Hawkins grinned faintly and in answer, tapped Drake lightly on the shoulder and indicated that he should follow him. The two men went out of the tavern and walked over to the single, wooden wharf where a ship was anchored. 'There,' Hawkins said. 'There is your ship. That is what I have in mind—the *Pelican*.'

'What?' Drake said, fury rising redly to his cheeks, his voice tight with suspicion. 'Either you jest, or you still wish to kill me, for this vessel is built like a whore, fat, small and French.'

To Drake's surprise, Hawkins continued to grin. 'Yes,' he said, 'perhaps she is fat, yet will you not agree that on a long voyage, space must be found for much food and water; above all for those things in which you must be self-sufficient. Tar and oakum for careening and caulking, much powder and shot, for you will be heavily gunned, then,' Hawkins' mouth parted and he showed his small, sharp teeth in a grin of pure avarice at the thought of gold, 'you must have space for that commodity of which we are all overfond.'

'But the ship!' Drake's voice was still suspicious, fearing as he did, that his slippery cousin was playing some trick on him. 'She is plump and unweatherly, likely to sink at the first real blow.'

'Not after I've finished with her,' Hawkins said, his thin face rapt with enthusiasm, 'for I'll cut her in two and let in another piece amidships 'till she has the required proportion of three to one. Queen's timbers, Francis.' Hawkins' eyes shone at the thought. 'Three years seasoned. Gonson will get them for me. Everybody else steals from the Queen and so shall I, for good cause.'

'Can it be done?' Drake was still not sure whether Hawkins was feeding him some elaborate fairy tale.

' 'Tis cheaper, well carried out, than building anew. What's more,' Hawkins pounded a fist into his palm, quite carried away with his own plans, 'we'll deck her over to reduce the high freeboard, like the *Foresight* here.' With his head he indicated the shining little model still visible in the tavern window. 'And also, much build up her poop.'

'Build it up?' Drake exclaimed. 'Yet have you not said that all superstructure must be lowered?'

'Two special reasons for this,' Hawkins said. 'A voyage of this kind will take years, not months. You will need quarters that are not only comfortable, but roomy enough for charts, books, instruments.'

'And the other reason?'

'Far more important. I have read the reports made by the survivors of Magellan's voyage. The seas down there run bigger than anywhere in the globe, wilder than any imagination can conceive. Running before waves that are the size of mountains, you will, with a low stern, quickly be pooped and sunk. A high after-cabin will prevent this.'

Drake found himself looking at Hawkins in a new light, remembering how his cousin, with an amazing exhibition of ship-handling, had cheated the Spanish plate fleet of an anchorage in San Juan de Ullua in the teeth of a terrible storm. He had the strange, and for him unusual, feeling that he was in the presence of a man who knew more about ship-handling than he did himself, yet confronted with this tubbily-built vessel, he still had his doubts. 'Laden with stores to her gunwales, how can she be fast?' he asked.

'Why I'll give her three masts,' Hawkins said, his eyes alight. 'Not just topsails, but a high foretopmast on top of your mainmast capped

216

with a brave set of t'gallants. And that's not all. There'll be a handsome lateen on the mizzen to help you steer close to the wind and, by the mass, we'll have a fine sprits'l to belly out over her bows, just to finish off the job.'

'Carrying that much sail, the masts will be drawn out of her like bad teeth.'

'Not so, Master Drake,' Hawkins said, his face set and grim with concentrated determination, 'for I'll give you fir masts, iron-hard from facing the tempests on the north slopes of Scotland's forests, yet at the same time as light and as pliable as a whip!'

At this, Drake, convinced at last, let out a great oath. 'By the bowels of Christ, Master Hawkins,' he said. 'You are a man to be much marvelled at. That you will build such a vessel I do not doubt.' He paused, his face settling back into gloom. 'Yet when she is rebuilt, will I ever sail in her as master?'

There was tension now. Oppressive. Somehow unpleasant after the easy flow of conversation. Hawkins appeared to be in deep thought and when he finally spoke, it was plain to Drake that he had picked his words most carefully.

'The Queen favours peace,' he sighed. 'So men like Burghley and Winter are listened to, while others like us have to work in obscurity. Hatton and I will needs have to expend the best part of our fortunes if the *Pelican* is to be properly reshaped and refashioned, yet I think the day may come when the Queen's grace will realise that she has been deceived: that Philip of Spain will stop at nothing to destroy her. When that day comes, we will have her ear once again and, who knows,' his thin lips fashioned themselves into a small smile, 'you may have the *Pelican*. Now away with you, Francis, to the bogs of Ireland, 'ere you are arrested.'

Both men stared hard at each other, as they had done so many times in the past, their eyes impassively locked in a way that could have meant anything. Then Drake turned on his heel and walked away to the waiting Doughty.

'Francis Drake,' Hawkins called after him, 'you may have your apology if you still wish it.'

Drake walked all the way back and put his arms round the other man's shoulders. 'Cousin, there is no more hurt,' he said softly. 'This ship is your apology.'

At the very moment that Drake took ship for Ireland with Doughty,

Philip, the sandy-haired Spanish spider, sat at his desk in a cold monk's cabinet deep in the Escorial at the centre of a great web of Empire filamented with threads of pure gold and silver. His eyes red-rimmed, his hands aching from writing and signing, his very bones ached from the pain of the work. He would have liked nothing better than to stride over the gaunt slopes of the saw-toothed Guadarramas and feel the raw wind and spots of rain on his cheek, but that was pleasure and must be rejected. Philip, with his mobile, sensitive Hapsburg mouth, knew himself to be a sensual man given to interesting lusts, who had once demonstrated an uncontrollable penchant for pinching the soft, butter-coloured backsides of English maids-of-honour, but now there was only penance, the greenish-grey granite of the massive Escorial nearing gloomy completion, the scourge with which he must flagellate himself until he died. There remained his one mission under God, to destroy the heretic Queen and her nest of piratical Lutherans and let the sweetness of Christ rule once again over the little kingdom of England.

Awaiting Juan de Recalde's arrival, he had with his usual meticulous care prepared himself for the interview. A cold ascetic hand shot out and unerringly selected from the mass of ornately sealed papers that festooned his desk, Recalde's report. 'Sacred catholic majesty,'—quickly his trained eye skipped over the usual formalities, his mind absorbing within the space of only a few minutes the entire closely-written detail of the nobleman's activities since Philip had sent him on that important personal mission to the Spanish Main. 'Humble servant of your majesty who kisses your majesty's royal hands and feet,' the document ended. A wan smile crossed the greyness of Philip's careworn face. Recalde was an arrogant man. So arrogant that he could not be obsequious without pushing his turn of phrase to the point of mockery.

In spite of himself, the King allowed himself to be annoyed and when Recalde was shown in, refused to look up from his papers and acknowledge him until Recalde had been forced to stay respectfully on his knees for at least a minute. Eventually he gave him permission to be seated, then said abruptly, 'Recalde, I am more than displeased. You failed to destroy Hawkins or Drake or any of the pirate leaders. Furthermore, I have just learned that considerable treasure was looted from a *recua* at Nombre de Dios. You have disappointed me.'

Philip, who had expected to see anxiety and contrition before

218

allowing his subject to bask in the balm of his forgiveness, was disappointed. Recalde's olive face remained expressionless, imperturbable. Others would have made excuses or abased themselves by admitting their failures, but Recalde knew he had done well in his stay on the Spanish Main and his silence was his way of letting the King know.

'But,' Philip went on, aware that the interview was not going precisely as he had intended, 'there are certain saving features. Not everything is bad. You did have Hawkins' fleet dealt with at San Juan de Ullua, not without considerable cost to our purse in ships of the line, and two of the pirate Draco's brothers lie dead. Furthermore, it is plain that you have much improved our defences over there and you cannot be completely blamed for the loss of the treasure-train since you were on the high seas when it was taken.'

Others would have eagerly snatched such crumbs from their master's table, but the statement had not required an answer and Recalde had merely given the faintest inclination of his head by way of thanks. Yes, Philip thought, there is arrogance there. The man is as dangerous as the corsair Draco who racks and flays my dominions. For that reason, I must use him well, use him to Spain's advantage.

'What,' Philip asked the nobleman, 'is the prospect of peace between Spain and England, in your opinion?'

'None at all, your majesty. In the end, we must fight.'

'Exactly. We must destroy England. Yet the Queen has fools for ministers who do not realise this and I intend to encourage them in their delusions. Mendoza goes soon to woo the Queen with gestures of friendship and my ships will pay England a visit shortly afterwards. One day, Recalde, they will wake up over there, and it will be too late. In the meantime there is much work for you to do.'

'I am your majesty's loyal servant to command.'

'Recalde, you have commanded the Biscayan squadron. You know about ship-handling in the grey northern seas. Also you have seen service with the Indian guard. Build me a great fleet that will smash the heretics. Take charge for me, of the royal dockyards.'

The slight smile that had rested on the olive mask of Recalde's face disappeared abruptly. 'The dockyards? You wish me to run your—' he paused, almost spitting the words out '—your dockyards?'

'Just for a year or two Recalde. You are the only man in the kingdom with the ability and drive to get things done.'

219

'That is true. And afterwards?'

For a moment anger flared in the King's face, then he rubbed his tired eyes with the knuckles of his hand to hide his emotions. The man's vanity was almost as bad as his insufferable self-confidence. It was true: there was no one else in the kingdom with the steel to take on El Draco. 'Afterwards,' he said thoughtfully, 'perhaps in two years or so, when you have done your work, I will give you a task nearer your heart. You can land volunteers in Ireland to drain Elizabeth's strength. You can reconnoitre the English Channel.' He leant forward, his wan face slack from fatigue and waxy from lack of sun and air, gaining momentary colour as hatred for the heretic, she-devil, English Queen built in his red-rimmed eyes. 'Oh yes, Recalde. One day I will invade England and you shall have your chance to settle scores with Drake. Now then, will you undertake this task?'

'On those terms, your majesty, I will.'

With the audience over, Recalde bowed his slim figure out backwards from the cold, white-washed, monastic cell, content showing in his eyes. He knew his King to be as treacherous as a two-headed snake, but could not see why the King should ever want to cheat him of his chance to sail against Drake in one final, climactic battle.

Philip watched him go. He had, he felt, handled Recalde in just the right way, even if he had needed to lie a little. For when the time was ripe, the Queen, he had been assured, would yield up the corsair in exchange for rights to trade and only then, after El Draco's body had fried in the flames of the Inquisition and the Queen had been duly deprived of his formidable services, would he launch his Armada and sweep the whole blaspheming pack of Lutherans to hellish ruin.

Philip the spider, pleased with his work, bent wearily back to spinning his web. There was silence now, except for the murmur of the incessant mountain wind fusing with the distant, dolorous chantings of a band of Hieronymite monks that he had lodged in the Escorial as an act of piety. The sound of their plainsong reminded him that he must soon go and take confession for telling Recalde that lie.

# 22

Ireland: a land of woods and bogs and green melancholy, of poor cattle and starving peasants ruled with iron, medieval ferocity by the Desmonds, the O'Neills, the O'Donnells; a land where seldom has the harp sung sweeter or treachery and cruelty been more foul and no one ever knew who started it, except the English were colonists and so must take the blame. Commanding a roving squadron of ships from a base on the Cork coast, doing bloody work better done against the richly-fed Don than the half-famished churls of whichever chief happened now to be in rebellion against the Queen's grace, hating the massacre and the rain and the cold, a special Irish kind of sadness descended on the once ruddy face of Francis Drake.

The very absence of those he had known and loved were reminders of the past. His brothers, burly, bull-necked John, silent Joseph, whose sword had always spoken better than his stammer: both of them had trusted him and now they were gone. Chamberlain, who'd stood shoulder to shoulder with him on the blood-soaked deck of the *Judith*, dead of the bloody flux. Higgins, only a little lad, stretched out, trumpet in hand, stiff as a board in the marketplace of Nombre de Dios. And Aruba, steeped in the innocent purity of original sin, hideously tortured to death. Every time the arquebus ball still lodged in his leg twinged under the incessant Irish rain, he would remember the fragrance of her breath, the satin of her touch. All gone. All of them gone. Everywhere weeping, mourning mothers and wives and only Francis Drake left, with nothing to show for it except the pain deep in his eyes and the reputation of a filthy, murdering pirate no longer fit for the gentle company of court.

No sense in continuing to live; he had resolved to finish it. Get it over. Go down fighting with a sword in his hand and an oath on his lips, yet one man, truly a special kind of fellow, saved him. Thomas Doughty: all things to all men, encased in a saintly face with slender flying buttresses for bones and fan-vaulted eyes, hollow and glowing, that showed the depth of his soul beneath a high, intellectual forehead. A man who spoke with the Queen's drawl and who, with a gentleman's ease of manner, could roister with all men and drink the potent poteen without losing his wits then quote a sonnet or two or declaim a poem in Greek or Hebrew to the confoundment of his companions. Certainly Doughty saved him, a jest on his mobile and articulate lips, sympathy in his deep brown eyes. No fancy boy this: he could fight too, his swordplay an Italianate, decadent thing, true, but his rapier no less effective. Doughty, an Englishman to his fingertips, as Renaissance as Michaelangelo; Doughty who had done the Grand Tour, who knew everyone and nearly everything, saved Francis Drake from squelching out to a lonely peat bog and for the sake of peace of mind, offering his body to the iron broadswords of hairy Gallowglasses still clad in mantles made from the skin of wild beasts.

And kindness, my masters. What kindness! Knowing how Drake worried over his poor, ailing, coughing, skeletal wife Mary, did not Doughty, in the course of travelling back and forth to court, find the time to remove her to a splendid new house in Looe Street, Plymouth, opposite the Guildhall, with two hearty servants to minister to her needs, trusting Drake to pay him back from his secret funds?

Over a roaring fire lit to stay the incessant Irish damp, there was always music. 'Be Peace. Ye Make Me Spill My Ale' they would sing, a merry partsong straight from the court of old King Harry himself.

222

Then with much tuning and plucking of gut and string, have at everything, with a mighty howl of sackbut, cornet, viol, cittern and bandora played by their comrades, from Tallis to the beautiful early motets of William Byrd.

Every time Doughty came back from court and told Drake, much sorrowing, that the Queen would still not have him home, he brought books. For Drake, with his fund of tales of distant seas, had quickly infected Doughty with the same irresistible urge to go deep-sea voyaging. Accordingly, his face alive with fascination, Doughty would dive into such tomes as *Le Voyage et Navigation faict par les Espanolz ec isles de Mollucques*, the earliest account of Magellan's voyage to the great South Sea, and with his insatiably curious young mind, have Drake explain once more the possibility of some Englishman repeating that memorable voyage one day.

At such moments, the gloom would leave Drake's face and his blue eyes would come alive as he told again and again of the time he had climbed that tall tree in Panama and seen for the first time the vast, endless ocean stretching away to Cathay and China. No one knew how far, he told Doughty, one would have to travel before sighting land. To the west and the south there were fabulous lands still unexplored. To balance the weight of the northern continents, a huge land mass, *Terra Australis*, must lie deep in the southern hemisphere beyond those terrible, stormy seas. No one had charts of these areas of the globe, he said. One would be sailing in unknown waters at the mercy of unknown winds, but what glory, what prestige, awaited the man bold enough to undertake such an intrepid voyage of exploration and discover these incredible lands for the benefit of Queen and country.

For a change had taken place deep in the soul of Francis Drake. Piracy was all very well for a young man, but a man must mature and there was more to life than leaping into the rigging of a fat treasure-ship with a knife in your hand and an oath on your lips. Never had he doubted that he had been born for fame and great things. Had he not remarkable qualities of leadership and a special knowledge of the sea and ships? Yes, in his own deepest thoughts, a truly great man is never modest with himself. Drake knew that destiny had prepared a great task for him: to sail where no Englishman had ever sailed; to force open the tightly-locked back door of the rich Spanish Empire; to explore that other half of the globe, still unexplored; a fabulously dangerous exercise in geography and ship navigation. The last great adventure into the unknown that man must take, my masters, until he takes wing and leaps to other planets? Yes. Truly that hazardous. Truly that important.

But how? He was a mere pirate, reduced to being one of Walsingham's murderous, secretive cut-throats, his life literally hanging on a single string that the Queen might snip at any moment. How then, to swim back into Gloriana's favour? Patronage in itself was not enough. Something, some power over her beyond the normal ken of man, was needed. Witchcraft? His stout Lutheran soul shrank from the word. Quickly, he reached for Foxe's *Book of Martyrs* to purge such un-Godly thoughts and then, as it happened, seeing his good comrade Doughty flicking endlessly through a rustling succession of parchmented notes, asked him what it was.

'Why 'tis the latest of many books written on navigation and the problem of establishing longitude, written by a most learned fellow. 'Twill shortly be published, and being a good friend of mine and knowing my interest, he has allowed me a sight of his notes.'

'What then, is its title pray?' Drake was mildly interested.

Doughty flicked back to the very first page. 'He calls it *Queen Elizabeth and her Arithmeticall Tables Gabernatick: for Navigation by the Paradoxicall Compass and Navigation in Great Circles.* 'Tis a fine sounding title, do you not think, Francis? I would have you read it one day.'

'I would read it gladly, Tom,' Drake yawned, the flickering firelight pressing heavily on his eyelids. 'Will you tell me the name of the man who wrote it?'

'Doctor Dee of Mortlake.'

Drake's chair crashed back against the wall as he surged to his feet. He could feel the shock of the name coursing down his shoulders, his arms, pulsating through his whole stocky, sturdy body. It was as if the Almighty had sent a blinding bolt of lightning clean through him. 'S'death,' he swore. 'By the faith.' He pounded a fist into the open palm of his other hand. 'He is the man to do it. Dee is the man. Dee will get me back to England and into the Queen's good graces.' He paused, his blue eyes shining the way they had shone and sparkled in the old days long ago, when he had been a young lad adventuring for the first time beyond the mud flats of the Medway estuary. 'And by the Mass,' he swore again, 'he'll send us off to circle the globe as well!'

224

'How dare he plump me like that,' the Queen spat. To relieve her feelings she dealt a powerful buffet to the maid-of-honour unfortunate enough to be placing a dish of freshly-baked manchet bread in front of her. Smacking the girl, little more than a child, who only hours before had dared to ask for permission to marry, made the Queen feel marginally better. As the maid-of-honour skittered sobbing from the chamber, the Queen looked once again at the portrait. Yes, that fiend Zuccaro had put so much flesh on her bones that she looked like a fat capon, ready to be plucked. An allegory, he had said. She had submitted to wearing the amply-cut russet gown with those ridiculous, gauze butterfly wings held in place behind her neck by some extraordinary arrangement of steel setting sticks and now, in a riot of artistic madness, he had painted eyes and ears all over her gown, a snake on her arm and all the wild flowers of England on her underrobe. The man must be a complete madman.

Very well—eyes and ears of England. She could understand that, yet to paint her as earth, the mother of all good things, with the ripe, plump body of a fertility symbol, was a liberty for which the fellow would shortly suffer the venemous lash of her tongue. For deep down, under her mask of conceit, the Queen was a realist: she knew herself to be a thin-fleshed woman, the slenderness of youth turning in middle-age to mere gauntness; her mouth, once so deliciously sensitive, settling into a dark line of obstinacy; the sculptured tracery of her high-bridged nose marbling under the weight of years into the curved beak of a bird of prey. Yet with the right skills, she could still look magnificent: a white cosmetic overlay to her skin, scented oils for her hands, a dab of benjamin and sweet marjoram cleverly combined to make a subtle, thrilling perfume and a touch of lye to soften the first tints of grey in her flaming red hair.

In riding habit, a cape and cloak of black silver tinsel lined with plush to keep out the keen March wind, she strode down the courtyard at Richmond Palace and hoisted herself athletically onto her favourite gelding. A state visit to Dr Dee. Why not? He was the most learned man in the kingdom and lately he had been nagging her for an urgent audience.

So to Mortlake with all the thundering, colourful, splendid trappings of a progress. The crowd rapturous, adoring, as the Queen, disdained all safety precautions despite the Pope making her assassination an act of piety.

'I thank you, good people,' she said in a high voice, nodding, inclining her head, smiling, always smiling. Rapport between Queen and subject, unbelievable.

Leicester lifted her off her horse. Getting plump, red-faced and bald, she thought. Better send him to Buxton to take the waters, but not before the fantastic entertainment it was rumoured he was preparing for her at Kenilworth in the coming summer.

Dee was standing there, his face sad. 'Your majesty. My wife is dead these four hours.'

'Then we must not come inside and intrude on your grief. Fetch us out instead your famous magic speculum, concerning which we have heard much.'

When Dee brought out the mirror, the Queen examined its highly-polished, coal-black surface with great care. She asked, 'Does this have all those powerful qualities that we have been told of?'

''Tis but an aid to my art,' Dee said diplomatically.

'We shall not tarry,' the Queen said, changing the subject. 'Dee, you must bear the death of your wife patiently. In time, all things heal. You will find that is truly so.'

'I thank your grace.'

'Now what is it on which you wish to have such urgent audience?'

'In short, it is this, your grace. After many years of calculations both astrological and mathematical, I most heartily recommend the advisability of a great voyage of discovery to the Southern Sea and beyond, by your majesty's explorers.'

The Queen laughed scornfully. 'We have no explorers,' she said. 'Only pirates. Now we are a friend, once again, of the King of Spain, we need them not.'

'I beseech your majesty to hear me fully. I most humbly beg your grace to consider such a matter most carefully.'

Elizabeth looked closely at her old friend. There was an urgency in his face that she had never seen before. Besides, with his wife lying stiff and cold in his bed, she felt the need to indulge him. 'Well then,' she said. 'Present us a report. Place in it all your "whys", all your "wherefors", and then one day, when you are ready, we shall debate the matter fully in Council.'

'Will your majesty grant me leave to assemble those whom I consider to be valuable witnesses?'

The Queen, whose mind was elsewhere, managed to miss, strangely for her, the whole, loaded point of the question. 'You have leave,' she said, smiling graciously, 'to bring whosoever you wish.'

So March time and quickly up river by barge to Greenwich for the ceremony of Royal Maundy. What a shuffling of towels and clanking of silver basins, what a praying by the chaplain, a frenzied whispering of instructions echoing off the rafters of the draughty hall, as forty-one poor people (one for each year of the Queen's age) took off their filthy, vermin-ridden boots and made ready for the washing of their feet. These feet, it seems, must first be washed by the yeomen of the laundry, then by the sub-almoner, then scented with sweet herbs by the almoner, before being fit for her majesty's slim white fingers. Yet kneeling on her cushion of state, surrounded by victuals and red-leather purses to be distributed to the poor, the Queen, caught in the freezing draught, is fast perishing from cold.

'Away with you,' she shouted with a great oath, losing all patience. 'By the bowels of Christ, if such feet were clean enough for the disciples, then so they are for a Queen of England.' So there and then she washed them all, down on her knees like any scrubwoman, trying not to wrinkle her over-sensitive nose at the acrid, putrid, cheesy, sweaty stink, secure and warm in the love of her common people.

For this year there was no time for fuss and pedantry. Now she must go and sit, as a tender old friend, by the sickbed of the Countess of Pembroke; and then away to Theobalds to confer with Burghley, temporarily immobile with gout; then forget all care and let matters of state go temporarily to hang, because her own sweet Robin was preparing this summer an entertainment, a pageant, a frolic, just for her, of truly awesome and breathtaking proportions.

Kenilworth. Nineteen days of madness, nothing less. Mountains of rich food. Oceans of sweet sack. Three hundred and twenty hogsheads of ordinary beer alone. Think of it. Just imagine the surfeit, the maids swooning out of their senses in the musky, sun-scented clover and hot young courtiers in flat, soft, slanting caps with downy feathers bursting over their ears and roving hands sliding around white bosoms or under galligascons to caress a treasure-house of fleshy, silky nether stocks.

And the fireworks sparking and whizzing, the marble fountains playing, the pageants, the masques, the birds humming, the music thrumming. A revel such as old England had never seen and would not see again. The Queen, caught in time by a perceptive courtier's line sketch, picnicking after the hunt, wearing a stiff bodice with high neck, long, tight sleeves and speading skirt, small brimmed hat with a plume to one side, young again while sweet Robin serves cold game and wine from a spreading table-cloth.

Yet the Queen must beware. Characters are everywhere, capering in woods or floating in lakes, waiting to adore her, for it is well-known that this is a Queen who likes to be adored. On her way home, Sylvanus, God of the Woods, springs from a tree with such passion that the Queen's horse rears in terror, yet Elizabeth, a magnificent horsewoman, effortlessly controls the maddened beast, a smile never leaving that pale, high-boned, glittering face, saying over and over again, 'No hurt, no hurt.'

What else from the chronicles of this amazing progress? Arion, riding a giant dolphin in the lake, preparing to address the Queen then entirely losing his nerve and explaining that he is not Arion at all, but 'plain, honest Harry Goldingham'. And the Queen throwing back her head and laughing as she has never laughed before. Not enough? You want more? Then here is the Lady of the Lake, announcing 'Your grace you are welcome to my lake.' And the Queen replying with mischievous glee, 'Well, we had thought it our lake, but will commune with you further on this, hereafter.'

On through those hot July days of long ago, the bear-baitings, the tumblers, the walks through twittering aviaries and pleasure grounds heavy with the smell of flowers and juicy strawberries; the Queen, the central, flawless diamond flashing in the golden sunbeams of a perfect English summer evening, the dust of jewels in her red hair as she leaps high in the galliard with sweet Robin of Leicester clad in doublet and jerkin of white velvet embroidered all over with silver and seed pearl. Robin, red-faced and puffing a little, yet still magnificent with the azure garter, the highest accolade a loving Queen can give, tied round a shapely knee.

On then to more rustic entertainments, for all this is not just for fops of courtiers with Marquis Otto beards and so much perfumed hair along their cheeks that they resemble a gaggle of bowelled hens. To the quintain then. A fine and devilish thing, this; and the Queen will be watching, never doubt. Think of a post fixed in the ground with a cross-bar turning upon a pivot or spindle, having a broad board at one end and a heavy bag of sand suspended at the other. One man comes in too fast and misses the board altogether, to a great round of jeers. Another comes in slowly in a cloddish, plodding sort of gallop on his old stallion, spear stretched out straight and accurately aimed, until the stallion flicks his great cod at a nearby mare and veers off with a shrill neigh, leaving his master to bite the dust. What drunken laughter, what beery, boozy carousal! Here's the next man, a stout fellow, red-faced, ruddy-cheeked. What's this? He must be well into his thirties and he's dressed as a page. Well that's a bit of a joke! Here he comes in his side-gown of Kendal Green, tight at the neck with a narrow gorget and secured all around with a red Cadiz girdle. Some sight this, the varlet full of beer up to his bright blue eyes, thundering down on fat dobbin, his borrowed cart-horse, a voice full of oaths and not going to quit either, as his spear hits the board good and true and round comes the bag of sand to smite him with a great whack on the back of the neck and catapult him from the saddle.

And the Queen's laughter turning sour as she examines this drunken fellow further in his page's fancy dress. Well, by Christ's bones, she thought, here is a funny thing. This fool is the very image of Francis Drake, but that cannot be, for Drake is in Ireland hiding from my wrath.

That night, told by her secretary of the plan by Dr Dee to send an expedition to the great South Sea, due to be on the agenda for the great Council meeting next day, she thought once again and in a flash of sudden, angered perception knew the truth. Drake had returned to trouble her fevered emotions.

So Dee had taken advantage of her generosity in allowing him to bring any witness he pleased and called Francis Drake back from exile. Well this time, she would not allow herself to be swayed by Dee's wizardry and skill in the occult. Fury was a stronger emotion.

The great hall of Kenilworth, gorgeously hung with the richest silken tapestry, at one end the state canopy erected over the royal throne where the Queen sat in Council. Beneath her, counsellors and ministers grouped together at a horseshoe of oak, the whole scene brilliantly illuminated by a superb gilt bronze chandelier hanging from the highly-carved oaken roof in the shape of a spread eagle, from which twenty-four torches of wax guttered and glittered. Sitting there, the Queen's counsellors glanced nervously at each other. Previously as sweet as honey, the Queen was today plainly out of sorts, her mouth pinched and tight, her dark, knowing eyes sour. Her comments, they knew, would be vitriolic, penetrating, merciless and very probably alternating with womanly hysteria.

'Well,' she said curtly. 'Let us start. Send in Dee.'

Dr Dee, shown in, was, after the usual effusive obeisances to the Queen, permitted to sit down, a solemn and learned-looking man with white beard and black skull cap.

'If we remember, Dee,' the Queen came incisively to the point, 'you have advised us that omens for a voyage to the great South Sea are unusually propitious. State then, why this should be the case.'

Dee was not going to be caught that way: surrounded by the hard, pragmatic, puritan, politician faces of the Council, this was no time to argue a case with the aid of necromancy or astrology. He lost no time in shifting to firmer ground. 'Although,' he said, indicating his strange, flapping gown, 'I speak to your grace in the clothes of a seer, I shall use the language of a navigator.'

'Yes?' The Queen waited, narrow-eyed.

'Your grace will be aware that for many years a sea-route has been sought to Cathay and the Spice Islands. Without spice for our winter food, we must all perish. Yet why is the price of this commodity literally worth its weight in gold? Because both routes of supply are unreliable and dangerous, the overland journey passing through hostile kingdoms, the sea voyage round the Cape of Africa, a jealously-guarded monopoly of the King of Portugal.'

'We are aware of all this,' the Queen snapped. 'Pray continue, good Doctor.'

'In my opinion, there is no north west passage through the Straits of Anyan, nor any easterly route through the icy seas north of Muscovy. There is, however, one way that is definitely proved. Over fifty years ago, Magellan passed successfully around the Americas into the Great Southern Sea. Performed once, why should not such a voyage now be repeated?'

'But the seas beyond are unknown,' Leicester exclaimed. 'What purpose to round the Americas if only to perish from hunger and thirst in a vast, unnavigated ocean?'

'Your grace,' Dee persisted. 'My Lord of Leicester's point is well enough made, but I beg you to consider further. Should your ships succeed in crossing this unknown ocean in the opposite direction, they would bring back a fortune in spices. Think also of the future trade that may be opened up with the unknown kingdoms lying on the west coast of the Americas, not to mention the vast lands known to lie south of Magellan's strait.'

'Magellan's notes tell us nothing of it,' the Queen said shrewdly. Something like a sigh went round the Council. Elizabeth, as usual, had been doing her homework.

'Oh, there is no doubt at all that such a continent exists,' Dee said pompously. 'My calculations prove quite conclusively that without the land of *Terra Australis*, the southern hemisphere would not balance with the northern: and that, of course, is an impossibility.'

There was silence while Queen and Council brooded. The word of a man as learned and famous as Doctor Dee was not to be taken lightly. The Queen's flag, planted on this enormous and unknown continent, would bring great wealth and prestige to all of them.

Burghley judged it high time to intervene. 'I would like to ask some questions, if your grace permits,' he said, 'on matters of ships and seamanship.'

All eyes turned to gaze on the immensely influential figure of the Queen's chief minister. As usual, he was dressed in black, although discreet gold buttons marched modestly down his robe and the hint, the merest hint, of ruffed, starched lace peeped whitely from sleeve and collar. His face, gaunt from the pain of re-occurring gout, seemed strangely stern, unusually compromising.

'By all means,' the Queen purred. 'Let us consult someone skilled in these arts. Who is waiting without?'

'Chiefly, there is Hawkins,' Walsingham said. Although his dark face was expressionless, he was relying heavily on the persuasive and much-respected Hawkins to wring from the Queen her consent to the voyage.

'Have him brought in, then,' the Queen said testily. 'Let us see him.'

John Hawkins entered, beard pomaded and waxed to a stiff point over the high, lacy, starched convolutions of his great ruff. Receiving permission from a thin, pointed, white finger, he sat.

'Now, Master Hawkins,' Burghley said, 'Magellan's voyage was a plain disaster, was it not?'

'A sailor would call it a success.'

'Indeed. Then pray tell her Grace how many men embarked and how many returned.'

'Two hundred and eighty men set out, your majesty. Of these, only thirty or so returned.'

'Did not Magellan himself perish?' The Queen leant forward.

'Yes, your grace.'

'And I ask you,' Burghley was as persistent as a ban-dog with a baited bruin, 'why has this voyage not been repeated in fifty years?'

231

'The dangers are enormous. The winds rising to colossal strength, the seas in these waters running to a height beyond belief.'

'Then, John Hawkins, why should you wish the voyage repeated?'

Hawkins compressed thin lips in thought before answering. 'My colleagues and I are merchants, wishing to enrich both Queen and subject with fresh ventures in trade. That has always been the way of it. Under my supervision, with my advice, such a voyage offers a chance of huge return on capital.'

Burghley eyed the thin-lipped, rat-faced Hawkins gently. Realising the man was competent down to his fingertips, Burghley, a little way back, had baited a nice little trap for him with more than his usual subtlety. Now, he was almost ready to spring it.

'Let us return to Magellan's voyage. You say it was a success?'

'That is so.'

'Why?'

'Because,' Hawkins said, 'it opened up the whole western coast for Spanish trade and colonisation. From thence forward—'

'Exactly!' Burghley cut in, his voice as crisp as a cracked whip, stern, accusing. 'That is exactly correct. So you may not trade there at all, may you, Master Hawkins? For it is all territory under the sovereignty of King Philip of Spain, is it not?'

'Sovereignty? That is a much over-used word, my lord.' Hawkins bared his rodent's teeth in fury at the way he had been caught. 'Do the Portingales control the whole length of Africa's coast? The argument is the same: both coasts equally vast. I do not remember such argument being employed when slaving brought in badly-needed revenue for the Queen's grace.'

There was a hiss of expelled breath. This was a direct challenge to the Queen. Elizabeth leant forward, thin, pencil-sharp, her whole bejewelled, ornately angular figure loaded with pointed menace. 'Have a care, Master Hawkins. We know how exceeding well you do love us, but have a care, for you go too far.'

Hawkins fell to his knees. He said, with an expressive sweep of his arm, 'I would willingly die for your grace.'

'Very well then. Enough of that. All of us do get overheated. Tell us then.' The Queen's whole manner had become, to those who knew the supple cunning of her mind, dangerously calm. 'Pray tell us, good Master Hawkins, which mariner do you have in mind to command such voyage?'

Hawkins set his mouth into a firm, thin line of resolve. What he was about to say, he knew, would be greeted with as much shocked consternation as if he had just smashed his fist clean through one of the priceless early stained-glass windows in Westminster Abbey.

'Francis Drake,' he replied. 'Your grace. There is no other mariner in your majesty's realm who has the slightest chance of succeeding.'

Francis Drake paced outside the Great Hall at Kenilworth, walking impatiently up and down under the suspicious gaze of Robert Laneham, official porter to the Council. He was not feeling too well, his normally clear blue eyes strangely bloodshot, his tongue as thickly furred as a monkey. It had all started when he had travelled up to Kenilworth with his old comrade John Oxenham and the trusty Doughty, who had brought the great news to him back in Ireland that Dr Dee had procured his return to England to give evidence before the Queen's Council concerning a possible voyage to the great South Sea.

As the drunken celebrations grew wilder and wilder, Doughty had nervously watched the two men, knowing the piracy that lay only an inch deep under Oxenham's grave exterior and the steely quirks of Drake's character which could never refuse a challenge. Doughty's fears were well-founded; bored with watching the tumblers twisting aimlessly about, their bodies as boneless as lampreys, they had moved to watch the Cornish wrestling that was taking place nearby. In no time at all, Oxenham grave and immensely respectable, had quaffed a large flagon of old ale, then following it up with several more, was soon stripped down to his britches, his beery paunch hanging pendulously over his belt, as he roared out 'Come on me old hearties, us 'll show 'ee how this be done on old Dartymoor.'

Drake, resigned to the inevitable turn that events were taking, and no longer restrained by the need to set an example of good ship's discipline on board his own vessel, had himself seized a large horn of ale and the two of them now stood side by side, flexing their muscles, looking forward to a first-class fight.

Doughty had stalked off, shaking his head, only too aware of how the afternoon would develop now that the beer had started flowing. The next thing he knew was when a great cart-horse had lumbered down on the quintain with Francis Drake, dressed now in the absurd velvets of a pageboy from some strange drunken quirk the celebrations had taken, obviously well the worse for liquor, receiving a resounding thump on the back of his neck that had sent him hurtling from his horse under the astonished and incredulous gaze of the Queen.

As Drake walked, wondering whether he would be allowed inside the Great Hall, he gingerly felt the bump on the back of his head. It was the size of a plover's egg and had given him a splitting headache. He felt distinctly out of sorts and if the truth were told, thoroughly bad-tempered. Giving way to impatience, he strode suddenly over to the doors of the chamber, stooped and peeked through the keyhole.

'Well, what's this then?' Laneham had a shrill, self-satisfied voice, smug like all petty officials who find themselves, by reason of their job, rubbing shoulders with the highest in the land. He placed a hand on Drake's muscular shoulder and rudely wrenched him back from the keyhole. 'I'll have none of that, d'you hear? Robert Laneham will have no priers-in at the chinks or at the lockhole.'

'Stuff a cow's turd up thy weaselly chops,' Drake roared. 'How darest thou lay a hand on the person of Francis Drake?' His hand flew to the rapier caught at his waist.

Laneham, game as a rooster, was not frightened. 'Now sit thee down straightaway on a form or a chest,' he commanded. 'Try that once again, and Master Drake or Master Duck, I'll be at the bones of you, I warrant it.'

At this enormous rudery, Drake's eyes bulged with rage. How dare this fellow, he thought, with his long cock's feather stuck in his velvet bonnet, his crimson doublet all pinked and slashed, his ruff elongated to absurd lengths, put on such airs? With one move he picked up the thin, acid frame of Laneham and held him effortlessly at arm's length, gobbling like a scrawny chicken ready to have its neck rung for the pot. 'Hark to this, porter,' Drake roared. 'I have it in mind to hold thee here dangling, while I teach thee some respect, for I still have one hand free to smite thee.'

'Put him down.' The girl's voice was pure, commanding, crystal clear.

Drake turned, releasing the shaken Laneham in astonishment. Although still shaking with rage, he had to laugh at what he saw. Standing before him was a slim, tall child, clear-skinned, slightly freckled, wearing a dress of peacock brocade, a demure heart-shaped cap sitting neatly on a young head. ''Tis indeed a strange day,' he growled, 'when Francis Drake takes orders first from a porter and then a child of ten.'

The girl stamped her foot, her face pinking with indignation. 'I am

234

twelve years old this Michaelmas, I'll thank you to know.'

'Out of my way then, for I mean to see the Queen and no whey-faced porter or silly young maiden is going to stop me.'

'Your piracies are well enough known here, sirrah. I pray you not to visit them on the Queen's person.'

Drake, who had reached the doors of the Great Hall, found himself halted in his tracks as though tied to the end of a stout rope. The girl was little more than a child, yet her tone held real authority as though accustomed to many fawning servants and retainers. When he turned again to examine the girl more closely, he found his gaze held by the clearest of challenging grey eyes and noted with pleasure the smooth purity of her skin, as clear and fresh as the streams cascading off the Devon tors in a springtime sun.

'Well now,' he roared, hands on hips, 'we seem to have a devilish proud maiden here. Be off with you, for where I come from, a young lady's stern is as swiftly paddled as a lad's.'

'Oh yes.' Her gaze withered him in its fierce contempt. 'You would do that, would you? Where then is the truth in all these legends we hear of the chivalry of the famous Francis Drake towards women?'

'Woman?' Drake shook with laughter. 'Well, you have the scold's voice of any wife, I'll warrant that.'

'Sir.' The girl's face flushed hot with anger. 'I advise you to treat me civilly, for I am tutored here so that I may shortly take my place as maid-of-honour to the Queen's grace.'

Drake, who had been secretly flattered by the fact that the girl plainly knew of him and his reputation, found himself examining the girl more closely. She must, he decided, be of noble birth, landed gentry at least, and showed signs of becoming a sensational beauty, with her skin freckled as the morning dew, her breasts swelling like tiny rosebuds in the gently creasing brocade of her dress. He was careful, however, not to allow his admiration of the child show either by voice or glance. 'Well then,' he said roughly, 'since you are on such close terms with her majesty, slip you then into the Council chamber and tell me how my stock stands in there. I doubt Master Laneham here, will try to interfere.'

The girl nodded and without further ado slipped quietly through the doors of the Great Hall. In minutes, she was out again, eyeing Drake queerly.

'What news?' Drake asked.

The girl bit her lip, plainly embarrassed, then blurted out with a

235

rush, 'The Queen says you are nothing but a great pirate and shall go nowhere except, with her mercy, back to your mewing, spewing peasant of a wife.'

They held each other's glance, the girl's face tip-tilted inscrutably in the fashion of the court, towards Drake's round, tanned, redness. 'By the faith,' Drake said softly. 'I mean to sail that Southern Sea and no one shall stop me.'

'Do not despair,' the girl said with the precise wisdom of a child trying to assume the poise of an adult, 'for women are much known for changing their mind and the Queen more than most.'

Drake managed a faint smile. The girl, he had to admit to himself, pleased him strangely. Contrasting her lissom, clear-skinned beauty, her obvious breeding, with the spindly, ailing, whining fishwife to whom he must now return, he could not help sighing, a loud, distressed sound that rose deep from inside his broad chest. 'Young lady,' he said, 'I am in your debt.' Bowing, he walked heavily away.

Elizabeth Sydenham, for that was her name, felt tears of sympathy sting her eyes as she watched him go. She had long known the legend of the flamboyant, freebooting, chivalrous Francis Drake, and hated to see such a lusty pirate so tamed and put down at the hands of shrewish women. Why does the Queen hate him so, she wondered.

*'Our prisons are festered and filled with able men to serve their country which for small robberies are daily hanged, even twenty at a clap out of one gaol.'*

Hakluyt (Chronicler of Elizabethan
voyages).

# 23

The Council, realising for the first time the depths of the Queen's hatred for Francis Drake, sat in amazed silence. Here, they sensed, was a matter not open to intelligent debate, but a womanly emotion in which they would be well advised not to dabble. Only Hawkins, who feared nobody, had the courage to speak at all. 'Then,' he said, 'since your grace shall not send Drake, who shall go?'

'Well, there is Grenville,' the Queen said smugly, 'but 'tis only months since we refused him permission to make this same voyage for fear of offending the Spaniards. No, he is a pirate. So we shall send Frobisher instead.'

'Frobisher?' Hawkins said in astonishment. 'But he's as much a pirate as the others.'

'And for that reason may attempt once more the north west passage, there being no Spaniards in the north to take offence.'

'Your grace, I beg you to consider again,' Dee cut in passionately. 'Francis Drake is the best of your mariners and the very stars in heaven do plead for his preferment.' Forced to play his last card, the white-bearded, rosy-faced Dr Dee could only hope that the Queen's belief in his occult powers would be sufficient to turn the tables, but on this occasion, as he was now to see, the Queen's unreasoning hatred of Drake was plainly stronger.

Under the astonished gaze of her Council, Elizabeth's eyes, at this further mentioning of Drake's name, had hardened into chips of black marble, her bosoms, wrinkling and shrinking now under their poisoning layer of alabaster paint, heaving in erratic rhythm to her short, panting breath. Send Drake? He who by his obstinate silence had denied her the right to womanhood, to children, to 'sweet

Robin', the husband she had wanted so much; who by condemning her to rule her kingdom like a man, had sent her spiralling into frigid, middle-aged spinsterhood? No. Dark, tumultuous thoughts cascaded through her febrile intelligence. No. The only place she would send Drake was to the gallows. Then she brightened, recalling that she had already ordered him home. From what she had heard, no fate could be worse than sending him back to the terrifying embrace of his common, frowsy, half-maddened fishwife.

Allowing her gorgeously-bejewelled fingers to flash under the Kenilworth chandeliers, she sniggered coarsely as she terminated the Council meeting with a single wave of a slim hand. Yes. Let Drake rot forever in tortured anonymity. Let him rot in hell.

Hell. There was no better word.

Over the years Mary's illnesses had grown worse, perhaps each spawning the other; but as one attacked the lungs, the other ravaged her mind. No peace for anyone. She would run through the kitchens and sculleries of her fine Plymouth house, scolding and bullying the servant wenches with the vengeful pleasure of one who has been a serving wench herself. Truly amazing, this relentless energy in one so thin, so hollow-eyed, with which she pattered round fine Venetian hangings, across rich Turkey carpets, clad like some demented ghost in her wraith-like nightgown. She punished whoever she met, whether husband or servant, with the agonising lash of her vitriolic tongue, coughing, spitting more bright crimson blood onto her pretty lace 'kerchieves with each week that passed. Then would come the times when she would lie collapsed in bed, sometimes for a month at a time; and Drake, coming in to comfort her, would sit, head bowed, as florid curses flowed around his ears for leaving her alone in the past with her illnesses, for finding no doctor to cure the ravaged hawkings of her lungs. For hours she would go on, wild, interminable reproaches mixed with ramblings of self-pity, and not a few bedpans flung at his head to make the nights hideous to all within earshot.

Brutally assaulted by the Upright Man when so very young, she had stayed suspended in time, her mind never maturing beyond that of a deranged child, a pathetic figure inviting sympathy. Yet for Francis Drake, who had to live with her, there was only torment and all he could do was to bow his shoulders and patiently endure what was God's will, his undoubted punishment for past piracies and wickedly adulterous fornication.

Always, there was a ray of hope, however faint, to bouy up and sustain him. The Queen might change her mind. The Queen was a woman and had changed her mind before.

Then the worst happened. John Oxenham, always so grave and respectable unless he was in his cups, or a murderous cutlass fight, lost his patience and took off for the Isthmus of Panama with some of Moone's collapsible pinnaces, planning to let loose the sweepings of the Plymouth taverns in a whirlwind of piracy on the treasure-ships sailing peacefully up the west coast of the Americas. Undoubtedly, without proper leadership, they would be caught and the Queen blamed by the Spanish for launching the expedition.

Elizabeth, who had nothing to do with it, was furious. More important, with Francis Drake tarred, as it were, with the same brush, the distant hope that she might one day allow Drake to go on his longed-for voyage of exploration vanished forever.

This then, was Drake's lowest moment: when life had no further meaning, when the only prospect stretching before him was the endless misery of infinite domestic torment. His life finished, his ambitions blunted, Francis Drake finally acknowledged himself beaten and gave up hope.

What happened then was something utterly extraordinary, so bizarre to those ignorant of the reason as to defy explanation. The Queen, being a woman, changed her mind.

Greenwich. Christopher Hatton, chief of her majesty's guard, on duty outside the audience chamber, whispering out of the side of his good-natured face to Drake and Walsingham as they wait to go in. ' 'Tis done. The task has taken me many days, but finally she is convinced.' Walsingham's dark face carrying a grim smile at the thought of his mistress finally coming to her senses.

She had appeased Philip for years, hoping for peace, had even deserted her allies, the Dutch, to avoid offence. But now Don John, Philip's bastard son, was destroying the Netherlands and the world knew, everybody knew, that his next ambition was to marry the Queen of Scots and join her on the throne of England: that after the Netherlands it would be the turn of little England and that Philip, for all his honeyed words, had turned out to be nothing but a treacherous, devious, vindictive dog.

The great doors opened. Drake and Walsingham went in and sank

239

to their knees. The Queen was dressed in white silk bordered all over with pearls the size of beans, over it a mantle of black silk with silver thread. On her head was a small crown; in her ears, two pearls formed into the milkiest, fattest, most iridescent of drops; her bosom satiny-white and uncovered as much as modesty would allow.

'Drake.' The Queen's voice was sharp and wasted no time. 'We would gladly be revenged on the King of Spain for divers injuries that we have received.'

'Yes, your grace.'

'You shall go on your voyage, but for exploration and trade only. Discover *Terra Australis* if you can, then go northwards, but never beyond thirty degrees of latitude where the main Spanish colonies lie.'

'Yes, your grace.'

'It is enough for Philip to know that we have forced the back door to his great Southern Sea. Then he will have to come to terms.' She regarded Drake balefully, dislike apparent in her black eyes as she eyed his bent figure. 'Of all men, my Lord Treasurer must not be told the destination of your voyage. You understand?'

'Yes, your grace.'

'Because of your blatant piracies we will not trust you as sole commander. A nephew of Sir William Winter shall go with you. Also, a third gentleman shall shortly be appointed to command the soldiers.'

'As your grace wishes.'

'No piracies, no treasure stealing, no killing of Spaniards. Philip is master of an army well beyond the match of ours.' She paused, her harsh voice silent for a moment before picking words again, carefully, venemously, her black eyes glaring at Drake in open and undisguised hostility. 'We are sending you, Francis Drake, only because it is reported to us that you are the best sailor in the land. We have no wish to prefer you, little enough to preserve you. Disobey our instructions in the slightest degree and as Almighty God is my witness, you will answer for it with your life. You understand?'

'In all respects, your grace.'

'Good,' the Queen said grimly. 'Then for good measure we shall repeat it. One dead Spaniard, one piece of gold stolen, one ship seized, just one mile sailed to the northward of thirty degrees, and you will lose your head therefor.'

'Yes, your grace.'

From behind her back a slim, ivory hand snaked out, holding a

240

piece of rolled parchment. 'Here are your written instructions. Now get out.'

Years of instability and hysteria were beginning to reap ruin on the Queen's features and her once-sensitive nose glowered hatred at Drake with all the curved menace of a vulture's black beak as, terminating the audience, she sent him away as though he were nothing more than an itinerant pedlar.

From the darkness of a shaded cloister, the girl ran out at him with the grace of a frightened deer, satin slippers pattering lightly over the mossy stone. 'Stay a moment sir, I beg you please.'

The clear sound of the girl's voice stayed his hand, which had moved towards his dagger with lightning speed. 'Lady. Although 'tis the Queen's court 'tis devilishly ill-lit and you risk danger, walking here alone.'

'Then sir, I beg you, come with me so we may talk where it is brighter.'

As her hand grabbed his with sudden gaucheness, without any hesitation, Drake realised that the girl must be little more than a child. As soon as they were illuminated by the flicker of smoking cresset clamped to a nearby wall, he pulled back the hood of her velveteen cloak and saw bold grey eyes, a cluster of freckles, a proud, arrogant little mouth, the petal soft skin of a slim, swan neck. He breathed deeply, strangely affected by her beauty, deprived for some reason of his normally bold manner. 'Why it is you,' was all that he could say.

'You remember me?' The girl's voice was challenging.

Drake grinned. 'Only just. Two years have passed, I think, since I saw you last and you have grown, I swear, like a weed in a wet summer.'

'Not the most elegant of compliments. On your forthcoming voyage you will certainly have the time to fashion better.'

Drake stepped back. 'You know of my voyage?' he asked in astonishment.

'You think I ran after Francis Drake because he is pretty?' There was scorn in her voice. 'If I wished to set my cap at a man there are courtiers a-plenty at Greenwich more handsome, and younger too.'

He looked at her. She was barely fourteen, yet her beauty and the sheer mockery in her voice openly challenged his manhood and he felt desire rise strongly within him. Shame came now, to blush his

241

cheeks and clog his throat, yet when he studied her face again, those grey eyes were still upon him, strangely understanding as though they could read his deepest thoughts. 'Soon,' she said, 'I shall be full-grown and you will no longer have to treat me like a child.'

He grinned, a ghost of that old devil-may-care smile flitting across his clear blue eyes. 'But you have already told me, when you are a lady, you will prefer elegant young courtiers to an old pirate like me.'

'If you are still alive, we shall see.' Her voice became suddenly serious. 'For you, sir, are in grave peril. Lord Burghley already knows of your voyage and the gentleman who told him of it goes with you, determined, with Burghley's blessing, to wreck your enterprise by any means he can.'

'You joke. You jest. Is this a child's passing fancy?'

She flushed with anger. 'I may be young in years, but my ears work well enough and this conversation I plainly overheard. You are warned sir. Warned.'

Drake laughed. A deep-throated rumble from his wide, robust chest. 'My thanks child. Be sure, if I were young, famous and fancy free, I would tell you a pretty tale.'

The girl's crystal-clear reply sent shivers dancing deliciously down his spine. 'As to age, only an older man may command me. Fame, you will surely have if you return from your voyage. As to freedom, that is for the fates to decide.' A whisper of velvet and she had vanished into the shadows before he knew it. Then from the darkness a girl's voice floating ethereally, magically through space 'And so Francis Drake, I shall wait a little longer and see what becomes of you.'

Now Drake left Greenwich, riding hard for Appledore. On his way there, his thoughts remained full of the exciting, bewitching beauty of the Queen's new maid-of-honour, Elizabeth Sydenham. The girl was gauche, childish, true, yet with a deliciously provocative manner that suggested that she would soon enough be a woman. And why had she singled him out, run after him, an old pirate twice her age, married to a common scold and in the Queen's bad books? A failure if there ever was one. Indeed there was no accounting for a young girl's fancies.

Her message, though, he would have to take seriously. She had overheard, there was no doubt about it, Burghley conspiring with another man, someone in his expedition who would be determined to

242

secure its ruin. A man who would be a menace from within, who to please My Lord Treasurer might already be planning to kill him. Well, he would deal with this plot as it happened. The important thing now was to get clear away from England as soon as possible, before the Queen once again changed her mind.

At Appledore, when he saw the *Pelican* again, he had to stand and catch his breath. A great piece had been cleverly let into her amidships. 'Queen's best oak. Three years seasoned,' Hawkins said proudly. 'Greatly lengthened in proportion to her beam. All rotten deck planking removed and keel timbers refashioned from mature pine and finest elm. Double-sheathed, too.'

'Double-sheathed?' exclaimed Drake in surprise.

'Ah, 'tis my own idea,' Hawkins said, grinning. 'For many months you may have to keep the high seas with nowhere to careen. In tropic waters, the teredo worm may well eat your false keel, but the true one underneath shall be preserved.'

'Why did we not think of that before?' Drake said, scratching the bushy, fair beard he had grown in recent years.

Hawkins shrugged. 'The world progresses. Now look you at her well, Master Francis and tell me what you think of her.'

Drake walked twenty paces away from the edge of the quay then turned and inspected the ship. She was long now, with a lean, greyhound look, despite the ample space for cargo, yet something disturbed the low, finely-balanced purity of her line. Then he saw it. Hawkins had built up two cabins in symmetrical layers at her poop, so as to provide extra space on the long voyage and more important, to stop the vessel from being overwhelmed by the mountainous seas that could be expected to sweep in at her from astern.

'She looks odd?' Hawkins asked, grinning slightly. 'Well never fear. In a rough sea, I promise you, she will dance as effortlessly as a lady of quality.'

Drake, excited and eager to explore the interior, asked 'May we go aboard?'

'By all means.' Hawkins led the way up the gangway.

Looking her over, Drake could see that nothing had been spared to make her fit for the incredible voyage. The masts were made from iron-hard pine and the sails, hand-stitched by craftsmen from best flax, would be unlikely to part in some life or death situation such as being driven onto a lee shore in a howling tempest. The range of hand weaponry with which she had been equipped was also impressive.

243

Swivel mounted falconets for sweeping enemy decks with shot, arquebuses, calivers, pistols, pikes, fire pikes, fire bombs, bows and arrows, yet when he reached the main armament, Drake stopped, rooted in his tracks.

'What are these?' he asked in an awed voice.

'Why sir,' Hawkins said, his rodent's teeth showing in a broad smile. 'Now I will tell you something. Hatton and I have dug deep into our pockets to have these beauties made.'

Drake, spellbound, examined the guns. Demi-culverins, the latest thing: seven of them, set in neat threatening rows along each side of the ship, two in the bows, two in the stern. Eighteen in all. They were smallish, true, not more than four and a half inch calibre, yet capable of throwing a murderously accurate broadside of ten pound cannon-balls deep into a Spanish galleon's hull at the incredible range of five hundred yards.

Patting their lean, deadly outlines, sleekly warm to the touch, Drake said, 'But why, cousin, have you been so generous? With these guns I could sink a ship twice my size.'

'Oh, you never know,' Hawkins replied airily, 'some helpless, fatly-laden treasure-ship might try to attack you.' Then he gave Drake a curiously intent look.

Then, and at that moment, Drake finally realised why Hawkins had made up their quarrel: why he and Hatton had lavished so much money on the *Pelican* and were investing heavily in the voyage themselves. Sure that Drake would not be able to resist the opportunity to bring back a mountain of gold, despite the near-certainty of his execution by the Queen if he returned with so much as one Spanish jewel, they were cynically, cunningly, almost pathetically, inviting him to commit piracy. Well he would prove that he was no longer a corsair: that Francis Drake was a gentleman of learning, a navigator and an explorer.

Not that he blamed these crafty courtiers for trying. After all, they had been generous with their own wealth in equipping the *Pelican* so superbly, but they just did not understand that Francis Drake was a reformed fellow who no longer stooped to such dreadful pursuits as buccaneering. They were certain that he was still a robber. A mere pirate. The thought brought a look of obstinate determination onto his ruddy face. He, Francis Drake, would shortly prove them all to be wrong.

In Plymouth, Drake lost no time in getting crews together. With Captain Winter bringing round the *Elizabeth* from Deptford, manned by sailors who were no more than murderous cut-purses recruited from the stews of Southwark, attracted only by the thought of easy plunder, he would have to be careful in the selection of his men. On a voyage of long duration, some form of mutiny was always a near-certainty, and to make matters even worse the Queen, in her foolishness, had split the command three ways, so that discipline would be especially lax.

When Drake sat down at his table outside the Dog and Whistle, close by the Catwater, there was already a long, patient line of men stretching down towards the harbour's edge, waiting to be interviewed. He could always tell the seamen by their canvas jackets and woollen caps, their sturdy, independent walks and tanned faces. Quickly he weeded them out from the beggars, the sly-looking pickpockets, the purse-snatchers.

'Name?'

'John Chester.'

'Why, you fought right stoutly in the *Minion* at San Juan de Ullua, with Hawkins, as I remember. And do you not have a wife called Jenny? Now make your mark here, good John.'

Beaming with pleasure that the great Francis Drake should recall, after all these years, the name of his wife, whom he was sure Drake had never met, Chester boldly scratched his cross on the parchment.

'Name?' Without looking up.

'Martyn, zorr. Me and my brother.'

'The two lads who raided San Sebastian with me in Tom Moone's pinnace? Aye, 'twill be handsome to have you aboard. Next?'

'Holderness.'

Drake's ruddy face broadened with a smile of pleasure. 'Why, Master Holderness, you were mate on the *William and John* when we rescued those poor seamen from the Inquisition. Pray sail with me again.'

'Aye, zorr. I'll come.'

Slowly Drake built up a structure of crew and command for the ships that Hawkins and Hatton had provided. He had not failed to note the lopsided smile, the crafty wink when he told each man that the voyage was merely a delivery of cargo to the Great Turk at Alexandria. If that was so, where, in fact, was the cargo? Stores there were in plenty, but no sign of a cargo. It was plain to them that Francis

245

Drake was up to something and being Francis Drake, it could be only one thing. Piracy—and for that, they'd follow him to the ends of the earth.

He hated practising deceit on such good men, but he had not dared to disillusion them. He hoped merely, that when they found out the truth, that this was a highly dangerous voyage of exploration with no chance of loot, yet offering every chance of death, he might still claim their loyalty. Many men stood out particularly in his mind. John Thomas, who'd fought nobly alongside Hawkins on the *Jesus*, yes, he must have a command. Others too, who'd been to distant parts and proved their guts and their seamanship: Horsewill, Minivy, Danielles, good old West Country names these and a few foreign ones too, Great Neill the Dane and Little Neill the Fleming.

He'd been particularly glad to sign up his old friend Tom Moone, the bald-headed ferocious little carpenter who had muscles on his arms that were as corded as tree-trunks. Moone had served with him in all manner of dangerous places where they'd collected loot or baited the Spaniard. Winter was bringing the *Bark Benedict* round from Deptford, an excellent ship for reconnoitring havens and harbours in unfamiliar waters; and manned as she would be, by the scum of London's gutters, a tough, experienced skipper like Tom Moone, expert in the handling of small craft, would be invaluable.

Still not enough. Dismissing the rest of the waiting men as so much riff-raff, Drake went round to William Hawkins, the Queen's governor in Plymouth, and obtained fat William's authority to raid the jails to make up his crews. Many a skilled and trusty sailor he found there, condemned to rot and starve on damp stone floors for some trifling offence. Men who knew the name Francis Drake, and for being taken out of the darkness and filth of dungeons, would be suitably grateful and loyal.

Then quickly to the gibbet at Pennycomecuik, where a cartful of poor wretches were already disembarking, ready for their slow death dance at the end of a rope so casually handed to them by some bored justice of the peace, thinking about his lunch. One man only was left in the cart and as Drake came up, the hangman lashed the horses so that they sprang forward, leaving the man dangling in mid-air, his feet kicking and lashing in agony. With a single stroke of his rapier, Drake cut the rope. He leapt off his horse, and bending over the hanged man, eased the knot from his throat as the man groaned, his chest rising and falling in a desperate search for a whisper of air to sustain life. To his surprise, the features were familiar, although he could not place them.

'A pox on you,' snarled the hangman. 'Do you defy the justice's order? He is king of a band of travelling gypsies and must be hanged this day.'

Then it dawned on Drake who the man was: dark and swarthy, as he'd first known him, but older now, with silver streaking his sweat-soaked hair. 'Ned Bright,' he breathed. 'By the faith, you did me a service long ago at the gates of Woodstock and now I shall return it. Will you sail in my ship as prime seaman?'

Recognition leapt into the glazed, bulging eyes of the man still contorting at his feet in his search for air, then slowly, he nodded.

'Good.' Drake smiled. 'You know me. Who amongst these others are good honest lads?'

Bright's mouth worked feebly, but the rope had bruised his vocal chords and little sound came out beyond his harsh croaking. Eventually words trickled out. 'All of them good country lads, stole through hunger only.'

'Then I'll take them too.'

He threw money at the hangman's feet. 'Here's a royal for your cut rope and your lost corpses. Deliver these men to my ship tomorrow morning.'

Raymente, Southern, Waspe, Gallaway, Fry, Gray: the numbers were at last mounting satisfactorily. He had all he needed now. With Winter's crew and his contingent of gentlemen adventurers, with musicians and ships' boys, he would have not much more than a hundred and sixty, all told. Pitifully few for a long voyage where over half the crew might be expected not to return, but Hawkins had taught him to avoid the traditional practice of overcrowding the deck spaces so as to compensate for sickness and disease. Take less, Hawkins had said, and you will have less sickness, less disease. Give them air, good food, fruit for scurvy; rummage the ship frequently and your crew may live to fight another day. Yes, he thought, Hawkins had taught him a lot. Most of what he knew.

Three more lads: John Drake, a young cousin, an artist who could draw headlands and coasts; Tom Drake, barely twenty-two, the last of his brothers; and John Brewer, a boy trumpeter to tootle away fanfares dressed in silks and satins as befitted the status of the admiral of such a fleet. And the job was done.

The stores. A myriad of things that he had needed to list then delegate to the attention of James Lydye, the local storemaster. Drake could only hope that Lydye had done his job, but noting the man's sly and crafty countenance and the reputation of such people for cheating, felt a distinct sense of foreboding.

The end of October: the *Elizabeth* had come round, bringing the *Bark Benedict* with her. Men stood idle and consumed precious food while the year drew in and they waited for a favourable wind, then, on the 15 November, the wind veered round to the north.

Time to go: so many things to remember that might be mentioned in his favour, if and when he returned, Drake thought. Dress the flagship overall, with a multitude of Tudor dragons snaking out in the crisp breeze from slender pennants and silken banners fastened to the mastheads and fighting tops. A discreet display of heraldic shields showing Hawkins' and Hatton's crests might not come amiss, prominently suspended from the freshly-gilded upperworks.

Now, at the last moment, take on board those precious casks of fresh water; always the first consumable to perish, to turn into wet, green, stale, mildewed scum.

'Small boats taken on board and lashed down in the waist?' he asked Cuttill, the ship's master.

'All secure.'

'Capstan crew ready by the windlass?' he bawled to the bosun. Normally the master's job this, but today he was taking no chances.

'Ay, ay, zorr,' the bosun shouted back.

Drake held his breath. Always a moment of paralysing excitement this, for any ship's captain.

'Up anchors,' he roared. 'Set the mains'ls. Royal salute.'

The ship came to life like an exploding ants' nest, men hurling themselves at the capstan, straining and chanting in unison under the spittle of the boatswain's curses, the patter of horny feet drumming like a sudden hailstorm on the ship's planking as topmen raced up the masts. Sails, at first no more than a narrow flare of white, budded into gorgeous flower, the foremast first to blossom, crumbling for a moment then proudly bellying out and cracking with monstrous, pistol-shot reports as they were pulled taut. Then glorious of glorious moments, young tousle-haired John Brewer clinging to the rigging with one hand, blaring out a proud fanfare to the Queen, while simultaneously the royal standard broke from the maintop and the cross of Saint George flared into white and red flame from the foretop. Now, from being inert pieces of timber, the ships, one after another,

248

achieved the miracle of graceful life as bowsprits dipped towards the sea and ripples curled back like long arrowheads from the forward movement of the ships' hulls.

Having gained steerage way, Drake led his flotilla, not straight out to sea, but in line astern across the green promontory of Plymouth Hoe, the gusty north wind carrying easily to the crews the ripe Devon accents of a crowd of relatives and friends assembled there to bawl their last good wishes. In seconds he would be abreast of the Chapel of St Catherine, a squat building dominating the harbour, where at this moment solemn prayers were being offered for the expedition's safe return, then 'Fire!' Drake yelled.

A moment carefully and precisely planned this, as the gunners touched as one man their linstocks and eighteen lethal, tigerishly powerful demi-culverins roared and jumped in a final and thunderous salute, the *Pelican* suddenly enveloped in a cloud of grey smoke as the sound rolled back and forth across Plymouth Sound.

Francis Drake had neglected no chance, no means of impressing on all those who sailed with him, the amazing power of his ship: the plain fact that if divided command was not able to work, one man had the will to enforce his own commands and the power too, even if he paid for it with his life to the Queen. He was, Drake realised, sailing to a moment of great destiny, both for him and his country. Whether he succeeded or whether he failed, Drake knew one thing: he would travel towards his fate boldly. History was not written by men with faint hearts ruled by hysterical women.

He roused himself from his thoughts so that he might give full attention to clearing the Mewstone and Rame Head. Soon, the treacherous, sharp fangs of the Eddystone Rock slid by, their presence shown only by the merest ripple like some huge shark waiting silently to pounce, then they were in deep water. Catching the full force of the fresh northerly, the green hills of Devon, with the purple line of Dartmoor behind them vivid and pencil sharp, slowly sank, becoming no more than a greyish blur as the music under the bows increased and the vessel pitched to the motion of the sea. Past the Manacles and the fearsome rocks of Dodman Point, the ships' boys changing the half-hour glass beside the compasses for the last time, when the westering sun lit with rosy glare the receding outline of Lizard Point. Away. Drake thought. Clean away. Nothing the Queen may do can stop me now.

Three days later, driven backwards by a huge gale roaring out of the south-west, his fleet lay battered and storm-tossed in Falmouth harbour, the fine taffetas of the foppish gentlemen adventurers stained with the awful puke and vomit of their wearers' first taste of an ocean's elemental power.

# Part Three

'... shall enter the Strait of Magellanas lying in 52 degrees of the pole and having passed therefrom into the South Sea then he is to sail so far to the Northwards as thirty degrees seeking along the said coast aforenamed like as of the other to find out places meet to have traffic for the venting of commodities of these under her Majesty's realms. Whereas at present they are not under the obedience of any Christian Prince, so there is great hope of gold, silver, spices, drugs, cochineal and ...*

Extract from document in the Cotton mss, not discovered until 1930 and probably the Queen's sailing orders to Drake.

# 24

Back in Plymouth Harbour once again, Drake, with, unfortunately, time to spare now while repairs were effected, clambered into the holds of his ships with a lantern guttering in his hand as he checked off the various commodities against the list he had handed the storemaster, James Lydye.

A hundred things: gunpowder and cannonballs safely stowed in magazines; spare canvas, timber, pitch, resin, oakum, nails, leather, all manner of tools required for careening fouled hulls on a distant shore; harpoons, nets and fish hooks—there would be times crossing the furnace-like calms of the tropics when their very survival would depend on the fish they could catch; woollen clothing for the freezing blasts of Patagonia; rough lead for casting shot, sheet lead for patching hulls; coal and logs for the galleys; all these items a storemaster could not readily cheat on. But when it came to food, it had been a very different matter.

In the hustle and bustle of imminent departure, not expecting to see these ships again for months, perhaps years, possibly never, James Lydye had worked a provision master's monumental deceit. Beer and wine were already sour in the barrel. Beef and pork in cask were little more than bone and gristle; the biscuit teeming with weevils. Only the honey and vinegar Drake had ordered specially to combat the scurvy was, by its nature, still in good condition.

Drake was incapable by his nature of anything but direct and violent action, and had stormed on shore in a towering fury. He had lifted the shifty skinny little storemaster off his feet and started to wring his neck like a chicken. Only Doughty had stopped him killing the man.

Since taking ship, Drake had learned to his delight that the Queen had appointed Tom Doughty to command the gentlemen adventurers. That was excellent. If he had to share command with anyone, there was indeed no man better with whom to share it, than his old friend, his kind and loyal comrade of proven wit and scholarship, the man who had pleaded for him at court and comforted him in his terrible exile in the Irish bogs. Yet Doughty had quite unexpectedly taken Lydye's side and by so doing had much magnified Drake's problems.

Without Doughty's co-operation he could not condemn the stores and involve his backers, Queen and court, in the enormous expense of restocking—not without a long delay. This had special perils: already in his imagination he could see Burghley persuading the Queen to call the whole expedition off; at this very moment the Queen's tentacled fingers might be reaching slimly in his direction to stay a voyage which within a few days had achieved much of the appearance of a disaster.

Perhaps, was it possible, that the traitor in the fleet, whom he still had to root out, had engineered the whole provisioning of rotten stores in order to abort the voyage at Burghley's order? Already he knew to his cost that Burghley had tricks and twists that no other man could match. In the end, he had taken the only decision he could: to go.

He left Plymouth quite unexpectedly and to the confoundment of his enemies, on 13 December an unlucky date. A date that could only be chosen by a brave man. He left unprepared, his stores rotting in the holds, butting into an offshore wind so foul that his ships' masters were down to their stern lateen sails in order to maintain bare steerage way. Only when the wind freshened and veered to a more favourable quarter, and the *Pelican*'s hull trembled under the firm tug of its main and foresails, could he be sure that he had stolen a march on his enemies, finally got clear of vicious thieves, scheming politicians and a hostile, hysterical Queen.

Drake sat down in his cabin and began to take stock. The problems looming up in front of him were incredible, almost unsurmountable, yet as he stretched out his short, strong, sailor's legs under the table, there was already a broad smile on his ruddy face. A pox on those who schemed against him. If necessary, he would take this whole expedition by the scruff of the neck and carry it forward by the sheer brute strength of his own personality. He knew he appeared to others over-confident, a man of swaggering arrogance. Yet those who dismissed him in such cursive terms were blind to his enormous and ultimate inner strength. Anyone wishing the voyage to end in failure would have to kill him. And Drake, above all things, was not afraid to die.

The small fleet of ships butted out almost due west into the Atlantic, aiming for enough sea room to enable them to weather the stormy lee shores of the Bay of Biscay when they turned south. This, with one day blurring uneventfully into the next, was the testing time, when men crowded into a ship less than the length of a tennis court learned to work smoothly and happily with each other in the knowledge that the heat of small frictions could quickly flare, in cramped spaces, into disastrous mutiny.

Between the officers and crew of the *Pelican* all went excellently. The ship's company had by now been divided into watches, each man picking a companion. Then, every sailor joined with one from the opposite watch to share a palliasse (if one possessed such a luxury), hoping to find a cosy spot wedged in under the guns or stanchions of the low-ceilinged 'tween-decks. There, in the airless darkness, one man would sweat or shiver, depending on the weather, curled up like some exhausted animal in his jacket of tarred canvas, while the other worked.

Slowly the voyage took on a fixed routine: the sounding of the hourly bell when the quartermaster turned the glass of filtered sand to mark the progress of the watch; the regular issue of one gallon of beer per man a day, and God help any captain who did not allow it. The portable galley boxes were brought up from the hold, weather permitting, to cook food on deck, where the ever-present danger of fire was slightly less terrifying. Morning and evening Master Drake, son of a preacher and sure of himself in the Calvinist faith, would read prayers to the assembled crew from his great Geneva Bible instead of inflicting on them the pratings of round-eyed parson

Fletcher. In this way men banded together against the common peril of the sea, searched for and found security and warmth in routine comradeships and the command of a good captain.

Hawkins' modifications to the poop had provided Drake not only with a small cabin for his personal use, but also with a large, airy, day room in which each evening he was accustomed to dine in great pomp and state. The knowledge was never far from his mind that he had been commanded by the Queen to confer on all matters with Winters and Doughty. So he would deliberately use these splendid dinners, with ships' captains and gentlemen adventurers eating off gold plate to the soft sounds of viol, pipe and tabor played by Drake's own musicians, as a blatant device to over-awe and impress, to stamp his power and authority on them all. Secretly convulsed with laughter at his own posturings, he insisted on enormous respect and only on the first night was one man bold enough to remain seated when Drake strode in, ruffed and pomaded, red-cheeked, ruddy-faced.

For a time they had been impressed, then as Drake's thin veneer of gentility was rubbed away by the workings of conversation to reveal the true yeoman underneath, the mood of the gentlemen adventurers, as if secretly orchestrated by some leader, changed from respect to barely-concealed contempt. Now they would discuss Aristotle, Archimedes, ancient philosophies, the principles involved in the art of alchemy, mocking Drake openly in Greek or Hebrew, while he sat red-faced, embarrassed, picking at his food. To Drake's amazement, his old comrade Doughty, instead of rushing to the rescue of his ill-at-ease friend, was himself always in the van with barely-concealed taunts, his saintly, vaulted eyebrows arching with pleasure every time some subtle barb lodged in the sweating, uncomfortable flesh of Francis Drake.

Shaking his head in dog-like confusion at the extraordinary change that had come over the manner of his old companion, he said, one night, when all were listening 'Doughty, 'tis not the same between us as before. Once, many months ago, when we were in Ireland, you would laugh with me. Yet it seems now your only pleasure is to laugh at me. What have I done to offend you? Tell me and it shall be quickly mended.'

Doughty, his face as pure and peaceful as some cardinal lying in state, had replied, 'What nonsense, good Francis. What an imagination you do have.' Then he had sniggered and added, playing to his audience 'The philosopher Attalus used to say that it was more of a pleasure to make a friend than to have one. Moreover, did not Seneca himself say "the wise man is content with himself"?'

As the gentlemen under his command roared their sycophantic approval, led by the raucous, weak-chinned Winter, Drake, looking into the eyes of his old companion, saw no longer there the slightest sign of any affection. Instead, the glaring hostile whiteness of their corneas were like gauntlets thrown down.

Before long the ships turned southward, ploughing their way across a peaceful sea with ominous lack of incident. The calm before the storm, thought Drake bitterly. For many hours a day now he would retire to his personal cabin, brooding alone with his thoughts. The sumptuous furnishings, the fine turkey carpet spread over the bare planks, the panelled bulkheads hung with tapestries of intricate design, did little to alleviate his mood of black depression.

Restlessly he strode backwards and forwards, spinning occasionally with muscular, spatulate fingers the twin, ornate bronze globes he kept in a corner, one depicting the zodiac, the other the known world. He was acutely conscious that he would shortly be heading into uncharted waters sharing a command where he was outnumbered by two openly-hostile men. The enterprise showed every sign of becoming a disaster.

Somehow, when he reached Africa, he must obtain huge quantities of fresh supplies before launching out on the endless journey across the South Atlantic and Doughty, who controlled the soldiers, together with Winter, would undoubtedly forbid the slightest use of force. Pilotage would pose a worse problem. Once beyond the Cape Verde Islands, he would be in waters unknown to all but the Portuguese. Brazil was known to have a treacherous coast prone to sudden and frequent storms, with perilous shoal water everywhere, and he had no charts, no maps. He glanced at his shelf of books: every single worthwhile tome on contemporary navigation was there. He even possessed a rare and valuable copy of Ortelius' map of the world, printed in 1570, clearly showing the great continent of *Terra Australis*, but Drake put little confidence in the self-satisfied dogma of chairbound navigators. No: there was only one thing for it. He would have to capture a pilot.

In his imagination he already heard Doughty's howl of rage, well-supported by his weak but dutiful shadow, Winter. Yet a pilot was plainly essential. Very well. There was no alternative now. He must claim overall authority.

That evening at dinner, at the end of his patience with Winter's shrill, inane giggle every time Doughty aimed some witty, sardonic sally in his direction, Drake scraped back his chair and demanded silence. Standing, squaring his broad, burly shoulders, he announced coldly, flatly 'Gentlemen. Henceforth I am to be known as "General of the Fleet".'

And they had laughed in his face. A great gale of laughter, led by Doughty and Winter, that had sent him down to his cabin in red-faced confusion. It had been absurd, he realised, to tangle with high-born gentlemen, products of Eton and Winchester, using mere words for weapons. In doing so, he had only made himself look ridiculous. Still shaking with rage he went over and patted the warm, brass flank of a piece of heavy ordnance mounted on its carriage, pointing outwards through a gunport in the overhanging stern. That talked stronger than any words, he thought. Let them ridicule him. Let them laugh; the Hunsdons, the Winters, the Careys, all those glittering, aristocratic young men drawn from England's finest families. He who controlled those wicked demi-culverins, controlled everything.

He might as well be hanged for a sheep as a lamb. Anyone watching Francis Drake at that moment would have noted how his eyes had suddenly regained more than a touch of their former clear, murderous blueness, and knowing how closely the pirate lay under the mantle of explorer, might have trembled.

Twelve days after setting out, the fleet made a landfall off Mogador on the Barbary Coast. The sight of the snow-capped peaks of the Atlas mountains rising high and pure in the distance above the desert haze sent the boats' crews into an endless buzz of speculation. They were well south of Gibraltar now, so there was no chance of a tame Mediterranean voyage to Alexandria. More likely it was a slaving voyage: West Africa, the Spanish Main and then home, with more than a bit of piracy thrown in. The old salts among the crews curled their lips in anticipation, winking quite openly at their commander when he came anywhere near. And Drake, knowing of the awful horrors to come, did not dare disillusion them.

When Drake towed three Spanish *canteras* behind him for some nine hundred miles, calmly eating the fish from their holds and then exchanging one for the *Christopher* so that Tom Moone might have a larger and more adaptable pinnace in which to do his scouting, Doughty and Winters protested furiously. Even worse was to come when off the high promontory of Cape Blanco, where fish teemed in fabulous numbers, Drake made the rounds of the Portuguese fishing vessels anchored there, appropriating several barrels of fish and four hundredweight of biscuit. Winters now told Drake that he considered all these actions to have been plain unlawful, that he was making an official protest and that each incident had been carefully noted in his ship's log.

'Log them then, my friend and go to damnation,' Drake had growled back.

Lying in his cot at night, Drake could feel the hysterical laughter rising up inside him at the thought of his exposed and defenceless position. Winter's uncle, Sir William Winter, ran the Navy Board, a ruthless man of immense prestige and very close to the Queen. Already, with the voyage hardly begun, he might fear for his very life when the log was formally read among the members of the board.

Soon the fleet set sail for the Cape Verde Islands. Ploughing through an awkward, choppy sea, Drake made a point of being everywhere, ranging across the *Pelican* on his short, muscled, mariner's legs, the fury and despair he felt carefully masked by his usual wide, red-faced grin.

'Now lads, what are you doing here?' he asked, coming across a pair of obviously raw sailors, their faces still white from jail pallor. From the ominous tap-tap of a cane held by the nearby bosun, he suspected that they would soon receive a tender rump apiece if he did not intervene and stop the hash they were making of their attempt to shoot the angle of the sun with an astrolabe. 'See here,' he went on, 'one of you must take a hold of the ratlins with one hand and the ship's rail with the other.' He showed them how to do it. 'So that one man resting against his comrade's chest may have a steady platform. Now then, my lads, here is a good way to obtain a sighting in an awkward sea. Place a card behind your astrolabe and when the sun's rays catch it true, the card will light up, you may measure off your angle and all will be proper.'

They watched him stump off with open love in their eyes, the renowned Francis Drake who could be haughtier than God himself with the gentlemen, yet had a touch of old Devon in his voice when he spoke to the seamen.

Over the next few days, with the sails of the little fleet bulging from

259

the north east trades, Drake made quick time to the Cape Verdes. Here, while the men searched for water, Doughty seized the chance to drill the gentlemen adventurers. Noting how well-armed they were, their obvious loyalty to Doughty and open contempt for his own person, Drake could feel the tension mounting higher and higher with each day that passed.

Soon the southern tip of the Island of Praia came into view, almost coinciding with a wild cry from the masthead 'sail ho'. A fat westward-bound merchantman was wallowing out of harbour bound obviously for Brazil. Boarding her, Drake found many useful things necessary for the long, arduous voyage ahead: clothes, canvas, much food and a hundred and fifty casks of Canary wine. The ship itself would be a useful addition to his fleet. Ignoring Winter's furious accusation of piracy, he renamed her the *Mary* and commandeered her, together with the most precious piece of cargo she contained, one Nuno da Silva, an experienced pilot who knew the Brazil route well.

They were setting out into the tropics now, weeks at a time of burning heat, little wind, no guarantee that supplies would last. Drake knew how men responded to idleness, to furnace-like temperatures and continuous, oppressive humidity. He remembered how Hawkins himself, in similar circumstances, had had to deal with terrible mutiny. Everyone knew how undisciplined Tudor seamen were: had not a great battleship of bluff King Harry's capsized because too many sailors had wanted to steer the ship at the same time?

In his fleet Drake carried many hard, lawless gentlemen adventurers, each man a high-born killer viewing him with the open contempt due to an upstart. As for Doughty, he knew well enough the murderous, consuming hatred that his former friend now held for him. Drake felt himself to be sitting on the smouldering peak of a volcano. As they headed out into the unknown and fiery wastes of the South Atlantic, he knew it was only a question of time before that volcano exploded.

The doldrums. The devil's sea. Day after day, the stores rotting, the water turning foul, the ships motionless under a sky of hot copper, their men praying for a catspaw of wind to help them summon up enough saliva to spit on the brassy smoothness of the ocean and so disturb, even for a second, its mirror-like surface. To Nuna da Silva, the dark, stocky pilot, the effect of the sun on these white-skinned northerners was frightening. From the first moment that its burning rays touched the upper works of the ship, gilding it with gold, it was an animal to be feared, to be tamed.

Their captain, he was interested to note, the famous Francis Drake, was an authoritarian, although he did not exercise his power in any cruel or sadistic manner. Drake was sufficiently experienced to know that idleness on tropical voyages bred either disease or mutiny and therefore, despite the inferno of continuous, unremitting, brassy heat, the men were worked hard.

First thing in the morning, a singing of the psalms: the captain, no lie-abed, distinctive at the head of his men with his ruddy face and fine countenance fringed by a full, golden beard, taking the lead in bawling out the well-known hymns. Then, noted Da Silva, the work would begin, with deck swabbers scrubbing the planks and sluicing them down with buckets of sea-water while some of the duty watch were sent to work the pumps. Even on the calmest days timber-built ships leaked a little water and there was no substitute for practice and tight, efficient handling that might well save their lives when they entered the region of unimaginably ferocious storms that only Drake and Da Silva knew awaited them.

The strange cleaning of the ship, the carrying of trays of burning pitch through the mess-decks to fumigate the fetid atmosphere, was an old slaver's trick, Da Silva noted. Well, Francis Drake was known to be a pirate captain of enormous experience, and the stocky Portuguese could only chuckle in his long, black beard at the fearful depredations Drake was likely to inflict on any Spaniards that came his way, for Da Silva was a man not without humour and with no especial liking for the Dons.

With idleness the enemy to be fought at every minute, the moment cleaning was completed a gunners' party was detailed off to polish the brass culverins, and to oil the trunnions and trucks on which they were mounted. After that, the small arms: crossbows, pikes, arquebuses, must be cleaned against the insidious, ever-corroding salt of the sea; the gunpowder freshly sifted, dried then tried in firing practice, the ship heeling violently over as its great guns belched shot and white smoke harmlessly across a turgid, oily ocean with its foul, festooning, clinging strands of cloying seaweed.

At noon Drake would walk over to the rail and shoot the sun, calculating by such means the latitude he had reached, although he had no ready means of discovering longitude other than by dead reckoning. Every day he would mark a small cross on his chart as he estimated the ships' progress. Some days, such was their lack of wind, one cross would be almost superimposed over another and at such times, as Drake carried his astrolabe back to his cabin, his limp from an arquebus ball still lodged in his leg would be more pronounced than usual.

Endlessly the routine of the ship repeated itself over and over again, one day merging agonisingly into another under the pitiless, relentless heat of the overhead sun. Soon after midday the first meal would be eaten, the portable galleys brought on deck, the smoke from the green faggots rising thickly from the forecastle chimney as the bread was baked. With the steep tubs of pickled meat freshly broached, the sailors would form an orderly line for their rations. Dull food this, quickly rotted in the heat, but Drake had shrewdly issued those too ill to work with hook and line, so that rations were frequently augmented by flying fish, bonito or delicious dolphin.

And what of the gentlemen adventurers? All through the long, torrid marches of the day they lazed under the shade of specially-rigged windscoops and sails playing at primero or reverent friars—an un-Godly game this, where every man was given a long but filthy dirty name and they would all have to repeat them one after another and the first to make a mistake through excess laughter would have his buttocks soundly spanked. After evening prayers and the men had been sent to quarters and the only ship's activity was the quartermaster stolidly turning the hour-glass as the last grains ran out, the gentlemen, having passed the day in idleness, would assemble in the airy poop to have the best of the ship's food and drink. At no time, Da Silva noted, did they accept orders from anybody other than Thomas Doughty and their attitude towards Francis Drake and all the sailors was one of complete contempt.

Men sweating, simmering and boiling in the hellish devil's cauldron of the doldrums, Da Silva knew, did not take kindly to such treatment and were holding onto their tempers only with difficulty. Accordingly, as thunderclouds grew oppressively over the becalmed ships, tension hung thickly in the air like invisible gunpowder dust ready to explode into mighty flame at the first small spark. That spark might have come when Doughty accused Tom Drake of theft.

The investigation showed Doughty's accusation to be blatantly false: just another step in his campaign to infuriate and enrage his old friend. There was only one thing to be done: unite Doughty with his main band of gentlemen adventurers on board the *Pelican*. There

262

were risks in such a course, but at least he would have the villains all penned in one place, under the eyes of his loyal sailors. Drake would then join his brother on board the *Mary* where life might, for a time, be more peaceful.

But Doughty knew how to goad and needle his man, aiming to drive the hot-tempered, violent Drake into some uncontrolled, ill-conceived action that would destroy him. Brewer, Drake's young boy trumpeter, sent on board the *Pelican* with a routine message, was quickly given a highly painful 'cobbey'—bent ignominiously over a gun barrel and thrashed 'till his buttocks turned crimson—by the arrogant gentlemen adventurers, with Doughty in the lead. To the raucously belligerent laughter of the gentlemen adventurers, young Brewer reported back to his master, trying bravely in his pain to blink back the scalding tears from his eyes.

By getting at him through those nearest to his heart, Doughty had finally ruptured the strained membranes of Drake's self-control. 'What,' he roared, 'do these well-born sprigs know nothing other than how to thrash arses? Doughty shall be sent to another place.' Exploding with rage, he ordered Doughty to be sent over in disgrace to the *Swan* an uncomfortable little supply vessel with an awkward motion that would make a man puke, even in a calm sea. And Doughty, after laying careful plans and always shrewd enough to avoid a direct personal confrontation, duly went.

Now, red-faced with anger, blue eyes blazing, oblivious to the terrible danger he was in, Drake went over on his own to face the gentlemen adventurers. Massed round the entry port, deprived of their leader by a man they despised, there was an ugly, threatening look about them. Twelve of them were waiting, murder in their faces, as he climbed up onto the *Pelican*'s deck. Many of them he knew by name: Antony, Carey, Markham, Watkins, Vicary. Most were second sons of powerful houses, doomed by the English inheritance laws to forage for their own fortunes. All were lean, sinewy, dangerous bravos who'd learned their rapier play from Italian sword-masters and, with the gallows something to be bought off with a bribe and a wink in the right places, were as ready to run a man through as look at him. Yet Drake knew that somehow he must impose his own authority: face them down or be killed.

Something like a low growl came from them, as though they were a pack of mad dogs, as he stepped on board. Drake noted the holes in their silken hose, their faded doublets and torn taffeta. He had strictly forbidden his sailors to play the mincing valet to them and the gentlemen, faced with the intolerable chore of having to dress themselves, and with too much pride to adopt the mariner's comfortable jacket of tarred canvas, looked tattered, out of sorts and quite plainly, homicidal.

John, Tom Doughty's brother, stepped forward. Drake had never fancied the look of him. A thin, crafty, bony head sitting vulture-like on a corded neck and long, muscled body. Something wrong there, the face weasel-beaked, with hair tufting the angled, sloping cheekbones. A face that looked at home with rotting carrion and dead flesh, the eyes bright with intended evil.

'Well good morrow, general. We wish to discuss matters in all peace. Shall we then go below?' The smile ingratiating, but the tone pleasant enough. Drake could not refuse, though surely the poop was a better place than the crews' quarters.

Down the hatchway, one foot easily after another, then— uugh—Doughty's boot smashing cruelly into the small of the back and Drake spinning down into darkness below, his ruddy face crashing with brutal force into the hard planking of the lower deck while above, a gentleman adventurer smartly slammed the hatchcover down, denying any sailor access. A diabolical trap had been neatly sprung, almost certain to end in Francis Drake's death.

Stunned, the impact of the fall a blinding starflow of flashing, exploding light as his forehead crashed against a deck bulkhead. John Doughty leapt after him from a five-foot springboard, heavily-booted feet thrust forward, aiming to hammer Drake's spine into shattered fragments of bone and cartilage, a curse torn out of him in the moment of free fall 'The Doughtys shall command here and Drake shall die.'

Self-preservation. The sense of it is built deep into some men. Very few. Drake had not lived a lifetime in the company of cut-throats and desperadoes without developing reactions faster than the speed of light. Even as he crashed agonisingly into the hard, unyielding floor of the lower deck, some part of his brain, some residual corner of his mind, took over, made decisions, sending survival signals flashing to arms, legs, fists, the endings of his shattered body knitting together under a nervous system that, though dented, was intact and functioning.

As he hit, he rolled and Doughty, dropping after him with the weight and force of a small dray-horse, glanced off Drake's shoulder and had to roll himself on impact in order to avoid injury. On his feet somehow, unable to see anything yet in the darkness through the blinding pain of a battered, half-concussed brain and now a lacerated shoulder hanging in screaming, useless agony. Duck. Weave. Adjust. All right, my hearty, Drake thought. I'm ready. Come and get me—or shortly, I'll come and get you.

Down there among the rows of great cannon lying in their wooden trunnions, no space to move or flash a sword, with the ceiling lower than a man's shoulder. There could be only one weapon: cutlasses.

A hint, no more than a loom of a steel blade, slashing at his bruised, bleeding face. Drake leapt back, hitting the great, central bulk of the mast with a crash, slipping and sliding over a heap of cannonballs then rebounding like a cat off a nearby bulkhead, looping upwards and outwards with his own blade, his other hand useless but somehow crouching behind it, using it as a sacrificial offering to save his vitals.

A curse. Doughty, a tall, rangy man, had straightened, trying to avoid Drake's blade, and dealt his head a smashing blow on the low ceiling. Drake charged, his blade scything for the other man's guts, his teeth bared. A fight. How he loved a fight! The years he'd had to wait for a fight like this. As the fog cleared from his brain his eyes took on a brilliant, homicidal blue stare in the darkness, and he laughed—and as he did so, the need for vengeance evaporated from the soul of John Doughty and his guts took on the consistency of water, knowing now that the man advancing on him had recovered from his surprise, and had the advantage down between the 'tween decks of being small, stocky and durable.

'Come on my 'andsome. Only let me come close enough and I'll give 'ee a shave.' Drake's voice seemed to have lost its gentleman's edge and was a thick, Devon, piratical burr once again.

'I yield,' Doughty whispered. 'I yield.' It had not been his intention to take on the ferocious, formidable and famous Francis Drake in single mortal combat. Far from it.

Nothing. Just the moaning breath of the homicidal killer stalking his prey. A blade whipped his arm, flaying his cringing flesh, cutting to the bone—and Doughty screamed and threw himself backwards into the darkness. A hand found his damp, sweaty hair and jerked his head over the fat barrel of a demi-culverin. Paralysed with fear now, he could do nothing but offer his gobbling throat to the final sacrificial slash of Drake's knife.

Drake left him there, a sobbing, terrified wreck. Softly he edged up the ladder and threw open the hatch. Seeing it was him, the gentlemen adventurers clapped hands to their rapiers as one man and advanced grimly towards the battered, bleeding person of Drake. Cutlass forward, he faced them, crouching, as dangerous as a jungle leopard. For one moment, stand-off. Then they would kill him. And Drake grinned.

Softly, like a grey-haired monkey from a tree, old Ned Bright the gypsy dropped from the shrouds onto the deck, a thole-pin held menacingly in his hand. 'Come on lads,' he said softly. 'Will you see your commander die?' All around him, like the first patter of heavy rain drops on a summer afternoon, sailors dropped from the mast, the spars, the shrouds, the ratlins, a protecting, adoring, loyal pool of men around Francis Drake.

A brief moment of facedown, like an eternity, then the gentlemen, their swords still sheathed, knowing that mutiny could not be easily proved against them if they desisted now, let their hands stray away from their weapons and adopting elegant attitudes of studied and open contempt, allowed this peasant, yeoman commander of their's to pass safely through them.

Drake, bruised, bloodied, his face swollen like a pumpkin, had survived, but for how long? True, the lads aboard the *Pelican* had proved loyal and showed their love for their famous commander, but many of them had sailed with him before and owed him favours, and that was to be expected. Yet on other ships there were mariners a-plenty who owed Drake nothing.

On board the *Swan*, the expedition's supply ship, held there under no specific charge by honest John Chester, sweating and uncomfortable, Tom Doughty of the saintly, vaulted face, who had inexplicably conceived such mortal hate for his old friend Drake, judged it time to take stock. The gentlemen were his, he knew. But how to gain the men? Doughty had the way.

As slippery as an eel, he began to plot and intrigue with all the mastery of a courtier accustomed to subtle conspiracy, setting men against master, master against captain: a touch of ridicule here, a lie there to rot like canker in a man's mind, and always promises of preferment back in England, if they would be Doughty's friend. And now, in concert, as if acting on some pre-arranged plan, he and brother John, immured in irons in the *Pelican*'s brig, began to hint darkly of satanic, supernatural powers at their disposal.

No one is more superstitious than a sailor and no sailor more superstitious than when he is sailing in an unknown, uncharted sea. If that sailor happens to be living in Elizabethan times when a neighbour may be readily pricked or ducked or burned for witchcraft, then the power of such superstition should not be doubled but rather, multiplied by the power of ten.

'Now, my masters,' John Doughty had sneered, his weasel-beaked features contorted with malicious fury as he had been dragged off to the brig, 'soon you shall have nothing but monsters and storms coming only from the nether regions of darkest hell.'

As they edged out of the torrid doldrums there was no relief, for as John Doughty had so malevolently predicted, storms had indeed begun: vicious, sudden, evil squalls that could only have been raised by some infernal intelligence; then sudden thick grey mists, the well-known *pampero* of the Brazil coast, that to ignorant and frightened mariners, suddenly separated from their comrades by these ghostly, impenetrable tentacles, bore all the hallmarks of the devil. And sea monsters? Any good necromancer could conjure them up, the sailors knew that: beasts with enormous horns and scales and great tails that inhabited the Southern Seas and swallowed whole ships, crunching them effortlessly between their yellowed, dragon-like fangs. And as both the Doughty's kept reminding them, the further south they went, faster and faster would they sail until they sailed right off the edge of the world into eternity.

Now, Tom Doughty, with his seed well-sown, proceeded to reap his harvest. Never more than hinting, too seasoned a lawyer to be caught openly conspiring, he let the sailors hear what they wished to hear most. 'Were I in command,' he hinted darkly. 'I would be taking you home to your wives and sweethearts. If we go any further south with Drake, we are all as good as lost.'

And Drake knew that it must certainly be only a question of time before his men mutinied and brought the voyage to a bloody end, unless he could still the dangerous and vitriolic tongue of Doughty, find some reason to convene a drumhead court-martial, and hang him.

For south was where they were sailing. Every day, further and further away from familiar waters, the skies glittering at night over their plunging hulls, full of unknown constellations, the quiet mutters of the men began to grow and swell into open snarls of fear.

267

As time went on, the hand of Satan seemed to lift temporarily from the expedition and Drake was lucky enough to find a sheltered bay which he called Port Desire, where he could clean his ships and send men out in search for food. The men were soon able to kill plentiful numbers of rhea, the South American ostrich: Fletcher the Parson recording that their legs were as fat and juicy as a leg of mutton, and everyone's spirits began to improve immensely. Drake, always a forgiving man, now regretted his previous homicidal impulses and had Doughty restored to his original status, in the hope that he might regain the friendship of his old comrade.

He was rewarded in no uncertain fashion. Doughty immediately marched onto the deck of the *Pelican* at the head of his gentlemen adventurers and demanded a straight answer to a single, terrifying question: if Drake still insisted that he was in overall command, would he now name his successor in the event of his death?

And Drake saw the lawyer's oily cunning in the question. If he declined to answer he would be shown up as a man of selfish arrogance; if he did not name Doughty he would be accused of bias; and if he did, his life would not be worth a sixpence from that moment on. In the end, promising to consider the matter, he had limped off to his cabin, his ruddy face sweating with anger.

Next day, standing on the poop, he kept a close watch on Doughty. To his fury, the man was moving from sailor to sailor, openly soliciting them. That was enough: the dam broke, releasing in Drake a tidal wave of roaring fury. 'Bind him to the mast,' he bellowed in a huge voice accustomed to riding over the shrieking din of an Atlantic gale.

No one moved. The gentlemen adventurers hostile, the sailors sullen and disaffected. At that moment, had Doughty shown boldness instead of cunning, he would have won; but instead he stood there, posturing like some noble martyr.

'Come on my hearties,' Drake roared, starting forward. 'Give me a hand now.' The sheer, raw, physical presence of their red-faced, stocky, blue-eyed commander moved the sailors into obedient action as though galvanised by some invisible current of irresistible magnetism, and for Doughty the moment was irrevocably lost.

For two days Doughty, lashed to the mainmast of the *Pelican*, sobbed, cursed, threatened, bribed and wheedled. Ordered to be detained on the *Swan*, pending trial, he had to be carried there while he kicked, thrashed and blubbed with all the blind rage of a spoiled brat. By his uncontrolled and thoroughly petulant behaviour, Thomas Doughty had succeeded in forfeiting much of his respect and most of his following.

*'The first time he shall be bareheaded at the mainmast with a bucket of water on his head. The second time his hands shall be held up with rope and two buckets of water poured into his sleeves. The third time taken asleep shall be bound to the mast by his plaits and certain gun chambers tied to his limbs; as much pain to his body as his Captain wishes. The fourth and last time he shall be hanged on the bowsprit in a basket, with a can of beer and a loaf of bread and let him choose to hang there till he starves or cut himself into the sea.'*

Typical Elizabethan ship-board punishments.

# 25

30 June 1578: Drake had the whole company assemble on shore for the trial of Thomas Doughty.

'Bring him forward,' Drake said coldly. Unusual for him, this frozen, neutral sort of voice. Accustomed to despatching men in the hot blood of battle, he now had to kill a man in cold blood, and his dislike of the task plainly showed in his manner.

Still struggling, his fine silk clothes torn and tattered, his thin, expressive, mobile face working with emotion, Doughty was dragged forward and pitched into the pool of grass enclosed by the men of the expedition.

'Thomas Doughty. You have sought by divers means to discredit me and to overthrow this voyage,' Drake said grimly.

'Such villainy by me can never be proved,' Doughty answered.

'By whom will you be tried?'

At this, Doughty's face split into a slight grin. Nobody could say he lacked a sense of humour. 'Why, my masters, by a jury back in England.'

Drake's face remained impassive. 'Nay to that. I'll empanel a jury to try you here.'

'I hope your commission is good?'

'It's good.'

'Then let us see it, or prove yourself a liar,' Doughty snapped, his face contorting with rage.

An awkward moment this, but the tide was running too strongly against Doughty now, to be reversed by a lawyer's probing. One roar of fury by the stocky, indomitable Devonian, his feet planted apart, his face tanned as red as a carrot, was enough to dispose of the point. 'You shall not see it,' Drake bellowed. 'Hood, Gregory there, bind his arms, for I trow this knave puts me in fear for my life.'

While they bound Doughty's arms tightly behind his back, Drake selected a forty man jury. One by one now, the witnesses came forward. John Thomas, John Chester, Ned Bright and many others. Master and seaman, seaman and captain, all of them saying the same thing. Doughty had bribed, connived, conspired. Doughty had sought by every means open to him to wreck the voyage.

Yet Drake knew himself to be committing judicial murder on an old friend. For where was the crime? Maritime law still had to be codified and mutiny was nowhere defined. And what gave him a right to kill a man appointed as his co-commander? Or to convene a court of law that had no sanction from the Queen and was allowing evidence—hearsay, rumour, lower deck scuttlebut—that made its proceedings sheer mockery? He had no right. No right at all. As the trial progressed and the accusing voices buzzed interminably on, Drake looked inwards and saw himself as he really was: Francis Drake, pirate and murderer, murderer and pirate. Try as he could, he would, it seemed, never be anything else. Hating himself, he pressed obstinately forward, hiding his shame, his misgivings, his awful self-contempt.

'Now Doughty, how say you that you had joint command?'

'When Hatton and Walsingham took the plan of this voyage to the Queen, she joined us both together with John Winter, all of us to command.'

'Where is your proof?'

'Unlike yours, 'tis on parchment, executed under hand and seal.'

'Then produce it,' Drake roared.

'How can I when it is back in England?'

'Ah, my masters,' Drake bellowed, turning to the jury, 'see how this fellow prates and wriggles. Who then has seen this parchment? Hatton?'

'No. Not Hatton.'

'Hawkins? Walsingham? Surely one of our good patrons?'

271

'Neither of them.'

'Anyone here?'

'No.'

As Drake smiled in triumph, the silence closed in on Doughty, condemning, accusing. 'Burghley did,' Doughty burst out in desperation.

'Burghley?' Even as Drake echoed the astonishing word, he felt the graveyard chill of it freeze his soul, the icy tentacles of court treachery sending cold, evil currents of dread down his spine. 'Burghley?' he whispered again, unbelievingly.

Doughty, in his desperate fight to prove his authority had forgotten all his lawyer's skills and had just made an appalling and damning admission. White-faced, he tried haltingly to remedy the situation, but Drake silenced him with a mighty roar. 'The Queen herself commanded that no one was to divulge this voyage to her Lord Treasurer,' he allowed his voice to sink into a whisper for a second then bellowed accusingly, 'and that command was to be broken on pain of death. Then you, Thomas Doughty, went and told him.'

As he hammered this final nail home into Doughty's coffin a vision entered the mind of Francis Drake, still blazingly distinct despite coming from the far end of the earth, of petal soft skin, a slim neck and warm, chestnut hair. A vision of a young girl with a proud mouth and not afraid to use it too, warning an old pirate in the dark shadows of Greenwich, of terrible, diabolical treachery. He had never suspected Doughty as the traitor. Doughty had been as enthusiastic to make this incredible voyage to the Pacific as Drake himself: but the man, he recalled, was a courtier to his fingertips and apt, when the time came, not to have the courage to match the length of his tongue. Moreover, courtiers invariably have ambitions. Drake saw it all now. For Burghley's colossal patronage, for the power and influence he might gain through the Queen's chief minister, Doughty had sold himself. Doughty was a Judas.

'Well, my masters,' Drake burst out. 'See how he plainly convicts himself. This is no longer mutiny. This is treason.'

They found him guilty. Under Drake's formidable personality there had never been any doubt that they would not. Doughty twisted and turned, dissembled, writhing under the shadow of death like the agile, cunning snake he was, but gained nothing other than the right, as a gentleman, to the axe, rather than the disgrace of a

272

hangman's rope.

The night before his execution, Drake dined with his old friend and in the morning took Holy Communion with him. Side by side, they knelt at an English altar, not far short of the awesome Straits of Magellan with its moaning, raging tempests of icy, incessant rain and beyond which lay an ocean where no Englishman had ever been and where every man was an enemy.

Doughty, being a gentleman, in the end died like a gentleman, elegantly and with superb manners. Killed by mob law, lynch law, undoubtedly denied his proper rights, all this is true, yet when Drake lifted his bloodied head and cried 'Lo, this is an end to traitors,' he knew that the execution had been absolutely necessary if the expedition was to survive. He knew one thing more. He would have to answer for this act to the Queen. If the Great South Sea did not drown him, it was more than possible that the Queen would hang him. Such knowledge is no great aid to a man's sleep.

Now, Drake knew, was the time to ram home his point: that he was supreme commander. That there must be obedience and discipline if any of them were to get home alive. Like all great generals in history, Drake had the eloquence, the magnetism, the sense of timing that, taken all together, inspire devotion in the hearts of men. The gift is not forced, nor can it be learned. This charisma, or whatever one calls it, is a natural thing, flowing straight from the heart. This quality, when he needed it most, Drake would now produce.

Once again all men were sent ashore and Drake, instead of Fletcher the Parson, preached a short sermon. Then he spoke to them, lectured them, appealed to them, united them. 'I must have the gentlemen to haul and draw with the mariner, and the mariner with the gentlemen,' he roared. Absurd. Who could ever have imagined such a thing? Yet they cheered him.

'Now then,' he shouted again. 'To whom do you look for your wages?'

'We look to you,' they roared.

And then, hands on hips, he had put a wicked smile on his ruddy face and said, to his eternal shame, 'Well, shall we fix these amounts now, or will you stand to my courtesy?'

'At your courtesy,' they roared back. They were following a corsair with a literally golden reputation and the loot, the pickings, that awaited them under the command of such a captain, would be uncountable.

'Those of you who wish to go home, may do so.'

'We'll stay, cap'n. We'll stay,' they shouted. What, scamper home like mice while the others wallowed in gold? Not likely.

'Right. Master Winter, I do discharge you of your captainship of the *Elizabeth*. And you, trusty John Thomas of the *Marigold*. All masters are discharged from their masterships, all officers from their commissions.'

After a moment's stunned silence, the officers began to protest, but Drake silenced them with his usual roar. 'Why shouldn't I dismiss you? Am I not your supreme commander?'

'Yes, cap'n.'

'Have I not just executed my old friend, Tom Doughty?'

'Aye, cap'n. You have.'

'Then I'll do what I wish.'

He had them now. In his hand. Ready to be moulded into a body of men fit to endure hell. He lectured them again, producing parchments that contained the distillation of ship's rules that other commanders had, in the past, tried vainly to enforce. Rules laying down terrible punishments for disobedience, for slacking, for laziness—and the men listened to him, hiding a smile from their faces. Drake was well-known to be a man whose bark was worse than his bite; but the lesson was, all the same, well taught.

Now, having shown his right to dismiss all his officers from their posts, he reinstated them. A flamboyant piece of showmanship typical of the man. Then he dismissed the ships' companies, telling them that they would sail towards the Straits of Magellan next day.

As they approached the grim, unwelcoming jaws of the terrible Straits, the expedition pared down now to only the most seaworthy of the ships, Drake felt shame sit heavily on his shoulders. He had murdered his best friend and deceived the sailors, Devon men, trusted and true, many of whom he knew by their first names, by hinting at vast loot that awaited them on the other side of the Straits. There would, he knew, be no loot at all. For being hailed as a gentleman, a great explorer; for such miserable, petty ambitions, he had ruthlessly killed, cynically deceived.

Now, as the stark, forbidding cliffs of the Straits clawed ever closer with black menacing arms, he forced himself to observe the pleasantries, the pretty courtesies of the fine courtier he was aspiring to be. First, he ordered the topsails of the ships struck upon the bunt as a salute to his sovereign lady, the Queen. Then he turned to his brother and asked a seemingly casual question. 'Tom, what is Sir Christopher Hatton's crest?'

Tom grinned and shook his tousled head, but a gentleman adventurer who overheard the question called out 'A deer trippant.'

'Then I rename this ship the *Golden Hind*.'

With such clever little courtesies, Drake committed himself to the fearsome Straits. His ships: the *Elizabeth*, Captain Winter, eighty tons; the *Marigold*, Captain Thomas, thirty tons; and in his own flagship, the *Golden Hind*, a hundred tons, Captain General Francis Drake—a man who now considered himself to be a murderer, a swindler, a deceiver and a cheat.

As the steep cliffs closed in on him, mountains rising stark, huge and saw-toothed to the north and covered with snow almost down to the gaunt, withered skirts of their foothills, Drake had one last moment to turn over in his mind the grim history of those who had attempted the dreaded Straits before him.

Magellan, 1520: mutiny and desertion, one captain taking such fright that he had turned back for Spain while in the middle of the Strait. De Loaysia, 1526: mutiny and desertion. Sotomayor, 1535: mutiny and desertion. Sotomayor himself killed, and the expedition almost annihilated. Camargo, 1540: of a fine fleet, only one battered, sinking ship finally limping into a Spanish port on the west coast. This was considered to be such a tremendous feat that the vessel was displayed in a museum at Callao and its mainmast set up as a flagstaff outside the vice-regal palace in Lima. Ladrillero, 1558: one last try, then enough. The Straits of Magellan were death: the Spaniards did not try again.

The blue eyes of Francis Drake went distinctly thoughtful and he was observed to stroke his golden beard with a certain unease as the *Golden Hind* edged closer and closer to the whirling, foam-flecked vortexes caused by the conflict of one great ocean meeting another; their enormous tides compressed into monstrous, confused battle by the constricting action of the narrow Straits. Then it was upon him and it was no time now for calm thought, only for the roaring of commands; the great veins of his muscled neck pulsing and bulging and swelling from the strength of his voice, as the ships, slewing drunkenly over, began to spin round and round in a deadly dance. Fight your way out of that, only to be hit by the first, sudden, tremendous gust of wind squeezed into terrible velocity by the flanks of the high mountains, as it howled almost vertically down on the staggering, pitching vessels, laying them almost over on their beam ends.

Day after day, more of the same. No respite. Not for one second. The same appalling combination of eddies, foam-flecked rip-tides, and on both sides of the channel, razor sharp rocks beckoning with eager, salty, glistening, blood-thirsty fangs as the sailors, wearing every stitch of clothing they could find under their tarred canvas jackets, fought the incessant, freezing, sleety rain, scrabbling at the sheets with blue, numbed fingers in a desperate fight to keep control of the exploding, rogue-like sails.

Further and further, with desperate bravery, the little fleet of Queen's ships edged ever deeper into the black, murderous heart of the Straits: Drake and Da Silva with their enormous experience and the same, shared, sixth sense of danger that is common to all experienced mariners, somehow avoiding false channels and beating, very often at the last moment, away from treacherous, rock-strewn giant whirlpools that led nowhere except to a watery death.

When the men, who had eaten no hot meal for days, were so exhausted from fatigue and cold that they could no longer carry on with their tasks, Drake seized the moment given by a brief respite in the ever-present moaning, howling winds to anchor in the lee of a great, gaunt cliff. There, in the violent rise and fall of the boiling, turbulent water, the ships' crews with the last of their strength managed to tie cable after cable to outlying rocks, so that when the next terrifying tornado blast smashed into them, their ships, for the moment at least, would be safe.

At this moment, when their strength had nearly left them and all seemed hopeless and lost, the local natives helped them, showing them where, even in this terrible climate, the scurvy grass still grew thickly under the shelter provided by the low-hanging branches of trees weighted with snow and black ice. Also, they showed them where large, aquatic birds could be found, rich in fat—for fat was what these natives ate, to walk in this paralysing damp and cold, to the amazement of the shivering sailors, practically naked. Many of these birds were killed and eaten by Drake's hungry seamen. Inevitably they had to give them a name. 'White heads' in English, but two or three Cornish lads still spoke the old Celtic tongue and in that language it was 'Pen gwynn', and the name stuck.

Now, fortified by their brief respite, the seamen re-embarked. And not many days later, the sails of his ships weathered and torn from

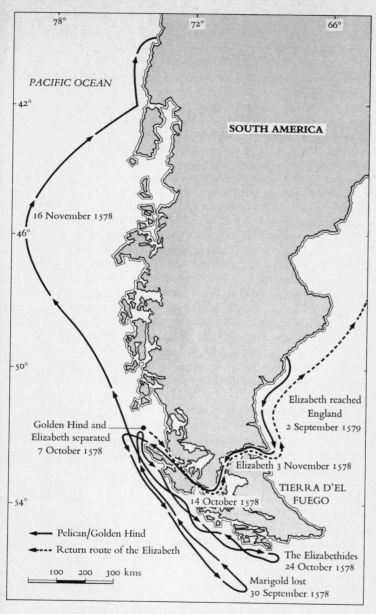

The Great Storm at the Straits of Magellan.

the squalls and icy tornadoes, Drake picked his way triumphantly through the graveyard of half-exposed rocks that lies at the western end of the Strait and to his amazement, emerged into the great South Sea. Magellan had done it in five weeks. De Loaysia in seven weeks. Drake in two.

As the first Englishman ever to sail this sea, Drake had intended to go ashore immediately and with much fine ceremony and trumpet-blowing, take possession for his Queen of the whole enormous continent of *Terra Australis Incognita*, which, as the learned Doctor Dee had assured everybody, began on the southern side of the Magellan Straits. He got no further than the pinnace that had been lowered to lie bobbing placidly alongside the hull of the *Golden Hind*.

When Magellan had first entered this ocean he had encountered such wonderful weather that he had called it the Pacific Ocean. But Magellan had been there at a better time and during freak conditions, for Drake was now well into a region of rain and snow which lies almost permanently across the Chilean Tierra del Fuego and gives an annual rainfall of over two hundred inches, most of that falling in the winter time. And in September, winter it still most assuredly was. Almost as though, high in the gaunt monastery of the Escorial, Philip's hooded and cowled monks had called down the wrath of God on these English heretics to punish them, to destroy them, obliterate them from the face of the earth for their terrible sin in trespassing on his most-catholic majesty's dominions, screaming out of the north west, the stupendous storm struck them.

What is a storm? An Atlantic gale? A stiff channel blow? A day, two, three days at the most, before the wind moderates? Experienced sailors could take that in their stride. So they got wet. They had no hot food for a couple of days. They were tough, experienced to hardship. The ship would be manned. They would cope.

Off Cape Horn, the sailors learned something. The rules were different. Many would not cope. Instead, they would die. The wind, a hurricane. A wind can only be so strong. An ultimate force, whining, howling, shrieking through the rigging and the shrouds like a thousand voracious, famished wolves in search of prey. Off Cape Horn, the sailors learned something else. The sea, like the rules, was also different.

The size of a wave may be determined mathematically by its fetch, that is to say, the amount of distance over which its energy has been allowed to build up. Take the distance of the Atlantic. Double it then double it again. Think of the size that wave may achieve once it has travelled halfway round the world. Bigger than a four-storey house, John Hawkins had imagined. Forget it. Try instead a small range of mountains, fill it with free, uncontrolled, raging motion whipped by a pitiless, freezing wind, the very tops of those waves surfing whitely in vast, spooming avalanches of froth down the enormous backs of the mother waves themselves. Then place upon this tormented sea three tiny, wooden ships, watch them thrown about like tiny chips of splinter, plunging madly ever south under bare poles, no control, steerage way long gone, and try to guess how long those ships will float, how long those pathetic ant-like little men inside them will stay alive. For this storm would not blow itself out like any little Atlantic blow. During this time it had, while the sailors lay wet through and exhausted on their palliasses, sicking up their guts and longing for a hot meal, any meal, been literally only flexing its muscles.

Three ships driving ever onwards, if one has to be precise, in a south-easterly direction, corkscrewing away into unknown, icy wastes, the tops of their bucking masts easily hidden one from the other by the colossal waves, writhing, pitching, the timbers shrieking and creaking, groaning further apart with every enormous switch-back. The vessels, when one wave met another of equally chaotic form coming from another direction, being picked up and tossed around like so many balls on a tennis racket, the wind and sky form-less, night and day becoming to the men a never-ending daze of unbelievable noise and motion.

Move closer now. Watch the tortured timbers work themselves free from their seal of oakum and observe the sea water hiss, spurt, then as the crack widens, roar into the ship. The ropes are working loose too, on those heavy demi-culverins. A rope may contain such enormous weights for only so long, before it stretches, frays, then breaks and then like some wild rogue elephant the first of these huge cannon will career on its trunnion round the ship, smashing men into pulp or ship's timbers into sawdust with complete impartiality.

These ships, at the mercy of this dreadful seaway, their men exhausted, famished and chilled to the bone, must surely be doomed. Not all of them. Not yet. For these are no ordinary men. These are lads from Devon and Cornwall. Francis Drake's sailors, no less. Incredibly, after endless days and nights, relays of stout fel-lows still desperately work the long-handled brakes at each pump

279

and somehow, pitched on beam ends, broaching to, literally somer-saulting, the men manage to keep that water-level down. Yes. There is still life. No longer under effective command, fast-failing, but the heart in two of those ships still beats faintly.

Fletcher the Parson and John Brewer, the young trumpeter, had been on watch when the third ship finally went down. The *Marigold*, thirty tons. Tiny, not much bigger than a pinnace, it had been a mira-cle that she had lasted so long. The two men could clearly hear the screams of their friends as they sank beneath the water, there to find a final peace from the terrifying waves. Captain John Thomas, Ned Bright the gypsy, both faithful friends of Francis Drake, died that day in the icy wastes of the South Pacific.

Three weeks of storm. Surely it must end now! The men can barely crawl, the pumps no longer manned. Water cascading freely into the well from all over the ship. Both vessels lying inert, dead in the water. Drake, finally beaten, lying exhausted on the turkey carpet of his cabin, knowing he will shortly die. His brain is clear though and he thinks of many things. His Queen, whom he had loved, protected and adored all his life, sending him away with a sneer, the pirate in him marking him as beneath contempt. His wife, well he'd soon have some peace from her. Elizabeth Sydenham. Amazing. Still a child, but he saw her clearly. Velvet skin, challenging grey eyes, vivid chest-nut hair. She had said she would wait for him. What had she meant? She had been very beautiful. All the freshness and eagerness of youth that he himself had long lost. None of this mattered now. Every-where around him men lay prone, starved, their stomachs empty, puking agonisingly on guts that no longer held food.

Day after day of palpable darkness, with no sign of the moon, the sun and the stars. And then, one night, through the torn rack of cloud, a star or two appeared and the wind veered and began to mod-erate a little. By morning, although they were still pitching devilishly in a confused swell, it had become evident to the comatose, exhaus-ted sailors that they had, by some miracle, survived the worst of the storm.

With the men too ill to move, to work, to speak even, it was Tom Moone once again who showed the way by his own example. Small, wiry, immensely strong, he was everywhere, his distinctive bald head shining, rapping and swishing a bosun's cane. 'All right my fine lads. Up with 'ee. Man the pumps. Get to work. To work now, me hear-ties.'

280

Amazingly, they responded, the men of the *Elizabeth* in turn being inspired by the sight of sail on the *Golden Hind*'s yard-arms to work their own ship, so that soon both vessels were under way once again, heading back the way they had come.

Wallowing desperately low in the water on a grey, vicious sea, they limped back towards the last sight of land. By the time, a week later, they had regained the western outlet of the Magellan Straits, both crews were in a state of terminal exhaustion.

Drake, amazed at the incredible resources of strength his crews had found, had taken Moone aside and asked him 'Tom, those men were near dead. How in troth did they find strength to set the sails and work the pumps?'

To this, Moone, his eyes glittering ferociously out of his gaunt, pock-marked face, had replied 'For the loot, master. Us always said us 'ould follow Francis Drake to the ends of the earth for gold.' Then he had grinned widely, showing such of his teeth as had not fallen out from scurvy and said, pointing at the wilderness of black rock and angry sea all around them, 'And master, here we be.'

Drake had averted his face and said softly, 'Tom, forgive me, for I have misled old friends and deceived dear comrades. For there will be no gold on this voyage. We come for trade and exploration only.'

Tom Moone had silently knuckled his forehead and walked away.

Within the hour, before the men had found time to go ashore and renew supplies of water, of food, the storm, incredibly, renewed itself in all its old fury. Once again, roaring out of the north-west, screaming like an army of berserk lunatics through the yard-arms and the ratlins, a monstrous gale sent the *Golden Hind* tumbling south again.

This time though, she was on her own. Captain Winter, with no more stomach for such seas, had turned the *Elizabeth* back into the Straits and with most of the gentlemen adventurers on board, was sailing for home, tail between his legs.

Alone then. Very low in the water now, wallowing sluggishly in a grey, foam-flecked desert of storm-lashed ocean, how long, Drake wondered dully, could they survive? No hot food for near a month now. Only mouldy crumbs of ships' biscuit, and even that had run out long ago. No water, for not a man on board had the strength left in him to trap the lashing rain and sleet. Fatigue, allied to starvation and scurvy, had finally reduced the men to a comatose condition near to death. Now, as the *Golden Hind* rose over the monstrous switchbacks then surfed back into the dark, chill depths of the ocean, each man awaited his maker in the position that his rank commanded. The men lay coughing their last in the dank chill of the 'tweendecks, where guns ran loose and water cascaded over them in rivers; such gentlemen adventurers who remained on board, all of a crumpled heap in their soiled silks and taffetas in the big day room; and Francis Drake stretched out on the turkey carpet of his fine cabin.

The ship, under no direction, manned by no watch, her plunging whipstaff held by no steersman, her timbers grinding and wrenching in eery harmony to the ever-present wail of the wind and gaping so open that fish swam freely in her flooded bilges somehow, unbelievably, incredibly, for some extraordinary reason, refused to sink. When days later, was it months, years, for he had lost all idea of time, Drake painfully opened his salt-cracked, rime-encrusted eyes and gazed painfully through the cracked ruin of the poop window, it was to see his ship bobbing placidly on calm waters, close by a cluster of small islands. Somehow, his poor, paralysed brain began to realise that the storm was over. That the *Golden Hind* had survived, and through no help of her crew or captain.

How, why, was she still afloat? He knew why. Hawkins had saved her. Hawkins with his masts of iron-hard pine fir, his ship's timbers three years matured, filched somehow from the Queen's dockyard: timbers that, double-sheathed, had opened but somehow held against the unbelievable assault of the sea. Hawkins who had built up that poop so stoutly that when enormous seaways crashed down on the stern of the *Golden Hind* the ship had merely shaken herself and kept on going. Hawkins, who with Hatton had poured out their life-savings into the construction of the *Golden Hind* in the hope that Drake would make them rich. Dear God, he thought to himself, for preserving my life, I must surely owe them something in return.

Drake stumbled to his feet. Slowly, painfully, he inched his way round the ship. 'Men,' he whispered, his voice cracked, croaking, desperately weak. 'This is your commander. The storm is over. Get up. Go to work. The ship must be manned.'

But nobody answered. They gazed at him like zombies, their eyes dull, glazed, seeing only death. And where was Tom Moone, rousting the men smartly about with his bosun's cane, sending them to their tasks? Nowhere. Nowhere to be found. Drake had never forgotten that look of hurt bewilderment that had appeared in Tom

Moone's eyes when he had been told there was no loot, no gold. Like a dog suddenly turned on and thrashed by a loving master, he had slunk away into the shadows.

All these men. They had come through hell for him, loving him like their own brother. And he had repaid them by cheating and deceit, only that he might no longer be looked on as a pirate, but accepted as a gentleman explorer by the fops at court.

From somewhere, black anger seized him. An amazing emotion that gave him sudden strength. He limped back to his cabin. There was the drum, used so often to beat to quarters in time of battle: Drake's drum, it was beginning to be called back in Plymouth. He looped the strap round his shoulders. Now he began to walk the ship, riffling, rat-tatting. A fine, stirring noise it made. Soon, he found the musicians. 'Up, my hearties,' he roared. 'We have work to do.' He kicked them mercilessly to their feet. Emaciated wrecks holding viol, shawm, sackbut and lute. 'Let's have a lively tune or two. "Hey trolly, lolly lo—", can you play it? "England be Glad", one of Old King Harry's favourites.' Somehow, his boot applied to their tender parts, he got them marching. A fine old tootle and riffle, as merry a scraping and a whining as a man had ever heard.

Round the ship they tramped, through the dripping 'tween decks, over the wreckage, across the overturned guns, slopping through the water; and over the sound of the lively airs, Drake's voice roaring 'All right my handsomes. Pick yourselves up. There's loot to be had. Spanish gold is waiting to make rich men of you all. There's treasure a plenty under Francis Drake.'

All over the ship, groaning, shivering from hunger and cold, men picked themselves up, stretched themselves and moved slowly out of the shadow of death. Unbelievable: look over there. The brothers John and Thomas Martyn, still inseparable from all those many years ago when they'd stolen ashore with Francis Drake to rescue poor sailors from the merciless San Sebastian Inquisition. Like him, no longer young lads anymore, but good Devon men still. Look at them. Minutes ago, close to death, but now dancing a merry jig, their horny feet pattering on the deck, one man's arm looped around the other's shoulder, their eyes shining brightly at the thought of loot. What men, and how he had deceived and cheated and exploited them. Just so that he could call himself a gentleman explorer!

Well, he had done more than enough exploring. Twice now he had plunged south to the depths of the fifty-seventh parallel, only to find

283

endless, icy, ocean wastes. Not a trace of land: *Terra Australis* simply did not exist. A myth in the minds of learned men. The way to the golden heart of the Spanish Empire was no narrow backdoor. It was a vast sea, needing only ships big and sound enough to sail it.

For hundreds of years, no man would discover anything more important. He had fulfilled a life's ambition; had proved himself a great sailor and a great explorer. Now he would be what he always had been. A ravager of Spaniards. A baiter and a scavenger of fat-bellied Dons. And who cared what they thought about him at court, idle, effete, so-called gentlemen, a Queen who had long disliked him and now openly despised him.

Others mattered more. Hawkins and Hatton, in whose debt he was. Simple Devon and Cornishmen, good and true, who had trusted and loved him. For them, he would show the world what had long been suspected. That a leopard cannot change his spots. Francis Drake was a pirate and always would be.

With an oath on his lips, his eyes the brightest of murderous, swashbuckling blue, he looked out once again at those islands where he bobbed placidly at the very uttermost tip of Cape Horn. Very well. The Queen would undoubtedly hang him, but she was still in his eyes a magnificent lady and deserving of fine compliments, and he liked to think himself a most chivalrous kind of pirate. Carefully, he sketched in the islands on his chart and named them—

The Elizabethides.

# 26

The hull of his *Golden Hind* a verdant, green forest of weed and barnacles, her timbers gaping open to the sea and those that were still intact, fissured dangerously with the boring worm, Drake managed to set enough sail to limp out of the storm zone. Stumping the poop deck, gazing about him, he had time now to take stock of his situation.

He was down to one ship, and that nearly a wreck, manned by less than eighty crew, some of them men, some of them boys, most of them half-dead. Drake stroked his beard. An interesting way to assault a vast and powerful empire, he thought, with a hostile coast stretching for thousands of miles with no port, no supply base where he might refit his shambles of a vessel. Then he chuckled. The odds were indeed amusingly weighted.

The first problem he dealt with was the scurvy. Off those islands at Cape Horn he had sent men ashore to pick, with the last of their strength, an abundance of berries and now, although hunger still made them stumble as they went about their work, teeth no longer fell out of the sailors' heads and they ceased to moan in agony from the awful pain in their arms.

Next, off Mocha Island, they found food, the Indians showering them with fresh meat and poultry. They paid a fearful price for it. The Indians, thinking them to be their Spanish oppressors, were treacherous and Thomas Flood, Tom Brewer, brother of the young trumpeter, and Great Neill the gunner died under a hail of arrows. Valuable, vital men that Drake could ill afford to lose.

Ever north Drake took the *Golden Hind*, away from the storms, into the sun, content for the moment to see the colour come back into his men's faces and muscle grow on their arms, so worried was he over his diminishing number of men. He was heading into danger now, nearing the fringes of the populous areas of Spanish colonisation, with his ship still no more than a wreck, the pumps needing to be manned continuously, the clear sea-water surging through her bilges, grim evidence of how frighteningly open her timbers were. Worse even than that was the absence, since the *Marigold* had sunk, of a small, speedy vessel to scout and reconnoitre ahead. Now, Drake decided, he must expend his one supreme weapon: surprise. Barter it in order to capture a large prize containing vital stores and also to obtain information.

The crew of the fatly-laden *Capitana*, lying sleepy and full of Chilean wine on her decks, were the first to experience the paralysing surprise of a boarding-party from the *Golden Hind*. Such attacks, as other Spanish vessels were soon to learn, had an atmosphere of appalling repetition about them. First, the bump of a rowboat against the side; then a bunch of ferocious pirates swarming on board, the oiled steel of their long cutlasses gleaming in their hands; their leader, ferocious little bald-headed Tom Moone, who dearly loved such operations as these, smashing his fist into the captain's face and snarling every time the same Spanish phrase in the ripe accents of old Dartmoor, '*Abajo Perro*—Get below, dog.'

With surprise complete; the crews battened down below; the *Capitana* towed out of Valparaiso harbour, to disgorge, when safely at sea, a vast cargo of wine and just enough gold, my masters, to whet a pirate's keen appetite; Drake proceeded to question the pilot. 'I want treasure.' In matters such as these, Drake was apt to be a direct man.

The pilot, Juan Griego, or 'Johnny the Greek' as he came to be called by the crew, thoughtfully drained the dregs from the tumbler-full of wine Drake had handed him. Coming from the Aegean, he cared little who employed him so long as there was good pay and enough wine. 'Well,' he muttered. 'There is the *Cacafuego*.'

Drake blinked. 'The *Cacafuego*?' For the name was indeed most vulgar, suggesting that the vessel could perform an anatomically impossible motion, namely fire a broadside through its bowels.

The Greek shrugged. 'Her proper name,' he yawned, holding out his tumbler for a refill of the excellent wine that Drake had come by in such quantity, 'is *Nuestra Senora de la Concepcion*. She always travels to the Isthmus at about this time of year.'

'Where is she now?' Drake snapped.

286

The Greek shrugged a second time. 'How should I know? Down here, we are only a distant outpost of the Spanish Empire.'

'What does she carry?'

Once again, Johnny the Greek held out his tumbler for the wine bottle. 'A whole year's output from the Peruvian silver-mines,' he said with elaborate casualness.

Now, promptly, Drake filled his glass. His blue eyes gleaming, glaring almost with concentration, he smiled at the pilot of the *Capitana*, a smile that suggested profit if he co-operated, violence if he did not. 'Tell me about her,' he whispered.

The *Cacafuego*. Somewhere up that coast a vessel was carrying a fortune so immense, so colossal, that no ordinary man might take it in, towards the Isthmus of Panama. A sum quite truly so staggering that only a treasurer accustomed to dealing in endless noughts could express the value of that cargo in terms of mere money. A needle in a haystack? Perhaps. But what a needle! From now on the thought of finding the *Cacafuego* completely obsessed Drake. During daylight hours he could think of nothing else. At night, he would dream again and again of those silver ingots gleaming massively, layer after layer, in her capacious holds.

Yet under his feet he had, not a ship, but a sinking, stinking wreck. There was only one answer. Calling to his cabin the two men he trusted most and on whom he was now chiefly to rely, he said 'Gentlemen. We have reached a bay where there is smooth sand and the rocks are few. Here we shall careen ship.'

They gasped in amazement. 'It cannot be done except in port,' his brother said.

'Well, I have heard of it,' Tom Moone admitted, 'but thought it more fable than fact.' At this, Drake had smiled and they knew that smile well. Patiently they listened while he explained what had to be done, then went away to give the necessary orders.

First though, a pinnace must be built. To give warning. To reconnoitre. Tom Moone's speciality this. In no time at all, one had been constructed from ships' timbers carried for that purpose and was soon ranging up and down the coast, checking for suspicious activity.

Now then: empty ship. Take off everything and then don't just swill the ballast through with sea-water but shovel out the stinking, excremental filth 'till she's light as a cork, for Francis Drake wants

287

no disease on board ship, so desperately short of men is he. Here, be careful. For this is the tricky bit. Take her in sideways to the beach at high-tide, then as the water recedes, quickly hammer wooden ramps into the sand close under her side and haul away on ropes attached by pulleys to her sides and mastheads until she lies snugly against those ramps at just the right angle to get at her sides and bottom. Now, flesh cringing under the unaccustomed heat of the sun, scrape away with immense patience, the shells, the crusty barnacles, the trailing green weeds, until every square inch of that hull is completely clean and the labyrinthine tunnellings of the teredo worm may finally be seen in all their frightening workings.

The carpenter's turn now: and Tom Moone knows more about this than most. Soon the beach holds a strange mixture of odours. The pleasant tang of melting tar, the appalling stench of anti-foul mixture being stirred and cooked. When all is ready, plug the drilled-out worm-holes; patch badly-damaged areas with thin sheets of lead specially brought for that purpose; force the rough, ropy oakum into the gaping spaces between the planks; then caulk with liquid tar and hammer everything home. Now cover the hull with a noxious mixture of grease, brimstone and tar to deter those foot-long tropical worms that would otherwise make sieves of a ship's timbers in days. Finally, and this is the worst part, get down into the very bowels of the ship and bucket out that ultimate and hellish soup of foul, greeny-brown, turd-ridden bilge water that remains; stumble over stinking, slimy planking, killing rats with a marlinspike in one hand, by the dim light of a lantern swinging from the other.

'Why shipmates, have you finished?' Drake roared genially. 'Then now you must turn her round and do the other side.'

Impossible? In any normal situation, yes, but not when you have a carrot in front of a donkey and the carrot happens to be the *Cacafuego*, a vessel deeply-laden to the gunwales with treasure. And the donkey is Francis Drake.

Bursting headlong through the thirtieth parallel went Drake, that invisible line beyond which if he trespassed, the Queen had solemnly vowed to hang him. His vessel was cleansed and clean, his men fit now, refined and toughened in the crucible of their hellish voyage. Less than eighty men and boys in a small ship on a hostile coast the other side of the world from home. Striding back and forth on the poop deck, still limping slightly from that ball in his leg, the sturdy figure of Francis Drake, blue eyes crinkling with excitement as he scanned the horizon for a ship. One particular ship. The opulently-laden *Cacafuego*.

The hunt was on. The fox—loose in the chicken run.

Dusk. A warm February night. Drake's pinnace slipped silently into the little port of Arica. A fat cargo ship lay placidly at anchor in the moonlight, which Tom Moone boarded in his usual ferocious style. He found some wine and a few small slabs of silver. That was all. Not the *Cacafuego*.

'Go on to Chule,' the terrified crew blabbered. 'There's a big treasure-ship in port, loading with five hundred bars of Spanish royal gold. That must be the great treasure-ship which you seek.'

A hundred miles up the coast and Moone's pinnace nosed into Chule as silently as a ghost, laying alongside the fat belly of a tubby cargo ship with the softest splash of muffled oars. Soon, within the hour, they could start transferring the first of a great hoard of gleaming, glistening gold and silver ingots into the hold of the *Golden Hind*, and all of them could go home and become fine gentlemen. Then came terrible disappointment. Not the *Cacafuego*.

Even as they surged on board and noted the freshly glistening timbers on her sides, they realised something else: they had been expected and the vessel had been quickly and recently off-loaded. Slowly the hard fact sank home that they no longer had the element of surprise. Relays of galloping horsemen can travel faster than the swiftest sailing ship and for days the news of El Draco's coming must have been radiating out and along the extended arteries of the Spanish Empire.

His rounded face reddening with rage, Drake impotently watched a long line of silver-laden llamas snaking up into the hills. With a nicely-balanced strike force he could have easily reached out and clawed back that silver, but with no more than a bare fifty fit men to sail the ship home, he dared not risk even the slightest of skirmishes. Bitterly, he regretted the loss of the *Marigold*, and Winter's cowardly scuttle back to England with the *Elizabeth*.

On again. Sailing ever northwards. Into the teeming, bustling harbour of Callao, the port to Lima itself, the capital of the vice-royalty of Peru, prowled the shadowy shape of the *Golden Hind*, intent on snapping up a plump, well-rounded prey, nicely-fleshed with gold and silver. There, Drake had been assured, a big merchant vessel was loading treasure at this very moment. His heart jumped when he saw

289

the sizeable cargo vessel moored up to the quay. Yes, there could be little doubt, here was the fabulous treasure-ship that they sought. Not the *Cacafuego*.

And worse was to come. The viceroy, Don Francisco Alvarez de Toledo, an energetic and capable man, had been patiently waiting for Francis Drake. As the *Golden Hind* lay becalmed under the lee of San Lorenzo island, he despatched two fat pinnaces, loaded with tough, vengeful Spanish soldiers, across the bay to board and capture her. Triumphantly, with much whooping and trumpet-blowing, they converged on their prey. In seconds now, all would be lost. They would end up, all of them, mouldering in a Spanish dungeon with only the Inquisition's hellish tortures to look forward to.

For the second time it was Hawkins who saved them. Hawkins who had bent an impossible four thousand square feet of sail on masts that were as hard as iron from the winds whistling round their trunks on the exposed slopes of icy, northern forests. Now, those extra t'gallants, clawing bravely into the very reaches of the sky, found wind that lower sails could not, and dragged him out of reach of the infuriated Dons. Like a long, lean wolf, the *Golden Hind*, water chuckling bravely once again past her bows, vanished into the black reaches of an ocean dusk, leaving the viceroy's beautifully-armoured soldiers cursing the name of the heretic corsair—El Draco.

Yet in the huge relief of escape from certain death, the mind of Francis Drake was still full of sadness. John Oxenham, a prisoner had told him, had been captured in the course of his mad assault on the Isthmus of Panama and now, incredibly, lay only a few short tantalising miles away in a Lima dungeon. At this moment, Drake was sure, the Dons would be interrogating him mercilessly, knowing what an intimate friend he had been to El Draco, hoping to learn from Oxenham of Drake's likely plans. And Oxenham, great, beery, waddling, softly-spoken, courageous Oxenham would be telling them, as he quivered and shook in exquisite pain, precisely nothing. If only he had a hundred more men to send on a swift incursion into Lima to bring back his old comrade! Drake boiled with frustration. He knew the Spaniards' methods of interrogation well enough. He tried not to think of his grave and respectable friend, stripped to his portly gut, draped naked backwards over a gun wheel while they whipped and tortured him.

'—S'wounds,' he cried out in terrible torment. 'What would I give to have honest John at my side with a few flagons of old ale under his belt.'

But he knew he would never see that roly-poly fighting devil with the deceptively solemn and pompous manner ever again and it took another old friend, Tom Moone, to stop him stomping back and forth across the poop deck, drinking bottle after bottle of Chilean wine to ease his pain; Tom Moone, another comrade equally dear, to say with unaccustomed softness for such a ferocious man, and with the familiarity that few might have dared to employ, 'Come to bed, you old sot, for you be as drunk as ten whores on a Saturday night on the Cat-water.'

They were sailing past fabulous country now: the surf rolling and booming against the rock-strewn coast with huge fountains of smoking spume, whilst rising above the stifling haze of the coastal plain, looking like distant clouds, so incredibly lofty were they, the majestic peaks of the High Andes clawed their way twenty-thousand feet into the blueness of the sky. Drake, who loved nature, had another matter pressing too heavily on his mind to enjoy the scenery. Where was that accursed treasure-ship? Her devil's spawn of a captain was enjoying incredibly good luck. Each day, as they progressed further north, Drake knew his chances of catching her must grow less.

Then a sail. A merchant ship. Deeply-laden too! The hearts of Drake's men leapt. At last, after endless disappointments, here was untold wealth. Then, unbelievingly, they watched the ship's outline grow steadily bigger. Coming towards them heading for Lima. Empty. Nothing to hide, nothing to fear. Not the *Cacafuego*. They boarded her anyway, growling at her terrified pilot, one Domingo Martin by name, like a pack of hungry, thwarted dogs.

'The treasure-ship?' quaked Domingo, a family man who had heard hair-raising tales of this maniacal pirate, El Draco. 'Why she is somewhere close, up ahead of you, hiding perhaps in the sheltered haven of Paita. Now may I have my ship back, for I am but a poor man who has spawned many children?'

'We shall keep you from your *mujer*,' Drake said with a grim smile, 'only until you have piloted us into Paita and we have run our fingers through its bowels.'

Two days later, the *Golden Hind* stormed into the little port. 'There she be,' Tom Moone pointed excitedly at a plump, well-laden ship skulking under the lee of a cliff. 'There she be. I'll go, cap'n.'

Four times they had boarded a chubby merchantman, the raw

291

stench of untold wealth in their nostrils, only to experience the misery of failure. Surely, this time, the fifth time, they would be lucky.

Señor Custodio Rodriguez, fifty years old and a ship's captain who had experienced most things, found the sheer terror engendered by a boarding party under the command of the ferocious Tom Moone, an utterly harrowing experience. A fist driven in his face, a voice snarling the same repetitive phrase at him time and time again, '*Abajo Perro*—Down dog.' He was sure his last moment had come.

His fears, however, turned out to be over-exaggerated and he found himself on board the *Golden Hind* being interrogated by a short thick-set man with a ruddy face, who, from being continuously denied the treasure-ship he sought, was plainly in a vile temper. Moreover, the news that he imparted did not help the man's temper. Not the *Cacafuego*.

'I cannot help you as to the whereabouts of the *Nuestra Senora*,' Rodriguez said loftily and not without courage as he fingered his aching jaw. He had been careful to use the proper name of the ship, being a man who dwelt in the bosom of his church and disliking the filthy and vulgar name by which sailors were apt to describe her. 'However, I will tell you this. She is well on towards the Isthmus and no ship, not even yours,' he eyed the formidable masts and spars of the *Golden Hind*, 'possesses the speed with which to catch her.'

'We shall see,' Drake said grimly, dismissing Rodriguez.

Now he had a terrible decision to make: explore every little inlet where the treasure-ship might even now be hiding, or cut straight across a wide gulf and head at all speed towards Panama. He was conscious at this moment that what he needed now was flair, sixth sense, a cat's hunting instinct. Others might call it by another name. Luck.

'Set the mains'ls,' he roared suddenly. 'And the fores'l and sprits'l too. Clue up the t'gallants. Give me every stitch of canvas that she'll take. I'll have that silver even if I have to sail the bottom out of her.' He took off one of those thick, golden chains that he liked to wear round his neck. 'And see this, my hearties.' He whirled the great chain round and round in his hand, so that the yellow gold glinted and sparkled in the sun. 'The golden chain of Francis Drake goes to the first man to spot the *Cacafuego*.'

With a great cheer his men ran to their duties, spreading out like ants across the shrouds, the ratlins; the top men swarming nimbly up

292

into the dizzy heights of the *Golden Hind*'s rigging. Sails billowed and flapped and cracked in the stiff breeze, then as they caught and held the wind, the ship leapt eagerly forward like the graceful deer after which she was named.

The end of February now, and surging across the wide Gulf of Gayaquil went the *Golden Hind*, deep into the heart of the Spanish Empire, with Panama itself not far ahead, and populous, flourishing settlements all along the coast. Drake's only hope was that the captain of the treasure-ship, knowing himself to be chased by corsairs, had under-estimated the sailing qualities of the *Golden Hind* and had made a bolt for it.

Spuming along in a stiff, following breeze, the *Golden Hind*, for the first time, showed her true paces. At her stern, the great lateen sail a tight, solid bulge, madly goading the vessel onwards through the sparkling sea, while for'ard, a gigantic sprits'l billowed and flexed, drawing the ship after it like some mighty muscle. High above the deck the mains'l bellied out clean, tight as a drum, without a wrinkle; while higher even yet, best flaxen t'gallants seemed to scrape the last spoonful of wind from the very heavens, the masts becoming live things, groaning and growling, bending and flexing from the terrible pressures.

Looking at that bubbling froth curling majestically away from the ship's bows, the enormous wake creaming out arrow straight behind him, a faint smile of pride replaced the look of pre-occupied worry on the ruddy face of Francis Drake. Surely, he thought. Surely, now, we must stand a chance.

And now the reward came. A yell from the look-out, voice cracking from excitement. 'Sail ahead!' Then they all saw it. A flash of white sail. A merchant vessel. A big one. Heavily laden and heading in the right direction. Suddenly, as one man, the whole crew began to cheer, until Drake cursed them into silence.

She was going fast, cramming on all sail in order to escape, but nothing on the whole Pacific Ocean moved as fast as the *Golden Hind*. Within half an hour they were alongside and Tom Moone, a cutlass in his teeth, was soon over her rail, with a gang of able-bodied lads at his heels, Francis Drake himself at his side. Incredibly, it was not the *Cacafuego*.

Drake had the captain, Diaz Bravo, brought on deck, together with his passengers. Some, he noted thoughtfully, were fat-bellied friars; the others, by the quality of their clothes, their body cuirasses expensively moulded to show off their chests and flatter the waist, a group of wealthy estate owners in transit for Spain.

Fighting down the terrible disappointment that pervaded his soul, Drake asked them collectively, his voice menacing and only barely cloaked with politeness, 'What are you carrying?'

Diaz Bravo replied, 'Only food and supplies for the dockyard.'

'Any valuables?'

'Alas, very few. We are all poor men.'

'Place what you have on deck.'

Very slowly, a small pile of valuables grew in front of Drake.

'Gentlemen,' he said politely. 'In a few moments I will have you conveyed on board my ship. Then we will search your vessel from stem to stern. If any hidden items are discovered, I will have you all hung.' As he spoke, a homicidal smile writhed mirthlessly from ear to ear across his rounded, ruddy face. A smile that most men were only privileged to see seconds before they were despatched to meet their maker. Something about that smile convinced the Spaniards that honesty might be the best policy.

Suddenly, the harvest seemed to grow most pleasantly. Money. Crucifixes made of rubies set in yellow Inca gold. A bag of emeralds, some of the jewels as large as a man's finger. Useful enough pirate loot, but Drake's men had not come halfway round the world for that.

'Now gentlemen,' Drake said. 'I seek this treasure-ship known by a strange name which suggests she may make turds of her cannon-balls. Where is she?'

Silence.

'I ask you for the last time. Where is she?'

As one man, the little group of gentlemen and friars remained obstinately silent. For a moment, Drake was undecided what to do, but noticing a suspicious bulge under the coat of a half-breed fellow lounging at the end of the line, strode over and extracted a concealed bar of gold. 'Hang him,' he said coldly. Within the minute, the body of Francisco Jacome cavorted and danced in choking agony at the end of the yard-arm.

'All right,' Diaz said desperately. 'I will tell your honour. Cut him down.' One expert stroke of Tom Moone's cutlass was enough to sever the rope and pitch the half-breed into the sea, where he was duly picked up, retching and gasping.

'I am waiting,' Drake said politely.

'Your honour is nothing but a pirate,' Diaz said coldly.

'*Exactamente*. The fact is well-known. Now where is the *Cacafuego*?'

'Two days ahead of you.'

At this, a groan of excitement escaped from the boarding-party behind Drake. Only two days ahead, yet Panama was no more than a week away. It would be close. Desperately close.

'How may I recognise her?'

Diaz sneered at him.

'Your honour could be next to dangle from the rope,' Drake suggested.

Diaz went white in the face. He nodded, accepting defeat. 'Your honour will easily know her, because she is three-masted. Such a ship is most unusual in these parts.'

'*Muchas gracias, Señor*,' said Drake, bowing low.

'There is one thing more. She is the only ship in this sea that carries cannon, and the ones she carries are both powerful and numerous. It is my earnest wish that she blows your honour's devilish crew of Lutherans to the hell where they belong.'

Drake grinned widely. 'I thank your honour,' he said.

# 27

It was 1 March 1579 when keen-eyed John Drake called down from his
dizzy eyrie on the mainmast, 'Sail ho.'

The fact that nobody took much notice was due to the endless false
alarms the crew of the *Golden Hind* had endured, the continuous failures they had experienced in their search for the treasure-ship, so
much so that they doubted now, whether she had ever really existed
at all. When, however, John Drake called down that the vessel was
three-masted, there was a distinct flicker of interest from the deck.

'What course?' Francis Drake called up.

'Full and bye for Panama, cap'n.'

Now, a buzz of speculation started on deck, quickly quelled by a
roar from Drake. 'I'm coming up,' he shouted.

It was no trouble for Francis Drake, with his strong arms and
burly legs, to shin up the mainmast, and within half a minute he was
sitting beside his young cousin in the fighting tops.

'Show her to me,' he demanded.

Silently, John pointed a finger over the port quarter. Drake studied the vessel. Seven or eight miles further out to sea. If anything
lying slightly behind his own ship. Deeply-laden, all sail crammed
on. Yes, definitely three-masted. If it was not the *Cacafuego*, it was
certainly where the *Cacafuego* should be.

Quickly he descended again to the deck. 'I think it is her,' he was heard to say to Tom Moone before retiring to his own personal poop deck, where he began to pace backwards and forwards, hand on chin, obviously sunk deep in thought.

Once again, the deck of the *Golden Hind* buzzed with excited speculation. Most of the men aboard were experienced sailors and Drake's problems were easily recognised: formidable problems that seemed impossible to solve. The basics were quite simple. The skipper of the other vessel, warned of Drake, would be suspicious, highly wary of any ship that approached her. If the *Golden Hind* spread less sail and allowed her to close, or turned and headed towards her, she would, without a doubt, head for the nearest port and with the sharp sweep of the bay in her favour, they would have little chance of catching her. If by some miracle they did, then they would be involved in a gun battle ending in the likely sinking of one or both ships—which is not exactly the way to capture a cargo of silver.

How then to allay the other man's suspicions? How to appear just another innocent merchantman? Somehow he must get close enough to lay a boarding-party over the side. What must he do? The crew considered the matter among themselves, then finding no answer, wearily, bitterly, broke up the discussion. Failure was becoming a distinct way of life to them, seeping into and eating away at their very souls.

'Do we still have those *botijas* aboard? Those wine jars?' Drake's voice sounded unbelievably relaxed, no longer under pressure.

'There be plenty of wine aboard, cap'n.' Tom Moone's reply was pained. It was as obvious to him now, as it was to the rest of the crew, that Drake, when confronted with troublesome problems, intended to drown them in wine.

'No, not the full ones Tom. The empty ones. I'll have them strung together and trailed over the stern. When that has been done, alter course five points towards the ship.'

As the meaning of their captain's order slowly sank home, the men began to cheer. Drake, by adapting to his own purposes the last desperate measure used by mariners to prevent their vessel from being blown onto a lee shore, had managed to produce a stroke of sheer genius. The wine jars would act as massive drogues, so that despite carrying a full set of canvas, the *Golden Hind* would be moving very slowly. As the other vessel imperceptibly overhauled her on a converging course, her captain, noting the slow progress of the *Golden*

297

*Hind*, would take her merely for another deeply-laden merchant ship and have not the slightest suspicion of what awaited him.

All through the long hot reaches of the afternoon, as the two ships pitched and rolled their way towards Panama, edging ever closer together, tension rose on the *Golden Hind*; an oppressive silence that lay heavily over the deck as the crew went about their work and tried not to think of that huge cargo of treasure wallowing imperceptibly nearer to their grasp with the passing of every minute. Then, as the equatorial sun sank, a fiery furnace low in the western sky, the three masts of the other vessel suddenly foreshortened into a single black line as, sharply and with no warning, she altered course.

'She has turned away,' John Drake shouted down.

Now the men of the *Golden Hind* knew only black despair. Somehow, the captain of the treasure vessel had become suddenly suspicious and in the enveloping darkness they would never catch her. Perhaps he had been diabolically clever, more artful even, than the redoubtable Francis Drake, playing the innocent lamb for Drake to slowly stalk, intending all the time to bolt for safety as darkness approached! Once again, and not for the first time, stark failure. At the thought of that great cargo of silver sliding effortlessly out of their grasp, the men began to mutter and look sullenly at their captain, in whose skill they were rapidly losing faith. From all over the ship, bitter and ferocious curses welled up towards the figure of Francis Drake standing silently on the poop deck.

'Wait!' John Drake's voice, strident with sudden excitement, reverberated across the deck. 'Is she? No. It cannot be. Yes, she is. Shipmates,' his voice cracking now from the tension, 'she turns towards us, not away. Do you hear? She has set course direct for the *Golden Hind*. Cap'n, she is coming straight for us!'

Slowly, in the gathering dusk, the two ships converged. Although their hearts were pounding with excitement, the crew went carefully and silently about their work under strict discipline, the beginnings of a formidable tradition that would make the Royal Navy, in years to come, the mistress of the high seas. Not by a whisper did they betray that they were anything more than innocent seamen manning a slow merchantman. Drake's execution of Doughty, his blood-curdling threats of punishment, the enormous dominance he had finally achieved over his men, now finally paid off. There would be no drunken seaman to ruin this operation the way the ambush on the

Nombre de Dios mule train had been ruined.

On the side of the *Golden Hind* shielded from the view of the other vessel, Tom Moone quietly launched the pinnace, waiting for his moment to send an assault force of picked men swarming over the unsuspecting Spaniard's rail. Drake hurried below decks, to where the rows of demi-culverins waited lethally in the semi-darkness, picking his way over the heaps of cannonballs and past the crouching, sweating gun-crews. In the heat the smell of powder, saltpetre, and the odour of many men in an enclosed space stripped to the waist, was overpowering.

'Where's the master gunner?' Drake demanded.

''Ere I be, zorr.' The pixie-like features of Danielles bobbed at his side. The man's face, as he knuckled his forehead, showed white from a life below decks, where it was not begrimed with dark streaks of powder from servicing, cleaning and cossetting these gleaming monsters.

'Who lays the best shot?'

'Beggin' yor pardon, zorr, I dew.' There was no element of bragging in the man's air of quiet confidence. 'But ain't we goin' to broadside her, zorr? Seven guns on the port side, then turnabout and seven more from starboard'll blow her near out of the water.'

Drake grinned. 'No broadsides, Danielles. I want her crippled not sunk. No use feeding all that silver to the fishes.'

A ripple of laughter went round the expectant gunners. Relief that their commander, their master, was in charge and apparently knew what he was doing.

'Now then, Danielles,' Drake went on. 'I want you to load two guns with chainshot and lay them to bring down first the mizzen and then the mainmast. Can you do it?'

Danielles scratched his one strand of curly hair. 'Yew be askin' for some smart shootin', zorr, but one of the masts at least, I promise 'ee that.'

'Well enough.' Drake strode away. 'Be ready within the minute,' he called back. 'We're closing fast.'

Now, trained to a hair, two gun-crews sprang into action. On the command 'load' each crew ran their demi-culverin back on its wheeled, wooden carriage by means of rope and tackle and the loader smartly rammed a canvas cartridge full of gunpowder down the muzzle. After that a wad of oakum, old rope twisted and teased loose, was thrust down, then, in quick succession, the chainshot, then

299

another wad.

Running from one to the other, Danielles delicately thrust a wire down and through each touch-hole, already primed with fine powder from the gunner's horn, and punctured the cartridge full of powder. 'Run 'em out.' he bawled.

Imperceptibly, two gun-ports opened. Quietly, quietly, the wheels smeared with thick oil to stop them squealing, each crew ran their gun forward, while Danielles, sweating from the need for urgency, sighted both guns in succession, the crews working away with wedges under the barrels and operating handspike and crowbar to achieve the right elevation.

'What ship is that?' The voice of the Spanish captain could be heard clearly even below decks, so close were the two vessels now.

'The ship of Miguel Angel.'

'That cannot be. We left her empty in Callao. Strike in the name of the King.'

'Strike yourself, in the name of the Queen of England.'

A shrill whistle. Prepare! A blasting trumpet-call from Brewer the trumpeter. Fire!

Now, to do the business. If Danielles aimed badly, they would all lose a fortune, perhaps their lives as well, when the other ship recovered its wits and unleashed a broadside. Over the long, lean, murderous line of the culverin, a solid black spot grew in Danielles' eye, dead centre of the mizzen-mast. Savagely, he thrust home his slow match.

'Boom!' The culverin recoiled fiercely against the breeching ropes with the noise of thunder, smoke billowing on all sides.

Leaping about like some madman straight from bedlam, Danielles aligned the second gun in the direction of the mainmast.

'Boom!' The shot too hurried, going wide. Yet the first one had done its work, blowing the mizzen-mast clean off the ship, sending it crashing into the ocean amid a mass of chaotic spars and rigging.

A quick hail of arquebus fire to keep the Spaniards' heads down, terminating with parade-ground precision to the shouted order 'cease fire' and then, paralysing in their terrible impact, Tom Moone and his bunch of piratical ruffians swarmed over the treasure-ship from the far side, the ferocious little carpenter laying about him as he shouted again and again the only Spanish he knew, or wanted to know, 'Abajo Perro—Down dog'.

In seconds it was all over. The Spaniards made prisoner. The bewildered captain brought on board the *Golden Hind*, just as Drake was taking off his armour.

'I am sorry,' Drake said affably to the poor man, 'but 'tis the usage of war. But you shall have my receipt in full.'

It had been a classical ship-boarding action, carried out with consummate skill. Now Drake crammed on all sail, the *Cacafuego* in tow. Only, he decided, when he had put three days of anonymous ocean between him and the avenging Dons, would it be safe, like a child opening a present, to see what the good Lord had provided!

When they opened up the *Cacafuego*, Drake and his men, not unaccustomed to the pleasant sparkle of captured treasure, were astounded, quite literally tongue-tied with amazement at what they found. Pounds of gold and tons, yes unbelievably, ton after ton of silver. Out here, in the unexplored Pacific Ocean, they had stumbled upon Aladdin's cave. His normally ruddy face pale with emotion, Drake gave the order to jettison the great pile of heavy stones the *Golden Hind* carried as ballast. To house all this endless treasure, there was just not sufficient cargo space in his holds. For its ballast, the *Golden Hind* would have to make do with silver bars!

Perhaps that fact above all made the crew realise what an incalculable fortune they had reaped. Whatever share their captain might be pleased to award them, would turn them, when they returned home, into rich men able to buy their own businesses, curse their servants, strut about in silks and taffetas.

It took three more whole days to shift all that silver into the *Golden Hind*. At the end of that time, she lay low in the water, stuffed and swollen, like some fat Michaelmas goose, with high grade Peruvian silver. With much flowery expression of goodwill, Drake, in the best of tempers, took his leave of the captain of the *Cacafuego*.

As he sheered off, a Spanish lad with something of a sense of humour, called out, 'Hey, *Capitan Draco*. *Escucheme*—in future, they call our ship, not "she who excretes fire", but "she who excretes silver", eh?' But Drake pursed his lips and pretended not to hear him. He was, after all, a most religious man, reared in the ways of the Lord and not, therefore, overfond of vulgarity.

Now he headed north. But why? With his ship groaning like the distended belly of an old whore after a Christmas feast, there was not an inch more room for loot. It was time to go home, and by some incredible good fortune, he had captured pilots familiar with the direct

301

route across the Pacific taken by the Phillipine galleons. Why then, go north. Why? Why?

To careen. Well yes, that is a partial explanation. Yet some other reason, some inner feeling, some sixth sense, some deep awareness of destiny not admissible of any full understanding, drove him ever north, past Panama, past Mexico, into the region of the thirty-eighth to the fortieth parallel, a little-known area not yet colonised by the Spanish and known to them as—

The Californias.

1578. The Queen returned to London after her summer progress to Norwich, racked by the normal number of petty illnesses. True, the ulcer in her leg which had done little over the previous months to improve her temper, had healed, but in its place she was now suffering from stomach vomitings and a persistent toothache. Freeze her in time then, at the age of forty-five, a frail woman with a glitteringly transparent pallor, every nerve in her bony body stretched taut from awful tensions, terrible hysteria, her string of petty complaints quite plainly induced by accumulated, unspeakable anxieties, the awful and lonely stress of monarchy.

In December the toothache reached a raging climax that left the Queen without sleep for forty-eight hours, and to deal with this sudden crisis of state, the Privy Council duly convened. She received them dressed in the very latest thing from the continent, a white partlet, a yoke with a turned-down collar, screaming with pain, weeping and stamping her foot in petulance.

'Was it,' the Council wondered, 'vanity, the thought of depriving that long, pale but still strikingly handsome face, of a tooth? Or was it, could it be, perish the thought, cowardice?'

They deliberated no further. Brilliantly, they sent venerable, grey-haired Aylmer, Bishop of London, to comfort and encourage her. Aylmer was a gentle old man who had tutored many children, including Lady Jane Grey, and the Queen, quite plainly, was behaving like a child.

'My lord Bishop,' the Queen wept desperately, imploringly, 'you have been sent, I do not doubt, to see this tooth parted from its companions. Pray, sir, desist, for I cannot face the thought.'

The old fellow knelt at her feet, his sympathy enormous, his compassion total, his love for her like that of most of her subjects—unbelievable. 'My liege,' he said gently. 'I have few enough

302

teeth left in my head, but those that remain are entirely at your service. The surgeon shall draw one out and your grace shall see it is of no great matter.' There and then, in front of the distraught Queen, he had the tooth removed, and in so doing, nerved her to follow suit.

This crisis then, was soon over, but worse ones, gravely threatening her kingdom, loomed like grey, heavy storm clouds on the horizon.

In the spring of the following year, Captain John Winter brought the *Elizabeth* home, to coincide with furious Portuguese protests to the Queen, regarding Drake's early plunderings on his way down the African coast. As the summer wore on and the trickle of reports on Drake's doings grew into a river of hard news, culminating with the capture of the *Cacafuego*, the Queen's fury grew into a maniacal insensate thing.

But for this sensitive, intelligent woman who, it seemed, was increasingly tortured with any number of self-doubts, hysterias, little illnesses and loss of confidence, one emotion had now become even stronger than anger. Fear. For Philip, the cane-haired spider of the Escorial, was in the course of putting into effect a whole series of actions, apparently disconnected at first, but which shortly grew under the terrified gaze of Elizabeth into a deadly web of menace from which there could be no escape, encircling tiny England.

In the Netherlands, Parma was busy demolishing the Protestant resistance that had bled the Queen's treasury almost dry, while on the Portuguese border, the redoubtable Alva was massing his élite tercios ready to take over the huge Portuguese fleet on the imminent death of the ailing King. In Ireland, the first small detachments of Spanish and papal troops had landed, together with seminary priests fresh from the English college at Douai, preparing the way for an even larger expedition shortly to follow. Meanwhile back in Spain itself, Recalde, that dedicated enemy of Francis Drake, had skilfully laid down a huge programme of warship construction, designed within a few years, to bring the heretic Queen to her bony knees.

In short, an amazing colossus of power was being built with the sole object of crushing Elizabeth. Invincible. Enormous. Without precedent. On all sides, closing in on her like advancing black walls of doom, Philip's armies flexed their mighty strength, prior to crushing her little realm.

What then, must a poor, distraught Queen do? Why, make the only gesture of conciliation at present open to her: send the completely guiltless John Winter to prison and promise compensation to the plundered Portuguese.

And if she could do that to innocent Captain Winter, what will she do to the person of Francis Drake? Philip knew. Oh yes, Leicester had told him all about the Queen's strange grudge against Drake. Philip knew all right. Philip knew everything. The master of psychological warfare he had ordered 'Before the corsair reaches England, it is not expedient to speak to the Queen. When he arrives, yes.'

Then his ambassador, the formidable Don Bernadino de Mendoza, would be sent striding into Elizabeth's court to demand peremptorily, without a doubt to receive, from a trembling, unwell woman—the head of Francis Drake on a silver salver.

Drake knew himself to be a condemned man, yet here, on the other side of the globe from his adored Queen, he could not help feeling a sense of detachment, of unreality. With a smile on his ruddy face, he would watch the jiggings and merrymaking of his delighted crew, while in the evenings he would dine in pleasant solitude to the soft scrapings of his ship's orchestra.

One day he found an outcrop of land jutting away from the main trend of the coastline so as to lie dead ahead of his northerly course. Normally, Drake would have turned to port and given himself searoom, allowing Moone in his pinnace to reconnoitre for a possible careening site. But as a pleasant inlet* grew into focus, Drake, for some unfathomable reason, felt himself impelled, against all the fundamental rules of seamanship, to take the *Golden Hind* gently in.

And there, before his eyes, the inlet opened up into a peaceful lagoon, absolutely perfect for careening, secluded, safe from Spanish attack and, wonder of wonders, as if placed there by the very hand of God, the low-lying land to starboard reared up and formed itself into an amazing image in miniature of the White Cliffs of Dover!

The *Golden Hind* heeled sharply over as her crew rushed to the rail to view this amazing phenomenon. A miracle. A divine portent. The Almighty must have plucked those sheer white cliffs from the English Channel just to gladden their hearts and give them the spirit to make the terrible, peril-strewn, sixteen thousand mile journey home. They

* An inlet to the east of Point Reyes and Chimney Rock, off San Francisco. The bay is called, predictably, Drake's Bay; the inlet—Drake's Estero.

were all superstitious men, even Drake himself was not immune.

Next day he spoke to Tom Moone, his friend. 'Tom, last night I had a dream. I saw, close to here, a great city full of people who speak our tongue. 'Twas most strange.'

'Ay, master. The sight of those white cliffs has given us all much food for thought. Were those folks you saw then, English?'

'I do not know,' Drake said softly. 'For my dream was much in the future and new nations grow great, while old nations wane. I tell you Tom, only this. They took pride, these people, in the inheritance of our customs, institutions and liberties.'

Tom Moone could only nod sagely. His master was indeed in a strange mood today and he must humour him.

This strange sense of mission, of purpose, stayed with Drake throughout the whole of the careening, a pleasant enough business made comic by the need of the local Miwok Indians to treat the white men as God. Soon the time came for them to take their leave.

Across the vast reaches of the Pacific Ocean, the *Golden Hind* boldly pointed her bows. Her men were not afraid. A ship that could survive the Straits of Magellan could survive anything, and that strange finding of an inlet containing a very duplicate of the white cliffs of Dover had convinced them that the hand of God must be watching over them.

Past many exotic lands sailed the *Golden Hind*, lands of opulence and riches too many and varied to record. On one occasion the ship impaled herself with great force on the fanged teeth of some concealed rocks and stuck fast, was almost certain to sink at the next blow of wind, yet Drake prayed and the *Golden Hind* was wafted off into open sea, quite unharmed. Again the mariners saw in this the hand of God, yet it had to be admitted even by them, that the Lord was proving unusually indulgent to a marauding, piratical corsair.

Away and across the Indian Ocean wallowed the *Golden Hind*, no longer a swift greyhound of the seas, but deep in the water from the tremendous load of silver she was carrying and the extra burden of valuable spices she had managed to cram onto her deck space, gifts from the many fabulous places at which she had called. Round the Cape of Good Hope and groaning from her precious burden, like some exhausted nag, she was able to steer north for home and England.

Now, on the last leg of his journey, awful realities came home to Francis Drake. He had not broken just one isolated order of the

305

Queen, he had succeeded in breaking all of them. Every single one of them! There was no hope. No possible defence or excuse. He was a doomed man and must prepare himself for the supreme penalty at the hands of a mistress that he had never ceased to love. No matter, he had always held his own life cheaply enough.

Other thoughts stayed at the front of his mind, rooted there as if possessed of some inexplicable importance. What had impelled him to nail that brass plate onto a tree close by those white cliffs? Why had he spent so much valuable time having words cut into the brass, claiming these lands for his Queen? What need had there been to insert in the plate an Elizabethan sixpence, so as to prove to future generations of English-speaking folk that Francis Drake had visited and loved that place? He had not done such a thing anywhere else on all his vast journeyings round the world.

Some inexplicable and mystical force had wedded him to that magical spit of land inside which there was a gentle lagoon with cliffs rising sharply into an amazing likeness of the white cliffs of Dover and which had given his men, separated by half the face of the globe from their loved ones, much comfort.

Ruddy-faced Francis Drake, blue-eyed and swaggering, pirate and explorer extraordinary, had, it seemed, indeed left his heart in—
San Francisco.

# 28

Juan de Recalde stood on a grassy promontory overlooking Smerwick Bay, gazing out to sea. Beneath him a snaky line of arquebusiers, weighed down with all their awkward equipment, halbardiers and pikemen, wound slowly, like the coils of a writhing serpent, towards the beckoning, vivid green turf of Ireland. As he watched, there was much whinnying and splashing, as to a tremendous commotion the small detachment of beautifully-accoutred cavalry was disgorged from the shallow draught barges; the horses, of Arab blood toughened with a leavening of the old destrier line of warhorse to take the weight of their rider's armour, lashing out with their rear hooves to express their fury at being plunged into the unaccustomed iciness of Atlantic sea-water.

If the English fleet were to attack now . . . Well, Recalde knew that, compared to his own well-found squadron of escorting galleons, the English fleet was insignificant. True, that pirate Hawkins was rumoured to be building a few small and weatherly warships on radical new lines, but they would have to keep their distance or risk being overwhelmed by the soldiers festooning the fighting tops of his galleons; and anyway, they were few and far between, the penurious Queen of the Lutherans not being able to afford the construction of more than one or two pathetic warships each year.

When he considered what he, in contrast, had achieved in the last few years, Recalde's olive face grinned mirthlessly. He had, with single-minded loyalty and devotion, built for his master a formidable fleet, yet took little pleasure in the fact. He, Recalde, a dashing man of action, had been pulled out of the Americas to serve his master in clerkly anonymity, just when he had been poised to destroy the corsair Drake. Every time he had gone up against El Draco, he had

307

damaged him. Did not Drake, even now, limp from the arquebus ball he had planted in his leg? Had not one of his brothers, the burly, bull-like John Drake, also perished at his hands?

Recalde glanced at his hand and yawned. No longer was there any feeling of emotion at that white scar, faint now, placed there so long ago by the eager teeth of the young Francis Drake. He was well into middle age now, rich beyond measure, secure in his position as trusted adviser to his King. He was past the years when ambition burned, the need for revenge festered a man's soul. His present wish was a simple one: to prove finally to himself which of them was a better man. He, or Francis Drake.

As he watched the gay splash of colour made by the multi-coloured tunics of the papal Swiss guard, as they climbed out of their boats, Recalde knew how terrified the English Queen would be when the news of their coming was leaked to her. As if the power of Spain, combined now with Portugal, was not enough to wipe her off the face of the earth, the Pope, with all his immense resources and riches, had announced his intention of actively participating in the heretic Queen's destruction.

Recalde hoped that she would dredge from some part of her ailing body the spirit to resist his master's certain demand for the head of El Draco; for then, Philip had hinted, he would send a great naval force up the Channel to link with Parma's army in the Netherlands and destroy the Queen.

Yet Recalde had heard that all the courage had seeped out of Queen Elizabeth's body. Fingering his hair-line moustache, grey now, as he plunged deep into his middle years, he realised that there was very little chance of his dearest wish being fulfilled: to settle finally, one way or the other, an old score with an old enemy in open battle.

Down to fifty-nine men now, water severely rationed, Drake battled slowly up the African coast. Yet only one more man died, the others keeping alive through sheer will-power. Coming home with a fortune is a sharp spur with which to prick a man into surviving just a few more days!

They reached Sierra Leone with only eight pints of stale water left in the ship. Easy though, from now on. Standing out well to the north west to avoid the main Spanish shipping lanes, navigating by the pole star until he reached latitude fifty north, Drake turned for Devon with a following wind, the *Golden Hind* tumbling uneasily through the turbulent waters of the continental shelf, low and sluggish in the water from the monstrous, the truly staggering, dead-weight of her cargo.

Soon, familiar landmarks came into view, sights that sent the men happy and contented about their work: the Scillies, Wolf Rock, the Lizard, then suddenly Rame Head and the fertile green arms of Plymouth Sound, the vivid purple-brown line of Dartmoor taking on shape and colour to the delighted exclamations of the men. Nearer and nearer to Plymouth surged the *Golden Hind* on the flood-tide, her bilges ballasted with silver, her after-quarters stuffed with gold bars, the odd nooks and crannies that were left, stuffed with precious cloves. As St Nicholas Island appeared to port and the lofty promontory of Plymouth Hoe rippled towards them like the fingers of a half-clenched fist, the anchor chain went roaring down with a quick splash.

26 September, 1580. Drake was home. The time, late afternoon, close to dusk, convenient for slipping in unnoticed, like an unwanted dog looking for shelter. Nearby, a group of fishing-boats.

'Does the Queen live?' Drake bellowed over to them.

The fishermen looked at the strange vessel in amazement, her sails torn and patched, her timbers bleached and cracked from years of hot sun and salt; and what, they thought curiously, what on earth must she be carrying to be that low in the water?

'What were that yew said, my lover?' one of them shouted back, cheekier than the rest in a ripe Devon accent. 'What ship be yew then?'

'Never mind my ship,' Drake roared. 'I ask again—does the Queen still live?'

'She be alive and well enough.'

At this, Drake heaved a great sigh. After nearly three years at sea, his very first question had been for the welfare of his mistress the Queen, who, in spite of her cruel treatment of him, he had never ceased to adore.

Quickly, he turned his attention to urgent matters: the men paid off and sent safe to their homes with their reward, before irate Queen's officers sealed the cargo. And now, Drake thought wryly, while I am still at liberty, to spend the last few weeks of my life with that other woman towards whom I also have a duty. He slipped away unnoticed to his nearby house, like a hunted fox crawling into his

309

earth, waiting only for the huntsman's terriers to drag him out for execution.

Within days of Drake's homecoming, Burghley drew up an Order in Council for the plunder to be restored to its rightful owners and in the meantime, to be lodged in the Tower. It seemed inevitable to Drake that he must soon join his cargo in that evil and terrible place, prior to being led out to the block.

What a tragedy is this, my masters, what an unkind trick of fate, that such fabulous flowering of art and the written word and music at court be entirely due to the intelligence and exquisite beauty of Queen Elizabeth; yet that lady, who used to love dancing, dances only reluctantly now, such prey is she to nervous depressions, melancholies of the mind and body, awful and nameless fears.

This magnificence, these fine prancings, the rustle of great ladies in silks and satins as they swoop and lift in the galliard, or 'solomon's jigge', the 'goat's leape' or the 'brawl' or 'nobody's jigge'; and the colours of the gowns, enough to blind a man! Provocations of mockado and satin in vivid shades of popinjay blue or lustie gallant or stammel; maids-of-honour in pretty little dresses of goose-turd greene and maiden-hair browne, sewn tight to show off their fine young dugs; while all around, the musicians scrape and fiddle and tootle on shawm, sackbut and viol, and the lively airs of Byrd and Ferrobosco and Allison and even young Master Dowland, grace the corridors of Richmond.

All this counted for nothing now, in her that had been its inspiration. She sat shrunken-faced, her black eyes lack-lustre, in a gown of grosgrain and silk of the most delicate salmon pink, a superb winged-collar of delicate lacework soaring around the thinness of her neck and caressing her elegant ears; her long, prominently-nosed face made slightly cavernous now by her exhaustion and terrible terrors, so out of place in the centre of all this scented prettiness and femininity.

She was still breathing hard, she realised, her shoulders quite shaking from being wafted clear up into the rafters in that great cat's leap that was quite mandatory by one's partner in the volta. My lord of Leicester had been in no condition to undertake such a strenuous dance and if she was puffing, Leicester, as he had fought to whirl her spare frame effortlessly up among the stars as Hatton or Oxford could so easily do, poor ailing Leicester, had been groaning like a blown carthorse dying in the shafts. For a moment, a slight grin appeared on her woebegone features, disappearing in an instant under the terrible weight of her cares, the pain of her multifarious complaints.

Listening now, while orchestra and dancers rested, her ears, long attuned to the normal hustle and bustle of the court, detected something unusual. The sounds of protest, of voices raised, the shuffle of guards, the confused rattle of pikes and halberds. The sound grew, passing through ranks of yeomen, sergeants-at-arms, then gentlemen pensioners, to materialise as the huge doors of the great hall burst open, in the tall and arrogant person of Don Bernadino de Mendoza, the Spanish ambassador.

A hush. A sigh. Whispers of foreboding. Across the whole length of the hall stalked the envoy of the most powerful country in the world, contempt on his dark face for the craven way these Lutherans had allowed him to force his way with such brutish ill-manners right into the presence of their sovereign.

He did not deign to bow to the heretic whore. An inclination of the head was enough. He looked at her. Pale. Deadly pale, visibly trying not to tremble. When he spoke, he barely managed to hide the sneer in his voice. Once she had been a spirited woman. Now, in only a few short years, she had turned into a dull-faced, cringing, middle-aged wretch, all her courage long since seeped out of her.

'Madam, in the name of my master, King Philip, I demand audience.'

Demand? The court gasped and waited for an explosion, but instead the Queen merely waved weak, febrile fingers at the dancers to go and the room was soon empty, save for Leicester and Walsingham waiting silently in the background.

'We are sorry not to rise to greet your excellency,' the Queen said feebly. 'Our body is plagued today, with uncommon gripes and pains.'

'I am desolated to see your majesty in ill-health, yet there is urgent business between us that admits of no delay.'

'And what business is that?'

'Your majesty knows well enough.' Mendoza's voice was curt, incredibly rude. 'I refer, of course, to the activities of the great corsair, Francis Drake.'

Mendoza noticed how the Queen's mouth seemed to purse in an emotion near to hatred at the mention of Drake, before she said faintly, 'Very well. Pray continue.'

311

'This pirate has plundered the whole length of my master's possessions in the New World. He has stolen enormous treasure.'

'Your excellency knows that a commission has been set up to arrange compensation.'

'Words, madam, mere words,' Mendoza sneered. 'My master well knows the workings of these so-called commissions.' He paused, then lowering his thick, bushy eyebrows, demanded brutally, 'Why is the corsair still at liberty?'

The Queen shivered slightly like a gillyflower in a chill autumn breeze. 'An order will be made for his detention.'

''Twould be wise, madam. 'Twould be wise. Permit me to remind your majesty of certain matters.'

Elizabeth shrank back into her velvet chair as if trying to avoid his gaze, and finding no escape, said weakly, 'Yes sir, what matters are these?'

In the Netherlands, Parma tramples in triumph over the ravaged corpses of Lutheran women and children. At home, my King, having conquered Portugal, now commands the mightiest fleet in the world. In Ireland the Holy Father himself joins with my master in sending an army into Ireland. In France, the catholics rule and you may expect little help from there. Even in your majesty's own realm, seminary priests openly detach from you the loyalty of one great family after another.'

'State your point, sir, state your point.' The Queen, shaking her head from one side to the other, could stand it no longer.

Mendoza noticed how her hands were openly shaking now and how she was trying to hide this by grasping the arms of her chair, so that the lithe veins in her wrists stood out like blue worms. He raked her with sharp, cruel eyes from head to toe, noticing the blatant absurdity of her hair soaked in lye, its fading redness glistening from a thick pomade of apple-juice and puppy-dog fat, her face enamelled into brilliant whiteness from some poisonous lead preparation. Yes, absurd was the word. Truly absurd. An ailing forty-seven year old woman dolled up into an awful mockery of youth.

'You are surrounded by a sea of enemies.' Mendoza spat the words out triumphantly. 'Your kingdom bankrupt. My master could conquer England within a week.'

'And what then, does Philip want of us?' the Queen cried out in terrible agitation. 'Only state his terms. Only let us hear them.'

'You must cut off the head of Francis Drake.'

312

'If we agree, what then?'

Mendoza opened his hands in an expansive gesture, the menace vanishing from his eyes. 'In that case, madam, the quarrel between my master and yourself is immediately terminated.'

'And the treasure?'

Mendoza spread his hands even further. 'I am authorised to state that an arrangement may be made pleasant to both sides. His majesty is well aware that the cargo manifests of gold and silver shipped from Peru are marked deliberately low so as to escape tax. My master will be satisfied with that valuation, and you may keep the excess, perhaps amounting to half the total shipment, and those dishonest mine-owners will have been taught a good lesson into the bargain.' He laughed at his own joke and continued, 'That is just the beginning. We Spanish are realists. You have learned a way through into the Pacific and we cannot roll back history. His majesty will grant you, from now on, fair trading facilities throughout his dominions.'

Even before the ambassador had finished, the Queen knew his offer to be irresistible. All she had ever wanted for her little kingdom. A right to trade, a decent outlet for her peoples' goods, her subjects' energies, and in addition, a handsome cache of treasure with which to replenish her empty coffers! All for the head of that ruddy-faced little pirate, Francis Drake, the cause of all her ills, her complaints, her lonely spinsterhood.

'You shall have my answer before morning,' the Queen said softly. 'We have little doubt that you will find it satisfactory.'

'You will cut off Drake's head?'

'Yes.'

'You had better—' Mendoza could not resist one last threat, the Queen cringed so agreeably whenever he fixed her with his hard eyes beneath their lowering thatches of dark brow. 'You had better, madam, for if these persuasions are not enough, why, we shall see what the roar of cannon can do!'

As he contemptuously turned on his heel, the short gasp that the Queen made was ample and certain proof to Mendoza, that he had finally terrified her into complete submission.

For Drake, the strain of waiting was terrible. Every day he would keep an ear open for the sound of Queen's soldiers marching across the cobbles to arrest him. John Hawkins had delivered to him a concise and very direct message from Walsingham and Hatton. Fly. Fly

313

for your life. The Queen and Burghley are united in their fury, their enmity. The Spanish ambassador demands your head. Arrest is imminent.

He would not fly. Francis Drake had never run from anyone in his life, and he would not run now, from his own Queen. Instead, he endured the miseries of his wife's company with resigned stoicism. His martyrdom would not last for long. Soon, he would be summoned to London, his head would be cut off and that would be that. And when the summons came, he would know only relief. For Mary had deteriorated badly. She was no more than a skeleton now, just skin stretched over bone. As consumption had bitten deeply into her body, so madness had continued to ravage her mind. But for her husband's purse, she would already have been despatched to some evil hole akin to bedlam. The poor woman had only brief moments of sanity now and had become only barely aware of Drake's return. As she continued to suffer at the hands of relays of doctors who would gather round her in their loose black gowns, examine her piss, rub their hands, mutter and confer, then bleed her, bleed her again and then finish by giving her an enema, the Elizabethan standby for chest complaints, Drake could only pray for her quick release.

A quick release for himself, also, was the fervent wish he expressed daily to the Almighty in his devotions.

Then, in the spring of 1581 his prayer was answered. A message from the Queen, short, peremptory. 'Francis Drake is to bring the *Golden Hind* round to Deptford.'

Right. Best doublet, two splendid rows of gleaming pearls, his hair singed and barbered, his beard and moustachios waxed and curled. He was a gentleman now, in his own eyes at least, and intended to die like one.

The *Golden Hind*? He would not have her crawl into Deptford like some mangy, weather-beaten cur come to lick its master's boot. This ship had sailed round the world, survived seas that most men believed were only legend. Two frantic days he spent, throwing his own money prodigally into the work, varnishing, painting, equipping her with brilliant new white flaxen sails. He had signed on a fresh crew, not wishing to hazard the lives of his brave sailors; only Tom Moone, his old comrade for so many years, accompanied him. Tom, who had spearheaded so many mad assaults onto the unsuspecting decks of Spanish ships: Tom, the only one of his original companions to survive, would, in any event, share his captain's fate and had expressed the wish to stand shoulder to shoulder with him, when it came.

When, a few days later, the *Golden Hind* docked at Deptford, she made a magnificent sight and, to be sure, there was a fine crowd there too. Drake knew well enough what a festive occasion the English liked to make of an execution and even if he was something of a national hero, so had many other outlaws been, in recent history, and their popularity had not saved them from the block!

The Queen was not long in coming. She must have been waiting nearby for the *Golden Hind*'s arrival, determined to impress her Spanish masters with her eagerness to punish the pirate. As she stepped aboard, he found he could not look at her in her bejewelled and majestic magnificence and his mind went back to that moment so many years ago, when the sheer luminous brilliance of her presence in that garden of Ashridge had similarly terrified him. He bowed his head, remembering only with enormous effort, to bark out the order for the royal standard to be broken. What a roar from the crowd greeted his ears as silken leopards, lilies and lions clawed gaily out in the stiff breeze, banners of the finest damask snaked into the wind marked with the vivid motifs of the ⌐ross of St George and, because the English throne still laid claim to France, the fleur-de-lys!

A block was placed in front of him. 'Kneel. Lay thy head there,' the Queen said curtly. But there was no executioner. What kind of strange business was this?

'The King of Spain has asked us to cut off your head, Drake,' the Queen rasped, 'and we have here a sword with which to do it.' She paused, then turned to a man standing next to her. 'Monsieur de Marchaumont shall carry out the task.'

And Drake, still not looking up, knew now for certain that the end had finally come, that his fate had been decided. Irrevocably. Beyond doubt. It had always been customary, he remembered, whenever an execution was to be carried out in England by the sword rather than the axe, to send over to France for an expert in that art.

As the first coolness of the steel sword stung his neck, realising that the Frenchman must be sighting for the blow, he froze, bent and red-faced, licking the sweat off his upper lip, intent on proving that he was not afraid to die and then, for Francis Drake time stood still.

For Mendoza, the Spanish ambassador, as the Queen's voice suddenly blasted after him, there was only massive surprise, so paralysing in its effect, that it froze him in his tracks. 'Come back sirrah. 'Tis we who shall choose when to terminate this audience.'

Turning, seeing the Queen's heaving bosoms, the glitter that had come into her black eyes, the colour that even now was surging into her pale cheeks, Mendoza was amazed at the change that had suddenly come over her.

'Now you shall listen to us, as we have had to listen to you.' Her voice seemed to singe the very air with the venom of its tone. 'In this audience, we have endured insults from you by tone, by gesture, by lack of courtesy and respect that no one in our realm would scarcely credit. To your knees then, fellow, and ask the pardon of the Queen of England.'

Mendoza looked around. In the shadows, both Walsingham and Leicester had clapped hands to their jewelled daggers. Would they kill him here, closeted in audience with their sovereign? The thought went quickly through his brain that these northern barbarians were capable of anything. Then he felt disappointment. Real disappointment. Leicester, his king had always thought, could one day be a puppet dancing to a Spanish tune, but now, by that gesture, Leicester had proved himself loyal to Elizabeth. What is the secret of this woman's magic, he thought to himself as he sank to his knees. No longer was her face dull, anxious. It was bright now, lit by a strange, ethereal, luminous fire that he could not fathom and which seemed to hurt his eyes. Her features had never been described as beautiful, but the pride, the arrogance, the compulsive magnetism that he had heard she had once possessed, seemed fully restored; Elizabeth appearing now as a self-possessed, highly dangerous animal in the fear she was suddenly able to induce.

Mendoza found himself shivering. 'If my tone was disrespectful, I beg your majesty's indulgence and offer most abject apologies,' he said quietly.

The Queen laughed. A harsh, triumphant, croaking sound. 'Mendoza, you are a fool,' she said contemptuously. 'You had before you a tired, frightened old woman, wanting peace at any price. Had you behaved with proper courtesy, you could have achieved for your master all that he desired. We were more than ready to give up the corsair, Drake. Yet your insults allowed us to remember two things. Shall we tell you what they were?' She leaned forward, giving the Spaniard a view of her glittering, bejewelled, prehensile fingers.

'Yes, your grace,' Mendoza said weakly, knowing it was expected of him.

316

'The first of them was this. If we gave you Drake and kept a small part of the treasure, we would still be at your master's mercy; yet if we kept both Drake and the treasure,' her black eyes gleamed as she stressed the word 'and', 'then we could afford to build a great fleet and still have an admiral to command it!'

'I understand,' Mendoza whispered. Here was a lion of a woman. Changed beyond recognition. Better to cringe like a dog at her feet and hope at least, to salvage something from the wreck of the interview. 'Your grace. I understand.'

'The second thing we remembered?' the Queen said crisply. 'Listen carefully, Mendoza and mark well what we say. To you we were a mere woman with a woman's heart and a woman's weak strength and you forgot the nobility of our line. We,' she thundered at him, 'are the daughter of King Harry VIII and his blood runs thick and rich in our veins.' She paused, then added malevolently, 'And we tell you this, Sir Ambassador. Threaten us with the roar of cannon once again and we shall put you in a place where you shall threaten no one anymore.'

Mendoza backed slowly out of the Great Hall, his face a mask of sweat from the tongue-lashing he had just endured.

By finding her courage when all was black and the outlook for her country hopeless, the Queen had ensured that she would be remembered by history, not as good, not as honest, not as particularly kind, certainly not as pleasant, but as Elizabeth the Great.

As the sword lifted from the neck of Francis Drake, he tensed himself for the quick, blinding pain and the sudden, black darkness; then the sword came down again, to lie flat across his back. He was not dead. What, then, was happening? For some reason the crowd noise had now grown enormous, booming and echoing round his ears.

'Arise, Sir Francis,' the Queen said, a wicked smile curling at the corners of her mouth.

What was that? Had he imagined it? He was sure the Queen had spoken to him, but the sense of the sentence had been carried away by the crowd's noise.

'Arise, Sir Francis. I dub thee knight.'

Up on one knee now, not daring to gaze directly into that strangely brilliant face with its inexplicable aura of luminous brightness. A hand proffered for him to kiss. A hand not blighted by the passing years, amazingly smooth and slim and with those same, wonderfully

317

tapering fingers before which he had crouched, swearing his eternal loyalty, all those long years ago, in the garden at Ashridge.

'The poor man is quite dazed,' the Queen observed to De Marchaumont.

Francis Drake was not dazed. Instead his mind raced with unanswered questions. Why had the Queen, who always fled from war, suddenly dared to flout openly and brazenly the mighty Philip of Spain, just to save the life of a disobedient mariner? It simply was not in character. He steeled himself to look upwards, noting the still delicate tracery of pale, arched eyebrows smudging the white-painted ruin of the Queen's features; that high, curved nose, once a flaunting arrogance in a face alive with girlish vitality, now settling, deepening, hardening into the sour gauntness of disappointed middle-age. Was there not an answering gleam in the masked depths of those black eyes? A merest whisper of a smile on those thin, bitter lips; a smile that only he could see and recognise? Was not the Queen, by this supreme gesture of defiance, paying her debts, saving Drake's life in exchange for that time so many years ago, when as a young lad he had saved hers? He would like to think so. She was a woman known to believe in balancing her books.

Bent over the scented elegance of her hand, his mind filled with memories. Memories of dearly-loved ones, no longer alive: poor, burly, brother John and stammering Joseph; lithe, fair-haired young Chamberlain; Aruba, the wild Cimarron girl who had taught him many things; and dear old John Oxenham with his vast belly and strange respectability that was apt to vanish within seconds of quaffing a flagon of old ale. How he would have loved them all to be here to witness this undreamt-of honour!

Still, there was little Tom Moone, scowling ferociously with pleasure; and surely—could it be possible—beyond the Queen, standing tall and willowy among the maids-of-honour, with the sculptured, milky white neck of a swan, a bouquet of freckles still, clear grey eyes and lush, auburn hair, was it not young Mistress Elizabeth Sydenham? How she had developed in the last four years from a gawky child into a poised and elegant beauty.

She seemed to be saying something, her hands outstretched towards him, her eyes amazingly moist. He looked harder, blue eyes crinkling with concentration, before he had it. Her lips were repeating over and over again, the single phrase, 'I will wait.'

# Epilogue

The dreams and ambitions of many of the characters in this book were destined to come true, although others would not be so lucky.

Elizabeth Sydenham, daughter of a well-known Somerset family from Combe Sydenham in the county of Somerset, was to realise her own particular dream by marrying Sir Francis Drake, himself rich and landed now, in February 1585.

Juan de Recalde's dream also came true, but with no happy ending. As the great Spanish Armada sailed up the Channel in the year 1588, Recalde, commander of the élite Biscayan squadron, broke from the rigid Armada sailing formation, turning his flagship, the *San Juan de Portugal* directly into the path of the advancing English vessels, there to belch defiance at Drake while his ship was pounded to a pulp. One of the few nobility to survive this disastrous expedition, Recalde returned home to Spain to die there a broken man.

John Hawkins realised both a dream and an ambition in being allowed to serve his Queen the best way he knew how. Placed in charge of the navy board in 1577, his genius for ship design produced a succession of weatherly and radically constructed warships. These splendid little vessels undoubtedly played as much of a part in saving England from foreign invasion as the Spitfire airplane was to do nearly four hundred years later.

Christopher Hatton achieved an ambition but not a dream. In 1587 he received the ultimate favour of a grateful and loving Queen when he was appointed Lord Chancellor. The dream? Never wavering in his adoration for Elizabeth, he stayed single all his life in the hope of marriage. In this, like all others, he was doomed to be disappointed.

For John Oxenham there was neither dream nor ambition. Only honour. Captured in his mad attack on the Panama Isthmus, he was repeatedly tortured by the Spanish in the hope of obtaining information as to Drake's intentions. He told them nothing. In the end, this fine ale-drinker of the vast waistband was condemned to death as a heretic by the Lima auto-da-fé of October 1580 and handed over to the civil authority for hanging.

And the greatest dream of all? Conceived and financed by two honest burghers of San Francisco, an exact replica of the long perished *Golden Hind* was constructed at Appledore in Devon and then sailed in 1974 round to that city, there to take up its final mooring. A moment which must have made the ghost of a certain blue-eyed corsair—they say he loved the Pacific Ocean best of all—smile broadly, providing, as he did himself, yet one more thick link in the chain of destiny which so indissolubly binds the mother country to the United States of America.

Somerset, England. 1979.

Of those men who formed the crews in the famous voyage of 1577–1580, under the command of Captain General Francis Drake, only the following names are known:

*Gentlemen Adventurers*

Anthony, N
Cary, G
Caube
Charles
Cliffe, E
Cooke, J
Doughty, J (John)
Doughty, T (Thomas)
Drake, J (John)
Drake, T (Thomas)
Elyot, L
Fletcher, F (chaplain)
Ffortescu, G
Hawkins, W
Hord, T
Markham, W
Saracold, J
Thomas, J
Vicary, L
Wattkins, E
Winterhey, R
Wynter, J

*Seamen and others*

Artyur
Audley, J
Blacoler, J
Blacollers, T
Brewer, J (Trumpeter)
Brewer, T

Bright, E (Ned)
Burnish, R
Cadwell, R
Clarke, R
Corder, P
Cottle, J
Cowke, W
Cowrttes, J
Crane, T
Cuttill, T
Danielles, R
Deane, J
Diego
Fforster, D
Ffloud, T
Flud, T
Fowler, J
Fry, J
Gallaway, J
Garget, L
George
Goddy, P
Gotsalk, B
Graye, R
Grepe, J
Grige, T
Hals, C
Haylston, T
Hayman, C
Haynes, W
Hogges, T
Horsewill, W
Huse, J

James, P
Joyner, R
Kidde, J
Kingesoud, R
Laus, J
Lege, W
Mariner, J
Markes, T
Martyn, J (John)
Martyn, T (Thomas)
Meckes, T
Milles, J
Minivy, R
Moone, T (Tom)
Mour, N
Great Neill
Little Neill
Oliver
Pitcher, W
Player, R
Pollmane, R
Raymente, G
Rowles, R
Shelle, W
Smyth, W
Sothern, T
Stewerd, J
Thomas
Waspe, C
Watterton, J
Wood, S
Worrall, E
Writ, R